SURVIVAL

Andrew Frediani

About *Survival*

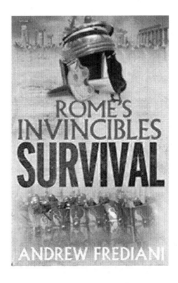

Caesar is dead. Revenge has armed his hand. His name is
Octavian.

Though little more than a boy, Caesar's heir is determined to
avenge his adoptive father, despite the imposing figures from
Rome's long political history who stand in his way: Mark
Antony, Cicero, Lepidus, Brutus and Cassius.

Despite some initial failures, Octavian does not give in, and
gathers about him a group of allies who are just as determined
as he himself: Maecenas, Agrippa and Rufus. With them and a
few others on his side, he forms a sect dedicated to vengeance,
with the aim of punishing, one by one, all those who have
Caesar's blood on their hands.

Octavian has resolved to overturn the established order, and to
finish what Caesar had begun…

I

"Caesar is dead."

Octavia froze at the words of her cousin Lucius Pinarius, who had just been ushered in by a slave, and she felt her grip on her daughter, little Claudia Marcella, start to fail. The child fell to the ground, tearing from her mother a cry louder than the little girl's own, but fortunately Octavia was herself tiny and had felt her knees start to give, so her daughter had thus fallen from no great height. The little girl's tears were more those of shock than of pain, but that did nothing to ease the despair of her mother, who hurriedly picked her up to comfort her, promptly assisted by her zealous maid Etain.

When she had made sure that Marcella was not hurt, Octavia handed her over to the maid and, giving him a grim stare, turned her attention back to her cousin.

"You shouldn't make jokes in such bad taste. You know how easily I get upset."

"I only wish that it were a joke, dear cousin," said Pinarius, looking embarrassed. Despite being born several years before her he seemed the younger of the two, as Octavia looked older than her twenty-five years.

He enunciated his words carefully, emphasising each syllable.

"Julius Caesar, our great-uncle, the dictator, was killed an hour ago, or perhaps less, in the Curia of Pompey, while the senate was in session. Do not you hear the cries in the street?"

She felt her knees trembling again, and looked around for a chair. Finding one, she grabbed its arm and, without taking her eyes from her cousin, sat down and concentrated her attention on the sounds coming from outside her home on the Aventine: yes, she could hear the echoes of shouts.

"Who? Who killed him?" she asked in dismay.

"I've heard a lot of names. Important names. Senators. What is certain is that there were several of them. And that the

1

others just sat by and watched."

"Tell me some."

"I dare not," said Pinarius, looking confused. "They seem so unlikely that I can scarcely believe it was them, and I have no wish to falsely accuse men who Caesar pardoned after the Civil War, gave gifts to or installed in the highest positions of the State."

Octavia hesitated. She was still unconvinced, although the noise from the street was growing louder by the minute, in confirmation that something serious had happened.

"Maybe he's not dead. You know how it is with this kind of thing – the rumours spread and become exaggerated between one account mouth and another," she ventured. "Perhaps they weren't successful…"

"He was stabbed by many people, cousin," said Pinarius, shaking his head sadly. "And this is the only certainty. It is said that his body lies in a pool of blood, abandoned in the atrium of the Curia, just below the statue of Pompey the Great. If it is thus, there is no chance that he survived. And we must now look to our own survival."

Octavia flinched. "What do you mean?" As soon as she had spoken, she heard a thud that shook the wall.

"Death to the supporters of the tyrant! Death to his relatives!"

Shouted threats rang out in the street, startling the woman, who instinctively held out her arms to Etain, demanding the return of her still crying child.

"Do you hear them? Would they have the courage to come out into the open thus if Caesar were alive?" said Pinarius. "Now all those who opposed his regime but dared not speak out for fear of reprisals will voice their discontent. And if it is true that those who killed him were his closest aides, there will be nobody left to defend the family. Nobody. We will be the first targets of the cowards Caesar kept in check with his authority. We must flee."

"My mother…" murmured Octavia, unable to react, as she was.

"Quintus Pedius has gone to Atia. He was present among the senators at the murder. He sent a slave to warn me and I decided to come to you myself. I knew you would not have believed a slave. Apart from his wife, we are Caesar's closest relatives. And therefore we are the most vulnerable, at least until the political situation is clear. We are the ones most at risk. Fortunately, your brother is in Illyria, so they cannot get to him."

Octavia wanted to get up from the chair into which she had sunk and run to organise the slaves, set them to preparing a carriage and get at least as far as the family villa in Velletri to guarantee a minimum of safety. But imaginary chains held her down, relegating her to the impotence that had characterised her whole life. As always, the solution to which her nature obliged her was that of waiting for others to take charge. "My husband will not let anything happen to us," was all she said to her cousin.

"Are you sure?" replied Pinarius. "Marcus Claudius Marcellus was certainly in the Senate today, and he has never been a supporter of Caesar. Caesar pardoned him during the civil wars, and perhaps, even if he was not one of the actual perpetrators of the murder, he is among those who are no longer hiding their dissatisfaction. The fact that he has not yet returned home proves it. Should he not worry about his family before all else?"

"Are you suggesting that he would hand us over to the angry mob?"

"Of course not. But even if he is not involved, he may not be able to object if they take against us. In this moment, we can be sure of nothing. Caesar was everything to Rome, and each Roman, even the most eminent, could but live in his shadow. Now the road to power is open to all."

"What do you think will happen?"

"That, no one can predict. We must first see who really took part in the conspiracy and how much support the conspirators have among the people and the Senate. There are rumours that they claim to have done it in order to restore the legal republic, but I doubt that the Republic will resume its normal course after years and years of veiled monarchy, and the magistratures have already been allocated for the next five years. There are too many ambitious men around; too many people who believe they can emulate Caesar, and too many that delude themselves that everything will be as before his advent. I believe it all depends principally upon how Mark Antony behaves," answered Pinarius, after a moment's hesitation. "Despite his fall from grace with the dictator in recent times, at the end of the day he is the most authoritative consul and personage of the institutions. And we must also see how Cicero affects events. Like your husband, he will certainly be rejoicing even though he was not involved in the conspiracy, and will certainly fight to restore the Republic. And finally, there are some loyal to Caesar who did not betray their leader: I could not say how many nor even who they are, but I think that among them there are the *magister equitum* Lepidus, designated consuls Hirtius and Pansa, his friend Asinius Pollio, and his wealthier supporters, such as Cornelius Balbus. What will they do? You're scared, eh? Well, so am I: I doubt that Rome will find peace for a long time..."

"But why... Why?" sighed Octavia. "Caesar had proven himself to be lenient. And he would be away fighting the war against Parthia and Getae for years. So why did they do it?"

"Why? According to the rumours, they killed him because he wanted to become king, and Rome cannot tolerate a monarchy. Not after all we went through so long ago to get rid of one," said Pinarius solemnly. "But in my opinion, each of the members of the conspiracy had something to gain from the murder of Caesar... Or felt somehow diminished by his existence."

Suddenly the two cousins heard new sounds, louder than before, and excited voices in the vestibule – people had gained entrance. Octavia grabbed her daughter and held her tightly to her breast. She had always shunned violence and conflict of any kind, and had earned a reputation as the most submissive of the austere matrons who stood beside the senators of the Urbe. She didn't like contradicting people, be they relatives, acquaintances or even strangers, and the judgment of others, the dignity of the family and her inner peace were vitally important to her. It took only a trifle to make her anxious, and now that she and her loved ones appeared to be in more danger than ever before, she was convinced that it was too harsh a test for her not to fail.

No longer able to contain herself, she burst out crying, and her tears splashed onto the face of her daughter, who began sobbing again in turn. Octavia loathed herself for her lack of decorum in front of her cousin and her slaves: if they were coming to kill her, she should show herself worthy of her ancestors and die like a true Roman woman – like the *Julia* she was. She decided that they must at least find her standing upright, her chin thrust forward. She wiped away her tears with the edge of her palm and tried to rise to her feet, but a formidable force kept her in her seat. Meanwhile, the cries inside the house increased. There was the sound of metal, of cleated shoes treading the beautiful marble floor of the domus, the clang of swords crashing into the armoured sides of soldiers.

Soldiers?

Octavia felt a chill run down her spine.

*

Gladiators. The Clivus Capitolinus, the slope leading to the top of the Capitol, was heaving with them. "They're Decimus Brutus Albinus's," thought Gaius Cilnius Maecenas, with one eye on the sinewy fighters and another on his muscular litter bearers, trembling with fear at the turn events were taking. And, truth be told, he was scared too – he who had certainly never been a lionheart. He had come to the city from Arezzo to personally conclude a delicate business transaction, and found himself in the middle of what looked like a riot. Or worse still, a civil war.

Caesar was dead, they were saying. And his assassins, some of the most prominent senators, went about Rome boasting of their actions, calling themselves heroes and defenders of freedom. But, despite being of the equestrian and senatorial class, Maecenas' economic interests meant that he was too rich and well connected to the great landowners of the Senate to ignore the nuisance which, for certain financial factions, the recently toppled regime represented. Rather than a gesture for the citizens, this murder had been a day of reckoning! It was for the great magnates that Caesar's dominion had been an obstacle, not for the common people, who had benefitted greatly from the broad reforms of the dictator and the peace he had established.

But the people were fickle. All it took was for some speechifier to direct the mood of the crowd and convince it to endorse the work of the killers, whoever they were. And now, the people in the streets were forming gangs, arming themselves with clubs and stones, and going in search of the senators Caesar had created. Of Mark Antony and his followers – of those, in short, who had supported the regime. But just as many armed gangs of Caesar's supporters, who mourned the dictator, were combing the city in search of the senators who had killed him, or even those who had sat by and watched without intervening. And being unable to distinguish Caesar's allies from his enemies and murderers, they were not splitting hairs and were going after anyone wearing a senator's laticlave tunic.

He knew that he too was at risk. His clothing didn't mark him out as a senator, of course, but the pomp in his coterie could quite easily expose him to the anger of the plebeians. His litter, with its finely embroidered curtains and wooden frame dotted with precious gems could attract attention. It usually gave him pleasure to show off his immense wealth, but on this occasion he would rather have gone unnoticed.

The common people were excited, and it was hard to tell those who were happy about the dictator's death from those who wanted revenge upon his murderers. Maecenas saw people beating one another, opposing factions fighting, citizens climbing the statues of the assassinated dictator to push them down while others attempted to stop them, crowds of people turning over the carts which were authorised to move about the city before darkness fell, probably taking advantage of the chaos following the murder for a bit of looting. Not surprisingly, even some shops were being targeted by groups of rowdies, and the wealthy Etruscan doubted that it was for political reasons.

And anyway, what were the gladiators doing on the Capitol? They were slaves, and yet were going around armed as though they were soldiers. Maecenas knew they were owned by Decimus Brutus because a few hours earlier that morning they had taken part in the games at the Circus Flaminius, offered by their master himself to celebrate the departure of Caesar for the war against the Parthians. Marcus Claudius Marcellus, the senator with whom he was supposed to be concluding the deal that had brought him to Rome, had invited him to the Circus; there, he had written, they could finalise the details of the passage of the villa of Cuma, in Campania, from the senator's ownership to that of Maecenas. But the Etruscan had been delayed for a few hours, and had sent a slave to announce to Marcellus that they would meet at the Forum after the games and the sitting of Senate.

The sitting which had been fatal for Caesar.

But it was unthinkable to go and look for Marcellus in the Forum now. The roads had become too dangerous. It would be better to hole up in one of his houses in the city, Maecenas said to himself, and wait for the storm to pass.

Or at least, until it was clear who had killed Caesar and what they were planning to do to all the rest.

He saw that the Vicus Unguentarius, the road to the Aventine which housed his most prestigious *domus* in the *Urbe* was blocked by a band of hooligans who had set fire to a building. They were looking around themselves, and Maecenas had the feeling they were seeking someone to throw into the fire so they could enjoy watching him roast as though on a funeral pyre.

Realising that they had noticed him, he shouted to his bearers to hurry towards the Clivus Capitolinus and the gladiators, whose grim faces would, perhaps, deter the mob from continuing their pursuit. The slaves didn't wait for him to repeat himself, and increased their pace, demonstrating considerable fortitude as they started up the slope. Maecenas peeked around the curtain, and saw that some of the gang of louts had refused to give up – one, indeed, grabbed a rock and threw it at the litter, narrowly missing one of the bearers, but fortunately the rear of the formation of gladiators was near, and as the distance between it and the troublemakers shrank, their pursuers slowed to a total stop.

At that point, there was nothing for it but to tag along. Maecenas motioned for his men to follow the fighters, which obliged him to go back up the hill. It was not what he had wanted, but he appeared to have no choice, if he did not wish to endanger his safety.

But once at the top, he was greeted with chaos.

The whole of Rome seemed to have arranged to meet there, in the triangle between the Temple of Jupiter Capitolinus, the Tabularium and the Tarpeian Rock. The gladiators and some squads of soldiers seemed to be keeping order, but the situation gave the impression that it might degenerate at any moment. Among the many sacred buildings, statues and columns scattered about the hill thronged people of all social classes, though senators were scarce and – protected as they were by armed men – they stood out from the crowd.

Maecenas's attention was drawn to the plinth of the main temple of Jupiter Capitolinus. Above, some Capitoline nobles, their clothes stained with blood, were attempting to address the crowd, but with the great clamour that filled the square only those in the front rows could hear them. For the moment, Maecenas relaxed: probably nowhere else in Rome were there so many defenders of the law as there; if nothing else, he would enjoy some form of protection in the case of danger.

He focused on trying to understand what was happening and who those speaking from the plinth were. Being informed, in business as in everyday life, was the best route to a life of success. And he intended to have a great deal of success. Not as a judge or a politician, much less as a conqueror or leader, but as a wealthy businessman able to buy anything or anyone.

Maecenas's dream was to become a builder, but not of buildings, or ships or any other material thing – his dream was to become so influential as to be able to build, or even just direct and shape, the lives of others, in order to determine the course of society and history. He was not interested in glory, nor fame nor notoriety, but only in the power that came from making others satisfied. It was not a matter of altruism – far from it: his ego was so strong that he felt no need to be in the front row. It would suffice to know that *he* was the one who made things work. The only one to whom others could turn to feel fulfilled. It was a feeling he had felt for the first time when he was twelve, before giving up his young man's *praetexta toga*. He had given a harp to a local shepherd lad he had heard singing in a melodious voice. The boy had left happy, and he had felt like a divinity: a god, even, with the power to change someone's life and the feeling of having become, in the eyes of the beneficiary of his generosity, an object of veneration. Later, he would be able to ask that shepherd boy for anything, with the certainty of being indulged.

Information, therefore, was always the first tool for being able to offer people that which they needed, as well as to anticipate their desires, and to serve them up on a silver platter. He peered closely into the distance to see who was declaiming to the crowd. From their bloody clothes, it was clear that it was the men who had killed Caesar.

He narrowed his eyes, squinted and could barely believe

what he saw.

*

Marcus Vipsanius Agrippa walked out of the astronomical observatory with a radiant smile on his face. Theogenes the astrologer had predicted for him a future rich in success, exceeding any ambition that his modest means might reasonably admit. Even better, the old man had hinted at achievements even greater than those achieved by any other Roman before him.

Gaius Octavian and Quintus Salvidienus Rufus, both waiting their turn outside the building on top of the mountain which dominated Apollonia, noticed the change in his mood immediately. Their young companion had been troubled when he had gone inside, afraid of discovering some unfortunate fate, and had emerged almost triumphant.

"What did you find in there? A bevy of naked girls, dedicated to your pleasure? I thought there was just an old man..." said Salvidienus Rufus, the new friend he and Octavian had made in Apollonia.

"They would not have been able to make me so happy, I assure you!" said Agrippa, struggling to keep his feet anchored to the rocky terrain of the rugged highland, despite his massive frame, which certainly gave no impression of lightness.

"Good news for the coming years?" asked Octavian: with his acute intelligence, he had immediately sensed the reason for so much joy. Agrippa knew that, with him, he could not mince words for long.

"Yes!" he exclaimed. "And if Theogenes did not enjoy such great respect and credibility among all people, I would scarce believe it myself, and might think that I'd been made a fool of."

"Pffff," sighed Rufus teasingly, "... whatever can he have said – that you will be Rome's new dictator for life after Caesar?"

Agrippa had not seen it in those terms and frowned for a moment. Imagining oneself successor of the Master of Rome was enough to set the legs of an ambitious young man like himself trembling.

"Something like that... yes," he said, almost half-heartedly and somewhat ashamed.

He saw immediately that his answer had deeply disturbed Octavian, and wondered if he would have done better to keep quiet. But it was done now. His friend, a nobleman belonging to one of the oldest and most distinguished families of Rome, was already on his way towards a glittering destiny: it was understandable that he would recoil at the thought of a man of humble origins like himself ascending to similar heights.

"Then it's clear that he's played you for a fool," said Rufus. "Imagine a poor wretch like you matching the achievements of Julius Caesar…"

"That's not what I said at all," murmured Agrippa, embarrassed. In the meantime, he peered sideways at Octavian, observing his reactions. And he did not like his friend's expression one bit.

"Theogenes is always right. It is well known," said Octavian in a flat voice, staring blankly at a point on the horizon. "That's why we came."

"But it can't be… What exactly did he say? And on what basis did he say it?" Rufus demanded.

Agrippa looked at Octavian. He usually did, before acting. Although they had been friends since childhood, he never lost sight of the difference in rank and class between them. His father had taught him to always remember that friendship with a noble did not authorise a commoner to neglect the hierarchy. In every situation, he must always keep in mind that the one in command was Octavian, and he must limit himself to following in his footsteps, even when he felt that he was able to overtake.

One step behind. Always one step behind.

By doing that, he had managed, at only nineteen, to become an army officer who was now preparing to lead one of the largest military campaigns in the history of Rome: the conquest of the Parthian and Dacian kingdoms.

He waited for a nod from his friend, and only then did he speak. "I gave him my date of birth, that's all. Then he studied some papers upon which there were drawings of the stars, and he told me many things. That I will be a great conqueror, unconquered in all battles. That I will leave Rome richer in buildings and services, that I will bring it power and glory, and will hold all the magistratures of the Republic. And that my descendants will reach even greater heights than myself…"

"There, you see?" cried Rufus. "It cannot be, so the old man must be senile. Or otherwise, astrology an inexact science. Whatever it was, coming here was a waste of time. If he predicted such things for you, I can only imagine what he will say about the great-grandson of the dictator and supreme commander…" he added sarcastically, urging Octavian to enter the building with a wave of his hand.

In Agrippa's opinion, the young officer treated his illustrious friend with a confidence that was completely unjustified, often forgetting that he was not only a close relative of the dictator, but also the designated *magister equitum*, or second in command, for the campaign; after all, Rufus was no patrician either, and they had only known one another for the winter they had spent together in Apollonia. Caesar had sent his great-nephew and he, Agrippa, to prepare themselves, together with the legions he had already sent across the sea, in view of what was expected to be his most important war – more so even than the Gallic Wars, which had already given the dictator a prominent place among the great leaders of history.

The new campaign would finally consecrate Caesar, and those who were with him would benefit greatly. Beginning with his closest male relative, Octavian, and the latter's best friend. Both had immediately bonded with Salvidienus Rufus, the tribune of the Martia, the legion to which Agrippa had been assigned with the same rank. Unlike the two of them, however, Rufus, who was older by just three years, already had plenty of military experience, having served as a recruit under Caesar in the war in Spain. They too had participated in the Iberian conflict, but only nominally: due to Octavian being struck down by a sudden illness, they had in fact only arrived on Hispanic soil while the decisive battle in Munda against the elder son of Pompey the Great was already underway, and their contribution was limited to assisting with the roundups and reprisals.

Rufus, on the other hand, had never hesitated to make available to them all that he had learned, dispensing generously to the two friends the entire body of knowledge he had acquired in the field. It wasn't much compared to what was taught to and expected from them by the centurions who sternly and steadfastly trained them – doubtless because the dictator had ordered it thus – but his attitude had helped overcome any initial distrust and cement a friendship which was already strong after a single season.

"I'm not going in," said Octavian suddenly, standing up and walking toward the slope.

"What do you mean?" exclaimed Rufus, grabbing his arm and trying to hold him back.

Octavian stared at his arm and then at his friend with eyes of ice, not saying a word. The other immediately realised his affront, and released him immediately, as though he were hot. Agrippa, meanwhile, looked up at the sky: Rufus was still a long way from understanding how to deal with Octavian.

"Why give up the chance?" asked the tribune, sounding more subdued and respectful.

"I don't want to, that's all," replied the young man, his tone still icy. Agrippa knew he must address the issue with caution.

And as a friend, he must at least try to convince him. "But we need to know what your future holds, Octavian," he said, moving closer. "You're our guide. And in the coming years you will be one of the guides of Rome too, thanks to the favour in which your illustrious uncle holds you. So knowing what you will become means also learning about the fate of Rome over the coming decades…"

Octavian thought, gloomily. "And if it is not so? If the gods have established for me a miserable fate?"

Agrippa understood what he meant. That 'miserable fate' meant 'less than yours'. Yes, it would be embarrassing, but it would be worse to remain in doubt at this point. Their friendship risked crumbling forever. He simply must go in there now, to Theogenes. They all must.

He wondered if Rufus understood the stakes in play. He had probably guessed, but could not really know the essence of the matter. They two were lifelong friends, mainly due to the fact that the equilibrium between them had never changed. But if anything happened now to alter the hierarchy, it would be the end. They might even become enemies.

"Do you want to stay in doubt forever?" Agrippa asked finally. He might as well put it bluntly. They were friends, weren't they? At least for the moment…

Octavian was silent.

Rufus felt entitled to intervene. "Agrippa's right, my friend.

If you want to be a leader, and if you are destined to be one, you cannot shrink from the occasion to see your aspirations confirmed." Yes, the tribune had guessed roughly at the extent of the problem.

Octavian felt that he had no choice. He stood still for a moment, staring at the horizon, then took a deep breath and walked toward the entrance of the observatory without saying a word. The other two friends were silent, and neither dared speak while they waited. Both understood the gravity of the moment: what had begun as simply satisfying their curiosity had turned into a perverse battle of wills, with only one result ensuring their survival: the victory of Octavian.

Curious, thought Agrippa as he waited. For them, the most extraordinary of adventures had started only a few months earlier: their active participation as protagonists in one of the events that would remain longest in the memory of the Romans. Caesar was planning to avenge the defeat and death of his close friend and triumvir Crassus in Carrhae nine years earlier, recover the Eagles lost by the Romans and conquer the Parthian kingdom in Mesopotamia and beyond. Not content with this ambitious plan, he then intended to extend the control of the Republic to the Danube, attacking the kingdom of the Getae and Dacians. An undertaking which, they planned, would last five years, and so Caesar had arranged things in Rome and in Italy, and even in the provinces, so that the State would have appointed magistrates for the entire period of his absence. All close collaborators of his who would not have a role in the campaign. The men he trusted – Marcus Giunius Brutus, Gaius Cassius Longinus, Gaius Trebonius, Decimus Brutus Albinus, Mark Antony, Aulus Hirtius, Vibius Pansa, Marcus Aemilius Lepidus and Asinius Pollio would control the Republic in his absence as consuls or proconsuls, making sure that the Senate respected the provisions approved by him before his departure.

And at the end of those five years of war, he and Octavian would return to Rome laden with glory, and at twenty-four still very young, to begin the *cursus honorum* – the itinerary of public positions that he now knew would take him to the highest ranks of the Republic.

It had all begun. It was the Ides of March, and within three days the dictator would leave Rome for Brindisi and set off for the Illyrian coast, where they and the rest of the legions participating in the campaign would join him. A month's time, and the eastward march of a vast and powerful army would begin. And they would be at the head of this vast and powerful army.

A noise from inside the building startled him. He looked over and saw Octavian emerge with great strides, pushing the door shut behind him. The young nobleman approached the two friends, his expression unreadable, as always: not even Agrippa could always understand what was going through his mind. He gave in to the impulse, aware, though, that if his friend did not want to speak there would be no way of getting anything out of him.

"Well? Did you give your date of birth?" asked Agrippa, his voice choked with emotion. It was the 23rd of September, as he well knew: he wished he had had the presence of mind to ask Theogenes himself while he was inside.

Octavian nodded.

"And?" urged Rufus, he too conscious now that their lives depended on what Octavian said.

The great-grandson of the dictator waited in silence a moment longer, then said, "He knelt before me."

II

"In the name of the *magister equitum* Marcus Aemilius Lepidus, I assume control of this *domus*!" Gaius Chaerea intoned solemnly, as he burst into the luxurious house of Marcus Claudius Marcellus without even waiting for the doorkeeper to inform his masters. The squad of soldiers he led followed him with the blind obedience the young centurion commanded, and with the efficiency of experienced and disciplined legionaries, forged by the campaigns of Julius Caesar.

He was not afraid of the predictable protests of the house's owner. He was charged with protecting the family of Caesar at all costs, and had behind him the orders of the deputy commander of the recently killed dictator, one of the highest authorities in that moment of an apparent power vacuum, where it was unclear who was to command: the consuls? The *magister equitum*? The senate? The magistrates? The same people who, it was said, had killed the dictator?

But that was not all. His zeal sprang from far more personal reasons. In fact it had been he himself who had suggested to his commander that he provide for the protection of Caesar's family, as soon as he had realised that the chaos following the murder threatened to suck them down before anyone else into a whirlpool of violence. And the young officer would have done anything to prevent that from happening.

Anything. Anything to have Octavia forgive him.

He heard behind him the sound of objects falling to the ground and shattering. He turned and saw that his soldiers, though accustomed to marching in formation and on guard, could not help banging into the statues and furniture along the walls of the vestibule. He shrugged – in times like this, much worse things happened in Rome. They burst into the hall, and the sight of Etain coming towards them made his heart jump.

She had always been courageous. Octavia could not have

chosen a more trustworthy maid or closer friend: it took guts to run toward a group of soldiers who had burst into the house of your *domina*. On the other hand, her mistress had chosen her as assistant and secretary, and that spoke volumes about her dedication to the House of Julia.

Chaerea saw the girl's expression suddenly relax as she realised that he was the leader of the squadron. There was no need to explain that he had come to protect them, but he had to do so in order not to give the others the impression that they were already acquainted. And also, if possible, to re-assure her.

"I am the centurion Gaius Chaerea, attendant of *magister equitum* Lepidus. Call your *dominus*," he said to the young slave. "Tell him that riots have broken out in the city because of the dictator's death. We have the task of protecting you and of making ourselves available to the senator. Therefore we are taking possession of this house." He hoped that Lepidus's real intentions were not clear: the *magister equitum*, though apparently the diligent interpreter of the dictator's will, actually intended to get his hands on hostages or bargaining chips he could take with him in the case of the killers of his leader gaining wide consent. But in the meantime the young centurion was there to protect Etain, and would prevent anything from happening.

"The *dominus* is not at home. I will inform the *domina*," replied the servant, with a look that seemed to him one of understanding.

Gaius was already feeling tense about the meeting, for which he had been waiting nine years. He had entered the house with a lump in his throat and his stomach burning. And now, the absence of Marcus Claudius Marcellus, whom Lepidus had specifically asked him to detain, unnerved him further: the hostility of the senator towards the dictator was known, and it was possible that he even supported the conspirators, or that he had thrown in his lot with them. And that complicated things.

The appearance of Octavia, followed by Etain with a little girl in her arms, brought him suddenly face to face with the responsibility of handling a situation he had been both longing for and dreading for nine years.

By the gods, she had changed! He had left her little more than a child, and now she was a grown woman. It occurred to him that, ironically, he was partly responsible for that transformation. She had not become as beautiful as her features and her gracefulness had promised as a teenager, but she had retained the elegant bearing that was typical of her family, that sweetness of expression which made him want to protect her, and the little pointed nose that, for a brief but irreparable moment, had made him lose his head.

"Well, centurion Gaius Chaerea, what is this intrusion? Are our lives really in danger?" Octavia spoke in a voice filled with apprehension that Gaius hardly recognised. It was the voice of a woman, but the tremble that vibrated in it reminded him of the girl he had known. He wondered if she was troubled by their meeting or by the dramatic events involving her family. Or by both.

Only then did he notice that there was another aristocrat standing beside Octavia and wearing the toga of a senator. The man was slightly older than her and looked as though he might be a relative: all of the *gens Julia* family possessed, to a greater or lesser extent, features which might well have been taken from the statues of gods. It was not for nothing that they boasted of being the descendants of none other than Venus herself. Which, if it was true, meant that Chaereas's lineage too now possessed divine blood.

Octavia realized that Gaius was looking at the man beside him. "This man is my cousin, Lucius Pinarius Scarpus. Speak, then."

Gaius nodded. He knew Lucius Pinarius as one of Caesar's closest relatives, but could not remember the faces of all the senators. He knew Octavia's other cousin, Quintus Pedius, because he had been a good commander under the dictator and had earned himself a certain reputation, but this Pinarius was not so well-known among soldiers like himself.

When he spoke, he hoped not to betray his emotions. "As I said to your servant, *domina*, we are here to protect you. You will have heard of the atrocious crime of which your great-uncle was the victim. Rome is unsafe for the moment, even more so for the family of the dictator…"

"And Lepidus is so thoughtful as to send an escort?" said Pinarius, with a pointedly sarcastic tone. "How kind of him to… *guard* us against any eventuality."

He hadn't fallen for it. What this know-all *didn't* know, however, was that he, Gaius, actually *was* interested in saving

Octavia, and so – despite Lepidus's intentions, the escort really would have a protective function.

"Senator, we are here only to protect the family of the dictator," he specified, answering Pinarius but staring at Octavia, with the hope that she understood his position. But the woman's eyes were dimmed with tears. Chaerea remembered how fragile she had been, and now he saw that time had not instilled in her any more confidence in herself.

And yet she surprised him by finding the strength to take a few steps toward him. She stopped a short distance from the centurion, and addressed those present. "We accept the protection offered by the *magister equitum*," she said, punctuating her words with occasional sobs. "Until my husband returns, I leave it to you, centurion, to decide what is to be done," she added, staring into his eyes for a moment, only to look away immediately.

"Thank you, *domina*," Gaius Chaerea felt compelled to say, before turning to his soldiers. "Dispose yourselves in pairs on either side of the door, and then at the back, along the wall of the garden. I'll join you after I have inspected the house for places which need guarding."

"This is an outrage!" shouted Lucius Pinarius. "You have no right! I will take my grievances to the *magister equitum*! And the consul Mark Antony!" Octavia, however, reached out and grabbed his arm, trying to calm him.

"We are in a situation, Senator," replied Gaius, pulling his robust figure to its full height, "in which we do not know to whom you will need to take your precious grievances tomorrow. The authorities may change by the hour, and perhaps it is not clear to you that we are again faced with the spectre of a civil war – one where it will be every man for himself, because it is not clear who is on whose side. The only thing that matters now is saving those who are most at risk."

Pinarius opened his mouth to reply, but gave up and looked at his cousin, who nodded in assent. "So I may not even leave to go home?" he said, with little conviction.

"I would suggest avoiding it, at least until the situation is clearer. As far as I know, they are taking important decisions on the Capitol," said Chaerea.

Pinarius snorted, then grabbed the centurion's arm and squeezed it with force. "You are right. I apologize. I realize that your presence is the lesser of two evils, in this moment. Allow me just to go and tell my slave to inform my family I will not be returning."

Gaius Chaerea liked people who knew how to apologize. Especially when they were powerful with deeply rooted pride. He decided that he liked Pinarius, all things considered. "Go ahead, senator. Know, however, that Lepidus also sent soldiers to your home, as well as that of your cousin Quintus Pedius," he said.

Pinarius nodded and left the atrium, leaving him alone with Octavia. They looked at one another for a long time, without saying a word. There was so much Gaius wanted to tell her, but he did not know how to begin: every possible opening gambit seemed vacuous and shallow. And then... he simply could not read Octavia's mood. She was very upset, of course, but that might just be because of the dramatic situation in which her family found itself. And then, she always had been so easily upset. That, above all, was why he could not forgive himself for what he had done to her, even though he certainly had not forced her.

"Octavia... I..." he mumbled finally, unsure as to how to continue.

She shook her head. "There is no need to say anything or to justify yourself. Just tell me how Marcus is. Etain tells me he is growing healthy and strong."

Gaius felt reassured and made to answer, but the noise of a struggle coming from the vestibule caught his attention. Was it possible that the house was already under attack, when it wasn't even clear yet who was leading the opposition to the murdered dictator? He left the atrium and rushed toward the entrance. When he arrived, he saw one of his soldiers on the ground with a gash in his abdomen, two more disarmed and three he did not recognise, their swords extended towards their fellow soldiers. One of the armed legionaries was holding Octavia's daughter while the other held Etain by the wrist.

"What is this?" he asked, with all the authority he could muster, but without drawing his sword.

The soldier with the child replied. "You've not understood the development of events, centurion. We are taking this family: the *praetors* who killed the tyrant are taking control of the city and they will be extremely grateful if we deliver them over. Draw your sword and throw it on the floor, or the child will grow up without her pretty little nose."

Octavia cried out in terror, and Gaius had no choice but to obey.

*

It hardly seemed possible to Maecenas that he had bumped into Claudius Marcellus in the crowd that had formed on the Capitol around the murderers of Caesar. But it seemed even more incredible that it had been Caesar's closest allies who had killed him.

"Marcus Junius Brutus... By the gods, Caesar pardoned him for having sided against him in the civil war, he made him *praetor urbanus* and future *propraetor* of an important province," he said to Marcellus while their litters, side by side, attempted to make their way down the Clivus Capitolinus.

Marcellus answered, but the Etruscan could hear nothing. The voice of his interlocutor, lying in the litter alongside, was drowned out by the cries of Caesar's veterans, now retired settlers who had gathered in the city to be present for the dictator's departure to the East and to receive the handouts he had promised them. However, he sensed from the movement of his lips that Marcellus was talking about Cassius, the praetor *peregrinus* who, even more than Brutus, had benefited from the clemency of Caesar during the civil war, and who had likewise been assigned the governorship of a province.

His litter swayed violently, and Maecenas suddenly found himself almost embracing a crude individual who another citizen was grimly pummelling.

"How much did you pay those murderers, you pig? Enough to forget what Caesar has done for you, was it?" cried the incensed man, who seemed to be prevailing in the altercation, while the other, indifferent to having ended up upon the Etruscan's litter, tried to force him back through the expedient of wild kicks.

In confirmation of the citizen's words, coins fell onto the stuffed fabric and between the cushions upon which Maecenas lay.

"You defend a tyrant! A man who deprived us of liberty!"

cried the victim, turning and exposing his back to the blows of his persecutor as he tried to recover his money from between the legs of the Etruscan. Now it was Maecenas's turn to kick frantically, more horrified by the discomfort caused by the proximity of an individual with an unbearable stench than by the intrusion itself. But he was also worried that one of the two might notice the chest hidden beneath one of the cushions: inside was the sum that he intended to give Marcellus for the purchase of the villa of Cuma.

The two men Maecenas had hired to protect him finally decided to intervene, though in their defence, they'd had their work cut out freeing the litter from people squabbling in the street. The two litigants were unceremoniously thrown to the ground and kicked mercilessly, but it didn't prevent them from continuing their quarrel. Maecenas looked around and saw that more and more people were fighting. Getting away from here was a priority.

"Is everything all right?" asked Marcellus.

"Yes, fine," replied the Etruscan, adding, "Apparently, the conspirators have managed to win over rather a lot of people to their cause thanks to the money they gave out after their speech…"

"Bah! But then, Caesar too won popular favour with his gifts. The people are scum. What are these veterans who praise him except the people he himself corrupted with the spoils of war and the settlements in the colonies he forced we senators to authorise?"

Marcellus was another of the senators pardoned by Caesar after the civil war, and it was not difficult to see that he was in no way sorry about the dictator's death, though he didn't go as far as Publius Cornelius Dolabella, the man the dictator had chosen as consul in his place after his departure for the Parthian campaign; Dolabella had climbed onto the plinth of the Temple of Jupiter Capitolinus along with the conspirators and had boasted of having participated in the attack, although others had denied it soon after. Other important personages had done the same, giving a clear indication of the feeling among the people who mattered in Rome.

Maecenas preferred to avoid this discussion with the man with whom he was preparing to conclude a business transaction. He had greatly appreciated the work of the late dictator, and if it had been up to him he would have had all the murderers unceremoniously imprisoned and executed. Apparently, however, Roman politics were taking another direction. He decided to continue reviewing the list of conspirators, now that they seemed on the verge of leaving the rowdiest area.

"I was more surprised by the presence of Decimus Brutus Albinus among the conspirators," he said. "He has won more than one battle for Caesar, and was such a close part of the dictator's inner circle that he had been given the governorship of Gaul for next year."

"Keep in mind that Caesar was betrayed by his main collaborator, Titus Labienus," replied Marcellus. "What is certain is that, if he managed to earn the hatred even of those of his aides he had most rewarded, he must have been an autocrat. And what of Gaius Trebonius? It seems that he kept Mark Antony occupied while the others were busy holding this little party for Caesar. Trebonius, can you believe it? He was Caesar's legate in Gaul for many years, and was even in Britain with him, and then magistrate, and consul, and future proconsul of Asia. A man thus rewarded by a superior should have nothing but unconditional devotion for him. And instead he did not hesitate to kill him. Precisely because he worked in close contact with Caesar, he must have been exasperated by his tyranny."

Maecenas, however, had the impression that the personages just mentioned as well as the others he had heard named in connection with the conspiracy had acted mainly because they were in the shadow of the dictator, who had condemned them to a life as half-men. It was one thing to be consul in a Republic which followed its normal institutional course, quite another under an oppressive figure like that of Caesar: history would remember him, and relegate those around him to mere supporting players, even if they did occupy the highest positions of the state.

They had probably done it out of pride and ambition, as well as solid economic interests. Maecenas was ready to wager good money that the killers – those who had stated upon the podium of the temple that they had acted in the name of freedom of choice – would not give up the positions of command that Caesar himself had assigned them for the next five years.

Unless, of course, people like Mark Antony and Lepidus or Cicero managed to turn the popular mood against them and put them out of action, but something told him that this would not happen: Antony, for example, had not been seen since, and it was rumoured that he had barricaded himself in his house for fear of attempts on his life. And Lepidus, who was supposed to take Caesar's place, had hastened to take refuge beyond the Tiber.

And these were the two men who, more than any others, would presumably have been aspiring to take the dictator's place.

Maecenas shuddered at the thought of what might happen: those two would not hand over power to Caesar's murderers so easily, and were surely preparing their next move. Which would certainly not be to flee! And in the meanwhile, the conspirators would have plenty of time to win over the favour of the crowd, which was by definition capricious: yesterday praising Caesar for the wheat that he distributed free, and now ready to go along with his killers for a handful of *sestertii*.

"At last the Republic is restored! It has been transformed and replaced by a monarchy for at least four years – ever since Caesar's crossing of the Rubicon!" said Marcellus, interrupting the flow of his thoughts.

Maecenas saw that they had begun the ascent of the Aventine Hill, where Marcellus had his home. The company of this man had begun to weigh upon him. He did not like him. He did not like his politics, nor his attitude. He was a coward who had always opposed Caesar, but who only dared come out into the open now that Caesar was dead. Evidently, the conspirators were well aware of his cowardice and had been careful not to involve him. Yet even he could sense the contempt that the senator harboured against him: Marcellus was of those patricians of ancient nobility who looked down upon the members of the equestrian class like him, who were Italics and not Romans, upon whom Caesar had relied more than upon the senators themselves. But at the same time, nobles like Marcellus did not let their prejudices affect their business: they held their noses and did not hesitate to enter into contracts with the recipients of their scorn.

But then, he told himself, that was what he himself was doing. Holding his nose.

He could not keep quiet in the face of Marcellus's absurd ingenuity, though. The statement needed correction, albeit with the proper manners.

"Are you certain you know what Marcus Brutus and Cassius, Decimus Brutus and Trebonius, Casca and the others really want?" he asked the senator, while the bearers continued to keep the two litters side by side. "They have announced no plans or projects. They have not said that they wish to give up the positions which Caesar had assigned them for the future, which suggests that they do not want new elections. And I do not think that they are so naive as to think that the Republic will resume its normal course as though these last years had not happened. Caesar paved the way for ambition. You will see how now many imitators he will have…"

Marcellus smugly dismissed his words with a gesture. "Nonsense! Democracy is too deeply-rooted in Romans for it not to resume its course, now that the tyrant has been got rid of. Caesar's assassins will not give up their positions simply because they give them immunity in the face of Caesar's supporters. If they did, they would be at the mercy of Antony and Lepidus, who would take them to trial whenever they liked and thus get them out of the way and seize power for themselves! But Cicero will bring all to agreement, you'll see. I know that he intends to propose an amnesty for the murderers…"

As far as democracy went, thought Maecenas to himself, the Romans had long since lost any right to call themselves masters: Marcellus pretended to have forgotten the dictatorships of Marius and Silla, the triumvirate of Caesar, Pompey and Crassus, the failed attempts of Catiline and of Lepidus' father, the civil wars, the proscriptions, as well as Caesar's lifetime dictatorship, which had dominated the last half century of Roman politics. He could not see how the future would differ from the years that had gone before. But this time he preferred to keep quiet and pretended to have been convinced by the soundness of his interlocutor's arguments. In business, lying was essential, he concluded, and he was there for business alone.

Which was why he stiffened when Marcellus stopped before an elegant *domus* guarded by two legionaries. If it was Marcellus's home, carrying out their transaction under the greedy gaze of soldiers was not ideal. And if the senator wanted to intimidate him… well, he had succeeded.

But he noticed that his host seemed bewildered too. "Soldiers! Why are you here?" Marcellus asked the two legionaries, descending from his litter.

"For your protection, sir. Yours and that of your family, by order of *magister equitum* Lepidus!" said one of them. Warily, the senator hesitated, then nodded and invited Maecenas to descend from his litter too. Maecenas silently ordered two of his bearers to take the chest containing the money and follow him to the door. He was aware of the risks of carrying a chest full of coins with him, but he had wanted to rub Marcellus's nose in his wealth and smother him with cold, hard cash so as to stifle his air of superiority towards the equestrians. People like that were in awe of no one, and tolerated those who had no illustrious ancestors only if they were filthy rich. He was, and had no intention of hiding it when it was useful. Flaunting his possessions in the senator's face might make his noble interlocutor show him the respect that senators usually only accorded their peers. The doorkeeper, tenser than he should have been, did little to re-assure him, though. Rather than feeling protected, he began to feel threatened. Marcellus looked nervous, a sign that he too sensed something amiss. In the vestibule, several busts lay broken on the ground, and a certain disorder was evident. Maecenas and Marcellus entered the lobby and two other soldiers barred their way.

"Who are you?" asked one of them, his face grim behind the visor of his helmet.

"What do you mean, who am I? I am the master of this house, imbecile!" answered Marcellus, already red with anger. "Who are you, rather, and what are you doing here?"

The soldier gave him a violent backhanded slap on the cheek which sent him reeling. Maecenas rushed over to support him and prevent him from reacting, and realised straightaway that he had done the right thing: the senator saw what must be his wife immediately behind the soldiers, a baby in her arms, and launched himself at them, only to find spears blocking his way.

"Calm down, my friend. You are not in command. The city is in chaos and it is the soldiers who decide the law, for now," said another soldier, who only then made an appearance. He waved his sword under Marcellus's nose and added, "Now be a good boy and shut up until we decide who to deliver you to. You're worth a lot of money, you know. And Caesar's killers are giving plenty of it out, or so they say…"

It was only then that Maecenas noticed the four legionaries, including a centurion, who had been disarmed and were standing with Marcellus's wife, Octavia – Caesar's great-niece – near the *impluvium*. There was disagreement among the soldiers, then: some did not agree with the abduction, and the subordinates had rebelled against their officer. In that case, it might still be possible to salvage the situation, and Maecenas began to wonder how. In any case, no one seemed to attach too much importance to him, who represented no bargaining chip. Unless they knew of his money, of course: it was necessary to put it to good use before they stole it.

He stared at Marcellus, who appeared shocked and was barely managing to hold his anger in check. Ironic, he thought wryly, that he, a secret supporter of Caesar's murderers, had become the victim of others who wanted to ingratiate themselves with them. He looked over at Octavia: she was not beautiful, but she had a grace which made her very interesting to a man's eyes. She was trembling and her eyes were moist, which revealed a lack of self-control and a fragility of which, without doubt, her husband could not be proud. She seemed totally inadequate for the role of one of the Republic's most visible matrons, a senator's wife and great-neice of a king. At her side was another senator, who looked to be one of the family. He must be another of the *gens Julia*, and was roughly the same age as Marcellus. He was looking around him nervously and could barely maintain his composure – he would probably have preferred to shout and kick up a fuss, but it was pride, and not fear, that held him back. Next, his eyes fell on the centurion. He kept close to Octavia and followed her movements closely. He was young for one possessing such a high rank, so his parents must be rich. He was not venal, then, and perhaps could be counted upon, especially if, as seemed to be the case, he had some personal interest in protecting her.

Finally, he examined the soldiers who said they were in control. Shady, wretched faces, certainly wholly uninterested in the political events of the moment but just as determined to derive the maximum economic benefit from it if it meant leaving behind their humble condition.

"What are they saying in the Capitol, Senator?" asked one of the armed legionaries, addressing Marcellus. "Who do the people side with? Have Caesar's killers a large following? If Mark Antony and Cicero are still holed up at home, and Lepidus is standing to one side, it shouldn't be hard for them to take possession of the city."

Marcellus turned his head away, staring at a point somewhere on the wall next to him.

The soldier stepped forward and gave him a shove. "Answer me when I talk to you, senator! You're not in the senate now, protected by lictors of the consul."

"Perhaps Senator Marcellus does not answer you because he is unable to," Maecenas hastily intervened. "In the Capitol there is such confusion that we cannot know how the situation will develop. And your actions may be useless, or even backfire on you", he pointed out.

"And who might you be?" asked the soldier, seeming only then to notice his presence.

"Someone who has an interesting proposal to make to you, and enough money to be certain you will lend me your ears," said the Etruscan.

The soldier looked at him diffidently. Maecenas could feel eyes filled with contempt but also with greed upon him, and was certain that he had their full attention.

"I'm listening. We'll have to pass the time until they bring us news about who's offering more anyway. And I doubt that'll be before tomorrow," said the soldier finally, relaxing somewhat.

"I'll pay you more. And most likely it will be the only offer that you will receive in the immediate future," said the Etruscan.

The soldier was silent. And the others too seemed all ears.

"I saw only chaos at the Capitol," continued Maecenas. "Among the people, only those who have received payments seemed to support Caesar's killers. Many others seemed to be waiting to see what turn events took, while the veterans were eager to take revenge on those who had killed their benefactor. No one knows what will happen tomorrow in the Senate and in the city. There may be a settling of accounts or, worse still, rebellion, and the powerful may well be too busy with their own feuds to be interested in your offer. In short, you might get something in a few days, or you might get nothing at all. I, however," and he went over to the slave who held the chest, "offer you a tidy sum right away – if you leave immediately." He ordered the slave to open it and the glimmer of gold on the surface seemed to dazzle the legionary's eyes, wresting from him and his fellow soldiers a cry of astonishment.

He rushed over to the chest and sank his hands into it, realising at once that he could immerse almost his entire forearm before reaching the coins at the bottom. He smiled to his comrades and shouted, "Well lads, there's enough in here to set us up for a bit."

The other armed soldiers rushed toward the chest and allowed themselves to experience the same heady feeling, and from the corner of his eye Maecenas saw the officer stiffen and take a step towards them. It was clear that he intended to take advantage of their distraction to attack them from behind. Maecenas judged the manoeuvre too risky – it was not what he wanted, so he made a negative gesture with his head, and the officer stopped, hesitantly.

Meanwhile, the one who seemed to be the leader of the mutineers spoke to him again. "And suppose I accept your kind offer," he said, "I keep the money, split it with my comrades, and then tomorrow take this family to whoever will give me the most money anyway…"

"Suppose that I don't let you…"

The legionary laughed. "Ah! And how will you do that? You're unarmed and a bit feeble looking to make threats like that!"

"Oh, I'm armed, much more so than you!" answered Maecenas, forcing himself to smile and appear confident. In reality, he had never been in a similar situation, and was testing his nerve for the first time. "I am armed with money… more money! This is simply a down payment: if you now free this family and take me to one of my properties in Rome, I will write a letter and a member of my staff will give you an additional amount."

The soldier looked at his fellows, who stared wide-eyed, attempting to hide their enthusiasm. But Maecenas knew he already had them in hand. It was all too easy: however many of them there were, whatever weapons they had, he had an overwhelming advantage over them – so much money that he could afford to throw it away.

And anyway, it was far from wasted, judging by the look of gratitude that an incredulous Marcellus shot him. The villa at Cuma was assured, and perhaps even something more: the other senator was also looking at him with respect, and gave him a nod of thanks.

The soldier who was closest nodded and said, "Well let's not waste any more time then. Let's take advantage of this gentleman's generosity immediately, before he realises that he is out of his mind. Come on lads, let's go. Centurion, there's plenty for you too, if you want to come along," he concluded, turning to the officer as, together with a fellow soldier, he lifted the chest.

But the centurion only glared at him without moving, and the other unarmed soldiers, though visibly tempted by the legionary's offer, followed his example.

Maecenas walked calmly towards the door. Now he had an adequate armed guard, which would keep him safe from the dangers of the coming evening. And he had made one of the most important senators happy – two, in fact, if you counted Octavia's other relative – earning the gratitude of a family as prestigious as that of the Julia, who in all probability would continue to play a leading role in the city even after the death of their most famous member.

He was satisfied. He had obtained much more than he had hoped for when he set off for Rome.

*

"Did you hear that? *Magister equitum!* A sickly naive boy at the head of a vast army in the event of Julius Caesar not being able to lead his troops into battle" whispered the soldier.

"Shhh!" hissed a fellow soldier, his face illuminated by the campfire. "Some things are better left unsaid. Remember that you are talking about the great-nephew of our supreme commander. Who knows that someone might go and tell him your words in order to ingratiate himself! And anyway – remember that if Caesar chose him, it means he has what it takes. Caesar never errs – that is why he has become what he has become."

29

Octavian stopped in his tracks as soon as he heard the dialogue, and with him so did Agrippa and Rufus, all three keeping away from the light of the fire by which the two soldiers were playing dice. The young man felt a tremor of anger mount inside him. He would have liked to lash out at the skeptical soldier, throwing in his face the prophecy he had just received from Theogenes and punishing him personally for his lack of faith. And at the same time, he wanted to reward the other soldier, who acknowledged Caesar's ability to identify talent. However, he felt Agrippa's arm hold him back, and knew he must avoid being recognised: it had been a memorable day, and there was no need to finish it with a brawl. Because when Agrippa was involved, that was how things often ended.

In fact, Octavian was waiting impatiently for the morning, when he could take a jaunt to Apollonia. He couldn't wait to talk to his teacher, Apollodorus of Pergamum, to whom his great-uncle had sent him to finish his studies. He was anxious to know what the scholar thought of Theogenes and whether he considered his predictions reliable and realistic. However, part of him was also afraid that Apollodorus would bring tumbling down the castle he was building upon the foundations established by the prophecy.

Ruler of the world.

In all honesty, it was hard for him to believe, too. It would be no surprise if an educated man like Apollodorus was skeptical. Yet people came from all over Asia and Europe to consult Theogenes: if his prophecies had turned out to be unsound, he would not have enjoyed such renown. He decided that he would behave as though it were all true. In any case, his great-uncle seemed to have him pegged for a bright future, and he might as well put it to the best use possible. He would make Caesar proud of him and never, despite his youth and his weak constitution, regret having made him one of his closest aides.

"Pay them no attention. A soldier always speaks ill of his commanders. You've just had a taste of what it'll be like when you are leading them," said Salvidienus Rufus, when they were far enough away to speak without the two soldiers hearing them.

Octavian opened his mouth to answer, but then noticed that Agrippa was no longer with them. He knew immediately in which direction to look: he knew his friend all too well. He saw him unsteadily approaching the soldier who had maligned him.

It seemed as though he was pretending to be drunk. He hoped Agrippa did not want a quarrel, at least this time: that would give the distinct impression that there was a regime of terror hovering over the ranks, and he wanted to win the soldiers' respect naturally, without forcing them to fear him.

Agrippa came close to the two soldiers and seemed to stumble, kicking one of the brands in the fire, which struck the disrespectful legionary and set fire to the hem of his robe. He rolled on the ground up to put out the flame then rose defiantly. "What are you doing, you idiot? I'll show you…" he breathed into Agrippa's face, before realising that he was dealing with a tribune. Suddenly, he became more submissive. "I mean… tribune… perhaps the legate of the legion would not be happy to see his officer drunk…"

Agrippa gave him a gentle slap on the cheek. "Come off it! No one's ever died for having a drop too many… Come on, soldier, nothing happened. Back to your dice," he answered with a wicked smile, perfectly imitating the thick, wavering voice of a drunk, and then walking away from the fire towards the two friends.

Octavian shook his head and smiled back at him. Good old Agrippa! If there was one person upon whose loyalty and affection he would have sworn, it was him.

"Very clever of you to punish that soldier for his views without seeming to do so…" he said, encircling his waist with an arm. "You never change, though… With you by my side I'm as safe as though I were in an iron barrel."

"Of course – like Atilius Regulus!" joked Agrippa. "Now that they've prophesied your dominion over the world, it's more in my favour than ever to keep you close, isn't it? On the other hand, if Theogenes prophesied a shining destiny for me, it's obvious that it will only be such if I stay by your side. It's very much in my interest to back you up…"

Octavian smiled again. His friend had been fond of him since they were children, when he was still just the scion of a minor branch of an ancient but impoverished noble family, sickly and clumsy to boot. He was certain that Agrippa wasn't his friend out of mere self-interest or opportunism but it was a question he would have to ask about anyone that he had met since coming into Caesar's good graces. Salvidienus Rufus included. He glanced over at him and saw that his face had darkened. Until that day, he had only had the impression that Rufus was sometimes jealous of the profound understanding between him and Agrippa, and wanted to be part of it. But this time there was something more: Theogenes' prophecy for *his* future had been less rosy. The astrologer, he had told his friends, had predicted a gratifying destiny for the near future, followed by ruin later on. He felt compelled to give him his full attention.

"If it's true what Agrippa says, dear Rufus, you have only to do as he does: stay by my side and you will elude this inauspicious prophecy, no? In any case, a glorious time awaits you, and it is up to you to put it to good use, don't you think?" he said, embracing him too.

Puzzled, Rufus nodded. "I see no reason why our paths should separate, dear Octavian," he replied. "But we cannot know where life will take us. We are about to embark on one of the greatest undertakings ever conducted in the name of Rome, and we will run every sort of risk under the command of your great-uncle. Each of us will be given responsibilities that will lead him who knows where, to do who knows what, and we will not always be able to decide in accordance with our own will. And it seems that my destiny will not be as fortunate as yours…" he concluded dispiritedly.

Octavian embraced both his friends. "What you say is undeniable. But so is the fact that there is a great bond between the three of us, and today we learned that together we can go far. We might even be invincible, if we remain united. What about that? Invincible! We will make Caesar proud of us with our deeds, and when we return to Rome, we will be considered heroes."

Agrippa did not hesitate to produce a roar of triumph. Rufus waited a moment before following suite, but allowed himself to be infected by Octavian's enthusiasm and, seeming finally heartened, joined in. The young man was pleased with his leadership, which never failed to surprise him: he still had to work out exactly how much of an influence he was able to exert on others, but during his short life there had already been many clues he felt augured well. Despite being somewhat reserved and far from a picture of health, people tended to love him and to give him credit. He did not need to go looking for them: they came to come to him to seek his approval. Perhaps because he gave the appearance of not caring much about their opinion of him.

It had even happened even with the great Julius Caesar. He had never really tried to get his great-uncle's attention, convinced as he was that the famous leader would never have confidence in such an apparently insignificant individual as he. Yet, the dictator had given him so many opportunities: summoning him to Spain at the end of the civil war, having him march with him for Italy and in his triumph through the streets of the City, and even conferring upon him the title of *magister equitum in pectore* for the upcoming campaign. Deputy Commander! He, who had never even picked up a sword! Well, he would not disappoint. Where his physique would not take him, his brains would. And he was sure they would allow him to achieve remarkable results. And in any case, for the things his frail body was unable to tackle, there was Agrippa: that friendship was the most precious thing that had ever happened to him, and he would do nothing to undermine it.

Anyway, as long as Caesar was at the head of the state, his back would be protected, and he would have plenty of time to learn what was needed without anyone taking advantage of his weaknesses to crush or humiliate him. Nothing was more likely than that five years hence, at the end of the campaign which would extend Roman sovereignty over Parti, Getae and Daci, he would have become one of the dictator's most important aides, if he had shown that he deserved it. On the other hand, hadn't Caesar himself wanted to enrol him prematurely among the members of the aristocracy? Had he not offered him the opportunity to preside over the summer games? Had he not passed a law that had anticipated his *cursus honorum*, just as with Scipio Africanus?

He had not done the same for Quintus Pedius, nor for Lucius Pinarius, the other older children of his sisters, the closest relatives of Julius Caesar after the painful death of Julia, his only legitimate daughter.

And yet, he had done it for him.

Whatever he had become, it was thanks to his great-uncle.

Caesar was his idol.

III

She had heard that someone had fainted at the sight of the torn, bloodied toga, and Octavia had no trouble believing it. Etain had been forced to support her when she had noticed the grim garment which had once belonged to the dominator of Rome displayed there among the other elements of the funerary scene.

The girl turned to her mother Atia, who was crying silently, her head resting against the chest of her second husband, Lucius Marcius Philippus, a good stepfather to Octavia and Octavian. None of them had been brave enough over the previous days to visit the gilded chapel Mark Antony had built in the Forum in front of the Rostra to host the corpse of the dictator, and where the citizens had been allowed to lay their offerings. In fact, it had been their friends who had advised against it, at least until the political situation was clearer: there were still too many hotheads about seeking opportunities to show their joy at the death of the alleged tyrant. And for her family, danger lurked in every corner of the city.

But then had come the opening of Caesar's will, and the wind had changed.

Not that the political situation was any clearer. A soothsayer himself would not have been able to outline the institutional landscape of the near future. The only certainty was that Caesar's bequest had dwarfed the amounts spent by his killers to win popular support, and now it was Brutus, Cassius, Decimus and the rest who had to watch their backs and move about accompanied by their lictors or gladiators. But on the other hand, they enjoyed broad protection in the Senate, and Mark Antony and Lepidus seemed inclined to agree with them, forgetting that it was the duty of the dictator's closest aides to avenge him.

Caesar had laid down Rome's institutional outlines for the five years to come, and established the succession of magistrates. In his own way, he had given the city tranquility and a long series of certainties: now it had all come tumbling down and everything had been called into question.

And that will, that wretched will, catapulted them – his closest relatives, who had always kept clear of the cut and thrust of politics – to the centre of the arena.

Octavia looked around her. There was such a crush of people close to the funeral pyre that she had no hope of spying the only man she actually wanted to see at that time, the only one by whom she would feel protected in the new, menacing world into which the events following the Ides of March had thrown her: a world that frightened her more than ever, full of terrifying shadows, hungry for power and glory, looming over her and her family.

After seeking him among the miserable and occasionally hate filled faces of the ordinary people, she began looking among the purple-trimmed robes of the senators, their faces at once brightened by their sense of relief at the death of Caesar and troubled by the fear of passing under a new master, or worse, entering a new civil war. No, she certainly wouldn't find the one she sought among them. She saw instead her husband, on his face the same contrasting emotions visible that she had already observed in his colleagues. Marcellus had been pardoned by Caesar for having sided against him in the civil war, but if he had more guts he would have happily participated in the conspiracy. Yet now he was afraid of the consequences, and perhaps was wondering whether it would have been better to have let the dictator get himself killed by the Parthians…

Octavia's ears were enchanted by the litanies sung by the *coryphaei*: "I saved them because there were those who assassinated me… let them be cursed for their treachery…" They were verses from a tragedy by Pacuvius that Mark Antony had wanted declaimed at the funeral, but they could be applied to the only men of Rome who had not participated in that ceremony: Caesar's assassins, the betrayers all of his trust. If she were a man, she would have found a way to take revenge for their disloyalty. But the only two men in her family, Lucius Pinarius and Quintus Pedius, seemed principally committed to discussing and contending their share of the inheritance.

A group of men began hoisting the gold and purple bedecked bed of ivory upon which rested the battered corpse of the dictator onto the pyre. Only then did Antony begin to speak, and Octavia to realise that those verses had been part of a very subtle strategy.

"I need not dwell, citizens, upon the merits of Caesar: he did that for himself, by working for you in death with the same zeal that he demonstrated in life," said the consul. "He fed you and made you wealthy, and we will never know how much wealth the certain conquest of the Parthian kingdom would have brought to the treasury and to all of us, and how proud you would have felt to have avenged through him the humiliation suffered by Rome with the defeat of Crassus at Carrhae and the loss of the eagles of the legions! But we know that his first concern was always you. He trusted his citizens to such an extent that he, the most powerful man in the world, would move among you without an escort. And not because he believed himself invulnerable as a god, but because he trusted you: so certain was he of being loved for the good he had done that he need fear nothing and no one. It was not through fear that he believed he held us in the palm of his hand, but through respect and love! And love and respect, those who took him away from us most certainly had. Yes, they did, because their motives were pure and noble! You heard them when they explained their actions, and none could believe that they did so in bad faith. This act of theirs was no personal one! These honourable men respected and loved Caesar, because Caesar, so generous to all, had been even more so to them, elevating them to the highest positions of the state. They acted against what he stood for, because they felt compelled to do so. Indeed, their gesture should be appreciated because we know how much it cost them."

It was not just pity that Antony wished to arouse, but also indignation, thought Octavia, and she received confirmation of her conviction when she saw the consul take Caesar's bloody toga from the *tropaion* upon which it had been displayed and hold it up, waving it in all directions. As she watched the men lay the casket on the pyre, she began to think that the day was not destined to end peacefully. And only then did she realise that one of the bearers was actually him, Gaius Chaerea.

She tried to catch his eye, but the centurion appeared to be totally immersed in his role. She wondered if that was an act of love for her, or a form of respect for a commander under whom he had fought in Spain, in the last phase of the civil war. She liked to think it was both: a week before, when he had appeared at her home, he had not managed to protect her, and had it not been for the intervention of that Etruscan, things might have got very unpleasant. But he had made her understand that he was willing to do anything for her, and his presence had stopped her from surrendering to the most total despair.

She had not thought about him for years. As though by ignoring him she could wipe away their crime. She had left Etain to care for the little boy, and only occasionally had given in to the impulse to ask about his growth; she had never wanted to know about the man with whom she had conceived him, in a moment of weakness for which Gaius blamed himself. In reality, she had never dreamed of blaming anyone. And if she had not wanted to see him it was only because it would remind her – she who had set herself the goal of being an upright Roman matron – of having failed in her duties. And then, Gaius had loosed within her emotions which were too powerful: she sought serenity, above all, and it was hard to reconcile serenity with the presence in her life of a man who could make her lose her head so completely…

"Let us burn him in the Temple of Jupiter!" shouted someone in the crowd. "He is a god, and must burn in Rome's main temple."

"No! Let us burn him where he was assassinated! In the Curia of Pompey! So the assassins are forced to realise what they have done."

Antony's speech was short, and Octavia, absorbed in her thoughts of Gaius, could not say if that was because it was interrupted by the people or because he had already done enough to excite their souls. And if that was his intent, he had succeeded admirably: many people around her were beginning to stir.

No, the day would not end quietly.

"If you think *you're* disappointed then how should *I* feel? *I* fought for him in Gaul, and this is how he rewards me…" she heard her older cousin, Quintus Pedius, complaining.

"But I was closer to him in civilian tasks," said Lucius Pinarius. "Without me, many laws would never have seen the light of day…"

"Don't make me laugh! It's common knowledge that you weren't one of his favourites, while I was assigned important positions during the war. You should thank the gods that at least he remembered you in his will. But, if he did, it was only because you were his relative, and he had little choice… Or else out of respect for the memory of his sister…"

"If you put it that way then you shouldn't feel flattered either, since he left you what he left me. If I am worth little, you're worth even less, because you risked your life for him in Gaul and for you there was no position among the magistrates he appointed for the next five years. You must have given a poor account of yourself…" insisted Pinarius.

"Oh, enough! In any case, it makes no sense to argue," said an irritated Pedius, changing the subject. "We must join forces to get what is rightly ours, at least. And considering that we cannot count on the boy Octavian, we will have to do it ourselves. Antony has had Caesar's wife hand everything over to him, and will already be getting his hands on the assets."

"Yes," agreed Pinarius. "His position provides him with an excellent excuse for prolonging the emergency and taking all he can. And he will certainly will take advantage of Octavian's young age to appropriate his part too. We should at least make sure of ours. We must talk to the consul as soon as possible. We might even come to some arrangement with him…"

"What do you mean?"

"Try to convince him that, if he gives us a part of Octavian's inheritance as well as some magistratures, we will convince the boy not to ask questions. It'll be no problem persuading him to drop any claim…" he suggested, before noticing that Octavia could hear him. His face took on a guilty expression.

"Are you joking? Antony dreams of emulating Caesar and succeeding him upon the throne the dictator had built for himself. He will be extremely annoyed at not having been named among the first heirs in the will, and will do anything to get his hands on the inheritance: he needs the means to impose his authority, and money is always the most effective means of all. Caesar bought half of Rome to get into power and stay in the saddle," replied Pedius indignantly. But Octavia could not tell whether her cousin spoke sincerely or simply because he knew she was listening.

She shook her head. Her two cousins were agitated too, but for different reasons than the others. It seemed that the growing tension in the air did not concern them: they were too busy discussing their petty plans to realize that the stakes in play were much higher.

She had the distinct feeling that the serenity she had always sought – and which Caesar, with his political efforts and his decisions about the private life of the family, seemed to have given her – would be a long time returning.

The shouts of the people were increasing in volume, and the crowd began to push toward the pyre, many simply wanting to touch their benefactor for one last time. Octavia was afraid of being knocked down, or of a brawl breaking out, and found herself looking instinctively not for her husband of several years but for Gaius Chaerea, the soldier she had just encountered again after so long. Surprised at herself, she clung to Etain's arm, and when she finally met the centurion's gaze, she seemed to read in his eyes a flash of understanding. Perhaps it was nothing more than a sensation, she knew, but she felt reassured.

Soon after, Gaius Chaerea grabbed one of the torches which burned near the pyre, ordered a fellow soldier to do the same and, before even waiting for the order of the magistrates and priests, they threw them onto the piles of twigs at the base. The flames took immediately, and in a moment the ivory canopy, the regal figure of the dictator and the *tropaion* bearing his bloody robe were engulfed in flames. The people began to shout more loudly, but stopped moving forward, awed by the fiery serpent which wound its way up towards the heavens, resigned now to it taking place in the Forum.

Someone began shouting accusations at the murderers.

Octavia peered at the expressions of the senators. Since Caesar's death, some of them had shown without restraint their satisfaction at the actions of Brutus and Cassius, Dolabella in particular. And now that the crowd seemed to have decided which party to follow, they were afraid to be associated with the real killers who, unlike them, were too influential and powerful a group to be punished with impunity.

She started trembling again, not for herself this time, but for her brother. In what world would the one Caesar had appointed as his heir live?

*

Agrippa shook his head: Octavian would never make a fighter. Despite hitting the training post like a madman, the only result he obtained was that of tiring himself out quickly. He motioned to him to slow down, but his friend only gave him a sideways look. The *campidoctor* in charge of their training was too much in awe of Julius Caesar's great-nephew, and Octavian himself had instructed Agrippa to demand the utmost from the instructor, but sometimes his friend, troubled by the unprecedented effort he saw in Octavian's face, did not want to play the torturer right to the bitter end.

"Gently, young Octavian, gently," said the *campidoctor*, fearful that he might collapse to the ground unconscious with fatigue, as had happened a few weeks earlier.

Agrippa pulled a face: that was just the kind of thing that would get Octavian's back up and make him go at it even harder. And, in fact, his friend doubled the frequency of his blows, making Agrippa stop training and stand watching him, waiting for the inevitable moment when he would have to run over to hold him up.

"Keep… going, Agrippa. There's nothing… to see. Doctor, Agrippa's… slacking!" Octavian shouted, trying to attract the attention of the instructor, but the words came out faint and broken. The man was within earshot, though, and could hear, and zealous as ever, he walked over to Agrippa and shouted in his face, "Come on, slacker! Take a lesson from our next *magister equitum*, the most promising of the recruits."

From the corner of his eye, Agrippa looked over at his friend and saw that even he was struggling to contain his amusement. He had to make an effort not to burst out laughing in front of the *campidoctor*, so he pulled himself together, bowed his head respectfully and began to punch the post. The instructor went away, apparently convinced he had earned credit from a close relative of the dictator. The poor fool didn't know Octavian well enough to realise that he had just made an enemy. When he arrived, Caesar would certainly be informed of the instructor's cowardice and ineptitude. Octavian knew how to be as generous and helpful to his friends as he was ruthless with those who disappointed or aggrieved him.

Agrippa had not yet seen his friend struggle with a real flesh and blood enemy, and in fact, he thought, he probably never has: with his weak physique, he gave such an impression of fragility that no one had the heart to really go for him, nor did they fear him enough to really want to hurt him. But Agrippa knew him well, and he knew that behind his uncertain health, good manners and delicate features, he hid an iron will. He wondered what expedients, legal or illegal, Octavian would be willing to use to defeat an opponent.

Seeing him almost collapsing onto the pole after missing a blow, he rushed over to grab him before he hit the ground, but when he took him in his arms, Octavian struggled violently, displaying unexpected vitality. "You don't need to hold me up," he shouted, breathing hard, "I've already told you, damn it! If I fall, it's right that I eat dust. I'll be eating plenty of it on the marches through the desert of Syria and beyond the borders, so I might as well get used to it now! Otherwise, how can I march with my head held high at Caesar's side?"

Agrippa held himself at a safe distance, so as not to offend him further. "Forgive me, my friend. But you must also avoid marching upon a litter: in a few days Caesar will be here with us, and soon we will start the campaign. If you get sick – and you know that it can happen – it won't look good to have you lying there among the provisions, coughing your guts out with a fever. Remember what happened when you set out to Spain: we almost missed the decisive battle of the civil war."

Octavian hesitated a moment. "I cannot disappoint Caesar. Or the soldiers, who are already so fond of me..."

They were fond of him because they felt protective of him, thought Agrippa, not because of his charisma, which for the moment was simply a reflection of the dictator's light. But he was careful not to tell him that.

"Caesar is loved by the soldiers because he has shared their hardships and hard work with them," continued Octavian. "I must do as much myself, if I want to win their respect and not lose their affection. They gave me their trust and I must show myself worthy of it. I will ride alongside the greatest conqueror in history, and I have no choice but to show that I am like him or die trying."

Caesar had also won the love of the soldiers by greasing their palms, thought Agrippa. But he said nothing. Meanwhile, Rufus Salvidienus appeared with a man Octavian recognized as one of his own freedman. Their friend's face was dark and he looked shaken. Suddenly, Agrippa noticed the silence inside the camp:

the shouts of the centurions, tramping of horses and soldiers and rattling had ceased. The only sounds were those of the recruits training in the outfield, where they themselves were.

"*Ave, dominus*," said the freedman addressing Octavian with an expression just as sad as that of the tribune. "I bring urgent news from your noble mother in Rome," he added, handing him a bag with a wax tablet.

Octavian took out the message and read it, and his expression immediately underwent a metamorphosis that frightened Agrippa. His delicate features hardened in a way he had never imagined possible, and his blue eyes shone with fire. He tottered on unsteady legs and a violent tremor ran through his body.

Agrippa peered at Rufus, who was about to open his mouth, then fell silent, staring at Octavian.

Octavian stared into the distance, towards the sea, towards Italy, the flames in his eyes remaining undiminished in intensity.

"Who was it?" he asked the freedman, his voice so hoarse and low that Agrippa would never have recognized it had he not been standing before him.

"There were a lot of names flying around when I left," the man replied. "But your mother and your stepfather sent me to Brindisi just hours after it happened, so I can say nothing definite, except that there were rumours about there being several of them, and people of rank, too. The only certain ones are Cassius Longinus, Markus Brutus and Decimus Brutus, while Mark Antony seems not to be part of the circle of conspirators. For all I know, there may be civil war in Italy by now. For this reason your parents warned you not to return."

Agrippa could take no more. "What's happened?" he asked.

Octavian turned his head and looked at him as though he had only then noticed his presence. Tears extinguished the flames in his eyes, running down his face and wetting his lips, as his mouth opened to pronounce a barely audible sentence.

"Caesar is dead," he said, before collapsing to his knees in front of his friend.

*

42

Octavia was grateful to Gaius Chaerea for having lit the funeral pyre and distracted the crowd before things took a turn for the worse. The centurion would get a good scolding from his superiors – perhaps from Lepidus in person – for acting without authorization, but perhaps they would also commend his initiative. She liked to think that he had done it for her, but when she had met his eyes in the crowd Octavia had not been able to hold them, and had turned her head towards Etain.

She must not let herself get involved. Not again.

And so she stared into the flames that wound higher and higher into the leaden sky of late Markh, giving off a heat that warmed the area around the pyre, soothing the tremors that seized her every time she thought about what awaited her family.

What would Octavian do now? His role as Caesar's heir, which seemed implicit in the testamentary dispositions, exposed him to the vengeance not only of the conspirators: Mark Antony, himself evidently determined to succeed his supreme commander, would see the boy as a rival and would attempt instinctively to hinder him. Indeed, hindering him would be the least of it – when he put his mind to it, Mark Antony could be like a rabid dog.

And what of Lepidus? He was an opportunist, and would not allow a young man without means and with such a great legacy upon his shoulders a chance. Not to mention Cicero, who abhorred any form of autocracy and would see an individual to whom Caesar had provided the resources to succeed him as a threat. And Aulus Hirtius, and Vibius Pansa, who perhaps could hardly wait for it to be their turn to enter the consulate, take advantage of it and rule the roost as the presence of the dictator had prevented them from doing until then. And then there was Cleopatra, the Queen of Egypt, who Caesar had shamelessly paraded about Rome, and not as a spoil of war or as a guest of rank, but as a powerful and influential concubine: what would she do now that she could no longer enjoy the support of the dictator and the father of her son Caesarion? Her presence in Rome was a further destabilising factor.

Too many rabid dogs in the political arena for a nineteen-year-old in poor health and with no experience – theoretically endowed with many riches but with little actually in hand – to hope to survive.

Her mother and stepfather had realised all this and, in informing the boy of his great-uncle's death, had suggested he stay far away from trouble. Yes, because there would be only trouble for him if he returned to Italy. He would be greeted by the natural hostility of Caesar's assassins as well as that of his aides, or at least those few who had not betrayed him but, she was sure, would not hesitate to betray his designated heir.

Especially because, in an environment where what counted above all was bargaining power, Octavian had nothing to offer. Without Caesar, he was nothing.

The others, instead, had prospered and accumulated power, money and patronage in his shadow, and could now launch themselves into the political arena with some chance of success.

When the wind began to blow in her direction, the intense smell of incense and roses which had been strewn on the pyre penetrated her nostrils, making her eyes water. The figures around her grew indistinct, and she felt even more isolated. She wanted to get home as soon as possible, but for her and the family a long day lay ahead: they would have to extinguish the ashes and take them to the Campus Martius near the tomb of Julia. And then, as was the custom, the relatives would visit the home of Calpurnia, Caesar's widow, to remember him over a rich banquet. And it would go on for a long time, because Octavia was sure Pedius Pinarius intended to make some kind of agreement with Antony, perhaps even one which was to the detriment of Octavian. She would have to intervene in some way.

"Death to the murderers!" rang out a cry nearby.

"Yes, may they die as they killed Caesar!" cried another.

"Let's drive them out of their homes!"

"Let's burn them! Let's burn everything! Let's get Brutus! Let's get Cassius! They're the main culprits!"

Yes, Antony had achieved his purpose: suddenly, having got rid of an alleged tyrant was no longer anything to brag about.

The crowd began to sway. Many expressed their devotion to Caesar by standing, stock-still and silent, in front of the fire, while others felt the need to show their gratitude to the dictator by rushing to avenge him. Brawls broke out, and the more excited people began to push through the crowd to grab a burning brand from the funeral pyre and head for the homes of the conspirators.

It wasn't long before many began following the example of those who had procured themselves torches, and those who had thus equipped themselves began forcing their way through the crowd, pushing the others aside. Many, frightened, hastened to dodge out of their way and ended up banging into those behind them, and some were shoved, losing their balance and falling to the ground, only to be crushed under the heels of panicking citizens.

Octavia saw a soldier try to stop the advance of a man carrying a firebrand. The legionary jabbed his spear at the agitator's arm and managed to hit it, and the torch slipped from the man's hand, rolling along the floor towards another man who was standing nearby. The hem of his robe caught fire. The man began to shout and jerk about, banging into a woman who stood beside him. In a moment, her clothes too had caught fire and, moments later, both were burning from head to toe, but despite this they continued to grope blindly about them, bumping into other citizens who shrank back in fear as far as the crowd behind them permitted.

Octavia found herself dangerously close to the two human torches, and realised that the heat she could feel was no longer that of the pyre, but of the two unfortunates. People were screaming, pushing, falling: there was no longer a distinction between the areas reserved for nobles and those for the common people: men and women rushed towards whatever exit they could find, while those who were still trying to reach the fire to obtain a flaming brand had by now forced their way among the ranks of the aristocracy. The soldiers, for their part, tried to contain the movements of the crowd, but in so doing reduced the space available to those who wanted to escape the fire and the brawling, inevitably increasing the chaos in front of the grandstand of the rostrum.

The smoke from the pyre, the blinding light of the flames, the penetrating scent of incense, the tears, the fear: all contributed to giving Octavia the feeling that a blanket of fog had descended over her eyes. She felt lost, and held herself close to Etain. "Let's try this way, my lady! There's your husband, over there!" cried the maid, but all she could see were shadowy forms and, like a blind woman, she let herself be dragged along by the girl.

A wave of heat washed over her. "Be careful! That man's on

fire! Let's go over here, to the left!" Etain had not realized that her mistress could not see. The certainty of facing a looming threat she was unable to clearly see sent Octavia into a state of total panic, and she began to feel as though she were suffocating.

"Your husband! He's trying to reach us! Come over here to the left," Etain kept shouting in her ear, but her mistress's legs did not seem to want to go along.

She felt paralysed.

"No! Right! Let's go right! The *dominus* has been dragged into the crowd. I can't see him: we need to get to the Basilica Julia!" continued her servant, trying in vain to rouse her.

The heat grew stronger, and a bright light flooded her face, dazzling and burning her. Etain shouted, people bumped into her, and she felt herself being tossed about, then lifted by two powerful arms.

And then she fainted.

When she regained consciousness, she found herself lying on her litter, surrounded only by Etain, her husband and the bearers. She was no longer at the Forum, and now everything seemed quiet.

"What... what happened?" she asked no one in particular. She did not know who would be able to answer.

"Don't you remember? The riots at the Forum, during the funeral..." said Etain, with her usual sweetness.

"Yes, I remember that. Then I couldn't see anything and I fainted. I thought I was going to die..."

"And you might have had it not been for the man who picked you up and carried you out from the crowd, and led me out too. Once we were safe, your husband was able to find us," smiled her maid.

"A man? What man?" asked Octavia, still dazed, but not enough to not be intrigued.

"That centurion who came to our house on the Ides on Lepidus's orders. The one who tried to defend us. He said that this time he had succeeded..." said Etain, acting as though she did not know him.

Gaius Chaerea!

"That man has the remarkable quality of being always in the right place at the right time. It's a shame he's not a gladiator – we could hire him as your bodyguard..." smirked Marcellus, but Octavia paid him no attention. Gaius Chaerea was watching over her, and it gave her strength and the security that her life had been lacking.

Now she was no longer afraid, either for herself or for Octavian. Whatever her brother decided to do, she would support him.

*

"There is someone who would like to see you out here, my friend," said Rufus Salvidienus, immediately upon entering the tent where Octavian squatted disconsolately on the ground, his back against a cot. Near him was Agrippa, who was pacing about and puffing like a caged beast.

The young man raised his head with a grim look, staring at Rufus without appearing to be aware of his identity. Agrippa moved towards the entrance of the tent. "Can't you see what a state he's in? Enough of all these people coming to offer him their condolences. He wants to sit a while alone, don't you understand?" he hissed angrily.

Rufus nodded and, without losing his temper, said, "This is no act of homage, though. This is different..." Taking Agrippa by the arm, he led him out of the tent. The expression on the face of Agrippa, who swallowed visibly and widened his eyes, convinced him that he had his attention. "I'd say that you should convince him to come out now, don't you think?" he said, still speaking softly.

Agrippa nodded, then cautiously approached his friend, crouched down, took his hand and whispered something to him. Octavian finally seemed to come to, looked up at Rufus, and impatiently rose from the ground, letting himself be led by his friend to the tent's entrance.

When Octavian emerged, his appearance was greeted by an ovation. Rufus had no doubt that he recognized, in the crowd that had massed in front of his tent, dozens of centurions and *optiones* from the cohorts of almost all the legions encamped around Apollonia. A puzzled look came over his face as a *Primus Pilus* of the Thirteenth Legion – the legion that had accompanied Caesar in his race across Italy after the crossing of the Rubicon – stepped forward, stopping a foot away from him.

There was silence. All waited for the officer's words.

"My lord, on behalf of all the officers, I wish to tell you that your pain is our pain," said the senior centurion loudly, so that all might hear him. "Caesar has made us proud to be Romans and has given us a place in history, and would have given us much more if it hadn't been for this cowardly murder. No leader will ever be more missed by his men, I assure you, because no leader was ever able to guide with the courage, tenacity, sense of justice and humanity that distinguished him. And therefore I come to tell you that we are willing to do anything to make the perpetrators of this heinous crime pay for their guilt. If you wish to take revenge upon those who have tried to deprive you of your future as well as your great-uncle, know that we are on hand to escort you to Italy and face any threat at your side. We will be proud to march at your command, as we were to march at his!"

At the conclusion of the centurion's brief speech there was another ovation, and Octavian stared long at his interlocutor, nodding with a grim smile, then scanned the crowd of officers, and finally looked at his two friends.

"We are all with you, Octavian. And with an army like this, no one will resist you, once in Italy," said Rufus. At first, he had been appalled by the news, but now saw an excellent opportunity to further their careers. It was once again a time of civil war, and in civil wars, smart men climbed the ranks rapidly.

"I agree with Rufus," said Agrippa when Octavian turned his gaze upon him. "In Rome there will be a power vacuum. Before those who killed Caesar – whoever they are – can consolidate their positions, we must act."

"Remember that it was speed which gave Caesar his victory when he crossed the Rubicon," continued Rufus. "His opponents did not expect him to descend into Italy, let alone with a single legion available to him. You have many more legions, and the Republic is certainly far less cohesive now than then. You have an even better chance of succeeding than he did."

"If they have eliminated Caesar, it is safe to assume that they will want to get rid of his closest associates and relatives. They will strike you if you do not you strike first. You have no other choice but to act," echoed Agrippa.

Octavian was silent again, his expression absorbed and his shoulders hunched under the weight of the sudden pressure. Rufus began to think that he had bet on the wrong horse. Perhaps his friend did not have the makings of the great man that Caesar had thought. Or perhaps, they were simply asking too much, and too quickly, of a sickly young man who had been spoiled and pampered since birth.

"And instead, there is another choice," said Octavian, finally. "I will not march against Rome, as my great-uncle did; I will not, because I do not know what awaits me there, while he did."

"So what are you going to do? Flee to Egypt and hole up there with the men who follow you, counting on Cleopatra being in the city and having perhaps been killed too? Or that the queen will give you asylum and troops because you are the great-nephew of her lover?" asked Agrippa. Rufus nodded: he could not have risked being so frank himself.

"I have no intention of running away either, as my parents, who urge me to stay here, suggest," said Octavian. "That would not be worthy of Caesar. But Caesar was an intelligent gambler, who ran only calculated risks. And the Rubicon was a calculated risk. He would not want me to expose myself to unnecessary dangers, and I will take no reckless steps. Attacking Italy now means antagonising all, even those who might support me."

"So what will you do, if you do not intend to escape or go to Italy?" asked Rufus, spreading his arms wide in exasperation, while the confused officers murmured among themselves.

Octavian raised his voice, so that everyone could hear him. "I must go to Italy, but without an army. I must move like the private citizen I am and work out who I can trust. Alone I can do nothing, not even protect myself from my eventual enemies. I will keep away from Rome until I understand the situation, and then I will act accordingly."

Dissenting voices were raised by the group of officers. "Do you hear them? They do not approve. They want you to march on Rome," said Agrippa.

"It would be an impulsive decision, dictated only by emotions," said Octavian, with an ever more determined expression. Gradually, the project was taking shape in his mind, and Rufus was certain that he would not change it.

"I am grateful to all of you who offer me your support in avenging my beloved great-uncle, and nobody in the world wishes more than I to make those who killed him pay. But I cannot start a war without knowing how many enemies I have or how powerful they are. Nor I can hinder those who might help me in my mission – because I assure you that, for me, this is a mission. I will have no other goal from now on than that of avenging Caesar. I swear solemnly, here in front of you who are my witnesses, upon Venus who generated my ancestors and upon Mars Ultor. But I must first define my target, and make sure that those who were genuinely fond of Caesar trust me. For the moment we know only that, apparently, Antony and Lepidus are not involved, nor perhaps Cicero. If that is the case, I can offer them my help and, if they accept it, we will work together to bring about justice. I do not want Rome to continue to be at the mercy of the strongest of the generals of the day, who arrives at its gates with an army, as has been the case since the days of Marius and Sulla! I want the Republic to resume its course. The Romans must be able to attend to their daily business without fearing that some army will overturn in an instant what they have worked a lifetime to build and accumulate! So I accept your offer and thank you for your trust and consideration, which I have yet to deserve. When the time comes I will ask you to fulfil your promise. But only when the time comes."

The speech had begun as an explanation and had gradually transformed into a speech to the soldiers who, in increasing numbers, had come to stand behind their officers. And the cries of dissent and disappointment had soon turned to approval, luke warm at first, then actually enthusiastic. Some of the officers came over to embrace Octavian, shaking his hands and patting him on the back good-naturedly. Somewhat puzzled, the young man returned the displays of affection, and managed to force a smile, reassuring even Agrippa.

"He'll never be a fighter, but what a speaker, eh?" he said to Rufus. "He even convinced me, when I'd have dragged him, head down, against the enemies of Caesar, without thinking. Listen to me, my friend – if we have a place in history, it'll be thanks to him! He has the gift."

Rufus would have liked to feel as excited. Yes, he had learned to appreciate Octavian's intelligence and was aware that it at least partially compensated for his physical deficiencies, but he was more and more convinced that in order to become a great man, words were not enough. He loved Octavian and Agrippa, but now that they no longer had the protection of Caesar, how far could they get, with their limitations?

He felt a bond to them because he found them likeable and stimulating, as true friends should be, of course, but also because the dictator had launched them towards a shining destiny, and he could see nothing wrong with appreciating this about them too. But now that their mentor was gone, he saw them for what they were: young, inexperienced, one frail, the other of humble extraction, and perhaps even poor to boot.

For the moment, no one would bet on them. Nevertheless, he owed them a little more faith. A faith conditioned by results, of course: if the results didn't come... well, he hadn't known them so long that he felt bound to them forever...

IV

The one-eyed warrior stumbled out of the forest, supported by one of his men, who was in an even worse state than he himself: the wound that drenched the left arm of this slaughtered horde's leader with blood looked like a modest cut in comparison with the gash along his thigh.

Astride her horse, the woman without a hand trotted over, but stopped when she saw other warriors emerging from the vegetation showing all the signs of defeat. She started counting them, but after the fifteenth wounded man had appeared she realised that no one else had survived the battle.

No one else.

She looked at her man, hoping for a reassuring nod: maybe, she thought, the others would come later. But she knew that he was always the last to retreat, and when he shook his head disconsolately, she knew for certain that they had failed.

Definitively.

There was no need to ask him. They would not have another chance. In those parts, when a clan or leader was defeated even once, no new warrior would join their ranks. No one wanted to follow a leader who had proven themselves unable to ensure them booty or to prevail over the other tribes.

So she no longer had the means to regain the sceptre which had been her father's. All her dreams had perished in the battle for which she had yearned so long. Perhaps they had been so eager to fight that they had neglected to plan sufficiently, as Caesar and their experience with Rome should have taught them.

He came over to her, only the warrior who held him up preventing him from collapsing to the ground, and she smelt the stench of sweat and blood from their bodies and heard their harsh breath, broken by fatigue and despair. He looked at her for just a moment, saying nothing, but the woman without a hand seemed to read the reproach in his eyes: yes, she had sent him to the slaughterhouse. Now she knew that what he had prophesied was true.

That was why he had prevented her from participating in the battle – he was sure they would lose, and did not want her to die. But out of love – love for her – he had fought anyway.

A hint of embarrassment, perhaps even shame, compelled her to say something. She scanned the other tired, tattered and wounded warriors lying on the ground around her in the clearing where she had awaited the outcome of the battle, and then turned to her man.

"I know. We should have waited. I was too hasty," she said. And the words cost her dearly. She did not like admitting she was wrong. It was unworthy of a Germanic princess.

The warrior looked up with his one eye: in the battle he had lost his eyepatch, and she was for a moment disturbed by the sight of the vertical scar and empty socket – she was no longer used to them.

"No point blaming anyone now. We must think about how to rebuild our army and then wait for a more propitious moment to do battle," he said in a grave voice.

She smiled bitterly. She knew that he was saying it for the benefit of the other warriors, to prevent them from sinking into complete abjection, but not even he actually believed it. She tried to change the subject. "How went it?" she asked, without any real interest in the dynamics of the battle.

"There is little to say. We were outnumbered from the start by your cousin's army, and when I ordered the attack, at least a third of our men went over to his side. At that point, it was impossible to retreat and we were forced to fight. This is the result..." he concluded, gesturing to the survivors – in the meantime, they had been joined by their women, who had begun to tend to their wounds. The others, those who had realised that their men were not there, had thrown themselves to their knees, weeping and tearing their hair.

The princess took from the wagon the herbs and bandages that the clan had made available, got off her horse and began to clean the injured arm of her man. The other warrior was cared for by his daughter, and the two lovers felt able to speak more freely.

"The widows will soon start to look ill upon us..." she said.

"And perhaps the companions of the survivors too, for that

matter," agreed the man. "They'll be angry at not having chosen to join your cousin. And very likely they will also convince their people that we are a lost cause. We can trust no one now: our heads might look like an appetising opportunity for whoever decides to cut them off."

She looked around her, and saw the resentful faces of men and women who only a few years before had fought with dedication under the orders of her father Ariovistus. They were glaring at her, angry that she had used the prestige of her long-dead father to drag them into this hopeless undertaking. After years spent with Julius Caesar and Pompey the Great, she had failed to win them back, and the few who had placed themselves at her service had only done so for the benefits they hoped it might offer them.

Benefits which she was no longer able to offer. "What do you suggest, then?" she asked her man finally, in a dispirited voice.

"There remains only one thing to do. Caesar could help us, if we proposed an alliance with Rome, once the tribes of the Suebi were unified."

The woman thought for a long moment, then nodded.

"We return to Rome, then. Alone?"

"Alone," he said, sensing the growing hostility of the men he had just led to almost certain suicide.

*

He had only been away from Italy for four months, Octavian thought, but it seemed as though he had been gone a lifetime. The world had changed in that short period, and above all it had changed for him: his life had taken a different course from the one he had expected.

This quarter of a year had led him off the organised, preordained path towards being the most powerful man on Earth onto one where he would be totally exposed to the mercy of his enemies. He needed to rethink all his plans, and perhaps even change his whole way of thinking, if he wanted to survive.

These were his thoughts as he descended from the ship which, to ensure anonymity, he had ordered to dock not at Brindisi, where perhaps they would be waiting for him, but in Lecce. In the past he had always expected his great-uncle to think of everything, and to organise his career so that he would become one of the most important men in Rome. Now he would have to give up his highest aspirations and think first of all about saving his skin. Later, they would see what he was capable of.

Perhaps not very much, without Caesar's protection and without wealth, patronage, political experience – and, moreover, with poor health. He shook his head. He would never have admitted it to his friends Agrippa and Rufus, who had escorted him on this risky trip back to Italy, but the death of his great-uncle had floored him completely. He had nothing and, despite wanting more than anything to avenge him, he had neither the means nor the resources to make his voice heard.

To the soldiers who had offered him their loyalty in Apollonia, he had shown himself determined, above all, to not appear unworthy of their trust and the memory of Caesar. But after the trip at sea and a great deal of thought, he now had to face the reality – he knew that he was nothing more than a flea, with little chance of influencing the fate of the many giants who were struggling for power. He wanted to confide in his old friend, but Agrippa still looked strong and confident, and he was afraid to disappoint him. He decided to remain silent. At least until he knew how things stood now that more than two weeks had passed since the dictator's death.

"We must move with caution. What now?" asked Agrippa, seeming almost to read his thoughts.

"Information. We need information, above all else. For all we know, we might be walking into a civil war," he replied.

"Then you'd better stay here. You took part in Caesar's victory march only a few months ago and someone might recognise you," said Rufus. "We'll have a quick look around and test the waters. Once we have a clearer idea, we'll decide what to do. All right?"

Octavian nodded, and the two friends vanished among the buildings beyond the port. He saw Agrippa enter a tavern and had no doubt that the young man would soon emerge with news: the taverns of the harbour were a mine of information thanks to their patrons, who came from every part of the peninsula's coast.

Suddenly, he was gripped by anxiety. What if Caesar's assassins had already seized the reins of the Republic? What if they were wiping out all those who supported Caesar? What if they had put a price on his head? He would run the risk of being stuck by the knife of any cutthroat, at any time. Perhaps, all things considered, he would have done better to follow the advice of his mother and remain in Illyria.

He wondered if he was actually a coward, or perhaps even just lazy. His frequent bouts of ill-health and the weakness and fatigue that frequently assailed him certainly provided him with a convenient excuse to escape hard work and to avoid risks, but without those limits, would he have thrown himself into more dangerous challenges? He didn't know, and that was the problem: he didn't know of what stuff he was made. But Caesar had believed in him, and Caesar would never have put much faith in a coward – he must have seen something that Octavian himself still did not know he possessed.

He had the impression, however, that whatever it was, he would find out soon enough.

When he eventually saw Agrippa and Rufus returning, he felt his legs begin to tremble, and a sudden emptiness in his stomach caused a powerful wave of nausea to wash over him. He coughed, as he always did when he was anxious, and as always felt as though an overly-tightened breastplate was crushing his chest. He almost wanted to run away before hearing what the two friends had to tell him. He was afraid of what he would discover.

"We have surprising news, Octavian," said Agrippa when he was still far enough away that he had to raise his voice.

Octavian felt uncomfortable. It wasn't wise to speak his name aloud.

"Yes, very surprising, my friend," echoed Rufus.

The imaginary armour grew yet tighter. He coughed again, feeling almost as though he were choking.

"There is still a Julius Caesar about," said Agrippa solemnly.

"Yes. It's you," said Rufus, smiling.

"What?" They could hardly have been more cryptic.

"That's right, my friend. Caesar adopted you. You are practically his only heir. The will was opened two days after his death by Mark Antony."

Octavian felt his knees give and Agrippa raced over to support him.

A moment later, when he was sure that his friend could

stand alone again, he released him.

"That can't be! What about Mark Antony himself? And Lucius Pinarius and Quintus Pedius are older than me…" he said, barely recognizing his own voice.

"From what people say, as well as the adoption you are to receive two-thirds of his assets, and the other third goes to your cousins," continued Agrippa. "Three hundred *sestertii* to each Roman. And Mark Antony is only second heir, while Decimus Brutus Albinus, who killed him, actually appears as *third* heir. It is of that, above all, that people speak: that Caesar was killed by those he considered worthy of inheriting his possessions."

"Unbelievable… unbelievable…" murmured Octavian. "And who else was involved in the murder?"

"We have heard many names bandied around. You know what soldiers from the provinces are like – they love nothing more than gossiping and showing how well-informed they are: but that doesn't mean that it's all true," said Rufus. "In addition to those we already knew of, we've heard mention of Trebonius, Servilius Casca and his brother Longus, Tillius Cimber, Lucius Pontius Aquila, Decimus Turullius, Publius Sextilius Naso, Sulpicius Galba, and others that I cannot remember. There were a lot of them. Just think, they found twenty-three stab wounds in Caesar's body."

Octavian's blood ran cool once more. Now he felt able to think clearly again. The whole situation was incredible, but there was little they could do if Caesar's assassins had also gained power. And if there were so many of them, he was afraid that he might discover they had been successful. He trembled at the next, inevitable question, and his friends' reticence bothered him, holding him back from rejoicing as he would have liked. "And they're still alive and walking free? What is happening in Rome?" he asked finally, after a long sigh.

"Ah, there the situation is very confused. I don't understand it myself, and in fact no one seems able to explain it clearly," admitted Agrippa. "It seems that figures as authoritative as Cicero have done their utmost to have them granted amnesty, and that they will be given the posts which Caesar had promised them."

"What? But it's unheard of! They kill him and then keep what he gave them!" snapped Octavian indignantly. "And the others let them do it! Cicero too! He always hated Caesar, perhaps he was involved in this conspiracy too."

"Well, everybody says that the murderers praised his name while they killed the dictator..." said Rufus. "But they say they did it to restore the Republic, and for them, Cicero represents legality."

"Yet it was Caesar who made the Republic work!" insisted the young man. "What will become of the State without him now? His murderers have taken possession of it! They want to put themselves in a position to do whatever they want. Does no one dare oppose them? Does no one want to avenge Caesar? What is Mark Antony doing? And Lepidus? And the people, that Caesar made rich?"

"Some people say that Antony is afraid and has made an agreement with them. But many others claim that it is thanks to his work that a civil war has been averted. And Lepidus is waiting to see what happens, without affiliating himself with any group. In short, of the people of rank none has actually taken a position against the murderers; on the other hand, from what people say, it seems that there have been attacks on the houses of Marcus Brutus and Cassius. They and the other murderers go out rarely, and when they do, they go only under escort of Decimus Brutus's gladiators," said Agrippa.

Octavian reflected a moment. "Antony is alone, and so he is afraid," he said finally. "He does not know who he can count upon... But I am sure that it is his firm intention to avenge Caesar."

"Yes... that must be why they say that two days after Caesar's death, he handed over his son as a hostage to the murderers and then invited Cassius to dinner at his house, while Lepidus invited Marcus Brutus over. No doubt to avenge him..." said Rufus sarcastically.

Octavian was silent, but his face wore an expression of disgust.

"What do you intend to do?" asked Agrippa, studying him carefully. "In these conditions, accepting the inheritance could be very dangerous..."

"That's true. And not just because of the murderers," added Rufus. "Antony will be extremely upset that he was not appointed principal heir. You'll need his help whatever you want to do, and I doubt that he'll be very willing to give it to you... He certainly won't want to put himself in harm's way for the latest arrival."

"But he must. If he didn't betray Caesar, he will want to avenge him when he has the opportunity," said Octavian with conviction. "And I, with the riches of Caesar, will make that possible."

"Are you planning on starting a civil war or something?" asked Agrippa. "They must be extremely powerful if they've been given a pardon, and they will be even more so when they come into possession of the provinces that Caesar assigned to them next year."

"I hope not. The money will help me to win over the people who matter to the cause of justice, as well as the commoners. And with Antony at the head of Caesar's supporters, we will gather many followers, isolating the killers and bringing them to justice at last, as they deserve. I will not rest until they have all paid for their betrayal, from the first to the last... Because theirs is not only murder – it is treason against their benefactor."

"But you have no patronage, you have no supporters..." Rufus shook his head.

Octavian lifted his chin proudly and looked at his friend with eyes that now burned with fire. Caesar had shown him the way, at last: his life had begun once again to follow a clearly-marked route.

"I am the heir of Caesar, now," he replied proudly. "You saw how willing the soldiers were to follow me. So will be those who loved Caesar. And so will the people, if it is true that they mourn for him and despise his killers. I must speak immediately with Antony, but also with Cicero. I must convince the first of all that I am no threat to him, and second that I am not a threat to the state simply because I will take the name of my adoptive father. With them by my side, we will wipe out all the perpetrators of this heinous crime and pick up the reins from where Caesar left them. He had just begun to restore the Republic and straighten out all its deformities – the dysfunctions that have given Rome decades of civil war and a gang of greedy, myopic incompetents as heads of the state. Well, we will ensure that his work is completed."

"*We*?" asked Agrippa, as excited as a child.

"Of course, we: I and both of you. And whoever else wants to join us. Are you not perhaps my closest friends?"

Agrippa nodded, convinced, and Rufus followed suit, though without bothering to conceal his doubts. "You're sure you want to take it on, this practically impossible battle?" he asked, his handsome face split by a grin.

"It is not impossible, Rufus," said Octavian drily. "With his decision, Caesar showed that he felt I was able to meet the challenge, and I have a duty to believe him. And to believe him wholeheartedly…"

*

Switching from Lepidus to Antony could be rewarding for a soldier, Gaius Chaerea said to himself as he tried to keep up with the consul's brisk step. Although he had not participated in his latest campaign, Mark Antony had been Caesar's chief lieutenant, and enjoyed prestige immensely greater than that of the *magister equitum*. And the things he did were immensely more interesting than those done by the *magister equitum*, too.

Certainly, being under his command made the centurion's life much busier. Gaius had just accompanied him to visit Cleopatra, the Queen of Egypt, whom the consul had wanted to bid farewell to before she returned finally to her own country. Her presence had upset the Romans, and there was no citizen who did not hope to see the back of her as soon as possible, especially now that there was no dictator to impose her upon them.

Gaius had been given the task of coordinating the guards in front of the queen's residence while Antony was visiting her. Throughout the period in which she had been in Rome, Cleopatra had stayed in a sumptuous *domus* on the Aventine, leading a rather lonely life after the lack of enthusiasm with which her performance at Caesar's triumphal procession had been greeted. Mark Antony had been with the queen in private for some time, and the centurion had been forced to scold his soldiers who, as the time passed, had struggled more and more to hold back their sniggers. He could hardly blame them, though: when Cleopatra had arrived in the City, no one doubted that she lusted after Caesar, the most powerful man in the Republic, above all to save her kingdom and maintain her independence. And if she had given herself so freely to a man so much older than herself, she would have no scruples about giving herself to the man who was now the most prominent in the city, especially if he was in his prime, handsome and strong, with a reputation as a lover of life and an inveterate womaniser into the bargain. He could not help but assume that the two had not simply been saying their goodbyes. And he resigned himself to being unable to prevent his men from spreading rumours.

Soon their farewell would be in the public domain... whatever had actually happened in there.

Antony had certainly left the appointment with an expression on his face which anyone might have read as contentment and satisfaction. But that might only be the dirty-minded interpretation of soldiers, accustomed as they were to speaking ill of their commanders, Chaerea said to himself as he escorted the consul to another appointment which might give rise to just as much gossip.

Antony was at the home of Marcus Junius Brutus, together with Cassius Longinus. The men in that moment most hated by the Roman people, though not by the Senate. And yet he, Antony, was the most powerful and respected man in Rome: he could do whatever he wished. People seemed to want a new Caesar, one whose authority would deter further civil wars, and he seemed the only one able to play that role: making peace with the conspirators, far from procuring accusations of cowardice and betrayal, meant that he had passed for a peacemaker.

Gaius Chaerea was not particularly interested in what Antony and Cleopatra had said to one another, but would have loved to know word for word what passed between the characters who had gathered in that room. He stared at the door that kept him out as though his eyes and ears could magically traverse the wood. This time, it was his soldiers who stood impassively by as he paced nervously back and forth, and when the door suddenly opened, for a moment he had the impression of actually possessing supernatural powers.

In the doorway stood Antony, and it took Gaius a moment to realise that he was ordering him to enter.

His nervousness increased as he walked towards the consul and crossed the threshold. He found himself in a sumptuous triclinium, its walls covered with decorated panels and multicoloured inlaid frames. Inside the frames, zoomorphic figures alternated with other anthropomorphic mythological forms. High pedestals supporting oil lamps lit the room so that it was almost as bright as day, and at the centre, on a series of benches arranged in a horseshoe and covered in orange cloth, sat the others, intent on picking at fruit set on a small round table in the middle of the room.

Gaius recognized those reputedly behind the crime of the Ides of March. If it actually was a crime: many seemed not to consider it one, and these men still walked about Rome unpunished, even being fawned over by the consul.

"Well, dear friends," began Antony, "if you remain unconvinced, perhaps you would do well to hear the opinion of those who live among the ordinary people. A soldier, more than we people of rank, has the opportunity to judge the mood of the citizenry. He is a centurion, and I imagine he can be supposed capable of a balanced assessment. What is your name, centurion?"

"Um… Gaius Chaerea, sir," replied the embarrassed and confused officer.

"Good, Gaius Chaerea. You see, gentlemen, unless he is an actor, he did not even expect to be called and is visibly confused. He does not even know what I am about to ask him, so you may trust him entirely: this is no staged scene. Well then, centurion," he continued, turning to him, "What do the people say of those who claim to have liberated them from the tyranny of Caesar? Now that the turmoil of the day of his funeral has abated? Have they accepted the new state of affairs and endorsed the fact that those who have declared themselves 'liberators' have not been punished?"

The question was a difficult one. Gaius had no idea what response Antony wanted to hear, or if the consul wanted him to tell the truth. And furthermore, he was afraid of antagonising these powerful men: Caesar's assassins were among the most influential people in Rome, and some of them held or were preparing to hold magistratures, which put them in a position to determine people's fates.

In short, whatever answer he gave, in all probability he would make some enemy or other who could destroy him in an instant.

Antony had put him in a difficult position, and suddenly he hated him.

"Do not be afraid, centurion. Here we all need the truth," Mark Antony encouraged him. Gaius deduced that he must actually want him to tell them what was going on, otherwise he would not have underlined the fact. Or else he would surely have mentioned something to him before the meeting.

The centurion felt the eyes of the two conspirators upon him. He looked first at one and then the other, and wondered if they had really killed the dictator because they were sincere republicans and abhorred any form of monarchy: Cassius, the mastermind of the conspiracy, with his proud features and unfriendly expression and Marcus Brutus, as elegant and gentle of manner as he was timid and irresolute in decisions, and greedy for money to boot. All the others had already faded from view: Decimus Brutus Albinus, the most devoted of Caesar's followers and the vilest of traitors, was already in Gaul, to take possession of the province that the dictator had given him after having won it in Rome through eight years of hard struggle; Trebonius, long impatient with Caesar's hegemony, despite having been rewarded to the last, had hurried off to govern Asia, before the date that Caesar had pronounced; Quintus Ligarius had headed straight to Africa, where the dictator had exiled him in the past before having pardoned him; and then the Casca brothers – Publius and Gaius Servilius – who had never been satisfied with the limited power Caesar granted them for the simple reason that they were incompetent. And finally Sulpicius Galba, Lucius Tullius Cimber, Pontius Aquila, Cassius Parmensis, Minucius Basilus and all the other background figures the dictator had not considered worthy enough to include among his aides, and who had decided they had a better chance of furthering their careers with him out of the way. But Chaerea could not remember all the names.

In any case, the men in front of him had been daring enough to betray and kill the most powerful, and probably best, man in the world. It was unlikely they would have any qualms about getting rid of him. But he had no choice and so, with a deep sigh, he finally spoke, but in the tone of one reading aloud his own epitaph.

"I… I and my men have had to put down several riots in recent days. Especially in the Suburra, where Caesar spent his childhood, we've had to enter taverns and remove drunken people who were… saying… dangerous things."

"What things?" It was Cassius who spoke. The worst of all: his rancorous and vengeful nature was well known, and many said he had killed Caesar because the dictator had given Brutus the urban prefecture. Those murderous eyes rested upon him, peering with malignant curiosity.

Gaius cleared his throat. Things were growing increasingly risky. "Err, well, *Praetor*... they were talking about positioning themselves in front of the homes of some of you and attacking you with daggers to... to pay you back for what you did to Caesar. They were muttering something about twenty-three stab wounds each."

There, he had said it. And he felt as though a knife was pointed at his chest, its pressure preventing him from breathing.

Cassius continued to look at him without saying a word. Marcus Brutus, however, seemed troubled.

"See? What did I tell you? Go on, centurion, go on," said Antony. He seemed satisfied with what he had heard. He at least had not been antagonised. As for the others... well, Cassius's expression was eloquent.

He hesitated. But he could no longer wriggle his way out of it. "Some spoke of not respecting your appointment as magistrates," he continued, under the watchful eyes of the consul, "and, to be honest, those were the least dangerous ones. No real threat to public order, compared to the others. We've quelled street brawls where people who were singing the praises of Caesar and his memory were assaulting some victim who didn't regret his passing at all. Others shouted that they wanted to throw down the boulders from the Capitol at you while you were walking through the Forum. Still others said that if the Senate doesn't try you, they themselves will see to convicting and sentencing you."

Antony interrupted. "I would say that is enough, centurion. The overall picture you have provided us is clear. Now, frankly speaking, do you think the climate in Rome for those who, rightly or wrongly, took the trouble to kill Caesar, is a healthy one? Can they peacefully exercise their offices?"

Gaius looked once again the so-called 'liberators'.

"Erm... I would say not, sir. No, definitely not."

"Their presence is a source of trouble, then?"

"Yes."

"And they themselves are risking their lives?"

"It would appear so."

"Fine. Do you see, friends?" he went on, turning to the other two consuls. "I've done everything possible to ensure peace and avoid trouble. But if you do not hurry to reach the provincial commands that Caesar has given you, I cannot guarantee your safety." Then he turned back to speak to Gaius.

"Centurion, that is all. You may go."

Gaius bowed his head in deference, feeling shivers running down his spine when his gaze met that of Cassius. He left the room sadly, aware of the limited value that his life now possessed. But perhaps, he said to himself when he had taken up once more his position outside the hall, for the moment the 'liberators' had other things to think about. Antony was right for the climate in Rome was far from healthy for them, and they would be safer abroad. Not surprisingly, the majority of them had already left. What could they care about a common centurion who had done nothing but report what the people were saying? And, all things considered, he had made it clear that he had acted so as to avert any threat to them.

But why was Antony so anxious to send them away? He hadn't punished them, despite having stirred up the crowd against them, and he did not seem to be an accomplice, as some had commented after seeing his benevolence towards them. But he wasn't taking them on either, and indeed seemed even to be worried for their safety. The consul's position seemed to be an ambiguous one which he couldn't pin down. Lepidus, it was clear, was keeping to the sidelines while he waited for the command Caesar had given him in Spain and saw how things evolved politically. Cicero certainly wanted peace and the full restoration of the Republic. But Antony... Antony's attitude was just mystifying.

He continued to dwell upon his fate and Antony's motivations until the door opened and the consul signalled that they were leaving. When he was out of the building, the chief magistrate of the Republic summoned his secretary, who had been waiting in the street, and said, "They're going. Brutus and Cassius will give up the *pretura* and take provincial commands, respectively, in Crete and Africa. Go and inform my brother Gaius that it is done: tomorrow in the Senate I'll have his appointment as city magistrate approved."

And suddenly, the picture was clear to Chaerea. Mark Antony would have unfettered power, because the second consul chosen by Caesar, Dolabella, had infinitely less charisma. Mark Antony's brother Lucius had long been tribune of the people, an important role which put him in a position to veto any law coming out of the Senate. And now, his other brother would become *praetor urbanus*. Meanwhile, with a pretext, he had sent away from Rome all those who could hinder him.

So that was Mark Antony's objective. His aims were revealed.

He wanted to be a new Caesar. The undisputed ruler of Roman politics. And all this, despite the fact that the dictator had not appointed him his heir.

V

Octavian rolled back up the papyrus that his sister's handmaid had just delivered to him. He decided he would not let others see the satisfaction he had felt since reading the very first words. In fact, it seemed like a good idea not to show any emotion at all in future, except with close friends: that was the most effective way to assume a dominant position, he thought – not only in conversations, but also of in front of an audience or any observer for that matter.

And in fact he saw that all present were regarding him with quizzical expressions. Absolutely all of them, from Agrippa and Rufus, who had been with him since the landing in Lecce and the people who had followed him for many miles after learning who he was and what he now represented, to the clients of the eminent personage with whom he had requested a meeting on his way back to Rome.

It seemed that the whole of Cumae had gathered in front of Cicero's villa, and their purpose was not to honour the greatest lawyer of all time but rather to witness the investiture of Caesar's heir.

The boy that the deceased dictator had chosen as his son.

Octavian looked around him, squinting at the crowd in an attempt to read their faces. What he saw was not diffidence, nor even simple curiosity. It was trust. And it occurred to him that perhaps, in their eyes, he was not simply the chosen one. Now that he was inheriting the dictator's main assets, those people, be they poor or rich, saw him above all as Caesar's successor. They expected him to walk his father's path, and perhaps were willing to trust him enough to allow him to make his way among the powerful people of Rome and take full control of the city, despite his young age.

They needed a new Caesar: after putting an end to civil wars, the last one had gained their eternal trust, but he had not lasted long enough, and the people already missed him. What they

67

feared most – and with good reason – was that the same chaos which had dominated Rome before his dictatorship would once again prevail. They wanted another dictator and they were willing to accept Caesar's choice and trust his appointed heir. Him, and not the lieutenants of the glorious leader – not those who had just betrayed him, and not even the ones who showed no great desire for revenge.

Well, he would avenge Caesar and at the same time guarantee the peace Caesar had granted his people. And just as Caesar had strived, bribed, killed, robbed and lied when he had to, he would use the same methods to prevail over those who would put their personal interests before the interests of the State. The dictator had proved that in order to keep control of ruthless and ambitious men you needed to use their own weapons against them. And they probably expected that the one he had chosen as his heir would do the same.

They were methods which repulsed him but it was the only way to overcome his rivals, who were more expert, influential and powerful than he. He didn't have enough money to bribe people yet, nor the means to kill – particularly Caesar's assassins, his real enemies – nor even the authority and connections necessary to steal… but he could start by lying in order to achieve his goals. That was the only weapon he had at the moment. The rest would become available in the future, if he played his cards right.

He was ready to flatter and lie to his first, precious, ally: Cicero. But before that, he must determine his targets. Agrippa and Rufus were impatiently waiting to know the contents of the letter he had just read, in which his mother and stepfather described the details of Caesar's inheritance, but he wanted to talk to them about something else. He turned to Etain.

"Did they also give you the other information I requested?" he asked her.

The handmaid nodded, took a second container from her bag and handed it to him. Octavian took it and opened it, unrolling the papyrus with one hand while holding the bottom edge with the other. He read it, then gathered his friends around him and decided to share that list, which he had been waiting for even more impatiently than the list of his inheritance, with them immediately.

"My friends, the confirmation of the scale of my inheritance fills me with pride," he began in a soft voice, not wishing anyone except Agrippa and Rufus to hear him, "but this is the document I was really waiting for. This is the list that will guide our actions from now on, regardless of how we must behave in public and around others. You must always remember the names I am about to read to you, if you are loyal to me, and you must never forget what they have done and what they deserve. I will not rest until every last one of them has received the punishment they merit for the crime they committed, and I hope you will help me with all means necessary, both legal and otherwise, to inflict upon them the same fate they inflicted upon Caesar. If they are not found guilty, it will be we who will see to their punishment, one way or another, even if it takes us decades. And if circumstances force us to praise them and wait for the proper time to act, you must never forget that they are our principal targets. If you loved Caesar as much as I did, I know that I can count on you."

"Of course you can count on me, my friend," broke in Agrippa. "You know that Caesar was an idol to me, and your goal is mine too. At whatever cost."

Octavian turned to look at Rufus.

"I will do whatever is in my power to punish the assassins of the greatest man Rome ever had," Rufus replied, feeling that it should be enough.

"If I could, I would put a reward on each of their heads: Gaius Cassius Longinus, Marcus Junius Brutus, Decimus Junius Brutus Albinus, Gaius Trebonius, Gaius Servilius Casca, Publius Servilius Casca Longus, Lucius Tillius Cimber, Publius Sextius Naso, Quintus Ligarius, Lucius Minucius Basilus, Rubrius Ruga, Lucius Pontius Aquila, Marcus Spurius, Caecilius Bucolianus, Bucolianus Caecilius, Pacuvius Antistius Labeo, Gaius Cassius Parmensis, Petronius, Decimus Turullius and Servius Sulpicius Galba. They must all die, from the first to the last. Do you agree?"

"Yes!" Rufus and Agrippa both shouted.

"Very well – when the time comes, we will swear it in front of the Gods, and Caesar will be among them. Now I can go to Cicero. Now our revenge begins," he stated solemnly, leaving them and heading towards the entrance of the villa to meet the ex-consul and famous lawyer.

Agrippa did not watch his friend go. Though he felt

profoundly involved in Octavian's desire for revenge, there was something that had been distracting him since the moment he had seen him receive the letter containing Caesar's last will. He looked at Rufus for a moment, and realised that his attention too was directed towards her. Towards the handmaid Octavian's sister had sent.

He had to act before his friend did. She was too beautiful to allow to slip away. He moved over to where she was standing, by the wagon which had brought her there from Rome, waiting for Octavian's orders and, seeing Rufus also heading towards her, placed himself between them so as to reach her first without giving the impression that he was running.

"What's your name, girl?" he asked as soon as he was in front of her. As he spoke, he took advantage of their proximity to look her over, discovering many pleasant details he hadn't noticed from a distance. She really was very pretty: her eyes were aquamarine, her hair blond like ripe wheat, she had a thin, regular mouth and a pointy nose, with wide, elegant nostrils, her chin was rounded and made her whole face perfectly oval. She clearly had Celtic origins. Through her tunic he could tell that the girl had little flesh covering her bones, despite her muscular arms.

"Etain, Sir," said the handmaid, after hesitating for a few moments, revealing delicate wrinkles around her mouth and a sweet smile. He liked her voice instantly – slightly nasal but melodious. He hesitated too, unsure as to what approach to take.

"The only thing that gives away you're a slave is the amulet round your neck. You carry yourself like a queen." Rufus had taken advantage of his silence to intervene. Just like when they were talking to the girls in Apollonia, Agrippa could never lower his guard even for a moment. But this time he wouldn't give up. This girl had something special about her: was it her sweetness? He decided he would find out at all costs.

"My friend mocks you. In my opinion, you look like a woman any man would want to have by his side," he said, feeling immediately that his words had been effective.

He had immediate confirmation: Etain looked at Rufus only for a moment, then she looked back at Agrippa, blushed and lowered her head in embarrassment. "You two tribunes honour this slave, Sirs."

"I would happily be your slave, Etain," replied Agrippa quickly. "With me, you would live a perpetual Saturnalia," he said with a wink, referring to the festival where slaves exchanged roles with their masters.

"I'd rather be your master. The master of your heart!" cut in Rufus. He was more tenacious than usual.

Agrippa was used to having a certain effect upon women, whatever their rank: he was tall and well-built, with a simple, frank expression which always worked with them, and it never took him long to conquer his prey. He was aware that, with his harsh, unrefined features, he wasn't exactly handsome, but his stature helped him feel self-confident. And most of the time he was successful. And this time, anyway, he very much wanted to be. But Rufus's words had clearly given him the lead: Etain was smiling at him, a sly look in her eyes.

He panicked for a moment, then said, "I would like to own the world instead, so I could offer it all to you!" It wasn't much of a line, but it would keep him in the game.

And in fact, the girl again turned her lovely smile on him. She looked amused by the fact that two important men were fighting for her attention, and didn't seem more interested in one than the other. The competition had grown tough, and on another occasion Agrippa would have found it funny. But not that time.

"In that case, *I* would take you to another world – one the two of us could conquer together and become king and queen!" Rufus pursued. That day he was clearly the more inspired. It was probably emotion that was paralysing Agrippa, but he couldn't face losing. Losing her. He grabbed her arm and pulled her towards him, looking intensely into her eyes. He smelt the delicate scent of her skin while he admired the beauty of her blue-green irises from close up. Then he said: "Enough now. Come with me, sweet Etain."

And he dragged her away. Rufus, too astonished to be able to speak, looked on while she sheepishly allowed herself be led, and Agrippa stopped only when they were too far away for Rufus to hear them.

"I'm going to buy you," he said, trying to kiss her neck. She tried to pull back, but without much conviction.

"You can't."

"Why not? Whatever the price is, Octavian will help me.

He's a friend of mine and he just became very rich," he replied.

"Octavian's sister, Octavia, owns me. I'm her personal handmaid. She would never give me up. For any price at all." The girl sounded upset, and Agrippa would never have wanted that. But he could also never argue with his best friend's sister.

He took her chin with his index finger and thumb and lifted the girl's face.

"What if things were different? Would it please you if I bought you?"

She remained silent. Her sparkling eyes rolled in all directions, then settled on him again. Little lines formed at the sides of her mouth and she smiled, half embarrassed and half impish.

That was enough for him. With his fingers he raised the girl's mouth towards his own and, as he felt no resistance, put his lips to hers and kissed her gently. She didn't pull back, so Agrippa increased the intensity of his kiss, opening his mouth and letting his tongue wander freely in that warm, welcoming place. He could always tell from the first touch of a woman, from the flavours and perfumes that enveloped him even from a kiss, if he would like all the rest. He knew immediately that, if it ever happened with her, it would be wonderful.

And he wanted to make it happen quickly.

He moved away, smiled tenderly at her and looked around, curious to see Rufus's reaction. His friend was standing where he had left him and was giving him a surly look. He instinctively felt he should run over and admit that, yes, he had played dirty, but he really felt something for that girl, while for his friend she would have just be one of his many conquests. But Octavian's audience with Cicero would soon be finished, and then there would be a meeting, or Etain would be sent back to Octavian's family with new orders.

And he had no intention of wasting that time with Rufus.

*

Octavian peered around Cicero's study, seeking something among all the bric-a-brac he could use to soften up his host, whose vanity was renowned. He was amazed by the quantity of papyri, busts and documents he could see on the office's tables, chairs and shelves, and was wondering how much stuff the famous rhetorician must have in his Roman house if he had this much in one of his many properties dotted around the peninsula. He asked himself if it was a simple question of collecting, or whether Cicero kept all that material in order to work at his writings wherever he was and at any time.

He walked over to a shelf and looked at the labels on the containers holding rolls. His attention was attracted by the closest one, whose label said *De imperio Cn. Pompei*. It was one of his speeches. The next roll's label said *Divinatio in Caecilium*. The other rolls on the shelf were labeled *In Catilinam* and were numbered progressively. He checked the next shelf: *Oratio cum populo gratias egit*; *Oratio cum senatui gratias fecit*; *In Verrem actio secunda*, from the first to the fourth... He looked at another: inexorably, there were *In Verrem action prima*; *De Sullae bonis, De lege agraria (Contra Rullum); In P. Vatinium...*

It was his works. Obviously, he carried them along with him so he could continue editing, modifying and rewriting them for those who would come after him, improving them from when he had first declaimed them. In a way, Cicero was lying to future generations. And the thought reassured Octavian: great men, like the one he hoped one day to become, built their personas, and presented an idealised, even completely false, version of themselves to those who didn't know them personally. In the future, the genius of Cicero's speeches would be praised everywhere, with none knowing how ineffectual they had actually been in court.

It was the same thing with leaders and politicians, Octavian had no doubt. Their fame was due more to what they chose to let people hear of their achievements than to their actions themselves. The more powerful they were, the more they could influence the perception others had of them. It was a good lesson in politics which would come in very useful in future.

"See how much work I carry about with me, young Octavian? Unfortunately, I don't have much time to dedicate to resting." A voice interrupted his thoughts. The young man turned to find the consul standing a few steps from him, staring at him with a mixture of curiosity and condescension. He immediately understood that Cicero had allowed him to enter his study alone to give him the chance to admire the scale of his works. It wasn't just vanity, it was a way of exerting an influence.

Another good lesson for the future.

"I can see that, consul," he said, attempting to appear zealous and walking over to shake his hand. "A man of your importance must have so many obligations that I consider being able to share a few moments with you a privilege, given my youth and lack of experience."

The old man shook both his hands vigorously, but his eyes studied Octavian with attention and diffidence. It was no mystery that Caesar's assassins had shouted Cicero's name as they had gone about the deed, and he hadn't hidden his approval of their actions. It was no coincidence that it had been he who had proposed amnesty for Caesar's assassins.

They said that Cicero hadn't taken part in the conspiracy, but Octavian wasn't wholly convinced. He would decide in due course whether to add his name in the list or not.

*

The tavern's owner looked them over for a long time before finally signalling them to follow him to the upper floor when he saw the jingling *sestertii* fall onto the table in front of him. Agrippa smiled reassuringly to Etain, putting to rest her remaining doubts. Though she wondered if she actually had any. She trusted this young man, who was only slightly older than herself and who made her feel as safe as only a grown man could. That was why she had gone along with him immediately and had put up no resistance. She knew she would have been less accommodating with the other young tribune: flattered though she was by his attention, she would have protested and, thinking him arrogant and full of himself, refused to let herself be dragged off had he attempted to behave in the same way.

It was different with Agrippa. It was as though... as though he had every right to do it. While she was following him up the stairs, his hand gently holding hers, she thought to herself how absurd the situation was: she had taken a message to her mistress's brother and had let an unknown man approach her whom she had then not only allowed to kiss her but even to take her to a room in a tavern. Perhaps he would think she was a Jezebel, but she didn't care: all she knew was that she wanted to be with him and was delighted by his attentions.

Strangely, sex had never been particularly important to her, not even while she had been involved with another slave two years ago, in Atia's house, a relationship which had ended after a few short, unmemorable dalliances when the man had been sold. Judging from the explanations the older slaves had given her, she realised that she hadn't even lost her virginity on those occasions. That was why she was so surprised at how naturally she had desired intimacy with Agrippa. And that she had forgotten that the reason she was disguised as a slave was to protect her from being pestered by men. When her former master had made her a freedwoman, they had agreed that Etain would continue to wear her slaves' *bulla*, as it could be useful in many circumstances.

Now she was Octavia's handmaid and personal secretary – an employee with a sort of salary, plus lodgings and food. Among the duties for which she received a salary there was also the possibility of becoming invisible to others – the way slaves usually were – and listening to their conversations: many powerful men, though very careful not to let freemen hear them, didn't care what they said in the presence of slaves. So whenever she had to run some errand for her ex-masters, the role of personal slave of a close relative of the dictator guaranteed her safety and respect, whoever she would need to deal with.

But now she had lowered all her defences. In front of him she already felt naked, and the knowledge that Agrippa would actually see her unclothed in a few moments allowed her to put aside all her shyness.

She entered the room unhesitatingly, and not even it not exactly being the ideal love-nest in which a woman might want to spend a night of passion was enough to put her off.

Nobody had bothered to open the shutters, and the sour odour of the soot from the lamps made her eyes water. The walls were blackened by smoke and a visible layer of grease covered the room's few pieces of furniture. One of the bed's legs was broken, and it was propped up on some large stone slabs like the ones used for paving the streets. The bedlinen was stained and the pillowcases were torn.

She looked at Agrippa, who looked back at her, smiled and opened his arms wide. "Would you rather we didn't?" he asked, showing surprising sensitivity.

She lowered her head and shook it, surprised at her own immodesty. As soon as Agrippa closed the door, she threw her arms around his neck and jumped up onto him, wrapping her legs around his waist and kissing him repeatedly on his cheeks, forehead and finally on his lips, her mouth never on the same spot for more than a moment.

She was a little disappointed by the young man's reaction – he smiled at her tenderly, held her to him and whispered, "You're such a child…"

She had thought she was acting like a sensual woman, but apparently had only highlighted her inexperience. She frowned for a moment, but Agrippa caressed her cheek with one hand while pressing her waist against him with the other so tightly that she could barely breathe. He slowly lowered her to the floor and she could sense his excitement as he lowered himself purposefully over her.

Once again, the woman inside her suggested what she should do. She had always imagined that during her first time with a man she would be clumsy, passive and timorous, but now she found herself taking the initiative. She undid Agrippa's *balteus*, which held his sword in its scabbard, then loosened and removed his tunic, looking delightedly at the healthy, naked torso she had revealed. The young man, now clad only in his loincloth, was clearly happy to be admired, and he proudly inflated his chest. She caressed it, gently at first, then squeezing his muscles and bringing her mouth closer to the scar between his magnificent pectorals.

He put his hand on the nape of her neck and pulled her towards him. Etain let her lips move across his hairy chest, then started kissing him everywhere. She imagined his next move would be to push her gently downwards, so she decided to anticipate him and started kissing his chest, then his belly, lingering on his navel. She kneeled down and found her face in front of his loincloth, which barely covered his turgid manhood.

She put her hands on his hips and, with some difficulty, managed to pull down the offending piece of cloth, leaving him totally naked, and for a few moments she admired his naked, athletic body.

"Dear boy, I'm not sure whether to give you my condolences for the loss of your great-uncle or congratulate you for being his heir."

It was the first full sentence Cicero had said, and Octavian already felt like strangling him: apart from the assassins, Cicero was the happiest man in Rome about Caesar's death, and the word 'loss' sounded wholly inappropriate. His condolences were pure hypocrisy, and his congratulations about the inheritance a lie, as he was far from pleased at the thought of another following in the dictator's steps. But Octavian controlled himself: without Cicero's help, he could make no way among the politicians of Rome.

He was disgusted, but he told himself that this was work. Just work.

"My dear senator, I feel how close you are, in this difficult moment for me and my family," he forced himself to say. "I hope I can always count upon your friendship, which I value above anything else."

Cicero motioned to him to sit down on a couch, sat down across from him and continued to observe him, now with severity and now with a hateful air of mock sympathy. "I know what a grave loss the death of the dictator was for the entire *gens Julia* family," the orator said. "Now, however, the Republic may resume its normal course, and we must all turn our common commitment to restoring the law and freedoms that your great-uncle, no doubt hindered by the emergencies caused by civil war, did not live long enough to."

If he hadn't been in front of the dictator's heir, Cicero would have spoken less euphemistically and would have said quite clearly that Caesar had deliberately caused the civil war and suppressed any remaining trace of democracy for his own ends. Octavian didn't agree, but he certainly didn't want to get into an argument with him.

"That is what I intend to do, as soon as my inheritance is in my possession, senator," he declared. "By his will, my father demonstrated that he cared for the good of the people, and the Romans are waiting to see his will fulfilled. As far as I am aware, consul Antony has not yet done it, so it's up to me to fulfil Caesar's instructions."

"Your *father*?" asked Cicero in surprise. "Ah, yes, he adopted you... Well, I am aware that the consul did not give out the three hundred *sestertii* a head that the dictator had so demagogically promised to the Roman people. On the other hand, Antony did agree to manage Caesar's patrimony with his widow, Calpurnia, so now we have to work out what belonged to him and what to the treasury. You can understand how the line between the two grew somewhat unclear over the last few years..."

"Forgive me, senator," Octavian almost interrupted him, regretting immediately afterwards that he hadn't been able to control his indignation, "don't you think I should be in charge of managing Caesar's patrimony, since I am his heir?"

"My dear boy... how old are you? Not even twenty, I think. You have only recently come of age to begin wearing your *toga virilis*, I hardly think you're ready to manage such large amounts of money – and money whose provenance is still not clear at that! The consul has great experience, and was one of Caesar's closest men. He is the highest Roman authority, so he will be able to manage the patrimony and decide who is entitled to what. And as well as him, there are a huge number of other people of high rank and experience who know the possible destination of his bequests in detail."

Octavian felt his blood start to boil in anger. It was his money they were talking about, and this idiot thought it was reasonable to let someone else manage it. Obviously Cicero considered him a child or an interloper who had come to ruin the established equilibrium and understanding between the powerful, no matter which party they nominally belonged to.

Nothing more than an annoyance, then. The fact that they didn't even see the need to tell him how his inheritance would be used showed that they probably didn't even consider him a serious obstacle. Well in that case, he thought, all he could do was use their lack of interest to his own advantage.

He thought carefully before answering Cicero's offensive statement. "Caesar didn't leave his properties and money to Antony, nor to anyone else – he left them to me. And it surprises me that you, senator, the most respected exponent of the Republic and democratic authority, are happy to see such wealth in the hands of a man as powerful as the consul..." he said. "Wouldn't it be better for somebody like me to receive it? One who would share the money with its legitimate owners – the Roman people and the veterans, who have as yet received no reward for their services?"

From the expression on Cicero's face, Octavian saw that his words had hit home. The great orator stared at the wall for a long time, tapping his nose. "I do hope the consul will listen to the senators and high magistrates who are working with him to restore legality," he said after some time. "We must, of course, avoid letting anybody obtain uncontested power, as has happened in the past, and I will do all I can to avoid it. The Roman people do not like tyrants, and I want to make sure no other dictators appear, you may trust me on that. Think of me as a guardian of the Republic."

He had fallen into the trap. Wise, astute old Cicero had been tricked by a young lad who had 'only recently obtained his *toga virilis*'.

"For that reason," replied Octavian with satisfaction, "I will be your devoted supporter. I wanted to talk to you first, before anybody else, because you are undoubtedly the most influential personage in Rome, above and beyond any magistrature. I am also sure you will safeguard the stability of the Republic and the respect for the institutions, and I would like to dedicate my modest powers to assisting you in the task. Consider me at your disposal for any matter in which you think I might be of assistance."

He saw Cicero's wide face open up in a smile of sincere satisfaction, and knew he had won him over.

At least for such a time as he had need of him. Because this meeting had confirmed all his suspicions.

*

Agrippa observed Etain leave aboard the wagon, where the girl was sitting by the driver after receiving Octavian's last orders for his parents and sister. He watched her go even after his friend had called him, thinking about the moments they had just spent in that seedy tavern which the intensity of their intimacy had turned into a royal palace.

Only when he had seen the blood which stained the

bedlinen had he realised that the girl was a virgin. He would never have imagined it from the way she had surrendered herself so easily to him and the violence of her passion. In the beginning she had seemed clumsy and inexpert, but she wasn't passive and embarrassed the way women who have never slept with a man usually are. Or at least, the way he imagined they were – he had never lain with a virgin before.

They had said goodbye to one other with the promise that they would find a way to meet again. And he meant it: he had often made similar promises to cajole girls into bed, even when he had no intention of seeing them again. But with Etain it was different: he really *did* want to be with her again, often, if the big events he and his friends were to face in the future allowed them to be.

How big those events would be was something he was waiting to find out from Octavian. When Etain's profile was no longer visible, Agrippa headed towards his friend, who in the meantime had been joined by Rufus. He only glanced at Rufus, who chose to ignore him: he was still annoyed about the humiliation he had suffered over the girl, and perhaps even offended about having been tricked. But that didn't matter: it was only a small defeat for him among his many victories. He would get over it, and maybe next time he would avenge himself upon his friend.

Suddenly he realised he didn't care any more about competing for the attention of other girls. He just wanted to see Etain again.

"Do you recall the list I read you before?" began Octavian, interrupting his thoughts.

"The names we must always remember to avenge Caesar? Of course," said Rufus.

"Exactly. We must add another. But only when we no longer need him. For the moment, consider him untouchable."

"Cicero?" deduced Agrippa.

Octavian nodded.

"Was he part of the conspiracy too? How do you know?"

"No, I don't believe he took part," admitted Octavian. "He's too much of a politician and a coward to do such a thing. I think Brutus and Cassius probably asked him to participate, but he only gave them his approval, and wished them luck. He practically confessed, by calling Caesar a 'tyrant' and indirectly accusing him of depriving the Roman people of their freedom. He could hardly hide his satisfaction, and the only reason he bothered trying was that he was talking to one of Caesar's relatives, by Jove! Anyway, it was him and his request for an amnesty that saved his assassins. It's like he put a knife in their hands, and he did so only because he wasn't brave enough to use it himself. Caesar told me that, before he even became a consul, Cicero used to accuse him of being an aspiring tyrant and thought he was the greatest threat to the state. I would be very surprised if he had played no role at all in the conspiracy. And in any case, do you think Brutus and Cassius would have done anything, if they hadn't been sure of his support?"

"Your reasoning is flawless," admitted Rufus.

"He undoubtedly bears moral responsibility for Caesar's death, if nothing more," Agrippa added.

"Yes. It is time to go to Rome and demand our inheritance," declared Octavian solemnly. "At the moment, Antony is powerful, and Cicero is afraid of him. He will help us, but first I need to know how he intends to behave towards me. It's time to face him. I hope he will be reasonable."

Agrippa doubted that a man like Antony, who Caesar's patrimony and his position as a consul gave basically absolute power in Rome, was capable of being reasonable. In his position, anybody would have been tempted to follow in the assassinated dictator's footsteps.

But he said nothing. That day he only wanted to keep thinking about Etain.

*

With visible suspicion, the one-eyed German warrior approached the domus which had once been owned by Pompeius Magnus and stood inspecting its entrance at length. It had been a long time since he had seen such an extraordinary example of civilization: during the past year, the largest buildings he had seen were the rough mud and straw huts where his Suebi countrymen lived. His one-handed woman embraced him, understanding his feelings perfectly: those buildings reminded him of great times passed in a previous life, a life he had lived until a year before, but which seemed much more distant. An existence full of triumphal marches throughout the Peninsula and along the streets of Rome, of conquests and riches, following the most powerful man in the known world; nothing could have warned him of the speed of the decline he had suffered since he had returned to Germany and agreed to let himself get involved in a venture he did not believe in and had only accepted because he loved her.

To indulge the foolish ambitions of a woman who had never been wise enough to aim at achievable goals. He would never hold it against her: his soul was too noble for such a thing. And now she couldn't afford to blame him for taking them on that pointless journey to Roma, for the thousands of miles of struggling and pain that had exhausted their horses to the point of death, leaving them to drag themselves here on foot… only to discover that the great leader to whom they had planned to offer their services had died, assassinated only two months earlier. Their few followers were respectfully waiting for them at a distance, wondering what their leader wanted to do now. She turned to look at them: they had lost almost all their Suebi warrior pride. They were dirty and shabby, their clothes torn and their weapons scuffed and dirty. Covered in dust from head to toe, their thick hair – once clean, decorated and bristling upon their heads, kept tidy with elaborate bows and lime – hung down, limp and miserable over their shoulders.

"Are you sure you want to do this?" she asked her man, who at present didn't seem to want to take another step forward.

"He will remember. We fought together during many campaigns," the warrior answered. "If Caesar is dead, the only one I can talk to is Mark Antony. He will offer us what Caesar no longer can."

"So why do you not ask to enter?" she asked.

"I… I am ashamed. I abandoned them and now I am here, begging them for charity. And in this condition…"

The woman sighed.

"You served them better than anybody else for over a decade. You saved Caesar many times. When you left, they had already defeated everyone and had no further need for you. I don't think any will blame you for that. All Caesar's followers will be grateful to you. And perhaps, if his faction is in difficulty, they won't be able to afford to do without you. Without us."

She didn't really believe what she was saying, but as it was her fault he had fallen into such depths of despair, she had to do something to raise his spirits.

Her man sighed too, then nodded, steeled himself and set off towards the guard's post. There were a few people hanging around the building, almost certainly Mark Antony's people waiting for an audience, but they made room for Ortwin as soon as they saw him: his imposing, barbaric appearance – or possibly the state he was in – his handsome face damaged by the absence of an eye, and the stink he was probably giving off after the long journey, drove everyone away, leaving him free passage until he was within shouting distance of the ostiarius who guarded the door.

"I want to see Mark Antony!" he shouted. The man lifted his head and inspected the German with blunt indifference.

"The consul is not at home at the moment, barbarian," he said, adding contemptuously, "And anyway, we don't receive beggars here."

"He is a consul now, is he? Good. My name is…" began the German, trying to control his rage.

"I don't give a damn about your name, you miserable barbarian. Get lost. Even better, get out of Rome. Beggars, especially wild ones, are not welcome here."

The woman saw her warrior leap forward like a wild beast with its claws out, and throw himself onto the guard. Roaring like a lion, he grabbed him and threw him to the ground, climbing on top of him and immobilising him completely before headbutting him, sending up a spray of blood that covered his face, then hitting him repeatedly. The small crowd of people ran to try and break up the fight, with the idea of earning the gatekeeper's gratitude, in the hope he would tell his master of their bravery.

While his woman watched, the German was dragged away, kicked and covered with spit and insults until she and other Germans, realising too late what was happening, decided to intervene. Given the way they looked, they needed to do little more than glare at the men holding him to frighten them off, and soon she was able to put her arms around her bruised and dirtied, but above all humiliated, man.

She had no idea long they stayed there, embracing one another in the dust, while their men kept back the crowd who had gathered around them and, from a safe distance, were shouting abuse and calling for the praetor's soldiers to intervene, and slaves came to medicate the ostiarius.

"What is happening here?"

The woman had been forcing herself to ignore the bystanders, but this voice was so authoritative that she felt obliged to turn towards it.

It was a lictor. He was standing over her with his fasces of branches and axe on his shoulder. Another lictor stood behind him, and a third behind him. She counted twelve altogether. Around them there were no longer the civilians who had been insulting them but a group of soldiers, many of whom bore centurion phaleras on their breastplates. She realised that Antony had arrived and so did Ortwin, who rose to his feet immediately and, though still unsteady from the blows he had received, pulled himself up to his full height and made an effort to answer.

"I… I am here to see the consul and offer him my services."

The lictor burst out laughing, as did the others near him.

"Oh you are, are you? And what makes you think the consul would want the services of a wretch like you? Especially after all this hue and cry you have caused!" he added, looking around him.

"The fact that he knows me and that I have already served him well," answered the German, summoning up all his pride.

The lictor looked at him, and then at his colleagues, who hesitated. And at that moment, the woman saw a man she knew well making his way through the guards.

"What are we waiting for? Who is this vagrant?" asked Antony, indicating the injured warrior. In the meantime, people around shouted that he had attacked the guard and deserved to be punished.

"Don't you recognise me, consul?" said the Suebi.

"Should I?" said Antony, looking him over skeptically. The woman couldn't blame him: not only had her man lost an eye since the last time he and the consul had met – covered in bruises, cuts and dust as he was, he looked like a beggar.

"Of course you should," the German replied. "We fought together in Gaul during Vercingetorix's great rebellion, we marched together for Caesar's triumph, defeated Pompey's army in Durrës and Farsala. How can you not remember me?"

Antony thought a moment, peering at him more intently.

"I can't believe it!" he exclaimed suddenly, "Ortwin, you tough old bastard!"

"In the flesh."

Antony looked over at the woman. "Ah, you're the barbarian woman without a hand... What was your name? Veleda, wasn't it?" he added, and she nodded.

"They said you had either died or deserted in Munda. Evidently, the second hypothesis was correct," the consul commented coldly. "You ran away..."

"That is *not* correct, consul. I fought until the end, and when the battle was concluded I presumed that my duties were too. I went back to my homeland..."

"You have not been lucky, by the look of it."

"I have not indeed. I came here to offer my services to Caesar again, but now that he is dead – and I still struggle to believe it – I think you are the most worthy leader I could wish to serve."

Antony smirked. "And you really expect me to take a derelict like you, do you? One who is a deserter, moreover? Forget it, my friend – you're finished."

Ortwin took a step forward, causing the lictors to move immediately to protect the magistrate and the soldiers behind them to draw their swords.

"Recruit me and I will surprise you. Don't be fooled by my appearance," he hissed.

"I don't need you. I have so much money now that I can afford to recruit the best soldiers in Rome as my bodyguards: do you see these men?" answered Antony, indicating the men with the phaleras. "They're all centurions. Only centurions. And they are at my exclusive service."

Ortwin hesitated. Veleda felt her stomach clench – she knew he was forcing himself to master his pride for her sake, and prayed he wouldn't humiliate himself any further...

But he did.

"Please, consul... I need a second chance," he begged.

Veleda saw Antony's disgust as he regarded the warrior. The consul shook his head and told his bodyguards, "Take this individual out of my sight. He abandoned Caesar and would do the same to me. In the name of our shared history and your services to Caesar, I will let you go, even though you did attack my gatekeeper. But do not show your face here again, Ortwin. You or your woman with her stump."

While Antony headed towards the entrance of his residence with indifference, his centurions leapt forward, seized the German and dragged him away. He tried to wriggle out of their grip but gave up after the first few kicks and slaps, staying passive until the soldiers threw him against the nearest cistern. He collapsed to the cobblestones. Veleda rushed over and sat down beside him, relieved to see that he was conscious.

"What now?" she asked.

"I don't know," he answered. "All we can do is offer our services to someone else."

VI

As soon as her brother appeared at the door, Octavia instinctively wanted to run and embrace him: she hadn't seen him for six months, and it felt like a whole lifetime, but that was a privilege reserved firstly for her mother Atia, after whom it was the turn of Marcius Philippus, her step-father. They didn't even allow the young man to cross the threshold – they went to Octavian and embraced him warmly, though Octavia couldn't help noticing that he seemed less than enthusiastic.

Those long months he had spent far from Rome had changed him. Had it not been for his eyes, she would hardly have recognised him. His expression was new too: Octavian had suddenly grown up. Not only in appearance, but more importantly in his soul, and his face reflected the change, of course. In those beautiful, sparkling pale blue eyes she could see a new depth and substance – they had lost their innocence. Determination sparkled in his gaze, wherever he directed it. Octavia didn't know if the boy she had once know had become a man yet, but he certainly wanted to with all his heart.

It was no coincidence that Octavian had announced his arrival in Rome and told his whole family to gather in Atia and Marcius Philippus's house so he could explain his plan to them. He had ordered all this as a man – he would never have dared to six months before. But he was Caesar's heir now. Or at least, he felt that he was.

"My dear son, I have been so worried about you," said Atia, allowing him to walk into the triclinium and greet the other guests, who stood up from the low sofas and moved towards him.

Octavian rushed immediately to embrace his sister, then turned to Atia. "Why, mother? Caesar's assassins have all escaped justice, as far as I know, and the people miss the dictator. Now Rome is safe for all of the *gens Julia.*" Octavia held him tightly, then let him go to greet Quintus Pedius, Lucius

Pinarius and her husband Markellus.

"The tension, however, remains," replied his stepfather immediately. "Antony is holding the Republic in a precarious balance. Cicero and the Senate do not like his excessive power, and Lepidus will not be satisfied with the position of *pontifex maximus* which Antony himself conferred upon him to keep him quiet. Caesar's assassins have taken office in important provinces, from which they could easily Markh upon Rome at the head of their legions, or decide to starve us."

Octavian shook his two cousins' and his brother-in-law's hands warmly, the turned towards Marcius Philippus. "I do not think we need be afraid, now," he said. "I am going to speak to Antony as soon as possible. I will take possession of my inheritance and will be able to pay the people and settle the veterans in the colonies. I will have the people's support and will be untouchable, and this will permit me to obtain a political appointment: I will represent the institutions and will take my revenge upon my father's assassins."

"Ah, yes?" replied Quintus Pedius. "And what makes you think Antony will allow you?"

"Or that the Senate will allow such a young boy to hold such exalted political rank?" continued Lucius Pinarius.

"That inheritance is cursed, my son," added Marcius Philippus. "It will only bring you trouble. You should give it up, if you want my opinion. Your mother thanks that it is too dangerous to accept it. Too many people desire that money. Too many powerful people, who could do away with you in a moment. Antony, for one!"

"And Caesar's assassins..." added Atia, fervently. "When they know that a boy dared accept the dictator's inheritance, they will make sure they get you out of the way so they can finish the job!"

Octavian stiffened. He looked at Philippus with burning eyes, something Octavia had never seen before. "You are not my father. You never were. And now, my father is Caesar. The sooner I officialise my adoption, the better. If he considered me worthy of him, I would be the greatest coward on the face of the Earth to turn down such an honour."

Octavia would have liked to tell him that their parents did not deserve such harsh treatment – they were simply worried for him. But her brother must have realised he had crossed a line, as he went immediately to embrace his mother and grasp his stepfather's hand.

"I apologize – I owe much to both of you," he said in a sweeter tone of voice. "But I owe Caesar much too, and the best way to repay him is by being as good as he thought I would be, and showing myself worthy of his trust."

"But you will have to face such powerful and unscrupulous men," His mother started to sob. "men who are familiar with the use of power… They will crush you if you try to stop them!"

His stepfather took him to a small divan. They sat, and the others followed. "I was a consul twelve years ago, as you know," said Marcius Philippus, "and I saw what they are capable of. I was so disgusted that I retired from politics a long time ago. You need to be cut out for it – to be able to sail the stormy waters of power. And those waters are *always* stormy, even when they appear to be calm, because there is always someone who wishes to have more, or to injure or get rid of somebody else. And all weapons are legitimate, especially those which are forbidden by the law. There is no morality there at all, unless it be for an audience. Either you develop the ability to put aside all your scruples, or you go under. I couldn't do it and preferred to leave that world before it crushed me. I am not your father, but I am taking the liberty of speaking to you as though I were because you are facing the most important decision of your life, and I would feel guilty if I didn't tell you all I know in order to allow you to choose wisely."

Octavian nodded, but Octavia hoped silently that her brother wouldn't be scared off and would take up the challenge. Had it been her, she probably wouldn't have had the courage, and she would have never dreamt of acquiring the unscrupulousness necessary to survive in that world. But she too felt that her family would be unworthy of Caesar if none of them avenged him and carried on his work. And she didn't really expect Lucius Pinarius or Quintus Pedius to stand up for their rights: just like Marcius Philippus, there were some conflicts they simply didn't have the guts for. When Octavian opened his mouth to reply, though, she saw immediately that he was made of different stuff altogether. He reminded her of his predecessor, not only physically but also in his attitude.

"I observed Caesar very carefully, and I tried to learn as much from him as I could," he said. "His death prevented me from learning as much as I would have liked and as much as, probably, was necessary, but I think I understand the mechanisms which allow a man to fulfil his ambitions and defend himself from those who would try to stop him. Caesar had his own personal ambitions – he wanted to prevail over others, that is true – but he also wanted to be the man to save Rome from self-destruction and to restore to its citizens that internal peace they had lacked for so long. He left me all the means I need to achieve those goals and should it should take my entire life, I will do whatever I can to realise his plan. *Whatever* I can, I assure you. He committed many crimes, that is certain, but I have realised you cannot defeat those who set obstacles on the path of righteousness unless you use the same weapons as they do. In any case, Caesar's crimes are minor when compared to those of his adversaries, because he was killed by those he pardoned – he gave power to untrustworthy men, who then killed him.

I learned from him what to do and what not to do – and how to choose my allies. Yes, because nobody can make it alone, but you must know how to choose the right people: trustworthy and skilled. Now I can count on the people and the soldiers' support, and I must take advantage of it immediately, before they start thinking I am undeserving of the trust Caesar put in me. I want to create a group of people I can trust completely, and who can help me to do what I cannot do by myself. I want to unite them with an oath and create a sect with a common goal: that of avenging Caesar and making Rome a stable and long-lasting empire, no longer vulnerable to threats of civil war or invasions like those of Gaius Marius's day. Even if we must fight other civil wars to obtain this…"

"You're forgetting about Mark Antony…" said Quintus Pedius. "There is already a man who is almost as powerful as Caesar in Rome. He's the one you will have to confront, if you wish to be visible. For example, he has denied Lucius Pinarius and myself our part of the inheritance, coming up with one excuse after another."

"Whatever I do, I will do it with Mark Antony, because he was Caesar's closest lieutenant and because he possesses the most prestige," Octavian pointed out. "I need him and he needs me, because the soldiers love me and the people have accepted the provisions of Caesar's will. He cannot oppose it, and if he has so far been careful to support Caesar's assassins, he will do the same with me."

"You have nothing. How can you say he needs you?" replied Lucius Pinarius.

"I have nothing? I have the support of the people! Do you call that nothing? And I have money, the money *he* will give me. I have the soldiers, who are faithful to Caesar's memory. I have everything a man needs to be powerful and in a position to dictate his conditions. And my conditions now are to avenge Caesar and obtain a high-ranking position to allow me to have my say on the Senate's most important decisions."

"A magistrate? But you're only nineteen!" protested his stepfather.

"People, money and soldiers."

The young man stopped talking, as did the others, who were still incredulous: none knew what further objection to make. Octavia examined the expressions on her relatives' faces and realised that they thought as she did.

The dictator had been right. If there was one man in the family who could, in the long term, follow in his footsteps, that man was Octavian. Once again, Caesar had proven himself more forward-looking than the others: in a frail, unhealthy boy he had seen a determined man, a man who would be pitiless enough to impose his will over that of his political adversaries and continue his work. Octavia didn't know if her brother would succeed: circumstances were against him, and the task was an almost impossible one. But she knew for sure he was the only one of them who would try.

*

The long wait had put Octavian's patience to the test, but the young man had decided not to complain and to try and appear friendly towards Mark Antony. He nodded to Agrippa, who nodded back in encouragement, then followed the slave outside, where he was dazzled by the blinding sun which illuminated Pompey's sumptuous gardens.

Antony was sitting on a bench in the shade of a plane tree with a secretary, who was noting down on a wax tablet the orders the consul was giving him as he read through some documents. When the slave announced Octavian's presence, he didn't even lift up his head, but only nodded, continuing to read and to dictate his instructions to the secretary: "… for these reasons, we think that the inhabitants of Sicily should no longer feel inferior to, nor have less rights than, those who were granted Roman citizenship for being faithful allies of Rome. We decree, in accordance with Caesar's desires, that they too must receive Roman citizenship and that Sicily will no longer be a province ruled by a *praetor*, but a part of the Italic territory."

Octavian's irritation began to grow. Not only was Antony flaunting his indifference towards him, but he was also giving orders for Octavian's sole benefit while pretending he was carrying out Caesar's will: allowing Siceliotes to obtain citizenship would make him many friends, but as far as Octavian was aware, it wasn't any part of the dictator's plans. Moreover, it underlined the urgency of the need for him to take possession of his inheritance and let people know he intended to apply Caesar's will to the letter: if he left everything in Antony's hands, the man's personality would crush him, perhaps for good.

Octavian felt like calling for his attention, but he forced himself to wait for the consul to speak to him and eventually Antony paid him the courtesy of lifting his head. After haughtily looking him up and down, he said, "*Ave*, lad. I'm pleased to see you looking healthy for once. I feared that the military life in Apollonia might have damaged you irreparably. How can I help you?"

It was worse than he had thought. Octavian prayed for the gods to give him the strength he needed to hide his indignation: he told himself that he had to get used to this – to being belittled and to having to hide his real feelings – and tried to convince himself that this occasion was the best possible training. A tough start, perhaps, but certainly no worse than the challenges he would have to face in the future.

"Father," he began, "… for such must I consider you, given the position you hold and your importance to me – I have come first of all to thank you for what you did for Caesar, both before and after his death, and also for me, however indirectly, by protecting the inheritance my great-uncle was kind enough to leave me. And I am also very grateful to you for your opposition to compensating the murderers; I am sure that if they hadn't kept you from acting, you would have done everything in your power to save him, or would have avenged him. But permit me also to criticise you for immediately coming to terms with the murderers and even giving them hostages, and allowing an amnesty be declared without taking the best interests of the people, who demanded justice, into account... You yourself saw how, after the will was read, the people were ready to actually burn down the assassin's houses, and yet not only did you not take up arms in support of the people, you did not even bring charges against Caesar's assassins, if charges are actually necessary for those who are caught in the act and confess to their crimes. You actually allowed them to escape, some of them to provinces which they continue to hold against the divine law after killing the one who had assigned them."

He hadn't been able to help it: he had spoken his mind. He was still inexpert at charming his potential allies, as he intended to do with anyone who might be useful to him. He had failed before he had even begun, and prepared himself now for Antony's outburst: after all, he had just launched into a critique of a man he already knew was not well-disposed towards him.

"I hope you are joking, lad," replied Antony, visibly irritated. "Have you any idea what the situation was like after Caesar's death? Of course not – you were not here: they said that I was the next victim, and that they could count on the support of many senators. I did all I could to avoid a civil war, and the senators now acknowledge that. And now here you come, arrogant and inexperienced, and dare to judge me..."

"No, no, I am not judging you, my father. I meant only to say that what was done then out of necessity can now be repaired. You and Dolabella acted correctly by taking Syria and Macedonia for your consulships, but was it really necessary to assign Creta and Cyrenaica to Brutus and Cassius? In any case, it is hardly in your interests for your possible future political adversaries to remain strong. I would have expected that you would have at least made them weaker, if you didn't feel like attacking them."

"It was a decision of the Senate!" snapped Antony. "And we did weaken them, actually, by denying them much more important provinces, like Syria and Macedonia!"

He's on the defensive, thought Octavian… It would be a good idea to press him some more.

"Of course, but it was you who called for a vote," he continued, "and it was you who was presiding over the Senate. Assigning provinces and gifts was like insulting Caesar for a second time and cancelling his political legacy. Moreover, you let that great betrayer Decimus Brutus keep Gaul!"

He hated himself for not being able to control his tongue. Getting Antony on the defensive didn't mean humiliating him. Nice work, he told himself: he wanted to head a party which would take inspiration from Caesar and yet he couldn't even get Caesar's closest associate on his side. How would he justify his behaviour to Agrippa, Rufus and his relatives?

*

Agrippa was aware of the delicacy of this meeting between Octavian and Antony, and awaited the outcome with trepidation. He walked nervously up and down the atrium of the domus attached to Pompey's gardens, which Antony had received from Caesar and made his principle residence. and circled the *impluvium*, leaning against the columns which surrounded it, his head down, angered by Octavian's decision to cut him out of the meeting at the last minute, fearing that his temper might compromise it. He had been strangely pleased when he had learned that his friend had decided to take only him along, and not Rufus nor his two cousins, and he had dreamt that he might meet the consul face to face. But now his disappointment stung him, although he could not deny that his outspokenness really might have made him say something which would have irritated Antony. He had to admit, even if unwillingly, that Octavian could manage certain situations better than he, and he was sure that his friend would apply to the letter the principles upon which he had decided to base his rise to power.

But he would still have liked to be present, though, to follow the development of the meeting which would decide their future. Octavian had only just gone off with the slave and he was already wondering if the meeting was going well. He decided to distract himself by thinking of Etain, but that too made him angry with his friend for not having taken him along to the reunion he had ordered at his parent's house as soon as he had reached Rome – he would certainly have met her there. There was not really any need for him to use her as a way of distracting himself from more worrisome issues, though – he found that she came to mind more and more frequently of her own accord.

"So you're a friend of our young cousin Octavian. What's your name, young man?" A voice made him lift his head.

Standing beside him was a powerfully sensual woman, whose approach he had not noticed. Either he had been too immersed in his thoughts or her step was incredibly light. He should in any case have noticed her perfume though, which seemed now to be climbing up his nostrils like claws reaching for his brain to tear it out of his head.

She wasn't beautiful, but he was certain she could have had any man she wanted.

"My name... My name is Marcus Vipsanius Agrippa, madam," he said after swallowing, "and yes, I am with Octavian," He was used to dealing with all kinds of women, but never with such a high-ranking matron, and he felt immediately intimidated. After Etain, who had provoked a different kind of reaction in him, this was the second time in a few days that the mere presence of a woman had made him lose control of his emotions.

When he realised who he was dealing with, his embarrassment grew even more. The woman did not introduce herself, but Agrippa knew she could only be Mark Antony's wife, Fulvia. One of the most talked-about women in Rome.

The consul had chosen a difficult woman, one who had been through two troubled marriages: the first with Clodius, tribune of the plebeians and notorious firebrand, who had ended up being killed in a street brawl, and the second with Curio, who had died tragically in Africa. It had been courageous of Antony to take her as his wife, after all the scandals in which she had been involved and the bad temper for which she was famed. On the other hand, if there was a man in Rome who was not afraid of women, that man was Antony.

Agrippa too had thought he had nothing to fear from the opposite sex – until he had met her: Fulvia frightened him, and he wanted to escape.

And at the same time, he wanted to tear her clothes off and take her violently.

"And what are you doing for Octavian out here alone? Are you his watchdog? His bodyguard?" Even her voice sent shivers down his spine: he felt a strange unease and restlessness. Her voice was low and hoarse, and Agrippa had the feeling that she made it sound that way deliberately. She must have been about fifteen years older than him, and she was using her age to her advantage so as to appear more confident and experienced.

"Absolutely not. I am his oldest and closest friend – we share almost everything," he answered, in a voice that came out sounding less convincing than he had intended.

Fulvia raised one of her perfectly shaped eyebrows. They were as dark as her hair, which was wound about her head in a complicated style. Her eyes, which appeared even darker because of the use of abundant kohl, stared at him for a long time – so long that he was forced to look away. He was behaving like a child.

"Really? How strange that Octavian would be such close friends with a plebeian…"

"We grew up together in Velletri and we have been friends since we were seven years old…"

"Hmm," nodded Flavia. "And you're sure you're not something more than just *friends*?"

Agrippa would have laughed, had he been less nervous. He and Octavian had been going with women since they were children, and in other circumstances he would have been amused at being called homosexual. But now he felt provoked.

He forced himself to summon back the self-confidence he usually exhibited in his dealings with the fairer sex.

"A respectable matron like yourself, of such noble blood, would never deign to verify my manhood. Unfortunately for you, the doubt must thus remain," he said, forcing himself to wink.

"On the contrary, I'm more than happy to verify. Indeed, that was my intention. Come, show me what you can do," she said, and with that turned around, dropped her mantle to the ground and raised her tunic to her waist, leaving Agrippa staring at her magnificent buttocks, which were not even covered by a loincloth.

Mark Antony rose to his feet, and Octavian could not help noticing just how different the consul – a large, powerful man – and he – a slip of a lad – actually were. He felt intimidated, overwhelmed both by Antony's bulky frame and the authority of his personality. That hadn't happened when he had met Cicero, which had deluded him into thinking that he could deal with powerful people easily. But with Cicero, he hadn't had to struggle to keep his emotions under control, and he had also been greeted gently. With Antony, instead, he had immediately felt the contempt that the experienced politician felt for the novice, and he hadn't been able to hide all the rancour within him for Caesar's assassination and the consul's inaction. Instead of drawing him to his side as he had planned to do, despite his opinion of the man, he was turning him into an enemy. And given the list of enemies he had just drawn up, he really didn't need any more.

"And why should I justify my actions to you anyway? Who do you think you are?" attacked Antony. "Do you think that Caesar left you not only his inheritance but his power as well? If he had, then it might be reasonable that I explain my actions as a politician to you. But we Romans have never allowed anyone to leave their power in an inheritance – not even kings, when we still had them! On the contrary, they killed Caesar because they thought he was behaving like a king and not like a magistrate. So I don't need to justify my actions to you, and I also exonerate you from having to be grateful to me. Whatever I have done, I did it for the people's good, not for yours!"

He had lost him. At that point the best thing to do was not let Antony walk all over him and try to make him believe that he would have to deal with him in the future.

"You did it because you wish to imitate Caesar, that's the real reason! And you have made all and sundry your friends to gain yourself wider support!" snapped back Octavian. "And you didn't punish Caesar's assassins as revenge for not being mentioned in his will!"

"What? I cannot believe I am being accused of such things! *I* am the one who fought to grant Caesar eternal honour and a public burial, against bloodthirsty, determined men who were all set to kill me as well! *I* convinced the Senate not to consider Caesar a tyrant and to respect his orders, including his last will. Without me, you wouldn't *have* any inheritance, you little idiot, and now you accuse me of not respecting Caesar's wishes in assigning the provinces? You'll have to make up your mind: if his documents about the assignment of the provinces are not valid, neither is his testament. And if his testament is valid in naming you as practically his absolute heir, then all his other documents are valid as well. You're accusing me of wanting to be a tyrant, but I have to take the Senate's and the people's will into account."

It was pointless, Antony was too able for him: with his ironclad logic, he had managed to overcome Octavian's rhetoric. Not only had Octavian not obtained anything, he had also made an enemy of Antony. But he still had the upper hand: everybody knew about the testament and that he was the heir. Antony could find whatever excuse he wished, but sooner or later he would have to give him that money if he didn't want to make an enemy of the people and the soldiers, who were waiting for their compensation payments.

At that point, their relationship was compromised. The only chance remaining was to try and obtain a material agreement, avoiding any hypocritical attempts at camaraderie. "It would appear, then, that I have no right to criticise you, so if you really have safeguarded my inheritance, please let me have it," said Octavian. "My main purpose is to avenge my father, and I am asking you to help me do that at least by allowing me to use my inheritance. I am not an ungrateful person, and I acknowledge you did all you could to safeguard Caesar's possessions by moving them to your own home. But since everybody knows I am Caesar's heir, I will look like a thief unless I carry out the dispositions of the testament regarding the people and the soldiers, who are still waiting for their compensations in Rome. Or alternatively, they will call you a thief, if you keep the money. I think we can come to an agreement: given all the risks you have taken, I will allow you to keep the precious objects, the ornaments and anything else you want. But I immediately need the four thousand talents Caesar allocated for the Parthian war to pay the three hundred thousand people who make up the population of Rome. I will pay the soldiers with the income from the sale of my properties, if necessary, and if that proves not to be sufficient, I will ask for a loan from you or from the public purse, with your guarantee."

He hoped Antony would be satisfied by his offer, but the consul's expression was enough to show him that he had been fooling himself.

"You know nothing! *Nothing!*" snapped Antony. "And you want to give me orders. You still have a long road ahead of you, lad! Don't you know that the treasury's funds are empty, because all tax money ended up in Caesar's hands? Yes, that's right, you feckless milksop – nobody dared investigate it while the dictator was alive, but now it's time for it to be done. Your inheritance will be challenged by infinite claims and appeals, because now all the private individuals who think they gave money to Caesar unjustly will feel brave enough to speak up. And don't think there's any treasure left in my house: straight after the Ides of March, a gang of magistrates and notables took it for themselves, with the pretext that it was the wealth of a tyrant. If you are smart, you won't give what's left to the people but to those who feel they are owed something by your father – the unhappy ones who might desire ill for you and whom you'd better have as friends. In the event, it will be they who allow you to send the soldiers to the colonies."

Antony had annihilated, overwhelmed and humiliated him. And yet Octavian just couldn't let him win. He remained silent for a few moments, and then shouted: "These are all excuses! Pretexts for not wanting to respect your obligations towards me! You allowed Caesar's treasure to be stolen in order to obtain friends and make agreements with the aim of obtaining absolute power! You distributed Caesar's money as it best suited you, not according his will! You're an opportunist and a thief!" he concluded, and then turned away from him and walked back to the atrium where he had waited, wondering what he would tell Agrippa.

Perhaps Antony was telling the truth, or perhaps the truth was in his own words. But all that mattered was that he was up to his neck in debt.

*

Agrippa looked around him, both terrified and excited at the same time. He realised he was sweating and felt ridiculous. He would never have dreamed of taking advantage of Fulvia's offer.

"But... your husband is only a few steps away..." he stuttered. "What are you doing? Are you out of your mind?"

"By all the gods," she replied, in a sorrowful tone, without even turning her head and continuing to flaunt her rear, "so young, and so cowardly. I wouldn't have thought that a young bull like you, with such a divine, athletic body, would resist the call of sex. For your information, one of my slaves is guarding the entrance to the gardens, and will alert me if anyone comes."

Agrippa felt confused. She was holding the reins, and this was the first time it had not been he who was leading the game. He would have liked to rush over to her, kneel down and sink his face into her generous body, but he couldn't help feeling that she was treating him like an object. Just the way he had treated most of the girls he had slept with.

"Young Agrippa, you are very disappointing. I thought you would have more initiative. I shan't wait like this forever... In fact, I am already growing bored," she said in a calm, blunt, severe voice.

Agrippa started looking around again. He thought of how embarrassing it would have been for Octavian if he was discovered. And he also thought of Etain's sweet face. And the determined, self-confident expression on Fulvia's face which had scared him so much... But the lusty form in front of his eyes made him make one step forward, then another, and another, until he found himself, he knew not how, grappling with her, an impetuous erection under his toga, touching what until that moment he had only been staring at.

"Mistress, somebody's coming!" hissed a voice.

At the words, she pulled away from him and rapidly tidied herself up. In an instant she looked the same as she had when she had entered the atrium. He, on the contrary, felt sweaty and clumsy; and moreover, his erection showed no signs of going away.

"Come back as soon as you can. Or I will come looking for you. I want you," she whispered a moment before Octavian appeared at the atrium's entrance. The young man's beautiful face wore a dark expression. He noticed the matron and said in a monotone voice, "My respects, dear Fulvia. Please forgive me if I do not stay, I have some urgent matters to deal with."

"Of course, dear Octavian," she answered, completely in control of herself. "Your friend Agrippa here was just telling me how busy you two are…"

Agrippa looked at his friend, and saw that he was scrutinising him, his loins included. His expression went from dark to surprised for a moment and Agrippa thought he saw the hint of a smirk of amusement. But Octavian soon grew serious again, and gestured to Agrippa that they were leaving.

"S-so?" stuttered an embarrassed Agrippa as he followed Octavian out of the building. "Did you manage to fool him as you did with Cicero?"

"Oh, of course…" answered Octavian with a bitter smile. "I might as well have sent you!"

VII

"We can thus conclude," the prosecutor's declared lawyer, "that the property situated along the Vicus Capriarius, by the Nymphaeum of Jupiter, was illegally confiscated by the dictator Julius Caesar following the proscription of its owner, Lucius Domitius Ahenobarbus, who was then exiled and has now returned to Rome to assert his rights." Even though the building was full of people, his words reverberated around the Basilica Julia, echoing off its high roof. "For these reasons, young Gaius Octavian cannot claim ownership of the building. The property must thus be removed from the inheritance left to him by Julius Caesar."

Octavian looked at Lucius Pinarius, who had offered to defend him in the lawsuits regarding their inheritance. The results so far had been bad. His cousin had forbidden Octavian to defend himself, saying that his age and his experience of attending lawsuits for years would provide better legal protection, but the courts were always chaired by the consuls or their friends, and the young man always lost, despite Pinarius's hard work.

Pinarius stood up and approached the court, which was chaired by Mark Antony. "Consul, I'm sure I do not need to remind you that the decree issued by the Senate after the death of the dictator declared all the dispositions he made while exercising his functions valid. For this reason I too will conclude by saying that if Caesar's instructions concerning the magistrates for the next five years were validated, and if his laws are to be followed, then the properties he confiscated following the conviction of enemies of the state, or those who were at the time held to be such, should be considered the property of his family, and thus of his heir."

The audience rumbled, some in support of Pinarius's claim, and others against it.

Most of them, however, urged Antony to approve Octavian's

claims, both because they regarded properties confiscated from rich and powerful people as currency and because the young man had already started to gain the crowd's sympathies by distributing what money he could in accordance with Caesar's bequest.

Antony asked Pinarius to return to his seat, and his face grew thoughtful. Quintus Pedius, who was sitting behind Octavian, approached his young cousin and whispered in his ear, "What do you bet he'll find against us again? But the people are starting to realise he doesn't like you…"

"Yes, but apart from the odd useless protest, the people – unfortunately – can do nothing," Octavian commented bitterly. "Luckily I still have some money my associates retrieved in Africa from the funds Caesar had allocated for the Parthian war. But there's not much left."

"What about the money Gaius Matius and Cornelius Balbus lent you?" Pedius insisted.

"That's finished. They did lend me some because of their affection for Caesar, but it wasn't much. And unfortunately, when I asked for another loan, I had already started losing lawsuits, so they must have thought I would soon be bankrupt. Which, if things go on like this, is very likely…"

"What progress are you making with the gratuities to the people?" asked Pinarius, referring to the three hundred sestertii that had been promised to each Roman citizen.

"It's not going well. I doubt I have paid more than fifty thousand people," he answered sorrowfully. "I'll need a lot more money to pay three hundred thousand of them, and if we can't get hold of at least part of the inheritance, we can't start paying." Some days he felt he had taken on a task that was too much for him: climbing the ranks of power at his young age and avenging Caesar were two undertakings he had probably accepted too lightly, and he sometimes he thought of the words of his parents, who had warned him to give up. This was one of those days.

He didn't really care if the crowd attending the trial were calling his name and, in its way, trying to intimidate the court. During the last few days he had found that more and more people were supporting him since the news about his having started to pay out the money promised in the testament had spread. Many people were sympathetic towards him – it seemed that they saw in him a new Caesar, and they encouraged him to continue his ascent and not let himself be scared off by the old holders of power.

In spite of all that support, though, he was realising how hard it was to acquire credibility in high places. Very few important people had agreed to finance him and lend him the money he needed to honour the testament's obligations, and the result had been that the testament had given him no rights but only obligations – obligations which might bankrupt him. His strength was based on the support of the people and the wishes of the soldiers, but they would both vanish in an instant if he couldn't keep them happy.

He didn't expect the situation would change that day either, and for that reason didn't react when Antony announced the verdict against him. He remained in his seat, head down, not joining Pinarius, who stood up immediately and followed Pedius to Antony's tribune to protest.

"This is an injustice!" He didn't even look up to see which of his two cousins was speaking. "The Senate's decree states clearly: the only acts by Caesar that are to be nullified are those which led to his claiming absolute power. All the rest are to be legitimised!"

"I understand your point of view, gentlemen," answered Antony mellifluously. "It would seem indeed that some of our verdicts go against the Senate's decisions, but the text of the decree does not, in fact, correspond exactly to what the senators decided. At that time, the people were rioting and we added the prohibition to nullify the laws published during Caesar's dictatorship to the amnesty, upon which we all agreed. But it would be more correct to interpret the spirit of the decree rather than following it to the letter, and to give the properties which were confiscated following a civil war back to the many who lost them instead of making one young man rich by giving him a patrimony of such proportions that he might decide to act unwisely."

"What are you talking about? That's just an excuse for attacking us! You are the only one taking decisions without needing to justify yourself to anyone else!"

Other people were protesting too, but Antony didn't seem to care. "I have no intention of attacking you – I don't wish to bother you once you have divided up the inheritance," he said.

"On the contrary, I'd say you two shouldn't worry: what is owed you will not make you too rich, and I am willing to give it to you right now if you will stop causing me problems."

Antony was becoming offensive now, thought Octavian. He was even trying to bribe his cousins to agree to some sort of separate peace with them, and not even trying to hide it – he must consider Octavian an absolute nonentity. The young man shook himself from his torpor and was about to get up and walk over to the stand like the others, but then he realised that doing so would give Antony a pretext to have him arrested or to publicly humiliate him. No, he wasn't ready yet to face the consul again.

Perhaps he never would be.

Antony was too powerful. Caesar's assassins were too powerful. The Senate was suspicious of a seditious young man who had begun to rock the political and social balances. And the people and soldiers, even though they all liked him, were inconstant by nature.

If he'd had more common sense, he would have given up. Only his determination to pursue his plan of avenging his beloved great-uncle gave him the necessary strength to go on. But for how much longer?

He saw his brother-in-law Claudius Marcellus with a man he had never seen before. "You weren't lucky this time either, I see," began Octavia's husband. "Your sister has been nagging me to do something for you, so I have asked this new friend of mine if he'd be willing to give you a hand. Despite his young age, he's a fellow with plenty of wealth and initiative. He even helped us out of a very tight corner during the Ides of March."

Octavian studied the person his brother-in-law was talking about who smiled back at him with ostentatious cordiality. He had no doubt that – if he really was as rich as Claudius Marcellus claimed – he liked showing off his wealth: he was wearing a toga made of a very precious fabric, with inlaid gems, and his tunic was of very sophisticated manufacture. Octavian had never seen one like it before, not even among the richest senators. And his face... His face was surrounded by curls which cascaded down from his temples, a style one might expect to see on a woman rather than a man. He thought he even saw some makeup on his face. And that was not all: his movements were cautious and circumspect, as though he were repelled by everything which surrounded him. Including the human beings.

He was a strange person. Almost ridiculous. And the strangest thing was that he was more or less the same age as Octavian.

"Greetings, Octavian," said the new arrival. "My name is Gaius Cilnius Maecenas, and I have been following your actions very closely."

"Why?" asked Octavian abruptly, without caring that he might appear rude. He was in no mood for chit-chat, and he didn't like the idea that someone was spying on him.

But his interlocutor did not seem to be annoyed by his aggressive manner. "Let us say that I like giving people the chance to fulfil their dreams. And you have a lot of dreams, but lack the means to realise them. For this reason, our path are destined to cross. And anyway, I like finding a man of my age who still has dreams…"

Octavian looked at his brother-in-law. "What is this, a joke?" he asked.

Marcellus opened his arms: "Maecenas has a… *peculiar* way of introducing himself. But I can guarantee you that there are few people as bright as he. Your sister will agree with me."

Maecenas smiled. He didn't seemed inclined to lose his good humour. "Yes, many think that if someone offers to help them they must be teasing. But ask around and you will discover that I have helped many people. Why do I do it? I want something in return, of course: somehow the people I help feel they have a debt to me, even if it is only a moral one, and they become my friends. Having many friends is important: you will see that as you climb higher and higher, as I hope you will. My motto is that what you invest today will usually come back tomorrow with interest. If I can bring out a man's unexpressed potential, if I give him the chance to feel fulfilled, one day I may also profit from his talent, or if not me, then the many others who will remember me as the man who allowed such a thing to happen. If this explanation does not convince you then know too that I liked Caesar, and I'm somewhat annoyed with those who killed him."

"So you are doing it for posterity," commented Octavian. He couldn't hide the sarcasm in his voice, but this man had cheered him up, which couldn't be a bad thing.

"Put it however you like," answered Maecenas, just as tartly. "Of course, it would be better for you if this posterity wasn't too far in the future – it is in the present that you need help, I seem to understand."

"And what kind of help would you provide to me?"

"Money, of course. It's what you need at the moment and it is what I can offer you most of. Not only my money, of course, but also that of the friends of mine I can convince to support you. I don't doubt they will agree to my requests: that's what friends are for, isn't it?"

Octavian thought it was too good to be true. There must be a catch. "Hmmm… And what do you want in exchange?" he asked suspiciously.

"I told you: your gratitude. Of course I expect to have my investment repaid with money too. I am certain you are a man of honour and you will repay me. And I don't mean interest. And when you are in power, you will perhaps remember that I was a valuable partner and will perhaps think it useful to facilitate my affairs – which I hope will also be yours."

Marcellus intervened. "Octavian, I have been doing business with him since March, and I can assure you that he has marvellous instincts. I am in debt with him not only for saving my life, but also for the precious advice he has given me about my investments."

"Is that all you ask, Maecenas?" Octavian asked again. "What makes you think you're backing the right person? Things aren't going well for me, as you can see – you might end up losing all your money as well as that of your friends only to obtain a worthless ally…"

"Well, all investments come with some risk," Maecenas admitted. "How much did your great-uncle risk when he crossed the Rubicon with only one legion all those years ago? But I trust you, Octavian. You could be the one lasting and stable element in a state whose centre is no longer visible. You think about increasing your support. Pay everyone, and everyone will be in your debt. And when you decide to make your adoption official, people will see you as the new Caesar and will follow you and hinder your enemies. And you will be able to obtain whatever you want."

Octavian looked at him in admiration. He didn't know how true this man's intentions were, but Maecenas had in any case managed to rekindle his motivation in a moment when he thought it had gone for good.

Octavian would have been grateful for that alone.

*

Ortwin and Veleda joined the queue, hoping to reach Octavian and his associates before sunset. Under the watchful eye of the soldiers, who were quick to calm any disturbances, people were crowding the Forum of Caesar, curious to see how the auctioning of the young patrician's properties would go. Even though their prices were relatively low, only a few people could afford to actually buy them, and the majority of them were there simply to admire the determination of this young fellow who, despite the best efforts of the most powerful men in Rome – and Antony in particular – was still not willing to give up his rights.

Ortwin could hear the comments of the people around them, which told him much about the man to whom he intended to offer his services. The more he listened, the happier he grew to know that he would have a new, real Caesar to serve. Destiny was finally giving him a chance to start all over again, with a man who could become as great as his previous commander.

If he took them on.

He realised that he couldn't be particularly appealing – he looked like a beggar and could only offer his possible client a sparse group of scrawny men who it took a considerable effort of the imagination to see as warriors. But he was hoping that Caesar had talked to Octavian of his achievements and that the young man would employ him on faith.

"Have you heard? Consul Mark Antony suspended the laws of the *lex curiata* so Octavian wouldn't be able to take Caesar's name. But as far as I'm concerned, he's his son anyway. They even look alike, don't you think?" That was the opinion one corpulent fellow expressed to a fellow citizen, who answered, "I don't understand why the consul dislikes him so much. He's a good lad, all he wants is to respect his step-father's will."

"You're right, he *is* a good lad!" said another person. "And despite everything they're doing to him, he minds his own business and tries to make the people happy at his own expense!"

"They're selling off villas and land at ridiculous prices! It's a bargain! Let's go and have a listen!"

"No, it's no bargain. Those are contested properties, nobody knows if they will be given back to the owners they were expropriated from! The ones who buy them now might lose them quite quickly!"

"But he's selling them to get the money he needs to pay the people. He's a decent man!"

"He's been forced to! You wouldn't believe what they've put him through. There's no honour in ganging up on a lad who's not even twenty yet!"

"Look how he holds himself! He looks older than he is! He must be wise – if Caesar chose him as his heir, there must be a good reason!"

People were definitively supporting him, though to look at him you wouldn't necessarily think he could become a great leader: he was too slender to resist a demanding military campaign. But he had a talent for leading, and Ortwin had intuition about these things, since he had served the greatest commander who had ever lived for many years. Caesar's charisma and charm had allowed him to rule both soldiers and citizens. Well, his grand-nephew had the same enviable characteristics.

"He won't take us – why would he?" said an increasingly disconsolate Veleda. "Look how many people love him! He certainly he won't lack soldiers, as soon as he starts paying them as well."

"He will. Caesar would have taken me back on."

"But he is not Caesar."

"He wants to be Caesar with all his might, though. It's obvious the general was his role model when he was growing up."

"Don't fool yourself." Veleda was discouraged. It seemed to her they had been roaming around with no purpose, further and further from that kingdom to which she was entitled as Ariovistus' heir, but which they could not reconquer. And if the respect of Caesar's memory and the desire to avenge him were strong enough motivations for Ortwin, as far as she – who had always hated the Romans – was concerned, they did not represent a way for them to triumph. She was no longer the determined, fierce Veleda he had always known, the woman he had always not only loved but also admired. She had always encouraged him and spurred him on, but now it seemed she didn't care about anything any more, and Ortwin had to look within himself to understand the reasons.

He was playing the role of leader, which was a novelty for him: it had always been her who led, thanks to Ortwin's awe of her high birth. "Listen, Veleda," he said, embracing her, "everything will be for the best. We will enter the service of Octavian, avenge Caesar and help him become the most important man in Rome, we will conquer new lands and will receive a reward that will allow us to reclaim your kingdom. Or to create a new one."

She pulled a sour face which distorted her beautiful features, but said nothing. In the past, he had never believed in Veleda's dreams but he had indulged them – he hoped that she intended to do the same for his.

He turned to the tribune of the auctioneers and noticed that, thanks to the movements of the crowd, he was now close to Octavian, and he decided to take advantage of the fact. He took Valeda's hand and pushed past the few people separating him from the young man. As usual, his unnerving appearance facilitated the task, and he soon came within earshot of Caesar's heir.

"Octavian! Octavian!" he cried. "Do you remember Ortwin?"

At first, the young man didn't seem to have heard him, but when the German repeated his name he managed to get his attention. Octavian stared at him quizzically, but gave no sign of having understood who he was.

"I am Ortwin," he shouted, hoping that it would do the trick. "I fought for Caesar!"

"Good!" said Octavian. "There are many of you, though! You'll have to wait your turn when I deal with the soldiers!"

"No! I was not a legionary, I was the head of his German bodyguard! I have to talk to you!"

A fleeting look of irritation flashed across the lad's face, and he came down from the stage, shadowed by a friend of the same age but much more powerfully built. Ortwin remembered seeing them together in the field in front of Munda, before the decisive battle against Pompey the Younger. There was a third lad with them.

Octavian went towards him and Ortwin moved towards the edge of the crowd until the two were finally face to face. Valeda, for her part, looked elsewhere ostentatiously. "She is probably ashamed by my begging," thought Ortwin.

"What did you say your name was?" said Octavian.

"Ortwin, my lord. Caesar must have spoken to you of me. I served under him in all his campaigns in Gaul, in Africa, in Asia and in Spain."

Octavian looked at his friends. "Ah, yes, now I remember: Ortwin. But you had two eyes then, I think. He told me that you were of great assistance to him during the campaigns. When he spoke of his most valuable lieutenants he always mentioned your name. But he also said that you had disappeared at Munda… He was sorry and disappointed, because he had wanted to give you a position of great responsibility when he returned to Rome. Do you remember him, Agrippa? Maybe you were there too sometimes when he spoke of him."

"Yes it's true," agreed the other young man. "He wondered if you were dead or had changed sides."

Ortwin puffed out his chest in an attempt, despite his appearance, to strike an impressive pose. "I had problems at Munda. You can see for yourselves that I lost an eye. But now I am here to offer my experience to his heir. I, my wife and my men."

Octavian looked at him pityingly, then cast a glance at Valeda and the seven warriors who were with him. He shifted his eyes to Agrippa and then to his other friend. "What do you think?" he asked them.

The two eyed the barbarians hesitantly, then shook their heads almost in unison, and Rufus said, "To me, they just look like they'd be a burden."

"I don't think they can be much help to us, the state they're in," agreed Agrippa. "And what use is a warrior with one eye? We need the money for real soldiers, as well as for the people. We can't afford to waste a single sestertius on people who can't help us."

Ortwin gulped and looked imploringly at Octavian. He almost wanted to throw himself at his feet, and the only thing that prevented him from doing so was the presence of Valeda.

And then he heard the words that he had dreaded.

"You have heard my friends," said the youth, spreading his arms. "They know more about fighting than I do. I am sorry, but you are a luxury we cannot afford."

*

Octavia felt an uncontrollable rage mounting within her. It surprised her, because she had never before lost control, except when she was afraid. This time, however, she was not afraid. She was furious. Her husband had finally made her lose her patience.

"This cannot be! We *must* help him! We are the only members of the family who have not made our wealth available to him!" she shouted at her husband, in a voice she hardly recognised herself. She had always seemed such a controlled woman, one who knew her place – an example of composure that all Roman matrons would have liked to imitate. If they had known of her past with Gaius Chaerea and had seen her in that moment of rage, though, they might have thought differently.

"You cannot ask me that!" said Claudius Marcellus, banging his fist on the table of his study. "After the persecution to which Caesar subjected my family during the civil war, I have worked hard to rebuild our situation. Why should I give it away to some lad who cannot possibly pay it back?"

"Caesar pardoned you! You should be grateful to his family, considering that you are part of it!"

"I never fought against him, like my brother and my nephew. I was simply a political opponent, who always behaved properly towards him. Why should he punish me? And now I am supposed to resolve all the problems of his descendants simply because he deigned to *pardon* me?"

Octavia was enraged by her husband's pig-headedness. She left the room and called Etain. "Go to Gaius Chaerea and tell him that I want to meet him at the Forum of Caesar, where Octavian is holding the public auction. Run!"

The freedwoman looked surprised: her mistress had never shown any intention of meeting that man before. Octavia returned to her husband's *tablinum*.

"I am going to my brother," she said curtly. "There are

properties which were part of my dowry that you cannot prevent me from giving him. But I implore you once more to be generous." It occurred to her that she obviously needed a cause to bring out her character.

And now, it seemed, she had found one.

"Don't do anything silly, Octavia," said her husband in a persuasive voice. "If there is a new civil war, and it looks like there might be, we will need some money put aside to protect ourselves." His tone had become more conciliatory.

"I have no intention of thinking in such a calculating way when my brother's future is in jeopardy. He deserves a chance, and I will do everything in my power to give him one."

"But your mother and Marcius Philippus are already helping him" Markellus's tone had become querulous.

"And for that matter, even Quintus Pedius and Lucius Pinarius have provided Octavian with their part of the bequest. Or at least, the little that Antony left them. And my mother and Marcius Philippus have given him almost all of their resources, without asking for anything in return. They, who were so opposed to him accepting the inheritance in the first place."

"Excellent!" insisted her husband, stubbornly. "So now your brother will have enough money to meet the commitments made by Caesar in the name of his heir! Why does he need ours?"

"Are you joking? Have you any idea how much he needs to pay three hundred sestertii to each Roman, pay the veterans who have settled in the colonies, reward the soldiers of the legions who welcomed his arrival and gain the assistance of at least some of the most influential senators? Caesar's properties are under investigation, and he is selling them off at ridiculously low prices. What he has is not enough – he is putting up all of his assets for sale: he will be ruined!"

"Exactly. He will give away everything he gets and end up with nothing. All will keep the money that he has dispensed so thoughtlessly and nobody will take him seriously in the future. Your parents were right: it would have been better to give up the inheritance…"

"And let Caesar go unavenged? And not discover whether Caesar was right to assign to him the role of his heir? He would have spent his whole life wondering if he would have been good enough to have deserved that trust."

"To be frank, these are problems which do not concern me," protested Marcellus. "I managed to pass unscathed through a civil war without losing too much, and I have no intention of getting involved in another. Do you know what will happen now? Antony hates Octavian, and therefore so does Lepidus. Caesar's killers hate and fear him. The senators look down on him. When the time for words is over and men start reaching for their weapons, people will forget that they ever received money from him, and that incautious lad will end up at the mercy of the richest, most powerful men, without an ally or a coin to his name. Only a poor deluded fool like you could imagine him prevailing over the likes of Antony, Lepidus, Cicero, Marcus Brutus, Decimus Brutus and Cassius!"

Octavia was disgusted by her husband's cowardice and opportunism. She left the room without another word, took the title deeds of her lands in Campania, called two slaves and ordered them to accompany her to the Forum of Caesar.

For the first time in her life, she felt alive and ready to act. And she knew there was at least one man who would support her.

*

Veleda saw her companion collapse. Ortwin did not fall to the ground or cry out or even put his hands to his face when Octavian told him that he did not intend to make use of his services, but she realised that the news had devastated him. She saw his blank expression, his vacant eyes and his stiff limbs, and knew that he felt defeated. He wasn't going to plead with them or insist: he had lost.

She could not allow that to happen, she said to herself. It had always been he who had supported her in times of trouble, and only the gods knew how many of those there had been. Now, for once, it was her turn. Ortwin would have been a celebrated commander of the Roman army had it not been for her – now *she* had to give *him* hope, otherwise, even though Ortwin was the one who had given up, she would not have felt worthy of him.

She went to his side and embraced him, and called out to Octavian and his friends before they climbed back up onto the rostrum. In the meantime, the auctioneer continued his work undeterred.

"What kind of people you are, you Romans?" she shouted at Octavian. "This man not only saved the life of Caesar again and again – he was devoted to him! It was me who forced him to abandon your dictator! It was my doing, otherwise he would be always have been at his side!"

She stopped for a moment, feeling her body shaking. She saw that Octavian was staring at her, without saying a word, while Ortwin had bowed his head and made no move to free himself from her embrace. Then she spoke again. "Do you not know what gratitude is? If you, boy, have received this huge inheritance that is also thanks to my Ortwin, who made a decisive contribution to Caesar's survival and to making him more and more powerful. Just ask any soldier, if you do not believe me! And he did it because he is a loyal person, unlike those who betrayed and killed him. How many like that will you find in the future, young Octavian? Are you absolutely certain that you can count on your subordinates? Ortwin's history speaks for him: he is more reliable and loyal than no other. He abandoned Caesar only when he was no longer useful – and then only to conquer a kingdom in his own country. He certainly did not betray him. And he stood by his side not for money nor because it suited him, but out of admiration and affection. He truly loved Caesar: often we quarrelled about it. I accused him of caring more for Caesar than his own people. And it was a bitter surprise to find that Caesar was dead. He would do anything to avenge him – to punish those who killed him and to assist he who Caesar chose to follow in his footsteps."

Octavian descended the steps he had climbed and went over to the couple, his two friends behind him. Veleda was still shaking, but could find nothing more to say. The young man looked at her and then at Ortwin, studying them carefully with those piercing eyes which resembled Caesar's. The woman felt her man awakening from his torpor and puffing out his chest again.

"Perhaps I was hasty, Ortwin," said the boy, rubbing his chin. "Your woman is right: truly reliable men are few and far between. And with the challenges that lie ahead of me, if I find one it's worth keeping hold of him. Do you feel up to facing new dangers for me?"

Ortwin swallowed. "There can be nothing worse than what I faced with Caesar, my lord," he said, his voice breaking with emotion.

"And is avenging your commander really your most important goal?"

"As Wotan is my witness: I will do everything in my power to make those who murdered him pay."

"Are you sure, Octavian?" asked one of his two friends. "It seems to me that his best days are already behind him – far behind him. What good is he to us?"

Octavian's face broke into a broad smile. "Dear Rufus, I have already decided what role to assign our friend here," he replied, giving the German a pat on the back and climbing back up onto the platform.

＊

Octavia climbed out of the litter as soon as the bearers set it on the ground. One of the slaves helped her up from the cushions on which she lay and passed her the papyri she had brought with her. Octavian was on the platform with his friends Agrippa and Rufus, busily examining the papers upon which his future depended. She saw him shaking his head and grimacing in disappointment, and sensed that the auction was not yielding what he had hoped. She looked at him with tenderness, and hoped with all her heart that his dreams would not break against the harsh realities her husband had spoken of. She was six years older than her brother, and had always been protective of him, even after marrying. She had always devoted herself to precautions, thoughtfulness and care for him, believing that Octavian's physical fragility had condemned him to a life of suffering. When she had seen him as a child, incessantly coughing and sometimes even spitting up blood, she would wrap him in her arms and rock him until he fell asleep on her youthful breast. And she had gladly looked after him during his frequent fevers, sitting next to the bed on which he lay until she saw signs of recovery.

In time, though, she had realised that the boy had an iron will and a lucid intelligence, two qualities which were more than able to compensate for his physical shortcomings.

Octavian had grown frail but tall, and despite his weakness he knew how to impress others with his poise and regal bearing. She had become proud of him, but had never ceased to watch over his growth: on at least a couple of occasions, even while pregnant, she had rushed to her parents' house when she had learned that Octavian was lying sick in bed, and had spent the night watching over him.

She had no intention of disturbing him before the arrival of Gaius Chaerea. She needed to be certain that he could embark on the incredible adventure which just weeks before he would not have even dared to consider. She was terribly excited by the idea of being able to do something useful. Her role as mother and senator's wife relegated her to an austere marginal role which didn't feel as though it belonged to her. If Octavian had overcome his fragility and thrown himself with such determination into this titanic undertaking, she too could overcome her fears to help him.

She saw Etain and Gaius Chaerea arriving. They had been quick – that was a good omen. She stared at the man who had made her a woman before her time, and felt that she harboured no grudge against him. On the contrary, she felt for him an affection the depth of which only now, after seeing him again, had she had begun to understand. She had never blamed him for what he had done, for the weakness that he gave in to – indeed, she recalled her first time as the most beautiful of all: in that fleeting encounter, which had produced so many consequences, she had enjoyed his tenderness, a sweetness that she would never have expected from a soldier, the attention that Gaius had paid to her needs and her responses. All things that she had found lacking in her subsequent lovemaking with her husband.

His inner discipline and the strict morality that her mother Atia had imposed upon her had prevented her from ever meeting him again, but now she discovered that the real reason for her avoidance of him was principally fear of her own feelings and the reaction that she might have towards him. Now everything had changed. *She* had changed.

"What has happened, my lady? More trouble?" asked a breathless Gaius Chaerea, as solicitous as ever.

"No. At least, not yet. I just wanted to ask you something."

"At your service, my lady."

Octavia looked at Etain to tell her to move away, but saw that there was no need: the girl had drifted off and was staring at Agrippa, whose massive figure loomed on the tribune to the side of the auctioneer. The lad had noticed her and stared back at her in turn. And his expression suggested that he liked what he saw.

The matron decided to speak freely to the centurion, "I I wanted to ask you… If I decided to support my brother in his struggle to claim what is rightfully his, would… would you be near me?"

She saw his confused expression. It was understandable. After having ignored him for all those years, she called him to ask him to be at her side. At best he must think she was mad.

"What… what do you mean by 'near', my lady?" he asked.

"I mean that, as you know, my brother will have to fight to assert his rights and enforce the provisions of our great-uncle. And I want to be by his side and help him in every way possible. But I need help, and moral support: the support of a courageous man who has known me for a long time and who makes me feel safe. A man who fought for Caesar and who, perhaps, would be happy to see his memory respected and to avenge him. A man to whom I have a stronger bond than I have ever wanted to admit: the only one in the world who can give me the courage to face the dangers and worries which await me in this challenge."

Gaius Chaerea eyes widened in surprise. He made to move closer to her, then stopped, aware of all the eyes around them. Octavia knew that her words had a powerful effect him and that he would have liked to embrace her, and she smiled: she still could not believe she had found the courage to say what she said, but she was glad she had. Indeed, she should have done it years ago.

"Not even in my wildest dreams did I ever imagine the possibility of deserving such a privilege, Octavia. I want to be to the person you need. I want it more than anything else, because I want to be near you, because I yearn to avenge Caesar and perhaps because – well, perhaps I can hope for your forgiveness," said Gaius solemnly, but also with visible emotion.

"You have nothing to be forgiven for," she replied. "You are the father of my first child, and I am glad that you are."

Gaius's face lit up in a radiant smile. She invited him to follow her towards the stage, stood at the foot of the stairs and called Octavian, who came down.

"What are you doing here?" he asked with barely concealed annoyance.

"I came to bring the deeds of purchase of my property. Sell them and use the proceeds to pay the soldiers."

Octavian looked at her in surprise. "But I thought your husband…"

"My husband has his properties," snapped Octavia, "and I have mine, and can dispose of them as I see fit."

His brother nodded. "You'll get every last sestertius back, I promise. Thank you, sister," he said, bursting into an affectionate smile, "I knew I could count on you."

"Don't thank me yet. There is a condition."

Octavian grew suspicious. "A condition?"

"Yes. I want to join the team. "

"The group? What team?"

"Oh come on, everybody in the family knows – the team you are putting together to face the trials that await you."

"It is no place for women. It is too dangerous."

"The fate of our family depends upon you. We run the same risks: if you fall, we all fall."

'But I wouldn't even know what to do with you."

"I can talk with the matrons and the wives of senators and get information. And everyone thinks that Etain – my freedwoman, whom you know well – is still a slave: I can use her as a spy. And that's not all," she added, bringing forward Gaius Chaerea. "This man is Gaius Chaerea, a centurion who fought for Caesar at Munda and would be happy to avenge him. He defended me during the Ides of March, when the soldiers tried to hand us over to Caesar's killers, and he saved me again on the day of the funeral, when I almost end up trampled by the crowd. So you see," she concluded with satisfaction, "by taking me you gain three people."

Octavian's eyes flicked back and forth between her and the centurion. He stood silently for a long time, then burst out into a frank laugh. "By the gods, sister!" he said hugging her, "I would never have thought you were so sharp!"

Standing beside the improvised altar he had had set up in one of the houses owned by his cousin Quintus Pedius, Octavian looked at them one by one. These, then, would be his traveling companions. Those who would help him overthrow the system. He had told them that he wanted to form a group, and that was what those outside the group believed too: Octavian and his colleagues, a group of mostly young people who were chasing a dream, one which was perhaps an illusion and a utopia: that of making their way in the treacherous maze of Roman politics to avenge Caesar.

And also – but this the others did not know – to continue his work of restoring the State.

Caesar's young heir had obtained the favour of the people by claiming to want to avenge his adoptive father and earn his own opportunities in politics. The Senate regarded him with diffidence, but could not put up much resistance to his ambitions. For him though, revenge presupposed another phase, another level: it meant completing what his predecessor had started and what he had not had time to perfect – building the empire that a city like Rome deserved and which he had always dreamed of. To do this, however, meant restoring the state – that state shaken by half a century of strife and civil wars. He would therefore need to remove the cause of all this discord: the governmental paralysis that a sick republic had caused. Two consuls elected annually who hindered and obstructed one another instead of working together, a senate that spent all its time arguing without producing useful laws, tribunes of the plebeians who were manipulated by those in power to pile vetoes upon vetoes and a population who listened to he who paid best. Moreover, legions who increasingly influenced politics, elections driven by corruption, inept judges who occupied positions of responsibility simply because they belonged to important families, provincial governors who looked after their own interests, antagonising the population under their jurisdiction, fragmentary borders which were always exposed to enemy invasions, an incoherent system of administration of the territories which, over the course of the centuries, had almost accidentally become part of the domain of the city, rebellions that the soldiers were never able to completely put down... There was much to do just to prevent Rome from collapsing in on itself, he knew. And instead, all those who should have been working to stem its decline continued vainly to waste time and energy in trying to get ahead of the others or to cultivate their own petty interests.

Killing Caesar's assassins was only one of many tasks that lay ahead – the most immediate and the most understandable in the eyes of those who mourned for the dictator. But many other tasks awaited too, and they were of a type that must be kept secret.

They would have to get their hands dirty, very dirty, if they wanted to survive and lead Rome to the top of the world and give her a golden age. Caesar would have wanted it that way, and he too had had to get his hands dirty in order to have his way. There was no alternative: Octavian knew that, and so did the others. They would all have to declare themselves willing to go beyond laws, rules and morality if they wanted to save Rome and provide it with the progress that might prevent it destroying itself. But to do so it would be necessary to leave behind normality, and anyone who joined the small group of his followers would have to know that it was necessary to abandon convention. Whenever there were scruples, remorse or attacks of conscience, it was necessary to remember that it was all for a good cause, and that afterwards the world would be a better place thanks to them, the only ones who wanted to make things right instead of breaking them or keeping them broken.

It was a cult that he was creating, in which the absolute *credo* was the veneration of the memory of Caesar and the good of Rome. That was what its members must remember each time they had to do something which, perhaps, they would otherwise be ashamed of doing.

From then on, Mars would have to prevail over all other gods. Mars, the god of war.

Mars Ultor – the avenger. Their god.

Octavian had told them to keep the ceremony secret: the members themselves were the only ones to know that they were part of a cult. Other friends he had not considered sufficiently trustworthy would provide external support: Gaius Matius, Cornelius Balbus, his parents, some senators who were close to the *gens Julia* and the *gens Octavia* families, and many others upon whom he hoped he could count, must never learn that they were working for a faction whose goals were higher than those of which they knew.

Antony had used the *lex curiata* laws to prevent him from being officially adopted, and in the eyes of many he remained nothing more than the heir of the dictator, but thanks to the network of alliances that he was creating with the money he had made from the auctions and loans from Maecenas, he would soon be able to force the situation and acquire that to which he was entitled: he would be called Gaius Julius Caesar. And no one would be any longer able to deny his right to take revenge on those who had assassinated his father.

At a gesture from him, the two slaves present at the ceremony hoisted onto the altar the ram that they had stunned. The beast's horns had been gilded and it was wrapped in colourful ribbons. Octavian lifted the hem of his toga over his head, covering it as though he were a priest. He had no authority to call himself one, and some might have considered it sacrilege, but he was creating a new cult, of which he was the creator and therefore also the minister, the ministrant and... whatever else he decided to be.

He picked up the knife he had set on the altar and raised it in both hands with a theatrical flourish that all those gathered could see. He looked at them again one by one, making sure that each was concentrated fully on the act, then said loudly, "Mars Ultor, I consecrate to you this ram that you may favour my revenge and my intention to complete the work of my father, and that you may give to all those who have decided to join me the courage and strength to fulfil the duties to which they pledge themselves. I swear to all that I hold dear that I will continue to offer you sacrifices until my work is done, and that when it is, I will dedicate to you an entire temple."

He took a deep breath and with a firm hand sunk the blade into the body of the ram. Blood splashed onto his face and sprayed over his toga, then gradually spread out across the surface of the altar. Octavian ran his tongue around his lips and his mouth, welcoming the acrid flavour: his red mask, like that of a victor, was auspicious and proved the success of the sacrifice. With the knife, he opened up the wound and cut open the animal's skin and flesh to expose its innards, then put down his knife and stuck both hands into the animal's bowels, feeling the heat within almost burning him.

The weak light of the oil lamps set on tripods next to the altar, in a room dimly lit by the faint glow of the lamps he had had set on the ground, helped to create a solemn atmosphere, making him appear, to the eyes of the initiates, a ghostly, disturbing figure. That was what he wanted – to instil in them a sense of awe and of responsibility, and to make them feel that they had embarked on a journey of no return: either they succeeded in their undertaking or they went under. The partnership between them was eternal, their friendship deathless. It was time for them to swear allegiance. For some of them – the ones who had already given ample proof of their affection – it was hardly necessary, but he wanted their bond to be consecrated before the gods.

He tore the guts from the animal and held them up, then passed them to the two slaves who placed them on the nearby brazier, and said, "Repeat after me: 'I swear to Mars Ultor, upon the lives of those I love most and my children today as well as those I have in the future, that I will do everything in my power to fulfil the objectives of the sect of Mars Ultor.'"

"I swear to Mars Ultor, upon the lives of those I love most and my children today as well as those I have in the future, that I will do everything in my power to fulfil the objectives of the sect of Mars Ultor," repeated all present.

"I swear to Mars Ultor that I will not rest until I have ensured that all the murderers of Julius Caesar have been punished: Gaius Cassius Longinus, Marcus Junius Brutus, Decimus Brutus Albinus, Gaius Trebonius, Servilius Casca Longus, Publius Servilius Casca Longus, Lucius Tullius Cimber, Publius Sextilius Naso, Quintus Ligarius, Minucius Basilus, Rubrius Ruga, Lucius Pontius Aquila, Marcus Spurius, Caecilius Bucolianus the elder and Bucolianus Caecilius the younger, Pacuvius Antistius Labeo, Gaius Cassius Parmensis, Petronius, Publius Decimus Turullius and Servius Sulpicius Galba."

Octavian listed the names one by one, waiting for the others to repeat each before moving on to the next.

"I swear to Mars Ultor that I will do everything in my power and I will adopt all necessary weapons and resources, licit or illicit, to bring peace to Rome and transform it into a lasting, prosperous empire, just as Caesar had intended."

123

"I swear to Mars Ultor that I will do everything in my power and I will adopt all necessary weapons and resources, licit or illicit, to bring peace to Rome and transform it into a lasting, prosperous empire, just as Caesar had intended," they chorused.

"And finally, I swear before Mars Ultor that I will never betray my friends nor betray this brotherhood, to which I consider it a privilege to belong. May Mars Ultor turn his arrows upon me if I do not keep my oath."

"And finally, I swear before Mars Ultor that I will never betray my friends nor betray this brotherhood, to which I consider it a privilege to belong. May Mars Ultor turn his arrows upon me if I do not keep my oath," they echoed.

"Now, we are all sons of Caesar!" he exclaimed, feeling his excitement growing. "Let us share the same dish to formalise our pact and consecrate ourselves to Mars Ultor." He motioned to the others to approach the altar, then to the slaves to pass him the half-cooked bowels of the ram. In his hands they were still hot, and he felt them burning his fingers and palms. He wanted to squeeze them, though, and to tear off pieces to offer to the followers. In pain, he closed his eyes, did what he had set out to do. He put the still smouldering pieces into a small bowl, then went round the altar and placed the bowl before it: the others were already lined up. The first was Agrippa, his oldest friend, the only man in the world he trusted with absolute, blind confidence. Now he would have to get used to thinking of the others in the same way.

Agrippa smiled, took a piece of hot meat and lifted it to his mouth, then stepped back. Behind him appeared Salvidienus Rufus: a friendship which was much more recent but almost as strong. The soldier ate the flesh and then moved aside, making way for Octavia. At the sight of her, Octavian felt his heart jump with emotion: she must love him very much to have decided to take part in such a dangerous game. Next was Maecenas: the Tuscan had been a revelation – in only a few weeks he had proven to be more than the equal of the remarkable introduction he had made for himself, solving many problems and providing Octavian with endless ideas… as well as a great deal of money.

Then came Quintus Pedius and Lucius Pinarius: his opinion of them had changed since they had decided, without any pressure from him, to give him their share of the inheritance. Next were Octavia's two associates: Etain, a freedwoman who could come in very useful and who Agrippa seemed to care deeply for, and Gaius Chaerea, a centurion who was genuinely fond of Octavia and who could play a valuable role in the standing army in the capital.

The last in line were the two Germans: Ortwin and his woman, Veleda. As the days went by, Octavian had remembered more of the tales of the Suebian's exploits which Caesar had related to him: if he proved to be worth even half of what he had been to his old commander, his salary would be a profitable investment.

When everyone had eaten their piece of the meat, he had each of them given a goblet containing the still-warm blood of the beast, and only when they had drunk did he consider the ceremony at an end. But he did not dismiss them right away: he stood there admiring his followers, and finally gave a broad smile of satisfaction.

They made an impressive team. Together, they would be invincible.

VIII

Agrippa got up from the bed and went to get the strigil. He took it from the chest and began to pass it over his chest, collecting the copious beads of sweat which still ran down between his sculpted muscles.

"When you do that, it makes me feel as though all this is just athletics…" said Etain, approaching him with an amused look of mock offence. Then she removed the strigil from his hand and took over from him, passing it with deliberate slowness along his back and then lower down, focusing on the lad's toned buttocks.

Agrippa smiled. "No… it's that I have to go to Mark Antony's house, and I need to look decent. Octavian wants to avoid having direct contact with that family, and he doesn't want to make use of slaves or freedmen as intermediaries for fear of offending the consul. So the task of maintaining relations inevitably falls upon me or on Rufus…"

Etain sighed. "I have something to do too, you know. For the last couple of days, Octavia has been keeping very close company with the wife of Lepidus, in the hope of extracting some valuable information from her to pass on to her brother. And so now she wants me to go by the matron with gifts: of course, I pretend to be a slave and, when I'm there I chat a bit with the servants. Who knows, perhaps they'll let slip something useful."

"You never know. Octavian always says that information is the most powerful weapon in politics," admitted Agrippa. "And we of the group have to do what we can. Maecenas is doing his part, sending his henchmen off among the people and the soldiers and reminding everyone, in the case that they had forgotten, that Caesar should be avenged and that Octavian is the only one actually willing to do it."

"It doesn't sound like much if you compare it to what Antony and the others have…" she said, throwing the strigil to the ground and rubbing her naked body against his.

Agrippa began to feel excited again. He tried, without much success, to pull away and then smiled and said with a sigh, "We had to start somewhere. And don't imagine that I like this approach either. I am a man of action, I want to be a soldier, fighting for Rome, or even just for the rights of Octavian, who is more than a brother to me. Perhaps he is comfortable acting like this, but I think there will come a time when we will have to get our hands dirty – and when that time comes I will be much more useful than I am now."

"As long as you are not fighting on the battlefield for the rights of Octavian, it means that we are avoiding civil war, and that can only be good," Etain said, finally detaching herself from him. "Would you rather that the roads of Italy were once again drenched in blood?"

"No, no, of course not," he hastened to agree. He craved battle and could not wait to fight his first, but he was not bloodthirsty and certainly did not want to give that impression to the woman he loved. "And yet... Octavian relies heavily on his intelligence. I believe that, no matter how able he is, without Caesar everything will return to how it was before him, or worse. Until someone has the strength to impose his will on the others and silence them all, as the dictator did, the powerful will seek to outdo each other by any means, even war, regardless of the consequences to the people. The republican structure as it is now does not guarantee stability – in fact, it tickles the appetites of the ambitious."

Etain took a perfumed ointment and smeared it on him, taking the opportunity to give him occasional kisses. He let her do it, lulled by the softness of her touch, then put on his tunic and combed his hair. Meanwhile he continued with his observations.

"Octavian deludes himself that he can control Antony thanks to his influence over the people. But Antony is too strong, especially now that he is about to get his hands on the army of Macedonia and the other consul Dolabella on that of Syria."

"Why are those two provinces so important?"

"Because the armies gathered by Caesar to invade the Parthian empire were stationed there. The cream of the Roman troops. He who controls them could control Rome, in the long term. And now, the one who controls them is Antony"

Etain wrapped his toga around him, leaned back and gazed at Agrippa with her beautiful blue-green eyes. Awed as she was by his majestic figure, she rarely looked at him, but when she did, he melted, and his chest felt as though it would burst from the emotion. He hugged her and squeezed her to him, kissing her again.

They had started seeing each other quite regularly at his house over the last month, and Agrippa felt that he could no longer do without her. Etain had removed any desire in him for other women, and at that moment he knew that he would have been faithful to her forever, had circumstances been different.

But circumstances *were* different: and he gave his leave, carefully avoiding revealing the real reason why Octavian had asked him to go to the Antony's home.

*

The games for the Victory of Caesar were subdued ones; but, Octavian said to himself, it was already much that they were being held at all, given Mark Antony's diffidence towards the figure of his predecessor. It would have been the first year since the victory in Thapsus of Caesar over his enemies in Africa that the games had not been celebrated, and it was only thanks to the diligence of Octavian that the Romans could delight in big game hunts and gladiatorial combat completely free of charge.

He sat in the seat of the *dissignator*, the funder of the games: officially, that was him, even though it had been Maecenas's money which had made them possible. He savoured the cheers of the audience, who were present in large numbers, and replied with sweeping gestures of gratitude. His popularity was growing by the day, and he was sure that within a few moments it would rocket. He called Ortwin – who, with his men, was stationed at the edge of the stage – and motioned for him to come over. The German and the others lifted the object covered by a cloth that had been deposited on the ground, made their way through the crowd and reached the stage where the authorities sat.

Octavian ordered a slave to remove one of the chairs next to his and waved to the Suebi to place the object next to him. Once in place, the young man theatrically removed the veil that covered it, revealing a magnificent curule chair inlaid with gold, upon which was a golden crown set with diamonds.

The effect was instantaneous. Only the nearest spectators noticed at first, but soon word spread from row to row, until the voices of the public began to increase in volume. Many began pushing to get closer to the stage and see the two precious objects that, for days, had been a source of contention – yet another – between Antony and Octavian: the seat and the gold crown of Caesar, which, the day after his death, the Senate had decreed should be taken to theatres and circuses on the occasion of the most important events.

The clamour of the people grew louder. All shouted the name of the late dictator and his young heir, and Octavian was pleased to see that the audience approved of his act of defiance against the consul. He had already tried to display the two precious objects at the previous games in the *Edile Critonio* only two weeks before, and the magistrate, with Antony's support, had prevented him. No one had dared come forward to organize the next games for the Victory of Caesar, and so he had offered to do it himself, despite not holding any magistrature, and Maecenas had suggested shouting from the rooftops that, as organiser of the games, he would display the chair and crown in spite of the consul's warning. People, said the Etruscan, would flock in large numbers, not simply to watch the games, but to see if he actually dared challenge the consul and see what the reaction was. In any case, Octavian was destined to emerge victorious, according to his friend.

And it had worked, of course. The Circus was packed and the people were willing to support him. The young man was waiting for the second effect that they were expecting: he watched the movements of the legionaries Antony had posted near the stage and saw that they had already gone into action; the consul had fallen right into the trap. The soldiers walked quickly up the steps, pushing aside those standing there, and stormed the stage. The centurion who commanded them stepped between him and the throne and declared loudly: "Young Octavian, the consul warned you not to display the chair and the crown of Julius Caesar. Not complying with his command is likely to create unrest. I therefore order you, upon pain of the confiscation of the material and a fine of five thousand sestertii for disturbing public order, to remove these items."

Octavian smiled and nodded. He motioned to Ortwin to cover them and take them away, and watched the operation in silence. The German went off followed by the legionaries and the centurion, who gave the young man a confused look before he departed the stage. After the soldiers had left, Octavian took two steps forward and leant over the railing. "Romans!" he cried, turning to the audience. "Do you see what has happened? For the second time, I have tried to display the chair and the crown with which my father was honoured, and for the second time the consul has prevented me!"

The audience roared. Good, he said to himself: he was prepared to address them. He calmed their voices with one arm and spoke again: "You saw the injury I suffered, and the insult my father's memory received! And you know that this not the first time: since I returned to Rome, the consul has done nothing but hinder me. He has gone as far as preventing an explicit decree of the Senate, establishing the displaying of the chair and the crown of Caesar, from being carried out. He does so for reasons of public order, he says. But we all know that he is working to avoid upsetting his friends the murderers. Caesar's assassins! And in his desire to do harm to me, the legitimate heir of the dictator, he dishonours Caesar himself – the very man to whom he owes everything. He is an ingrate, almost as much of one as those who betrayed and killed the dictator. And his intentions are clear: even the Senate has learned to be wary of him, and the illustrious Cicero does not hide his hostility towards him. Now that he controls all six of the legions of Macedonia we must expect him to attempt to follow in the footsteps of his predecessor. Is that what you want? Do you feel he has the same qualities? And above all, do you want him to be a new Caesar with the support of those who killed Caesar?"

The spectators began to shout and rant against Antony, and against Dolabella too, but at the same time, they shouted praise of Caesar... and of him. Just as Maecenas had predicted: Antony, already unpopular with the Senate for his autocratic tendencies, was now completely alienating the people. While the more wrongs he, Octavian, suffered, the more his popularity grew. The people were with him; Now he had to win the support of the Senate and of the soldiers. And Maecenas had a strategy for that too…

He kept telling himself that he was doing it for Octavian. Since he had told his friend that Fulvia, Antony's wife, had tried to seduce him, his friend had encouraged him to begin a relationship with the matron to try and glean information about the consul's plans.

Nor was that all. He also had another pretext in his defence: Fulvia had contacted him, and she was not a woman it was wise to contradict. She had began by sending him a message to remind him of their appointment. He had not answered, and so she had sent another, in which she had threatened to tell Antony that he had attempted to rape her. That was when Agrippa had spoken to Octavian, and his friend had urged him to take advantage of the situation, in every way possible.

"You're hardly just doing it for the cause – she is a beautiful woman. Had she attempted to approach me, I wouldn't have thought twice…" said Octavian, and he had to agree. After all, his friend knew he was an incurable womaniser, and a prey like Fulvia, one of the most coveted in Rome, was more than attractive to his eyes. The trouble for Agrippa was that it was he who felt like the prey. And furthermore, Octavian didn't know about Etain – or rather, he knew, but did not know how deeply his friend was in love.

Nevertheless, he could have got out of it had he really wanted to. Octavian would never have forced him, and if Fulvia had lied about him to Antony, well, relations with the consul could hardly have been worse than they already were. After all, the consul was himself a well-known womaniser, and his wife did not enjoy the reputation of being faithful. No, the truth was that Fulvia intrigued him. He was unable to identify all the reasons which had led him to agree: he only knew for sure that attraction had nothing to do with it. No, attraction, and especially love, were reserved only for Etain. With Fulvia it was curiosity, male pride, and the desire for challenge and adventure. She was an aggressive, fierce woman, with whom intimacy would inevitably be a battle; and with his desire to fight, this meant he had found the perfect outlet for his exuberant personality.

In any case, he had taken it for granted that a single meeting would have been enough for the woman to satisfy her desire and forget about him soon after. The thought calmed him and soothed his sense of guilt towards Etain: just once, to scratch this itch of curiosity, and then he wouldn't think about it any more either.

Fulvia had not given him an appointment in the Gardens of Pompey, of course, but in another, less sumptuous house that, in all probability, was part of the two spouses' enormous fortune. Fulvia had twice been widowed and had inherited considerable wealth from her previous husbands.

Agrippa reached the Celio and knocked on the door of the *domus* that had been named in the last message, in which she wrote that she would await him in the afternoon of the first day of the week. Otherwise, she threatened, there would be reprisals.

The slave who opened the door looked him up and down and he didn't need to say anything: clearly Fulvia had described him to the servants. Agrippa followed her in silence, beginning to feel a lump in his throat, and he could not tell if it was the discomfort caused by guilt or excitement about the unusual encounter that awaited him. The slave led him through the lobby and then into a hallway, stopping in front of a room which she urged him to enter.

Like last time, Fulvia had her tunic on, but hiked up to her waist.

Again, those magnificent buttocks were on show.

"Welcome, Agrippa. I thought I'd let you pick up where you left off. Don't you think that's a good idea?" she said without turning around, her face nestled in a pillow, as soon as she heard his footsteps in the room.

Agrippa swallowed. "You don't like wasting time, eh?" He could think of nothing better to say.

"Why should I? You boys don't like wasting time, and neither do I. We both know why we're here, so why beat around the bush? Take me, Agrippa – and make sure you surprise me."

Agrippa was annoyed by the term 'boy', but he realized that nothing, at that moment, was under his control. He was at the mercy of a dangerous woman who gave the impression of always getting what she wanted.

In fact, he felt ready to immediately execute her order. He

took off his toga and his loincloth, but not his tunic, went over to the bed and lay down on top of her, while she continued to sink her head into the pillow, giving the impression of not wanting to see. He felt used, but had no illusions about being able to change the situation. He slid his member into the gap between Fulvia's buttocks then used his hand to direct it where he thought it might satisfy the woman's desire for originality. He had to push and shove more than a little, but Fulvia did not seem to feel any pain, or if she did she took pleasure from it, because she began to sigh with that hoarse voice of hers that Agrippa had come to know in their brief previous encounter.

He had expected to feel pleasure himself – Fulvia was a marvellous-looking woman who deeply excited him. But, to his surprise, he found himself performing the act almost mechanically, as though he had lent a part of his body to her, keeping the rest aside for himself. He was appalled, and realised immediately that this was the first time he had made love to another woman since he had begun his relationship with Etain. He had quickly gotten used to the intimate tastes, the smells, the skin and behaviour of the freedwoman, and thought they were the nicest he had ever known. But now he was disoriented by sensations he did not recognise, and which lacked the same intensity: partly it had been curiosity which had made him agree to go to Fulvia, and now he had discovered what happened to him with a woman that was not Etain. And he hoped it would all be over soon.

If ever he had needed confirmation of his love for her, he now had it. If nothing else, that adultery had served to make him fully understand his feelings. Ironically, he almost felt that, instead of weakening their love, it had actually strengthened it.

Fulvia's moans increased in intensity, and he moved faster to keep pace. She touched herself, and then let out a cry of liberation which was feral, almost a roar, before collapsing completely inert beneath him. Agrippa was surprised once again that he felt no need to continue and reach his own pleasure, and nor did she urge him to do so. He stopped moving, pulled himself out of her and lay down beside her. Only then did she lift her head from the pillow and look at him with a mischievous smile.

"You... worked hard," she said, staring at him with narrow, proud fierce eyes. She was not afraid of anyone, this woman, thought Agrippa.

"So did you," he lied. And hoped that she had not noticed his lack of involvement.

"I liked you right away, Agrippa. As soon as I saw you. I like your proud bearing," she went on, stroking his arms.

"Attracting the attention of one of the most beautiful women in Rome is a privilege, Fulvia," he answered flatly.

She noticed. "Oh, do restrain your enthusiasm, boy! I am overwhelmed by your passion!"

"I don't like it when you call me 'boy'" he protested with a forced smile, lazily returning her caresses.

"I'm almost twice your age… What should I call you? You and your little friend are playing at being grown-ups, but you are still boys…" she quipped.

Agrippa assumed an even more serious expression. "Boys who are making your husband's life difficult, I think," he couldn't help saying.

She sat up, pushing out her chest, highlighting the ample bosom beneath her tunic. "Ha! Antony will sort everything out, you'll see. It's no problem for him to buy the Senate and exert an influence on the legions," she declared.

That single statement from the woman had made the meeting fruitful. Agrippa wanted to ask more, but feared she might become suspicious and paused thoughtfully. What was Antony preparing?

"But the people do not love him as before" he ventured.

"The people are always changing their minds," said Fulvia contemptuously. "He has his ways of winning over the citizens. Soon he will have them all," she added cryptically.

Agrippa was silent for a moment, staring at the opposite wall. "What is it, my dear? Are you afraid for yourself or your little friend?" urged Fulvia, rummaging under his tunic. "Fear not: I will look after you!"

"Me, afraid? Are you joking?" exclaimed Agrippa indignantly, letting her. Meanwhile he reflected on the possible developments of the situation.

"Hmm… I have just remembered that you have not yet reached your pleasure," purred Fulvia, approaching his member and stroking it gently. "But we will take care of that now…" she added, lowering her lips to it.

"I keep thinking that I do not like this business," said Maecenas as he watched Octavian don the toga. The house of the young heir of Caesar was besieged by a multitude of people, ready to escort the young man to the Capitol to attend the event for which many had been waiting for months. The Etruscan had to raise his voice to be heard.

"And I say that everything is in our favour and that Antony is a fool," said Rufus, who was beside himself with excitement. "Octavian needs him more than he needs Octavian, and an agreement is more in our favour."

"Yes, but it was he who wanted the agreement, remember," objected Maecenas. "A good reason to be wary, especially after what Fulvia told Agrippa."

"The truth," said Octavian, "is that we need each other, and he knows it. The legions respect him but love me, the Senate distrusts both of us, the people love me and not him. Only together can we conquer all three components of the state, and he knows that as well as I do. As Fulvia told Agrippa, he is keeping the Senate happy, partly by stringing them along with his bill to abolish the dictatorship and partly by threatening them with the transfer of the Macedonian legions to Brindisi. And that is fine with me, because if the Senate is afraid of him it will end up taking me seriously when it realises that I am his only true opponent. Lepidus let himself be bought off by being appointed *pontifex maximus*, Caesar's assassins are on the loose thanks to him and of course have no intention of attacking him... Who has the strength and the means to counterbalance his dominance? I, of course! Or at least, that is what Cicero thinks, and as long as he is hostile to Antony, the consul will never dominate the senators, and will be forced to turn to me to get from the people that which he cannot get from the Senate. And then, he plans to use soldiers to impose his will on Rome, but does not have an real understanding of the affection that the soldiers still feel for Caesar, and therefore for me as well."

"Exactly!" interjected Agrippa. "And you must use it at the appropriate time: Antony is not the only one who can use the soldiers as a way of applying pressure. Lepidus will soon reach his province in Spain – with him out of the way that leaves the field open. And with the meagre provinces that have been assigned to Brutus and Cassius, they can do little to threaten Rome. Things are looking good for us, are they not?"

"I do not trust Antony, I have already told you," insisted Maecenas. "We must be careful what we agree to give him: he cannot have changed policy overnight without good reason. And let us try to get the most possible benefit from this agreement."

"But we cannot push our luck either, my friend," mused Octavian, who was now ready to leave. "Remember that my first goal is to have Caesar's murderers declared enemies of the state, and to then pursue them like the criminals they are. And I cannot do that without Antony: I must necessarily subordinate everything else to that result."

"He knows that. And that is why he will ask you a high price. You must be ready to haggle," said Maecenas. Meanwhile, they left the house, and as they crossed the threshold they were greeted by a cheering crowd, who chanted in praise of the imminent reconciliation.

"Haggle?" asked Octavian as he called for Ortwin, Veleda and their men to come and protect them. "What do you mean?"

"You must not settle for just the law against Caesar's murderers. You must ask for an even higher price, if he really needs your help."

"And do you have any idea what?"

"I think I do," whispered Maecenas, pushing his way through the crowd.

IX

Octavia realized that, at this point, it had become a habit for her. She had started looking for Gaius Chaerea at every public occasion, as though expecting to see him constantly watching over her. She knew it was impossible, that she shouldn't even be thinking it – but she couldn't help it. She had begun to see him as an indispensable presence in her life, and was more upset than she would have liked by the idea that, sooner or later, Gaius would be leaving with his legion. She longed to talk to him before he went away – and not just talk, but tell him the truth... The memory of the moments when she found herself in his arms, so many years before, had now faded so much that she was no longer sure that it had actually happened the way she remembered it, and if Etain had not consistently reported to her on the progress of Marcus, the son generated by that meeting, she would have questioned whether it had ever taken place.

Her mother Atia invited her to stand beside her in the front row, in the most enviable position for witnessing the reconciliation between Antony and Octavian. For the event, to which both intended to give maximum visibility, a special area had been set up in the centre of the Capitol's summit, at the foot of the statue of Jupiter. Legionaries surrounded the area destined for the meeting, preventing any busybodies from going beyond the limits set by the urban praetor Gaius Antonius, the brother of the consul. In the huge crowd were many soldiers, veterans of Caesar, who had called for a reconciliation between the only two men who could avenge the dictator, as well as those on active duty who were awaiting a posting.

Octavia told herself she should just focus on the event. She had worked hard at trying to talk Lepidus's wife into convincing her husband to persuade Antony to make peace. And yet, at that moment she felt overcome by nebulous memories of the day when, thanks to Gaius, or from her own fault, she had become a woman. A garden full of flowers, a clear sky, a boundary wall covered in ivy and jasmine, an accidental fall and Gaius's help... and tender caresses, a hint of a kiss, and then a longer, interminable one. And then his delicate hands everywhere, and a spreading feeling of pleasure which began to concentrate between her thighs, and brushing casually against his turgid member; she hadn't even realised what it was until she had seen it emerge from his tunic. And then she had felt it between her legs, not even understanding how she had taken it into herself, and after a moment of pain she had felt pleasure, and then pain again, and then pleasure, and pain, until she was flooded with an incredible wave of heat, which from within her washed over her whole body, leaving it in ecstatic bliss.

Her parents had only become aware of the situation a few months later, and had sought to avoid a scandal by sending her off to the country on holiday on the pretext of a long illness. But they had forced her to divest herself immediately of the child, once it was born, and to never see him again, which she had agreed to do despite the enormous suffering it caused her. Fortunately, Gaius had not backed down and had taken upon himself the burden of raising the child with a wet-nurse, paid for with the funds that Octavia sent regularly via Etain.

"There they are! They're coming!" said Lucius Pinarius, who was sitting next to her stepfather Marcius Philippus, near Quintus Pedius. He was referring to Octavian and his friends, the most important members of the sect of Mars Ultor, as they had got into the habit of calling their small fraternity. A faction which, in reality, had extended its membership over the last few weeks to include a long line of unknowing members, bought or won over by Octavian and his friends, who, in one way or another, were working to facilitate his rise: they included several senators who feared Antony and mourned the dictator, and who willingly supported the opinions of his rightful heir, the centurions would have given a year's pay to see him at work, with their help many citizens and artisans had become friends of Octavian and were ready to vote for him in a hoped for future election, and members of the equestrian class who did business with Maecenas and who the wily Etruscan had convinced to finance the campaign...

She was sure that Octavian would arrive first on the Capitol.

Antony hadn't even needed to demand it: it was the young man who had to wait for the adult – the private citizen who was obliged to wait for the consul, the highest authority of the Republic. The boy had never questioned that. What Antony had demanded was a public apology, and that was harder to swallow. But swallow it Octavian had, so convinced was he that he had much to gain from such an agreement.

The young man let his closest friends and associates take their places next to the eminent spectators, then he settled down to wait alone under the statue of Jupiter. Like everyone else, Octavia began to look around, but unlike the others, whose eyes were seeking the massive figure of Antony, she continued to scan the crowd hoping that among the guards there was also Chaerea. In vain. She told herself that, had he been there, he would have revealed his presence, but then dismissed the thought, thinking that he had sufficient reason to keep some emotional distance. After all, she had never once deigned to visit the child, and it mattered little that her parents had prohibited her to do so: she could have done it secretly – it would have been even easier after she was married.

The reason she hadn't done it was fear – fear of destabilising her life which, at that point, had taken a well-defined turn, wholly in line with what was expected by her family and that her dignity demanded. Now, however, the situation was different: the death of Caesar and the legacy of Octavian, the cult of Mars Ultor, the injustices to which Antony subjected her family and the possible civil war were all factors which had contributed to awakening her from her lethargic state and making her aware that she could not ignore the events that were tumbling upon her. Now, it was not only permissible, but even a duty to go and see her son.

She heard grumbling from the rows behind them, and realised that it had been a long time since Octavian had taken his seat in the appointed place. Antony was making them wait, no doubt intentionally.

Few cheers and many grunts greeted the eventual appearance of the consul, escorted by his two brothers, Gaius and Lucius. Shortly behind him rode the magister equitum Lepidus and the other consul Dolabella, and then the future consuls, Aulus Hirtius and Vibius Pansa, who Antony had probably brought with him to intimidate Octavian: he wanted to show him that the prominent people in Rome were his friends and show him what he would have arraigned against him should he continue to oppose him.

The eminent characters who accompanied the consul took their places, one after the other, in the first rows of the audience – mostly as witnesses – and, while Antony went with an ostentatious lack of haste towards the statue of Jupiter, Octavia glanced over at her brother, and noted that his fists were clenched angrily. Antony was taking advantage of the occasion to humiliate him in every way possible.

All she could do was hope that Octavian would stay calm.

*

"Stay calm. I must stay calm," Octavian said to himself.

Antony was deliberately provoking him to react aggressively in front of everyone; perhaps he intended to show to the Romans that he was the victim and not the aggressor. Or maybe he wanted to give himself the satisfaction of punishing him for his irreverent attitude before making an agreement with him.

He tried to look him straight in the eye to show him that he was not afraid of him and that he understood his game. Antony looked back at him cursorily and, as he approached, took advantage of his greater size and height to look down at him with a show of superiority. He clearly intended to intimidate him, and perhaps would have been successful with another. But not with him, Octavian said to himself–- not with Caesar's designated heir. Caesar had not been afraid of Pompey the Great, of Vercingetorix, of Pharnaces of Pontus nor of Cato of Utica, so why then should he be afraid of a hedonistic drunkard like Antony? If he intended to live up to his father, it was the least that Octavian needed to endure.

Antony shifted his gaze elsewhere in a show of indifference, but it was obvious that he expected the younger man to be the first to speak. In front of everyone, he had to look like the beggar. Octavian had expected this, and had no difficulty in doing so: the people would appreciate even more his deferential attitude towards a man many felt was almost his persecutor. Everyone would think that it showed respect for Antony's role, rather than for Antony himself – for the magistrate rather than the man – and would give the impression of an individual who respected the institutions. Just what he needed to differentiate himself from Antony, who – as Cicero always said in the Senate – was showing very little regard for the Republic.

"Hail, consul," he began, taking a contrite attitude. "Thank you for taking into consideration my request for an interview. It is very generous of you to give me some of your precious time." This was complete invention: it had been Antony who had sent out signals of reconciliation. But the consul might like the people to think the opposite.

"Greetings, young Octavian," said Antony, emphasising the word 'young'. "It appears that you have finally decided to calm yourself. I hope that with this meeting you intend to put an end to your provocation?" The agreement provided that they spoke publicly for the first part of the interview, so that all present could clearly perceive the difference in authority between the two. Octavian had agreed, but the consul was certainly not facilitating the task.

He struggled to hold fast to his determination not to fall into the trap. He knew that his followers were watching and judging him: if he wanted to be their leader, if he demanded their esteem, friendship and loyalty, he had to prove that he deserved them.

"Illustrious consul," he said, "I ask you to forgive the vehemence which I have shown since learning I was Caesar's heir. My youth and the vast responsibility that fell on my fragile shoulders made me forget the respect due to a magistrate of the Republic, an older man and a relative whose deeds have ennobled my family."

Antony nodded gravely. If he was satisfied, he didn't show it much. "A young man cannot expect to break into the political arena and lay down the law to men who have not only been forged by experience, but honoured by the people themselves with institutional roles, and whose actions can be challenged only by other representatives of the institutions and by the people themselves. Anyone wishing to apply pressure only on the basis of his name, and as a private citizen, commits an injustice and undermines the very principles of the Republic," was all he said. He wanted to string it out. Forgiving too quickly would have been a sign of weakness, of course.

Octavian was forced to continue. He hoped he would not

have to bow and scrape too much to get his damn forgiveness. "You are quite right, consul," he continued. "I ask you only to understand that my mind is conditioned by the unquenchable desire to avenge my father, and the despair that I felt and still feel at seeing his killers not only free, but actually in the positions for which my father had deemed them worthy, has certainly caused me to behave inappropriately and mistakenly."

Antony looked smug. "With your immense experience, dear Octavian, you dared to judge the work of those who had enormous public responsibilities – above all the obligation to avoid further bloodshed, which, after decades of civil war, the Romans could tolerate no more. It is easy, as a private citizen, without having one's finger on the pulse of the situation and without being fully informed, to criticise the actions of those who bear on their shoulders the burden of decisions upon which might depend on the fate of tens of thousands of people."

By the gods, how he was spinning it out!

"As I said, consul, my vision was clouded by my lust for revenge as the son of Caesar, and for justice as a Roman citizen. I did not understand the mechanisms underlying the policy, and wished to speed up the inevitable punishment for those who had committed the most heinous of crimes. But now I understand, and from now on will trust the judgment of those who have more experience than me." He hoped that would be enough for Antony. But in the meantime, he had made it known to all that he did not intend to deviate from his goal of having the murderers condemned. He knew that in this the people were with him, and in fact murmurs of approval arose from the audience, particularly the soldiers.

This put Antony in difficulty, and Octavian could barely suppress a smile of satisfaction: the charade orchestrated by the consul looked likely to backfire on him. Antony clearly realised this and finally assumed a less dismissive tone.

"It is the will of all to do justice in one way or another. Let no one forget that Caesar's murderers wanted to kill me too, and yet even so I addressed them openly to save the citizens further suffering. I have always put harmony above all else – I did it with them and even more so do I do it with you, young Octavian. We must all be united in this delicate moment, to restore the state, which has been so severely tested by this tragic event." Immediately afterwards he stepped forward and offered his hand, which Octavian did not hesitate to grasp.

It was done, or at least the part related to the performance was. Loud cries of joy came from the crowd, and for a while the people celebrated, chanting the names now of one and now of another. But especially that of Octavian, which, the young man thought, would do little to please Antony.

Eventually, people began to drift off, but Octavian had no illusions: what he had been forced to endure so far was only the warm up.

The real meeting began now.

"So, you little bastard," whispered Antony as soon as they felt they could lower their voices. "What are you planning to do, in concrete terms, to repay me for all the trouble you've caused me?"

Octavian looked around him. The tension among the spectators had relaxed – many had left, while others chatted cheerfully with one another. But others still – the most perceptive and thoughtful, as well as the most involved political figures – kept their eyes on the pair, in an attempt to interpret their attitude and work out what was really going on behind the pantomime. And among the latter, of course, there were his friends.

"I would appreciate it if you would treat me, for once, with the respect due to the man your historic commander chose as his heir," he said through clenched teeth, while trying to keep his face relaxed for the public.

Antony too was aware of the situation and continued to maintain his composure even while spitting barbs from his mouth. "Even great men can make mistakes," he hissed, "and you have done nothing yet to prove yourself worthy of his decision, boy; nothing except being a pain in the arse to those who know more than you."

"That remains to be seen. What is important now is to agree to avenge Caesar. It seems that you need someone to remind you of the fact repeatedly, otherwise it seems to slip from your thoughts; and therefore you can be sure that I shall continue to 'be a pain in the arse'," He mustn't let himself soften: Antony couldn't wait for an opportunity to push him about.

"Precisely: what exactly will you do for me?"

"Curious that I should have to bargain for justice for your commander…"

"Boy, feelings are one thing, matters of the state are another. I do not want to be remembered as the one who caused a new civil war. Caesar's killers are currently very strong: they have diverse legions available and can starve Rome by interrupting the flow of grain."

"Yes, because *you* allowed them to *become* strong," thought Octavian, but he said nothing, answering instead, "Exactly why we must join our forces and become stronger in turn – to put pressure on them and avoid any more impulsive decisions."

"'Join forces'? That's a good one," said Antony, mockingly. "You're new at this game, what forces do you have to join?"

"If I did not have any," replied Octavian, aware of his own strength, "I would imagine you would not have sought an agreement."

Antony could do nothing but roll with the punch. "Let's say that you have managed to make the people believe that and gained their sympathies. But the people are fickle and you need me if you want to retain their affections. Do not hinder me if I need support, and you will have your revenge."

"'Our' revenge, you mean. And why would you need the support of the people? You don't seem to have cared much about it since Caesar died. To me, you seem more concerned about having the support of my father's murderers."

"On behalf of the people I need to take away the provinces from your father's killers," said the consul. "Only then can we weaken them, and strike at them later. I'm going to ask the Senate to exchange Macedonia for Gaul, in order to be stronger against them, and since the Senate will not give it to me, I will turn to the judgment of the people and have it assigned me by vote. Meanwhile, Dolabella will go to Syria and keep an eye on Trebonius in Asia."

Octavian raised an eyebrow. Antony was playing a tough game. He had been given Macedonia, then had called the six legions back to Italy, and now he was asking for Gaul, which had been assigned to Decimus Brutus, along with its respective units. It was evident that the Senate would not go along with it: Caesar had set off from Gaul to conquer Rome, and in addition Antony now possessed units also to the south. The city would be trapped in a vice.

Caesar's crossing of the Rubicon years ago would seem like a mild threat by comparison.

Now Antony's strategy had become even clearer. He didn't give a damn about the dictator's murder, Octavian said to himself. He was steering a middle course between the various elements at play – Caesar's killers, the Senate, the people, Octavian and Lepidus – coaxing or threatening one and then the other, to acquire, one step at a time, a power equal to that of Caesar. And it meant nothing that he had proposed a law which abolished the dictatorship to please the Senate: there were many other ways of achieving supreme power.

However, for the moment the only way that Octavian had to take revenge on the murderers of Caesar without compromising his political ascent was to make Antony more powerful: the various parts of the state were too tangled up in mutual vetoes to be really effective against the assassins, and the young man sensed that it was in his interest to indulge the consul, for the moment. But taking in exchange the greatest possible advantage.

"You ask a lot, Antony. That will give you immense power, do not delude yourself that I am not aware of the fact. Can I be sure that you will use it to bring the killers of my father to justice?"

"That was my intention from the beginning. Do not forget that they wanted to kill me too, at first."

"In any case, I assume great responsibility in allowing you to acquire such power," went on Octavian. "Of course, I expect you to abolish the suspension of the *lex curiata* and allow me to proceed officially with the adoption. I have the right to take the name of my father."

Antony nodded, visibly relieved. "That seems fair."

But Octavian did not intend to let the consul off so lightly: Maecenas had suggested an excellent way of neutralizing or at least limiting his power. "But that is not all," he added.

Antony's face grew annoyed. "How's that?" he protested. "You'll be a son of Caesar, you will have your revenge… What more do you want?"

Yes. It was true that he considered Octavian nothing more than a child, whose caprices were to be silenced with a symbolic sop. And this could be an advantage: as long as Antony underestimated what he and his friends were up to, and the real influence that he was able to exert over the people and the legions, Octavian could avoid being seen as a threat by the consul and obtain more. "I am the son of Caesar," he replied testily. "And as such I think I have the right to anticipate my access to public office. I have the support of the people and I intend to put myself forward as candidate for the tribune of the plebeians. I hope you will not stand in my way."

Seeing the expression of dismay on the consul's face he realised that his words had a certain effect on Antony, and immediately looked around to see the reaction of the audience, hoping they had not sensed the tension that was once again mounting between them. Fortunately for him, Antony too remembered that they were being watched and soon regained control of himself. "Tribune of the plebeians? Are you joking? At your age? And anyway, you are a patrician – you cannot," he said.

"Of course I can. As did one of the previous husbands of your wife, Clodius: I'll even have myself adopted by a commoner for the occasion."

Antony fell silent, with good reason. The tribune of the plebeians – as they were both aware – could do much to hinder the consul's consolidation of his power: it was the only judiciary of the Republic which was empowered to veto laws, and Antony himself had used it on behalf of Caesar to block decrees against the then proconsul in Gaul. None knew of its effectiveness more than he.

"I cannot allow that,"said the consul finally.

"As you wish," said Octavian, coldly. "And I cannot allow you to take Gaul too, after already receiving the army of Macedonia."

"I do not see how you can stop me: I will appeal directly to the people."

"Good for you. You clearly have no need of my influence over the citizens, then. Nor my good relations with Cicero."

More silence. A silence fraught with tension, which would have put a dent in anyone's self confidence. Octavian was pleased to discover that he was holding up: he was certain that Antony would give in, and this confidence made him feel worthy of Caesar.

"Very well," said the consul, finally. "Give me the support of the people and, once I have Gaul, you will officially be son of Caesar and tribune of the plebeians, if you can get yourself elected."

He did not like the fact that his goal was subordinate to that of Antony's, but he felt that he could not antagonise him further. "And immediately afterwards will you announce a law calling Caesar's assassins 'public enemies'?"

"I certainly will."

Octavian hesitated, unsure whether to trust him or not. But he concluded that he had no choice. And anyway, Antony would cut a poor figure before the people if he failed to comply with the terms once he had achieved his objectives. He held out his hand and waited for the other to take it. The consul waited a moment and then reached out to grasp it. Immediately afterwards, a new roar of applause rang out in the square.

Apparently, they had made an agreement. And if an agreement had been reached, it should be satisfactory for Octavian and for the brotherhood. Octavia was pleased, despite the fact that, during the meeting, she had not been able to stop her mind wandering between the events she was witnessing and her memories of Gaius Chaerea, which appeared with increasing vividness in her mind. She had removed them for years, and now they were back, like an increasingly violent flood which overflowed the banks of her memory.

And the clearer the outlines of those images grew, the more she wanted to relive them. And to finally know the fruit of their love.

She was the first to get up when Octavian and Antony took their leave, both with forced smiles. Her brother came over to his family, but in her mind she was already elsewhere, and could barely wait to get away. Octavian received the congratulations of his parents and cousins, especially for the demeanour he had managed to maintain, despite Antony's obvious provocation. Of the hypothetical benefits that he had gained with the agreement, they would speak elsewhere. But just no longer having the consul as an opponent was a victory of no small importance.

Octavia didn't listen to what her brother and the other family members were saying and, when she saw that it was time for farewells, she told Etain to call for her litter. But she had no intention of returning home. As soon as the bearers appeared before her, she ordered them to take her into the Suburra.

Etain immediately understood her intentions. "Are you sure, *domina*?" she asked, nervously.

"Yes, I am," replied Octavia, her voice cracking with emotion. "You give them the exact directions," she added. She had never wanted to know the address, to avoid being tempted to go there.

"You know that this could have serious consequences?"

"I know," she replied. "But *everything* that we're doing for Octavian could have serious consequences. So this is the least of it." This time her voice was firmer. But as time went on, her determination grew stronger.

They were silent for the rest of the journey, except when Etain spoke to the slaves to tell them the way. They went into alleys which to Octavia, who looked out occasionally from between the curtains, seemed eerie, dirty and sordid. The faces that appeared before her eyes were damaged by poverty and the brutal conditions in which the plebeians lived: worse, much worse than slaves of the upper class neighbourhoods, who at least had food and lodging guaranteed in beautifully appointed homes. Here, however, the buildings were often half in ruins or showed fire damage which had never been repaired. There were no toilets or running water, the streets were covered with rubbish and excrement and the stench of waste matter clogged the nostrils.

The people wore worn and tattered tunics, the children played in the street, challenging each other to fights, their faces covered with bruises and cuts. Had her son Marcus grown up like that? The adults had dull expressions, on their faces the vacant stares of those without hope. They all looked older than they actually were – their hair was thinning and greasy, the women's faces smeared with disgusting homemade makeup, which distorted the features and made them look prematurely faded. The noses of most of the men were bent by the many street fights they had encountered in their lives, and none of them looked to be of a healthy weight: they were either too fat or too thin.

And they all looked at her with hatred, no doubt angered by the ostentatious wealth she exhibited as she passed through their territory. She began to feel scared.

But at the same time, she became convinced once again that she had made the right choice by joining the cult of Mars Ultor. If there was a man in Rome who could change this deplorable state of affairs, it was Octavian. Caesar – who came from the

Suburra himself, having spent his childhood there – had tried, and now it was up to his heir to give the Romans – *all* of the Romans – the dignity they deserved as inhabitants of the most important city in the world.

Those who had governed until then cared exclusively about maintaining the privileges they had inherited from their parents and consolidating their interests, dispensing only crumbs to the people – and sometimes not even those. Indeed, what with the civil wars that had shaken the state for decades, they had even taken away from the citizens who lived in the meanest conditions the few resources at their disposal, lowering the level of security, raising taxes and crippling the economy.

These were the faces of people starving and living in fear of not making it to the next day – and it was unacceptable that this was happening in the city that housed the richest and most powerful men in the known world. It was those poor people who paid the price of the ambitions, rivalries and power struggles of a few members of the ruling class. They were expendable, good only for votes; all it took was to dangle the mirage of a small improvement in their living conditions in front of them and they would vote for anyone.

It was easy to buy them, the poor beggars. But Caesar had grown up among them, and had attempted to do more, and had at least managed to stop them from starving to death. And with the presence of soldiers in the City, he had ensured a higher degree of security and therefore guaranteed the city greater prosperity. The businesses of artisans and shopkeepers had been able to flourish and provide work for many other people. Now that the powerful were back at each other's throats, playing their games, uncaring of the negative consequences they might have on the people, the most feared spectre of all walked again among those unfortunates – lack of hope for the future.

But Octavian would change all that. He would put Rome and the Romans back on the right path, the path which the gods had intended for them, and which men, with their pettiness and their infinite short-sightedness, had hindered and eventually blocked altogether.

Her brother took a wider view – he was far-sighted and aimed for the common good, and perhaps that was why Caesar had chosen him to continue his work. None of the politicians that Octavia knew were interested in making the empire that

Rome had almost accidentally created, work properly, because each of them was too focused upon what concerned him. Right from the start, though, Octavian, had decided that his role would be to make the state more efficient and powerful. That was how he would become great – not by becoming rich and powerful, nor by dominating others. If those other things happened, well that would simply be a kind of reward for the man who had shouldered this enormous task, which the others, with their negligence, indifference, laziness or simple prejudice, had not even attempted.

Etain pointed out the entrance of the *insula*. The building was no more dirty than the others she had seen along the way and was at least in one piece, albeit with a few cracks on the facade and the odd tile falling from the roof right outside the entrance. Octavia descended from the litter and realized she was struggling to stand up. She was trembling and realized only then that she had done all of this unbeknownst to Gaius Chaerea. He was the baby's father, after all, and she should have warned him, before going to see the child. He had a right to know that she had failed to do what she had told him she would years earlier. He might not agree.

She also realized that it was precisely for that reason that she had not told him: she was afraid that he would have prevented it. Who knew what went on in the head of a man she had neglected for so long? Anyway, she entered the main door and saw that the little assistance she had always sent with Etain, as well as the not inconsiderable salary of a centurion, had served to ensure that little Marcus at least lived in dignified surroundings. It was clean enough, though from under the stairwell there was a strong smell of urine, stored in vessels and waiting to be picked up by the tanners.

As she climbed the stairs, her stomach grew tighter with each step, and when she reached the door of the apartment where the child lived with his nurse, she was rigid with emotion. Etain knocked, and after a few moments, a woman came to the door. Octavia examined her at length, and in turn felt assessed. Here she was then, the person Gaius had chosen to raise his son, after the defection of his real mother. She tried to work out if she was also his woman, and from the hostility of her glare deduced that she must be: the person before her had realised with whom she was dealing – her elegance and the presence of Etain at her side could not leave no doubt – and she was not at all pleased.

"Have you come for Marcus?" asked the woman, adding, with a hint of sarcasm, "Or for Gaius?"

Gaius's woman was beautiful, there was no denying it. With a beauty that was raw and rustic but authentic, devoid of the trappings that only a matron knew and could afford. She obviously didn't know how attractive she was and, just as surely, she was more attractive than Octavia. She resembled her, only she was... more beautiful. Her features were more regular, her physical form more slender and harmonious. She must be the same age. There was a fresh twinge in Octavia's stomach, but this time she was not sure that it was because of the thrill of seeing her son.

"For Marcus," said Etain. "Could you call him?" she added, anticipating Octavia's question.

The woman looked at the freedwoman, then at the matron, who remained silent. At that moment, the sister of Octavian felt an unpleasant urge to make use of Etain to speak for her in order to highlight the difference in rank between them: a kind of revenge, she realized, for not being able to exceed her in beauty and to make her pay for her nearness to Gaius and Marcus.

"He is playing in the street," she said flatly, an unreadable expression on her face. "Come with me." She walked to the window and looked out. Octavia and Etain followed her and then looked down over the windowsill. A group of children were running about and squabbling in front of the building: just the sort of thing, Octavia thought in horror, she had hated since her entry into that district.

The woman did not speak. She let Etain indicate Marcus to his mother. The freedwoman extended her arm and index finger and said, "There he is. He's the one with the green tunic and curly black hair."

Octavia leaned further out over the windowsill and tried to focus her attention on the child. She saw a beautiful creature, the son which her marriage had not yet given her: a child who looked older than his nine years, robust – he seemed healthy and thriving, and displayed his strong personality to the other children. She felt tears streaming from her eyes, and the vice in her stomach melted in the heat of tenderness. And suddenly, she cursed herself for having missed his first nine years, the ones where she could have taken care of him and rocked him, even taking the place of the slaves and wetnurses herself.

"I'm going down to meet him," she said impulsively, and broke away from the window.

She had already reached the threshold of the front door of the apartment, when from behind she heard shouting.

"No, please, don't!"

The woman had changed her tone radically. The neutral way she had received them had become passionate, almost desperate. Octavia turned and saw that the expression on Gaius's woman's face had changed. Her detachment of earlier had turned into a pleading look. "Don't tell him who you are and whose son he is, I beg you, *domina*!" The woman insisted.

"Why shouldn't I? I cannot take him away from you, but I want to at least talk to him."

"He thinks he's my son. I brought him up and cared for him, and I have always regarded him as the son that I will never have, ever since he was two years old. I know that you've helped us many times and I am grateful, but now he is my son. Don't put ideas into his head, please. He is happy: he has a father and a mother who are united and take care of him…"

"Happy? In *this* pigsty?" said Octavia, glancing disgustedly around the apartment. She did not really believe it – in fact, the house was beautifully decorated and clean, but she wanted to hurt her, because she was with the man she loved.

Perhaps the same man who loved her.

The woman had a surge of pride. "Gaius is very happy, he calls this his palace," she replied, looking Octavia straight in the eyes.

Octavia turned, walked through the door and, without saying a word, went back down the stairs which led out to the street. Once outside, she felt a hand on her shoulder. It was Etain "*Domina*, please…" she pleaded, but her mistress did not answer. She did not even look at her.

She felt furious, but did not know exactly with who: she was afraid it was with herself. She took a few steps toward the boys, busy playing with a ball, and then stopped and watched Marcus. She advanced again, and stopped again. She turned to the window of the apartment where she had just been, and saw the woman watching her. She took another step, then another, and just then a child missed the ball, which ended up at her feet.

It was the boy with the green tunic and curly black hair who came to collect it. She saw him running toward her, bend down, pick up the ball and only then realize that standing over him there was an elegant and fragrant matron of the kind he had perhaps never seen, except from afar.

Octavia watched him with a rapt expression, not uttering a word. Despite the lump in her throat, she felt that she wanted desperately to talk to him. "You really are a very handsome boy, Marcus," she managed to say in a choked voice.

Marcus's face took an expression of amazement. "You know my name, my lady," he said. "Why do you know it?"

Octavia felt disoriented. She looked again at the window, and saw the woman, her hands in her hair despairingly. She hesitated, and heard Etain murmuring, "*Domina*"

"Well... Your father sometimes escorts me and my family, and he has described you to me so many times that I seemed already to know you," she said.

"Ah," replied the child. "And what's your name?"

"My name is Octavia, and I am...I am..."

She felt Etain's eyes and those of the woman at the window upon her.

"... the great-neice of Julius Caesar."

"Then you are fortunate, because you are the relative of a very important man... And also unfortunate, because they killed him. My father was very upset about that," said Marcus, who then smiled and ran off to play with his peers before she could say anything else.

Octavia took another step forward, then felt Etain's hand hold her back. "*Domina*... I think that's enough for today, don't you?"

The matron thought for a moment, looked at the child again, then turned to her maid. "Yes, it's enough. Let us go," she answered, and walked towards the litter that was waiting a few feet away.

Climbing aboard, she tried to wipe away the tears that flowed down her face before Etain could notice.

She didn't manage to, but she appreciated the affectionate smile that her friend gave her.

X

Octavian looked up to the sky. The red disc of the sun began to appear over the roof of the tallest buildings, and a faint rosy glow illuminated the brightest dawn that he had seen since his return to Rome. He turned towards the Capitol, and saw they were raising the red flag – the same one that, in that moment, was flying on the Janiculum, the Etruscan part of the city, symbolizing, in accordance with tradition, that no enemy was approaching and that the centuriate assemblies could begin.

He had gone to bed the night before with the conviction that finally he had reached the keystone of his destiny – a new phase of his life, where he would begin his ascent to the heights his adoptive father had intended for him. In the future, he would speak of that day as the starting point of his political journey, and at the same time as the completion of his first diplomatic masterpiece: his reconciliation with Antony.

And he gone to bed so excited by the idea that he could not get to sleep. After a couple of hours of tossing and turning, he had got up, put on his tunic and robe and gone to the Forum, to watch the work ordered by the consul in preparation for those clandestine centuriate assemblies that would give Gaul to Antony and the position of tribune of the plebeians to him.

And while he was there, in the dim torchlight, watching Antony's men rope off areas of the Forum to demarcate where the Saepta – the pens for voting – would be, he reflected upon the possible consequences of this blatant violation of the law by the consul, with which he had actively and intentionally collaborated. With this little trick, he ran the risk of losing the support of Cicero, who certainly would publicly express his disapproval; and his disapproval meant that of the entire Senate, which was already ill-disposed towards Antony and anyone who supported him. But it did not matter – in that moment, he needed the consent of the people and the help of the consul more than that of those old fools.

Yes, he was setting off on his political journey by encouraging an illegal act: by convening the assemblies in the Forum and not in the Campus Martius, in fact, Antony was leading the Senate to believe that they were judicial tribal assemblies. Instead, the consul intended to summon the centuriate assemblies for his election as proconsul in Gaul, and he was helping him by showing his face and urging people to participate in the vote. But Caesar too had sometimes needed to force the issue, and it was clear that there was no way around it if you wanted to get things moving in the gangrenous world of Roman politics.

He heard the trumpet blowing from the tribune of the Rostra. The augur had just finished divining the omens – which Antony, of course, had ensured were favourable – and one of the heralds had recited the last ritual prayer, the propitiatory *carmen*. The president of the voting had urged one of the criers to call the people to court, and the other waited for the horn to stop blowing before reading aloud the announcement.

"What say and command you, Quirites, if I ask you that the present consul Mark Antony be made proconsul of Gaul Cisalpina instead of the designated Decimus Brutus Albinus?" said the herald, his stentorian voice ringing out across the still almost deserted square.

Or rather, not quite deserted. Some of those poor souls who rose in the hours before dawn to pay homage to their patrons had noticed the presence of Octavian in the Forum and had spread the word, and already others were approaching the Saepta at the entrance where the young man had chosen to position himself.

"Greetings, young Octavian, Caesar's heir. May the gods protect you!" said a man with a worn tunic. "It is always a pleasure to attend one of your assemblies."

"I thank you for your support, my friend," said Octavian, smiling amiably, "but I'm not here for an assembly. Our good consul Mark Antony is presenting himself to take Gaul from Decimus Brutus, one of the murderers of my father, and I am here to support his candidacy. I hope that you will vote for him."

"If I must be honest with you, I would never vote for that brutish drunkard. He is arrogant, and thinks only of looking after his own affairs..."

"And he never did anything to avenge Caesar, the only politician who ever really helped the poor people like us!" said another, who had just arrived.

Octavian was prepared to play the role of Antony's defender: he would have to do it all day, and he decided that this was as good a time to start as any.

"We need to forgive him for what he has done and to praise him for what he has managed to do in truly adverse conditions, like those which followed the death of my father," he explained. "The very fact that he intends to take the government of Gaul from one of Caesar's murderer's shows that he will work to honour Caesar's memory, does it not? And later on, all of my father's murderers will be convicted, and I will be able to help the people as Caesar did, because with Antony as an ally I can take a position which allows me to work for the common people. This is just the beginning: voting for him is like voting for me," he concluded. In the meantime, a knot of people had built up and, after a bugle call, others approached the entrances of the various sectors reserved for the thirty-five tribes into which the population of Rome was divided.

"If it is thus, then I will vote for him. But let it be clear that I do it only as a favour to you, Octavian," said the first commoner.

"I too will vote for Antony, even though I have no time for him," echoed another. "If that's what it takes to allow you to do something for us, I will hold my nose and make him proconsul. And let's hope that he doesn't make us regret it!"

Octavian shook hands with both of them and invited them to enter the compound of the respective tribes.

"Long live the son of Caesar!" shouted one of them as he took his place. The others repeated his words, attracting the attention of passersby who had in the meantime began to flock to vote. The bulk of the crowd moved around Octavian, who was soon receiving a constant flood of congratulations and handshakes – and even being embraced, almost suffocated, by his more impulsive advocates. Ortwin and Veleda's men, who were stationed nearby, had to intervene to break up the throng around him.

The young man was pleased by those demonstrations of consent. He tried to see if Antony had arrived, hoping he might have noticed the scene and thus realised his debt towards one he persisted in treating like an annoying, interfering little boy.

At the same time, however, it also occurred to him that the people were not showing warm affection only for him, but also for what he represented: it was the son chosen by the Caesar they were praising, not Octavian; it was Caesar's works they were attributing to him, not his own. He enjoyed a broad consensus without in fact having done anything to deserve it. He felt a frenzied need to prove something, and he decided that he would begin to press for the position of tribune of the plebeians the same evening.

With that, he would really be able to limit Antony's power, and to block the laws of the Senate which consolidated the privileges of the powerful and neglected or actually harmed the plebeians. He would also be able to propose laws which would improve hygiene, supply, the roads, the administration and the building of the city, thus gaining even wider acclaim and becoming a defender of the underprivileged. Perhaps the ambitions of Maecenas, who employed vast resources and energy to please others, were not so crazy after all: there was always a return, both practically and in terms of affection, and it was easier to waste resources by not investing them than by using them for the improvement of men and society.

As though summoned by his thoughts, his Etruscan friend appeared in the crowd, along with Salvidienus Rufus. They gave him a nod of greeting then they too began to walk about the Forum, urging people to vote, assuring every perplexed or undecided citizen that they would be doing Octavian, Caesar's son, a favour. They had agreed upon this the previous afternoon, and Maecenas had brought along a bevy of his friends, people who he had made happy and who followed him everywhere, including some of the most distinguished senators: to please him, even his followers spread around the buildings of the Forum, persuading people to vote.

He thought he saw Lucius Pinarius and Quintus Pedius. As uncomfortable as they were in the role of criers, they too had started to throw themselves into the job. Octavian smiled at seeing them so awkward and clumsy, unlike Maecenas, who appeared to be totally at ease. And unlike the Etruscan, he was sure that his cousins had undertaken that particular task in order to increase the likelihood of their recovering the sums they had given over to him by relinquishing their share of the inheritance.

By now, the sun was high in the sky, and the deep blue that enveloped the Forum and its imposing buildings presaged a day of triumph for the destinies of the sect of Mars Ultor. Apart from Octavia, who obviously could not walk about disseminating propaganda, all of its members were now in the square. All but Agrippa. But his friend had an even more delicate assignment to carry out…

*

Agrippa had had enough of the role that the cult of Mars Ultor had given him. It was wholly unedifying, especially for a man who yearned to become a warrior. He had expected to make himself useful by fighting, and instead, since Octavian had discovered he was Caesar's heir, he had been ordered only to have sex for his friend's cause. He looked dejectedly at Etain, and was tempted to confide in her, but decided that she would be the last person in the world who would understand. In fact, he hoped that she wouldn't notice anything: if the girl found out, he risked losing not only her high opinion of him, but also her love.

It had cost him to reveal to Octavian that he was in love, and had only done so to avoid the risk of his friend speaking casually of his relationship with Fulvia in front of Etain. He had already known that his friend, skeptical of his feelings, would mock him. In addition, Caesar's heir had scolded him for not having aimed higher: "When we are more influential and powerful, you too can, and must, marry for prestige. It will be helpful to the cause and will procure new support," he said. "So get these strange ideas out of your head. I, for one, will never fall in love: it would be an obstacle for the high duties and responsibilities which await me."

But that was a problem Agrippa would tackle later, if it proved to be necessary. The point at the moment was that Etain was on the verge of finding out herself. He and the freedwoman were, in fact, on their way to Antony's home, at the behest of Octavia, who had taken the initiative of sending the consul a shipment of Falernian wine as a gift from the family. The chances of Fulvia behaving explicitly with him in the presence of Etain were, perhaps, remote, but nonetheless possible, and that was why he felt so tense – never as on that occasion had he so hated the idea of being taken off by that woman into a morning of rapacious lust.

"You're worried, aren't you?" asked Etain, leaning from the cart and taking his hand. "I can understand that: you'd rather be at the Forum with your friends following the voting, than taking an inventory of the forces in Macedonia and Gaul with Antony's secretary." That was the pretext that Agrippa had agreed upon with Octavian for visiting the consul's house.

"Yes. Yes, that's right," he mumbled, holding out his arm to her as he trotted along on horseback beside the wagon. "If Antony loses, so does Octavian, and we are back where we began. And above all, Caesar's assassins will be sure to go unpunished."

Etain smiled, with that smile which always made all his worries evaporate. "I'm sure that the consul will win. Octavian is now so popular that he can direct the voting as he wishes."

Agrippa gestured to the driver of the wagon to halt. They had arrived at the entrance of the Gardens of Pompey. "Let's hope you're right," he said as he dismounted, then he walked over to her, took her under the arms and lowered her gently to the ground. Etain took the opportunity to kiss him joyfully on his nose, then her mouth came down looking for the young man's lips. Mildly embarrassed, Agrippa looked around him: there were a few passers by, but they didn't seem to be paying any attention to the couple's effusions, so he went along with her.

It was hard for him to break away, and he felt even more disgusted about what he had to do, but this was an important day, he told himself, and any information he could snatch from Fulvia might be decisive for their future. For a moment, it occurred to him that the more radiant the fate of the sect might be, the less chance there would be for he and Etain to live their love in peace. She was completely unaware of the fact, and he hoped that the girl would not think about it, at least for the moment.

Agrippa took a deep breath and walked past the entrance, calling for the attention of the gatekeeper. He presented himself before the man could do or say anything which might make Etain suspicious – recently, Fulvia had taken to having him come straight to the house when she was certain that Antony would not be returning. The man gave him a surprised look, but nodded and went back in to announce them. He returned, followed by a slave, and indicated that Agrippa should enter, while he told Etain and the driver of the wagon to wait for the arrival of two gladiators from Antony's personal bodyguard, who would carry the shipment into the storerooms.

Agrippa walked through the halls which were now all too familiar to him with greater anxiety and discomfort than usual, in part thanks to the presence of Etain and in part because the centre of the action, this time, was far from here. As always, the slave left him at the door of Fulvia's bedroom, and the young man wondered in what position he would find his hostess this time. She had the odious but exciting habit of being ready upon his arrival, without any preliminaries, and didn't even like talking at the beginning: she expected him to enter and, in silence, to take her. If at all, they might chat a little afterwards. It was a perverse game that Agrippa detested but which, at the same time, was becoming a kind of addiction: on the surface, she made herself into an object, when it was in fact he who was being used.

He looked at the bed and did not see her. Amazed, he scanned the rest of the room before spotting her lying on a table by the window, naked, her legs wide open and her head thrown back.

She looked dead, but of course she was not, and the rules of the game prohibited him from asking questions or investigating.

He just had to take her.

And so he did. With the fury she expected, and with the violence that he wanted to express. And he hated himself for it.

*

Etain waited a long time before the two thugs appeared before the cart to unload the cargo. They looked at her lustfully and eyed her up and down, then they pointed to a low building, telling her to take the cart over there. As soon as the driver had complied with their request, they set about the wineskins, ordering her to stay where she was. They lifted one each, and carried them into the building, and soon after, re-appeared and took the other two, but Etain saw that they had been drinking. They disappeared again and this time took even longer to re-appear. When they came back from the storeroom they were definitely drunk, and their beards were so soaked in wine that Etain could smell it from a distance.

Staggering, they grabbed two more wineskins, and with an unsteady gait disappeared once again inside the doorway. Etain looked at the driver, who smiled in amusement, but she found nothing amusing about the situation: it was time to return to Octavia, and those two idiots were stopping her. She could hear them, now clearly drunk, laughing loudly inside, and waited in vain for them to come out again. She tried to distract herself by thinking of Agrippa and the tender moments spent with him, fantasizing about the possibility of binding him to her permanently, having children and welcoming him home on his return from some future military campaign. She ignored the nagging voice that said it was all an impossible dream: after all, they were both plebeians and free, and perhaps their union was not as absurd as it might seem.

But she could take no more waiting: there were still several wineskins to unload, and she began to fear that the pair were too drunk to continue working. Impatiently, she left the driver where he was before he could say anything, and went over to the door of the storeroom. She could hear the gladiators mumbling nonsense to one another, and burst into the murky interior of the building, barely lit by the soft sunlight that filtered through the small windows. She saw the two sitting on the ground facing one another, each with a cup in hand, leaning against the wall and with a wineskin at their side.

"Aren't you ashamed of yourselves? If your master knew..." she said, in the most peremptory tone she could manage. "Come on, get up and unload the remaining wineskins. And be careful not to open another, otherwise you'll have my masters to deal with as well."

The two looked at her, their faces, at first dull, gradually growing interested. Suddenly, Etain realised that she was alone in a dark building with two drunken giants, and she was afraid. She took a step back, then another, but in the meantime one of the two had awkwardly climbed to his feet and was staggering in her direction. The girl turned to make for the exit, but he leapt forward and got to the door before her, closing it. Etain felt the lascivious eyes of the gladiator upon her, followed, a moment later, by his hands. Other hands grabbed her from behind and threw her to the ground. She felt a stabbing pain in her head, and then everything went dark.

*

"I think I'm in love with you, boy."

Agrippa was deep in thought, lying in bed next to the naked body of Fulvia, when the words hit him like a cyclone. All he could think was that even in the moment she refused to use his name and continued to call him 'boy'. Then, though, he began to assess the weight of those words.

Fulvia was one of those lethal women with whom it was inopportune to fall in love, and it was even less desirable to be the object of one of their infatuations. While Agrippa felt flattered to have made one of the most desirable matrons of Rome lose her head, he was also aware that the love of such a capricious lady could easily turn into its opposite.

"Do you not answer me?" asked Fulvia. "I do not remember having said it to many others in my life so far."

Agrippa was forced to turn his head and look at her, wondering what had happened to the lucky others.

"I never would have imagined it," he replied. "When we make love, I always have the impression that there might be anyone in my place." It was true: she never looked at him and thought only of her own pleasure, as though she had paid him to be with her. It was the same way the young man had always behaved with the women in the brothels, and now he felt he was being repaid in the same coin.

"Why, what would you like me to do?" she said, getting up on her elbow and looking at him for the first time since he had entered the room. "Whisper words of love? Gaze at you with dreamy eyes?"

That was what Etain did, thought Agrippa, and he had no doubt that she was in love with him. He wondered if Fulvia knew really what love was, or whether it was that women loved differently: some were able to express their feelings while others were not, and maybe Antony's wife belonged to the second category.

However, what mattered was what *he* felt. And he felt love for Etain. He did feel something for Fulvia, but it was certainly not love. It was, most likely, a mixture of perverse fascination and gratification, which gave him the opportunity to channel towards her all his more sinister instincts, reserving for Etain those which were purest. If he could have, he would have escaped from that disease which made him feel so dirty, but he was sure that a part of him would actually regret it.

"Maybe I was wrong to tell you. I'm just being ridiculous," she added, and Agrippa became aware of once again not having responded.

"No, it's just that... I didn't expect it. I thought I was your... trinket."

"Well, now that you know that you are not, what have you to say?" she pressed him.

"I... I'm confused. You must understand that I have always tried not to get too involved in this story: a woman of your rank and your position, the wife of the most important man in Rome, you acting so distant..."

"And maybe the age difference..." taunted Fulvia. "Of course, you could never feel anything strong for one so much older than yourself..." She did not say it with a smile.

"That doesn't matter," he said indignantly. "What matters is the fact that I'm Octavian's man and... and that your husband was hostile to my dearest friend. And I'm not sure that he isn't still," he added, starting to get into his role. He must never forget why he was there: it made him feel less guilty towards Etain. Just a little.

"I have told you more than once: you are backing a loser. Abandon him and come over to us," she said, stroking his chest again.

"Why? Octavian and Antony are no longer enemies, and now both will have what they aspire to, each thanks to the other – your husband the proconsul of Gaul and the army of Macedonia, my friend the tribune of the plebeians and revenge upon the murderers."

Fulvia gave a smug grimace. "I told you, Octavian is a loser: you will realise that for yourself soon enough."

"What do you mean?"

"That he is too young and too naive to expect to enter politics and to influence a man as experienced and expert as my husband."

Agrippa had a revelation. "You mean that Antony is not going to respect the agreement?"

Fulvia smiled contemptuously. "Why should he? By this time he will have got what he wanted, with election to the proconsul of Gaul. Listen to me – leave your friend: Antony will lead the conquest of the Parthians as Caesar would have, sooner or later. That walking corpse Octavian will only lead you to anonymity. And when Antony leaves for the North, the two of us can see each other as often as we like. Or, if you prefer, I will make sure that he takes you along with him. Anything to please my boy…" she concluded, attempting to embrace him.

Agrippa sat bolt upright, knocking aside Fulvia's hands. The woman was right. They had been naive to give something to Antony without making sure that he would respect the agreement, relying only on his honour: the consul did not care about what people might think.

On the other hand, it wasn't exactly the kind of thing you could draw up a contract for, and they had no choice but to trust him.

"What's the matter?" asked Fulvia, caressing him again. "What have I said that has upset you?"

But Agrippa got out of bed, put on his loincloth and grabbed his tunic. He had to run immediately to the Forum; perhaps it was not too late to tell Octavian and the others to stop the propaganda in favour of Antony and change the outcome of the voting. "Leave me be," he said, coolly pushing her aside again. "I have to go."

"No! Don't go!" cried Fulvia, throwing herself at his feet to try and restrain him. "Stay here, let Octavian go under! It will be easier to convince Antony to grant you a prestigious position!"

For a moment, Agrippa considered Fulvia's proposal: Antony's lieutenant and his wife's lover. Soon conqueror of the Parthians and perhaps magistrate of the Republic, praetor or maybe even governor of some province. All quite likely. But Octavian too was seeking to ascend to the highest possible peaks, and to take Agrippa there with him – but his friend had no chance of doing it as rapidly as Antony, and perhaps he had no chance at all, seeing how things were going.

Octavian, however, had been his friend from childhood, and

he had also taken an oath before the gods. And then, there was Etain.

He had no doubts about his choice. He broke free of Fulvia's grasp and headed for the door. At that moment, he heard a knock, and immediately saw the door flung open. A slave, panting and with blood on his clothes, burst into the room and turned to Fulvia, who was still lying on the floor in tears.

"Domina," he muttered in embarrassment, "the slave who brought the gifts of Octavian's family…"

Agrippa stopped in the doorway and grabbed the slave's robe. "What's happened?" he asked, shouting in his face.

"An… an incident—" mumbled the fearful slave.

"Take me to her! Hurry!" ordered Agrippa, dragging the man out of the room.

"What do you care about a slave?" he heard Fulvia moan loudly behind him, but he took no notice. They raced together to the storeroom, and, heart pounding, he went in and saw Etain lying in the shadows, her eyes closed and swollen, wounds and bruises on her face, her tunic torn and blood on her legs. Next to her was the cart driver, wiping her brow with a rag soaked in water.

"They took her in here… I was outside and I realised too late…" he sobbed.

"Who was it?"

"The two gladiators ordered to unload the wineskins."

Agrippa leaned over her. Etain's breath was heavy and laboured.

She needed treatment. He caressed her gently, then bent down and whispered in her ear, "I'm here now. You don't have to worry." She moved her hand slightly and laid it on his arm, but could not tighten it. He kissed her gently on the forehead. He desperately wanted to embrace her, and moved closer, but stopped for fear of hurting her.

"We must call a doctor, immediately. Hurry!" he said to the driver, who got to his feet.

At that moment, he heard the voice of Fulvia behind him. "Ah! That's why you care so much about this slave! And to think that I humiliated myself in front of you." Her tone had changed radically: she was now the woman he had always feared.

He realised that he had to get Etain away from there. Fulvia would make sure that she was not taken care of immediately, or even worse, would prevent it altogether out of pure jealousy. He had to take her immediately to Octavia and have her treated, and stay close by to comfort her. But he also had to race to Octavian to warn him of Antony's betrayal and prevent him from being elected, if there was still a chance.

What to do, damn it?

*

Octavian gave a nod of assent to Antony, who was sitting on the grandstand as a candidate. The voting was going excellently, and although the flow of voters was not enormous, most of those entered in the precincts of their respective centuries and tribes were happy to go first to greet Octavian and listen to his advice. And since there was no need to reach a quorum, the job seemed done. Antony would receive Gaul from the people and would be officially given the task of getting rid of Decimus Brutus.

And Octavian would be tribune of the plebeians.

The consul, however, had done his bit. He had caused rivers of money to flow into the pockets of chiefs and centurions, who had therefore energetically encouraged their underlings to vote for him. And unless some of those present had come to spoil their voting tablets or to express a protest vote against the candidate – which was more than possible – Antony would be elected by an overwhelming majority over his fictitious rival – a friend of his that he had chosen as the challenger.

There was not long left until the closing of the polls, which took place at sunset. Octavian decided it was his turn to vote. He reached the section of the *saeptia* reserved for his centurion and his tribe, and walked all the way along the rope delineating the voting pen, stopping in front of the officer, to whom he showed his identification. He received in return his wax tablet, which he carried with him by its characteristic side ring, and climbed the steps to the bridge built to access the forum.

The elevated position gave him a few moments of increased visibility, and he heard his name being cheered. He clenched his fist in satisfaction and held up his arm with the voting tablet, showing it to all, then reached the podium where the president

– the tribune of the plebeians – the two candidates and two other officials were. One of the latter handed him a stylus, with which, moving behind the railing which bordered the grandstand, he carved into the wax the letters "MA", indicating Mark Antony. He then returned to the centre of the podium and threw the tablet into a basket already half-full of others. He gave a nod to the consul, who smirked back at him, and set off again towards the bridge.

Before descending the stairs, Octavian cast an eye at the counting operation, which took place just behind the stage. The tellers declared aloud the name of the selected candidate, which was noted down by others in the registers; the polling was that of the first class of the centuria of the tribe prior to Octavians. With satisfaction, he calculated that at least half of the eighteen equestrian centuria and seventy of the first class had voted. And Antony's name had always, invariably, emerged.

As he walked out of the pen, Rufus and Maecenas approached him. "It's going well, I would say," said the first. "The odd one spat in my face while I was urging people to vote for Antony on your behalf, but overall they were a minority."

"And many told me that they would be very happy to vote for you as a tribune of the plebeians," said Maecenas, while a slave busily brushed his toga, wrinkled by the constant contact with the crowd. Curious, thought Octavian, that a man so willing to help others should be so disgusted by human contact.

The young man was about to answer, when he noticed a small procession proceeding in his direction, with at its head two senators, recognisable by the large purple bands on their togas; those behind them must be their respective friends, without whom practically no powerful man would walk about Rome. As they approached, he recognized them.

"It is Vibius Pansa and Aulus Hirtius, the newly-appointed consuls.And they seem to be looking for you…" Even Rufus had recognised them.

"Ah… " said Maecenas, shaking his head. "Problems on the way, I fear."

"Don't worry. I'll hold them off," said Octavian, trying to appear confident. Wasn't that what a leader was supposed to do?

"Hail, Octavian," began Aulus Hirtius, holding out his hand. "Rumour has it that you've been here since before dawn…"

Octavian had never spoken to him directly, and immediately found the man obnoxious. Hirtius was one of Caesar's henchmen who boasted no other merit than that of having served as a scribbler during the dictator's term as Gallic proconsul, writing down part of what would become Caesar's Commentaries. He had no military nor political merit, but Caesar had decided to reward his loyalty with the consulate.

"Of course: my aim and my task is to avenge my father, and the only one who can take Gaul from the murderer Decimus Brutus is Mark Antony," he said bluntly, as he extended his hand to Gaius Vibius Pansa too, another of Caesar's followers who had done little to deserve the esteem of the dictator, but who had been rewarded beyond measure.

"For these things, there is the Senate, do you not think?" said the other.

Octavian had never spoken to him before either. "The Senate? Are you speaking about the same Senate which approved the amnesty for the killers of my father and allowed them to leave Rome undisturbed?" the young man replied defiantly. "That same Senate which cheered on Brutus and Cassius as 'liberators'? Distinguished senators, how can you expect me to feel protected by people who have defended those who deprived me of the one I most loved and esteemed?" he added, trying to sound more reasonable.

"There is no need to tell *us*, young Octavian," said a piqued Hirtius. "We loved Caesar, and supported him through thick and thin. Of course we want justice for his death! But political necessities convince us not to be uncompromising for the moment, and now the circumstances are changing: when the time comes, we will take the necessary measures to ensure that this murder does not go unpunished."

Octavian heard Rufus stifle a laugh, and he knew only too well why – Hirtius's words were just so much meaningless fluff intended only to hide his cowardice and his intention to do absolutely nothing at all unless it was in his interest. They were all the same, these senators: people who sought only to stay afloat. Perhaps he too should adopt the same tactic for the time being.

"My dear Senator, I am young and understand only with difficulty the mechanisms which regulate high politics. You must forgive my vehemence: you are professionals, and I am simply an amateur – a neophyte moved by filial love. And right now, I see Antony as the only real obstacle to the rise of Caesar's assassins. For this reason, I support him."

"In that case, boy, since you admit to still having to learn a lot, know that with your condescending attitude you risk giving him immense power, which might be dangerous for all, even for you," said Pansa. "I mean, I can understand that you in particular would want revenge rather than justice, but perhaps the remedy you've chosen is worse than the disease"

Octavian thought he would remember the word 'boy'. "I respect and appreciate the advice of an experienced politician like yourself, illustrious Pansa," he said, resigned. "But it will surprise you to learn that I have considered this possibility in depth, and it is for that reason that I will stand as a candidate for tribune of the plebeians. It will be a way of controlling Antony; in any case, he is the only one able to influence the army and who has military men at his disposal to tackle the murderers if they decide to put pressure on Rome. Which at the moment they are amply able to do, as you will agree."

A perplexed Hirtius and Pansa nodded in what was actually camouflaged dissent. "I hope you do not have to soon repent of your decisions, young Octavian. I truly hope so…" said Hirtius, and held out his hand to take his leave, immediately followed by Pansa.

Octavian bid them farewell with all the amicability he could muster, thinking contemptuously that not even those two cared about Caesar, in spite of what the dictator had done for them. The only difference between them and his murderers was probably that Hirtius and Pansa had not had the courage to take part in the conspiracy.

And he was overwhelmed by a powerful desire to add them to the list too…

*

Etain opened her eyes, while Agrippa struggled with his doubts about whether to run to Octavian or to take her home. The young man forgot for a moment his friend and moved closer to her, brushing her swollen cheek with his lips. She managed to smile, despite everything. "Don't worry, my darling, we'll get you out of here right away and a doctor will soon make you feel better," he whispered, trying to express a sweetness that, between his anger at what they had done and his anxiety about what was going to happen to Octavian, he struggled to find within himself.

"You prefer a filthy slave to me? And after what I told you, you slap me in the face with your disinterest, abandoning me in bed for a little hussy like that?" Fulvia's shouts brought to him the actual severity of the situation. His situation.

He looked at Etain, now conscious enough to understand the words of Antony's wife. Her expression was already pained because of her injuries, and it did not change. She just turned her head to the side, to avoid Agrippa's gaze. The young man tried to ignore Fulvia, who continued: "Come back to me, boy. We had not finished! Forget about her, I tell you! Please, I… I need you!" she ordered, her usual hardness falling away. But he did not turn around. He tried instead to look into Etain's eyes, moving his head to enter her field of vision, but she kept turning away.

"Go… go to her," she muttered finally, through tight lips. In the meantime, the cart driver had returned, excusing himself for not finding any doctor nearby.

"Never," said Agrippa trying gently to turn her face.

"Come, come to me, I beg you." Fulvia's voice had become shrill, despite its depth.

Etain did not allow him to touch her, and simply stared into the empty space behind Agrippa. "Please, Etain, I'll explain afterwards…" the young man insisted, "but now just let me help you."

"I'll be fine," she said, and tried to pull herself up on her elbows. "I'd rather take care of myself." But she couldn't manage. The driver approached her and helped her up, as did Agrippa, but she ignored him. "Take me to the *domina*," she said to the carter. Meanwhile, Fulvia had begun to cry, entreating the young man almost obsessively to return to her.

Agrippa wanted to explain everything, but Fulvia wouldn't give him a chance. He had to run to Octavian. And Etain did not seem to want to see him any more…

Yes, he would explain everything to her when she was calmer. Now it was time to go. He helped the driver lift her up, carry her out of the storeroom and gently lay her on the cart.

She continued to ignore him, and Fulvia had fallen into a gloomy silence. "Do as I say," he said to the driver, "get her to Octavia's as quickly as you can." Then he turned to Etain. "Forgive me – it's not what you think," he whispered, but she did not deign to listen, and continued to stare into space, seemingly almost more traumatized now by the revelation of his relationship with Fulvia than by the violence she had suffered.

Agrippa shook his head sadly, then set off quickly towards the avenue leading to the exit.

"Where are you going, boy?" he heard Fulvia's voice shouting hysterically behind him. "Come back here, do not leave me! Do not leave me!"

He paused and turned around, but only to say, "Enough. I am not a 'boy'." Then he reached his horse, climbed into the saddle and rode at speed to the Forum without looking back.

*

Ortwin, who was guarding the grandstand, was fascinated by the electoral system set up by the Romans. Although he had served Caesar for years, he had never had the opportunity to attend the voting for the election of a magistrate – and in any case, under the dictator magistrates had mainly been appointed, not elected. Nothing remotely similar existed among his people, or among those immense forests in neighbouring countries, where the law of the clan prevailed: the strongest dominated the others, and did so for as long as they could prove themselves such. No voting, no elections, no candidates. But if nothing else, the system that the Romans called barbaric that guaranteed that the people were led by the best: the Germans would never have had a blunderer at their head, while the Romans, instead, often elected incompetents, who they were then forced to keep until the end of their mandate – and sometimes, if they had influential friends, even beyond. In Germany, however, if a leader proved not to be up to the job, he was unceremoniously removed from his position.

It was a great thing, this democracy, he told himself, but it gave too many rewards to a bunch of unworthy people. And it was amazing that the Romans had managed to dominate the world, despite the many fools leading them.

He was still wondering how that was possible when he saw Agrippa galloping towards him. Octavian's closest friend had been seconded to other duties of which he knew nothing, and that was why he had not seen him in the Forum all day. "Where Octavian?" he asked breathlessly, and Ortwin pointed him to the back of the stage, where the counting of one of the last of the first classes of the tribes' votes was underway.

Agrippa dismounted, took his friend aside and talked animatedly to him, and the two called over Maecenas and Rufus. They formed a huddle, and then, alone, Octavian went over towards Antony, who was standing by the stage with some of his friends. The young man took the consul's arm and forced him to follow him until the two were right next to the German.

"What do you want, Octavian – can't you see I'm busy?" said Antony, visibly irritated.

"So, now you have your proconsul in Gaul. I expect you to keep your part of the bargain. Go up onto the stage and announce elections to substitute the tribune of the plebeians. And I expect you to recommend to all the people still present at the Forum to vote for me," he demanded.

"Now? You must be joking…"

"Why not? They expect a speech from the newly elected proconsul," insisted Octavian. "You might as well make reference to me in it, don't you think?"

"It seems contrived and out of place to me," said Antony, turning away.

Octavian took him by the arm again. "Not in the least. Remember that you won today thanks to me."

"Thanks to you? Hardly – your speech was irrelevant. With all the money I paid to tribal leaders, I could never have lost," said Antony drily.

Ortwin saw Octavian's handsome face twist into a grimace of indignation. "So it's true that you had no intention of honouring the agreement!" the young man protested through gritted teeth.

"Agreements are made with those who have something to offer. And you, boy, have nothing to give me. Why should I tie myself to you? You're nobody, apart from the name that you claim to bear." Antony seemed calm now: he felt that he was unassailably triumphant.

"Oh yes? We'll see if I have nothing. The people are with me, not with you. And you might also have some surprises from the soldiers of whom I mean to take command."

"The soldiers? A country boy like you who can hardly lift a shield? The legionaries appreciate strength and valour, and you are able to give them neither!"

"We will see. Meanwhile I will present myself for the elections, and I do not see what you can do to stop me," said Octavian boldly.

"I certainly can! You are not old enough to apply, and I, as the highest magistrate of the Republic, publicly forbid you from doing so. Try it, and you will incur serious penalties!" said Antony dismissively. And then he left.

Octavian remained immobile. He looked over at Ortwin, who gave him a discouraged look in return. Apparently, thought the German, the lad had let himself be played like a greenhorn. He recalled his earlier reflections on the quality of the leaders in Germany and in Rome. The first produced leaders like Antony – strong, determined, experienced and unscrupulous –- and the second leaders like Octavian – inexperienced, full of scruples and often naive.

Yet Rome always prevailed in the end.

XI

Agrippa looked around to check that no one was about; even though it was night, the Campus Martius was frequented by the wagons of household goods which were not allowed inside the walls during the day. He waited for a convoy of them to disappear from his view, although the poor lighting of the place would have hidden him from anyone who might pass nearby. He checked that his mask was tightly attached to his face and that his knife was in place in the folds of his robe, then he threw the grappling hook up over the wall. He pulled it until it found purchase and, when he felt that it had caught, he tested its hold was firm. Satisfied, he put his toes into the cracks of the boundary wall and began to pull himself up.

When he reached the top, he lay down to avoid being seen and began to observe the layout of the gardens of Pompey, squinting to adjust his eyes to the darkness. It took some time to orient himself and locate the entrance. But it was not through the front door that he intended to gain access. The place was swarming with guards, even though for the moment he could see none, and it was necessary to use the greatest possible caution. If he was to avoid getting Octavian into trouble – or into even more trouble than he was already – he had to avoid being recognized.

He focused his attention in the direction where he remembered seeing the servants' quarters, in the part opposite the *curia* building. Slowly he began to distinguish an edifice where he spotted the cracks of windows. He remembered seeing some slaves coming from the wing to the right, and guessed that the gladiators were in the one to the left, so he carefully hooked the grappling hook to the top of the wall and lowered himself, landing in bushes and brambles. He was in a distant, neglected corner of the gardens, which lent itself best to hiding his movements from any possible sentries.

He pulled down the rope and grappling hook and hid them

behind one of the bushes, then set off cautiously, crouching down and not taking the most direct route, the path between the hedges, until he had reached the centre of the building. He began to relax: if there were guards, they were certainly on the other side – the noble part, where Antony and Fulvia were, not that of the service personnel. But he did not know how many men capable of fighting he would find inside, so he forced himself to keep his guard up. He drew his dagger and approached a window. The shutters were only pulled to, and he pushed them slightly apart and peered inside, counting on the starless night to hide his movements and hoping that the creaking of the wood would be attributed to the wind.

Once his eyes had got used to the darkness within, he made out several silhouettes lying on beds. Too many people, he said to himself, and moved to the window of another room. He looked inside and saw there were only two beds, and from the long hair emerging from under the covers deduced that they must belong to women. Good, that was the room for him. Carefully, he opened the shutters, climbed slowly over the sill and walked stealthily over to the nearest bed, where he reached out and put his hand over the woman's mouth.

She started but could not scream. She was elderly, and Agrippa saw the terror in her eyes. Good. He put his lips to her ear and hissed, "Tell me where the gladiators's lodgings are, now! And if you raise your voice I'll slit your throat."

He shifted his hand slightly away from her mouth, and she whispered, "You have to… you have to leave this room and go to the last one on the right."

"If you have lied to me, I will come back and kill you. And if you scream when I go, I will come back and kill you. If you wake up your roommate, I will come back and kill you. But if you keep quiet, two rapists will get their just punishment and perhaps avoid, in the future, molesting your younger friends."

A flash of recognition illuminated the terrified woman's eyes, and her limbs relaxed. "If it comes to that," she said with a bitter smile, "those two have had their filthy way with me too"

Agrippa relaxed, although he struggled to believe her words. "Just the two of them in the cubicle?" he asked. "No. There are four of them. But one is out of Rome tonight on an errand."

Agrippa gave her a gentle pat on the shoulder, then stood up and walked over to the door. He opened it cautiously and looked down the corridor. No one around. He headed right, until he had reached the last room. He stood for a moment at the door, reflecting on strategy: the two gladiators who had used violence on Etain would have been weakened by the whipping that Antony had given them, but there was a third in there who was in full strength. He had no choice but to kill all three.

Only whipped! The indignation welled up inside him: the consul had limited himself to giving them that mild punishment and sending a formal apology to Octavia for the 'incident', as he had called it! He should have had them killed, and no doubt would have, had that 'incident' involved the family of one of his followers, and not that of his most serious political opponent. Because that was what Octavian was once more, after the low joke Antony had played upon him.

And now, Agrippa had decided to punish them as they deserved. Without telling Octavian, because he might have hindered his plans.

He would never have done it had relations between the consul and his friend remained on the level of propriety. But they were compromised. And anyway, with a little luck, Antony wouldn't connect his action to Octavian.

Perhaps.

He had to act quickly: hit and run before the entire staff of the domus swept down on him. Antony was the most important man in Rome, and the place where he lived was, as a result, one of the most protected and well-guarded in the city. But Agrippa put the thought out of his mind. He took his dagger and held it in his right hand, then kicked open the door and burst into the room. There were four beds; he had no time or way to figure out which were the two responsible for the violence inflicted upon Etain, the only ones he really cared about killing; he would have had to check their backs for the signs of Antony's whipping, but he had neither the time nor the inclination. He practically threw himself atop the nearest, and the man was still asking himself what was going on when Agrippa's dagger stabbed him in the throat.

Flooded with a violent spray of hot blood, the young man rolled off the bed and rushed to the foot of the next. The other gladiator was rising, but too slowly: Agrippa stabbed him from below, turning the knife in his body for a few moments before dragging it back out, along with some of his entrails. At that point, he was expecting the third to attack or to scream, but there was no reaction. He checked the two beds after peering into the shadows, and only then realized that they were empty: the sheet on one, however, was in disorder, a sign that someone had recently lain in it.

Before cursing his bad luck, he checked the backs of the two gladiators he had killed. On the first he saw the marks, a clear sign that he was one of those responsible for the rape. He walked to the other, turned him over and, in the dim light of the moon through the window, examined his skin carefully.

It was as smooth as that of a newborn baby.

Agrippa gave a soft curse, clenching his fists in frustration. The other offender had obviously gone to relieve a call of nature. He wondered if it was better to wait for him to return and surprise him or to go and look for him: in both cases, there was a high chance of being discovered and not getting out of the domus alive. He doubted that anyone had heard the sounds of the brief struggle: he had been absolutely lethal, and his victims had time only to issue a few groans.

He was still deciding what to do when he heard footsteps echoing in the hallway. Was it someone who had heard something, or the gladiator who was returning? He listened carefully to try and make out the footsteps: they seemed to be those of a single person – or, at most, two – who were approaching without worrying about keeping quiet. He was tempted to go out and face them, but could not make the mistake of being seen by someone else in the building: the best thing to do was to wait inside the room, lurking behind the door. If he came in, that meant he was the man Agrippa was looking for.

He heard voices. They were two of them, curse it. And after a while, they stopped to talk right outside the threshold of the room where he stood.

"Do you want to come in? You could keep me company in bed. Maybe blow on my wounds a bit. You know, they burn so badly…"

"I can't, not tonight – the *dominus* wants sturgeon eggs for breakfast tomorrow morning, and I have to get up before dawn to go and get them. But tomorrow night I will, count on it." This second voice seemed to belong to a very young boy.

"I'll be counting on it for tomorrow, then." Agrippa heard

moans and heavy sighs. He crouched where he was, clutching
the knife. He heard the lighter footsteps walking away, but the
other man did not enter. Maybe he had stopped in the doorway
to watch his lover. Finally he saw the door open. The silhouette
of a large man appeared, and he yanked him inside, pointing
the knife at his throat: now that he had him in his grip, he
wanted to look the man in the face before slicing him open.

"What do you want?" the man asked, paralysed by surprise.

"Justice," he said, bringing his face close to that of the man.
He smelled his fetid breath, which reeked of undiluted wine.

"I've done you no harm."

"Yes, you have. You raped my woman."

"I've already paid for that!"

"Not enough," replied Agrippa, just before sinking his
dagger into the man's throat. The gladiator let out a gurgle, a
gush of blood bubbled from his mouth and his body slumped
lifeless on the floor.

Agrippa walked out of the door, closing it behind him. It was
done, but it was not over: now he had to get out of there. But
just then, at the end of the corridor, he saw a slender youth
appear, walking directly towards him. They looked at one
another for a moment. The other froze, staring at the bloody
blade of his knife, then let out a scream and ran away.

Curse it! It must be the lover of the gladiator, who had
decided to come back and keep his friend company for a while
after all. There was no time to lose: Agrippa returned to the
room, climbed out through the window and stood immobile
for a moment, getting his bearings, before heading off for the
section of the wall where he had left his rope. Meanwhile, the
light of torches flickered through the windows: the boy had
raised the alarm and people were beginning to wake up.
Agrippa was keeping low, trying to stay beneath the level of
hedges, when he noticed two figures walking along the paths of
the gardens. They were carrying spears and they were looking
for him.

He quickened his pace, while the number of torches being
lit continued to increase. The wall was getting closer. Finally, he
reached it, but finding the exact spot and the bush where he had
hidden the rope in these conditions was no mean feat. He
searched on all fours amongst the briars, getting scratched and
cut and cursing softly to himself as he did so, but found

nothing. It could be just a few steps behind or ahead of him. He chose a direction at random, and meanwhile heard the voices of his pursuers drawing closer, though he could not tell if they had spotted him or had just happened to come in his direction.

With increasing panic, he continued to rummage among the plants, no longer caring about the wounds inflicted by the dense vegetation. Nothing there either. He turned and retraced his steps, still on his knees, and finally found it.

But he also found a pair of feet.

"Here he is! He's here!" cried a voice above his head. Agrippa dodged instinctively, just a minute before the tip of a spear penetrated the ground in the exact point where he had been surprised. With his dagger still in his hand, he swung a blow to the man's crotch, ramming it up between his legs so violently that it lifted him off the ground before he collapsed to the floor with a piercing scream. Meanwhile, Agrippa grabbed the rope, got to his feet, threw the grappling hook over the top of the wall and began pulling himself up. Immediately afterwards, there was a shout and he heard the clang of metal against the stone beside him. A spear had hit the wall.

He hastened his ascent, while the voices below him grew in volume, and once he had reached the top, he looked behind him and saw shapes prowling through the bushes. He jumped down and began to run. But still he heard the shouts of his pursuers behind him, and he realized that another group had left through the gate. He raced towards the busiest area in front of the Temple of Venus, which enclosed the gardens on the side opposite to that of the Curia of Pompey. There he saw an almost uninterrupted row of wagons parked in the road. He took off his mask and threw it away, then walked over to one of the wagons and pressed his knife into the driver's side. "Give me your cloak," he ordered, and the driver did not hesitate to obey. He put on the garment, hiding the patches of blood that stained his tunic, lifted its hood and carried on, walking past another of the wagons and then turning off into a side street.

He caught sight of Antony's men walking among the long line of wagons, looking disoriented. He had lost them.

It was done. Etain had been avenged. Winning back her love, though, was another story. One which was much, much more difficult.

*

"I am glad so many of you have come here, citizens, because what I have to tell you deserves all your attention. I am here to warn you about, and to tell you to guard yourselves from, the person to whom, on the sole basis of his name, you have given so much credit."

Antony's message was all there in the first words of his speech. Maecenas looked at Octavian and shook his head. Agrippa looked worried, while Rufus, instead, seemed intrigued, from what the Etruscan could just make out from beneath the hoods all four were wearing to avoid being recognised: it would not be healthy to be seen at the foot of the *Rostra* in the Forum where Antony had just set out on what had been widely heralded as a public denunciation of Octavian.

"Lunacy… It is he who has betrayed the agreement, and now intends to denounce you," said Rufus. "He's got a hell of a nerve!"

"Be quiet. Let's hear what the old fool has to say. I'm very curious to know what he is going to come out with," said Octavian, his eyes fixed on the stage.

The four returned their attention to the consul's speech: "All of you have been witness to his constant attacks, which began as soon as he returned to Rome. Evidently, having learned he was Caesar's heir must have gone to his head! Right from the first moment, he has never accorded me the proper respect. Me, one of his oldest relatives, the chief magistrate of the Republic: he has criticized, accused and even insulted me for months without even knowing why he does so, like the spoiled child he is – stamping his foot because he did not get what he wanted right away. And yet, I have acted – as I have always acted since the death of Caesar – for the good of the state, and tried to mitigate the conflict, just as I have worked for peace since the Ides of March! So I agreed to reconcile with him and to accept his apology – which, however, proved to be false."

"That's a very personal interpretation of events…" said Maecenas.

"Shhhhh!" Octavian silenced him.

"Yes, they were false! Because his behaviour grew even worse after I was elected proconsul of Gaul! Clearly driven by envy, he even made an attempt upon my life!"

A murmur of surprise rose from the crowd. "What is he talking about?" hissed Octavian.

"That's right, citizens!" the consul resumed. "Who knows what dark design drives him! He bribed one of my gladiators, who two nights ago tried to assassinate me! Luckily, my other two bodyguards realised what he was at and killed him, they themselves dying to save me."

Antony stopped and, with consummate oratory skill, let the audience take in the explosive news. Octavius looked around him to see the expression on the faces of the people. Some were incredulous, others angry, others – although not many, in truth – were calling the magistrate a liar.

"That's right, citizens! Incredible as it may seem, that is what he who boasts the title of Caesar's heir and would also take the name itself did! Octavian tried to kill me! It is a blessing that I must now leave for Gaul: If nothing else, I'll be out of his clutches. I believe he is more dangerous than a murderer like Decimus Brutus. With Brutus, at least I can hope to make an agreement. But with this lad, we have seen that agreements mean nothing: he betrays them with an ease that saddens as well as angers me."

Octavian shuddered with rage. He wanted to tear off his cloak, climb onto the stage and shout his innocence. Rufus and Maecenas realised that he was on the verge of doing something drastic, and grabbed him by the arms. Agrippa, however, seemed strangely detached and deep in thought.

"What fairy stories is he making up now? There's no limit to what these hyenas will sink to in order to get rid of a political opponent" said Rufus.

"I told you," said Maecenas, "there is no morality nor scruples in politics – everything is legitimate. If necessary, you can conjure up an accusation out of nothing, without even needing a pretext."

With lowered eyes, Agrippa spoke for the first time.

"In truth, I gave him a pretext"

Meanwhile Antony continued: "But I cannot put off beginning my term in Gaul. Now I know that I am in danger, I no longer feel safe in Rome. In Rome, in my own city! Octavian might try it again, and now I am not even certain that I can rely on the men to whom I have entrusted my safety, after what has happened! I feel that I am stalked and spied upon at every street corner because Octavian, with all the money at his disposal thanks to his inheritance, can corrupt anyone. Do you see how he uses Caesar's money? To kill the one who has proved his most faithful servant! That was why he was so keen to get his hands upon it! Therefore, I am forced to leave as soon as possible. I must live among the soldiers who fought under my orders and those of the dictator, not among the people I represent." His crescendo had been well thought out. More and more spectators seemed to approve of what he said. They had a lot to learn from him, thought Maecenas. But now he was also curious to hear what Agrippa had to say.

The Etruscan and the other two friends looked quizzically at the young man, who continued to stare in silence at his feet with the air of a little boy guilty of some misdemeanour.

"So?" urged Octavian.

"I… I killed those three gladiators," murmured Agrippa. For a moment the four friends were silent. Around them, the citizens discussed the questions Antony's speech had raised. Some continued to think his accusations absurd: they said that Octavian needed Antony alive, not dead, in order to avenge Caesar's murder. Many others, however, believed the charges, explaining, though not always justifying, them with all the wrongs that Octavian had suffered. For his part, the consul regarded the crowd from the platform of the Rostra, looking unabashedly pleased: he had managed, in one way or another, to put a crack in the solid popular front which supported Octavian. Now, he need say nothing more.

"In the name of all the gods, why?" Rufus was only the quickest to ask Agrippa the question that was on the lips of the other two.

"I wanted to punish the gladiators who raped Etain," mumbled Agrippa. "He only had them whipped."

"Etain? Octavia's slave? And why should you do that?" asked Rufus. Maecenas, however, was beginning to understand.

Octavian grabbed Rufus's arm. "Never mind," he said angrily, staring at Agrippa. "Why did you not tell me before?" he asked his friend.

"Because you would you have forbidden it."

Octavian's reaction was so violent that it began to attract the attention of the people around them: "Of course I would have forbidden it!"

Maecenas grabbed his wrist, and he realized he was going too far. He moderated his tone. "What do you think we are about? There is no room for personal vendettas, here! We are on a mission!"

"Personal vendettas?" replied Agrippa. "So what is it that you are proposing to do to Caesar's assassins, then? In my own small way I'm acting like you! And then, she was... she is one of us, and we could not tolerate them hurting her."

"Don't talk nonsense! You didn't do it because of us, you did it because she is your woman!" insisted Octavian. "And revenge against Caesar's murderers is the first motive for our mission, the main goal of our cult: our common purpose. Those gladiators deserved punishment, I agree, but this was not the time. But you had to do it your way, without taking the needs of the rest of us into account!"

"You're an idiot," echoed Rufus, who only at that moment had realised how strong the bond forged between his friend and the woman who had rejected him was.

"I... I am sorry. But when I saw her in that condition, I thought only to avenge her," said the young man, attempting to justify himself.

"You're sorry? You're *sorry*? If only you knew how sorry *I* am!" continued Octavian. "Maecenas is right – people like Antony need no excuse to stick the knife into those they wish to harm... so just imagine if you actually give them one! You have jeopardized our mission by acting on your own initiative, without consulting the rest of us. That is not what we need," he said solemnly, "you are too impulsive to be reliable. I do not think you can any longer be a part of the cult of Mars Ultor."

Rufus could not repress his expression of satisfaction.

Agrippa's face grew desperate. "I have given all I can for the sect. And what happened to Etain happened because I was carrying out the unpleasant task with Fulvia that you had assigned me. I lost her because she saw me with Antony's wife: and now you also want me to lose my place beside *you*? Is that what I deserve for having served so well the aims we set ourselves?"

"You have seen for yourself who and what we have to face and the difficulties that lie ahead. We will be able to overcome them only if we remain united and avoid taking impulsive decisions. Therefore you can no longer be one of us. I do not want you with us," insisted Octavian.

"Octavian, Agrippa made a mistake, but perhaps you could give him another chance…" said Maecenas, trying to soften their leader's stance.

"No. My mind is made up." The young man was adamant, though the tremor in his voice betrayed his pain at the decision he had just taken.

"Forget it, Maecenas. I do not need to beg from anyone. Not even Octavian," said Agrippa bitterly, then turned and disappeared into the crowd.

The three friends remained silent as they watched him go. Maecenas saw indecision on Octavian's face, and perhaps regret for what he had just said in his anger. One of the first things he had noticed when he had joined the sect was the bond of extraordinary affection which connected Octavian and Agrippa. He was certain that if he could turn back time, Octavian would change his mind, but he was equally sure that, by now, he would never go back on his decision, in order to avoid giving the impression of being a weak leader. It was a very bad business.

"Now what do we do? Antony is winning over the people with this trick of his, and if he goes now among the soldiers, he will recover consensus among the troops too. There'll be no room left for us," reflected Rufus.

Maecenas had an idea. "Not necessarily, Rufus," he murmured cryptically, "not necessarily…"

It was time to take the offensive. On several fronts. And each of the members would have to play their part.

XII

"What's that you have in your hand, soldier?" shouted the centurion, waving his vine staff menacingly at the legionary, who had been absorbed in reading a small piece of papyrus, as though ready to break it over his back.

"Another soldier gave it to me, centurion. I was just trying to work out what it was," protested the intimidated legionary.

"Give it here," ordered the centurion. He read it out in turn, aloud.

"Let's have a look… 'Legionaries! For years, Julius Caesar led you from one victory to another, and has given you the chance to parade in five triumphs in three different continents, he gave you money and laurels, he dispensed rewards and promotions to anyone who deserved it, made you the most celebrated soldiers of all time, and yet you allow his assassins to wander the world unpunished for his murder? What are you waiting for to take your grievances to the leaders who refuse to bring to justice those who deprived you of the greatest commander of all time, the one who would have led you to the conquest of the great Parthian Empire? Remember that his son, the new Caesar, awaits you, ready to guide you to your righteous revenge and give you back the laurels that the murderers have taken away.'"

The soldier was shaking now, expecting punishment for possession of seditious material: the consul Antony had just arrived at the camp of the Martia legion, near Brindisi, where, along with four others, the unit had landed from Macedonia. In the previous days, these propaganda leaflets had circulated more or less freely, and many superiors had turned a blind eye even when they had not agreed with the content. But now that the commander was present, controls were becoming increasingly tight.

"And what do you think of what it says here?" said the centurion. "Sincerely, I mean?"

"What do I think?" asked the legionary, surprised that his superior took the trouble to ask him but also frightened: whatever he said could be used against him. "Well, I'm loyal to our new commander. After all, he was the most prestigious of Caesar's lieutenants."

"I said, 'sincerely', soldier."

"Well… Since you insist… I think we should march against the villains who killed Caesar. Whether Octavian or Antony does it makes no difference to me, as long it is done. And Octavian has certainly shown himself to be more eager than Antony…"

"That was what I wanted to know," said the centurion. The soldier flinched, afraid that he was about to get a beating, but his superior officer walked past him, ignoring him. The officer went over to the Praetorian gate where there were other soldiers who, at the sight of him, hid behind their backs notes like that he had confiscated from the first legionary. He smirked, passed through the gate and set off toward Brindisi, a few hundred yards away from the camp which, along with four others, surrounded the inland side of the city.

He entered a building near the walls and climbed three flights of stairs, stopping before a door. He knocked and after a moment, it was opened.

"Gaius Chaerea! So it's true that Octavian managed to get you transferred to the Martia! Very well," said the person on the other side.

Purposefully, Chaerea walked inside. "As you are supposedly no longer part of the sect, it is your presence which is more surprising here in Brindisi, dear Agrippa. And judging by the number of notes with which you and your assistants have filled the camps, you've been here for a while, I would say. But come, let us talk: Antony has just arrived in the city, and will soon give a speech to the soldiers to try and recover the situation."

"Fine. It is up to us to frustrate his efforts, "said Agrippa, showing him to a triclinium.

*

"And how do you find life as a farmer, soldier?" said Octavian to the owner of the farm he had gone to visit near Casilinum.

The man was about fifty, with few teeth left in his mouth and even less hair on his head. "I find it good, son of Caesar. I was finally able to marry my woman and legalise the position of my three children. And this Casilinum colony is truly prosperous: I was lucky. But..."

"But?"

Octavian's magnetic eyes narrowed.

"But... Well, I miss them, those days. I was part of the thirteenth. I was with your father when he crossed the Rubicon, and none of us was in any doubt that we would succeed. We had such confidence in him... And if you only knew how many battles I fought in Gaul under his orders: I saw Vercingetorix lay down his arms at Caesar's feet in Alesi, and at Avaricum I was one of the first through the walls! And in Britain I faced the chariots of the Celts, jumping aboard them and killing both the drivers and the bowmen..."

"Good days, eh?" assented Octavian.

"You can say that again! The truth is, I'm too young to be retired and be a farmer. I still have a lot to give the army."

"And I bet you could do a lot to avenge Caesar."

"You can say that again too. I would do anything to have revenge on the scum who butchered him. Twenty-three stab wounds... Like beasts."

"True. And you know that when he died I was the only one of the patricians to proclaim repeatedly to whoever would listen that his killers should be punished. But I need an army to enforce my rights and to convince others to do so. Especially Antony, who seems afraid of Brutus, Cassius and the rest."

"Well, if you're setting up an army, you can count on me. I'm sick of being here looking after my brats and listening to my woman moaning. Nothing ever suits her. Yesterday, for example..."

"Would a thousand sestertii suit you, to begin with? I will be leaving for Rome in three days. With an army at the gates of the city, the Senate will have to listen to me."

"A thousand sestertii? Of... of *course!* You're just like Caesar! I'm with you, Octavian."

Octavian summoned the bursar, who was waiting outside the property with the wagon and escort led by Ortwin and Veleda. "A thousand to him too," he ordered, and the man pulled the already-counted money out of one of the chests.

The youth took it and handed it to the man, who grabbed it excitedly. "I will be waiting for you the day after tomorrow at the main gate of the city, then. You will have as much again when I see you. To Rome!" declared Octavian, squeezing his hand. Then he left the holding and climbed onto the wagon.

"How many does that make?" he asked the bursar as they headed towards the next farm where Caesar had settled the veterans.

"Three hundred and twenty-two. Then there are the two thousand who came from Calatia as soon as it was rumoured that you were here. We'll have to pay them off all together."

"Of course," agreed Octavian. "Now let us go and speak to the veteran who lives next door; otherwise, if he sees that we went to his neighbour and not to him, we will lose him." He turned to Ortwin. "You go to the city and announce that tomorrow I will speak to the people, and I will suitably reward those who share my goals."

Octavian watched the German ride away on horseback along with his woman, growing gradually smaller and smaller, and nodded to himself contentedly. Yes, all in all the barbarian had been a good buy; it was a pity that soon they would have to part...

*

By now, the senators had left the curia and swarmed one after another towards their respective homes, except for the few who lingered to talk on the steps of the building. It could not have been a particularly intense session, nor one which tackled burning issues, because their faces were calm and relaxed, and sometimes even amused. These were not times when a politician could afford to laugh overmuch, thought Salvidienus Rufus to himself, and the fact that the senators granted themselves this luxury spoke volumes about their lack of insight. Octavian was totally right when he insisted that there were few in Rome who actually made any attempt to work for progress and for the common good.

The lictors of the consul Dolabella were waiting for him at the base of the stairs. That meant the magistrate was still inside.

He resigned himself to waiting, and in the meantime his mind, left free to roam, went to the slave girl that Agrippa had been smitten with. She was beautiful, that girl, and apparently it was all over between the two of them. Moreover, his friend had fallen out with Octavian and seemed to be out of the sect. Rufus had ambivalent feelings toward Agrippa – on the one hand, he was sorry that he was no longer one of them: they had shared many adventures together, and he was fond of him. At the same time, though, Agrippa had always been one step ahead of him, both in Octavian's affections and esteem and in the affections of women, and he felt relieved at not having to compete with him any more.

It occurred to him that it couldn't hurt to make a move with Etain now.

At that moment he saw Dolabella appear. The consul who, appointed by the dictator as his successor, had always seemed to him a fool. He had heard tell that, immediately after the assassination of his own patron and protector, he had claimed to have been involved in the conspiracy, despite having been kept in the dark about it. He had also been one of the fiercest in quelling the unrest of the populace which had followed Caesar's funeral. But now he appeared to be annoyed both by the ascendency of Antony and by the activities of the killers of the dictator in the provinces, which made it difficult to take possession of what he had the Senate assign to him, namely Syria.

Dolabella took his leave of the two senators he had been speaking to and walked alone towards his lictors. Rufus set off in his direction and intercepted him. "Consul, I need to talk to you. I am Salvidienus Rufus and I come on behalf of Octavian, Caesar's heir," he said, stepping between him and the guards.

The consul looked at him suspiciously. "Caesar's heir?" he replied, sarcastically. "There has been no formal adoption as far as I am aware. He simply inherited his wealth as next of kin. Yet for some reason I have the feeling that he wishes to become his political heir too…"

Rufus smiled. "Try asking the soldiers in Syria, when you assume the governorship of your province, who is Caesar's heir – it would be unwise to make similar claims in front of them: they might get offended…"

Dolabella's face grew darker still. "What is this, a threat?" he asked.

"No, it is advice," replied Rufus, maintaining his affable tone. "Rumour has it that Brutus and Cassius are running around Syria and Macedonia, neglecting Crete and Cyrene which the Senate assigned them, and Trebonius is firmly established in Asia, busily fortifying the city and collecting forces on their behalf. I imagine that you will struggle to take what is yours, especially if you don't have the support of your soldiers."

"So?"

"So declare yourself avenger of Caesar and ally of Octavian, the only one who has proclaimed this without hesitation, and you will gain the collaboration and perhaps also the respect of the legionaries. You're shrewd enough to realise that without their enthusiastic contribution in what could turn into a civil war you'll soon be done for." Rufus did not really believe that Dolabella was shrewd, but he needed to flatter him, at least a little.

Silently, the consul reflected. "And it is disinterested advice, this of Octavian?" he asked finally.

"In a way, yes. His primary interest is that Caesar be avenged, and where he cannot go he gladly delegates the task to others."

"Well I don't take orders from some neophyte who has just appeared on the scene!" reacted Dolabella, piqued.

"No, of course not, of course not," Rufus hastened to reassure him. "We have simply suggested dispassionately how to act for the best, if you do not wish to lose your authority over the soldiers. You must know what is happening in Brindisi: the legionaries make no secret of their support for Octavian and their desire to avenge Caesar. And Antony has declared himself a sworn enemy of Octavian, more so than of Caesar's killers, and is now suffering the consequences. Do you want the same difficulties? You must have seen, in recent months, that the soldiers love Octavian more than any other commander. More even than Antony."

"Are you saying that he will turn the soldiery against me if I don't support him?" The consul's face had taken on a troubled look.

Good.

"No, no, of course not! Octavian, of course, has every

interest in you occupying your province at the expense of the murderers of his father, and will do everything in his power to favour that. To this end, he would ask you to accept as a gift a small group of barbarian auxiliaries, who have already been in the service of Caesar. They will be with you to protect you and handle any dirty work that Brutus, Cassius and Trebonius might necessitate. In a nutshell, you stand only to gain from working with us…"

"I should avail myself of a bodyguard loyal to Octavian? You are joking, I hope…"

Rufus changed his tone. Dolabella, if he had understood correctly, was one of those who went in whichever direction the wind blew. "I'd say you have no choice consul. Either you do this or you will find yourself having to quell rebellion among your soldiers. We need you alive, for the moment, so you can be sure that our auxiliaries will protect you. I couldn't say the same of any other bodyguard you might care to choose."

Dolabella looked at him, and his eyes had lost their proud glow of earlier. The threat had taken effect.

Rufus had him in the palm of his hand.

*

Agrippa dumped the hay from the wagon as soon as he had entered the camp of the Martia legion. He was about to tell the others to stack the bundles near the warehouse and to call the unit's crew when his attention was drawn to the crowd that had gathered around the praetorium. He walked over and saw that Mark Antony was haranguing the soldiers; intrigued, he made his way to a position which would allow him to listen to the words of the consul, who was standing on a makeshift grandstand in front of the building.

No one paid any attention to him; the job that Maecenas had procured for him as an obscure supplier of hay for the army offered him an excuse to wander about the camps without being subject to military discipline, distributing propaganda leaflets when necessary. In that way, the Etruscan had offered him the opportunity to continue working for their cause unbeknownst to Octavian. Maecenas was certain that their leader suffered because of the lack of Agrippa and would, sooner or later, forgive him, so he had done everything to keep him with them, at least informally. The young man had accepted, initially with some reluctance but glad in his heart to have an alternative to accepting Fulvia's proposals and joining Antony. And he was also eager to prove to his ex-friend how indispensable his help was.

Agrippa looked at the troops and was surprised to see that they were all listening to Antony's speech in silence, without whispering amongst themselves nor shouting out in approval, as was usually the case during commanders' speeches. He looked more closely: their expressions were grim, or at least puzzled. Apparently, the propaganda was having an excellent effect. Antony, meanwhile, was saying, "Four hundred sestertii are ready for each of you if you follow me to Gaul where, if necessary, we will fight to take the province from the governor that the Senate has now declared illegitimate. Four hundred sestertii! I should content myself with your gratitude for having called you back to Italy, saving you the hardship and risk of the Parthian campaign, and instead I mean even to reward you!"

The consul stopped to study the effect his words had produced, but the reaction was not what he had expected. The cries of the soldiers were music to Agrippa's ears.

"Four hundred sestertii? You old miser!"

"Octavian is offering two thousand! Shame on you!"

"Why do you never speak of avenging Caesar? What kind of man are you?"

Many were actually laughing, while others shouted out jokes of all kinds. Agrippa himself had to struggle hard to suppress his laughter at this embarrassing situation.

The consul was furious. His lictors signalled to the troops to be quiet, but it was a long time before he could speak again.

"This is the effect of the propaganda of that snake Octavian upon my troops! He has undermined the discipline and loyalty which you owe to your commander in chief. But I will not tolerate such an attitude! I want the names of troublemakers! Throw out of your ranks those who have distributed these damn notes!" he shouted almost hysterically, raising his arm and showing one of the papyri that Agrippa had been giving to the soldiers.

Agrippa wasn't worried about being recognized: he had acted through intermediaries, and no one had seen him distributing anything except hay in the legionaries' camp, but he realized that Gaius Chaerea was in danger – some soldiers anxious to ingratiate themselves might reveal that the centurion had been all too tolerant of them circulating. But in any case, it seemed that the legionaries were disinclined to denounce anyone; even those who, in previous days, had most vocally railed against Antony and his inaction towards Caesar's assassins.

"Out with the guilty, I said!" shouted the consul, angrily and repeatedly, but his cries were lost in the clamour of the soldiers. Agrippa thought that this demonstration of his impotence would please Octavian, and regretted that his friend – or at least, the man he hoped was still such – was not present: if ever they made peace, he would describe the scene to him in perfect detail.

After a futile wait, Antony turned his back on the ranks and went striding into the praetorium, followed quickly by the tribunes, while the soldiers remained on the parade ground to talk. Agrippa spotted Gaius Chaerea's centurion's crest. He would have liked to speak to him about how ridiculous Antony had made himself look, but refrained from calling for his attention. Suddenly, he saw excited movement in front of the commander's building. Out came the tribunes, and the *laticlavus* tribune waved his arms to silence the soldiers, this took some time and even then many legionaries continued to speak.

"The consul orders you to deploy yourselves in *centuriae* and cohorts! Now!"

The legionaries looked at one another, but they did not move, awaiting the instructions of their centurions. The tribune repeated the order, and only then did the officers give the order to their respective units, which went to line up behind or alongside one another. When all the soldiers were in position, the tribune spoke again.

"Soldiers! The consul considers your behaviour sedition! You are disobeying your supreme commander, protecting the enemies of the state and undermining the legendary cohesion of a unit of the Roman army! Therefore, he believes that the only way to restore discipline is to implement the punishment of decimation: every tenth soldier and centurion will be put to death."

And while the tribune spoke, his *angusticlavus* colleagues went down the steps and walked along the front row; one of them pulled out a soldier, and the others followed suit, pulling out from the line every tenth man. The shocked legionaries lost their boldness and went silent. There were no more protests from the ranks, only the begging and moaning of some of those who were being dragged away by Antony's bodyguards, who had come to back up the tribunes. Then came the turn of the first centurion, who was simply the one misfortunate enough to be occupying the position closest to the steps.

Agrippa realised with shock that Gaius Chaerea might well be selected, and began to think desperately of a way to get him off the hook.

*

Cicero's house in Arpino, the birthplace of the great orator, was more modest than Quintus Pedius and Lucius Pinarius had expected. A small, rustic domus, unlike the spectacular villas that the senator had built in Campania and elsewhere on Italian soil after making his fortune and becoming one of the most important men in Rome. However, the two cousins of Octavian realised as soon as they entered the vestibule that Cicero had furnished it luxuriously, with fine statues, frescoes and furnishings worthy of the most luxurious residences of Rome.

Not that they cared. They were there for a very specific and extremely sensitive task, and they wanted to prove themselves worthy of the trust that Octavian had placed in them: all their attention was focused upon meeting the man whose support could be crucial to consolidating the precarious position of their cousin, and so they silently followed the slave who led them to the magistrate's *tablinum*, both ignoring their surroundings and running over in their heads the instructions they had received from Octavian while exchanging the odd worried look.

They arrived in Cicero's presence with a certain awe, which the senator's affable welcome did nothing to diminish. Their host, buried among piles of sheets of papyrus and with a scribe beside him, got up from his desk and came over to meet them, shaking their hands and inviting them to sit down.

"My dear fellows," said Cicero, "I am honoured that you would undertake the difficult journey from Rome in such dismal times simply to have a word with this old relic of a republic which no longer exists."

"In fact it was precisely of that we wished to speak to you," said Quintus Pedius. "That is… of the Republic and its problems," he added, realising he had expressed himself badly.

"My dear fellows," Cicero sat down again and shook his head, "we live in difficult times, and after the end of the civil war I thought I had seen it all. But I'm seeing a lot worse now. This is why I prefer to stay on the sidelines, here in the house where I was born, away from the murky machinations that shake Rome."

"But perhaps, if I may," said Pinarius, "precisely because there *is* this state of great confusion and because danger looms over the city, your authority and experience would be of valuable assistance, in the case of you deciding to return to centre stage. Or so, at least, thinks our cousin Octavian, and we cannot but agree."

Quintus Pedius nodded quickly.

"Ah, Octavian… He's a good lad, truly he is, although his popularity among the people and the legions – and his obstinacy in wanting to pursue those who, rightly or wrongly, believed they were acting for the good of Rome – worries me. And then, this need to emulate Caesar… Isn't having Antony as a threat to democracy enough?"

"I assure you, Cicero, that the young man has no intention of emulating Caesar," Pinarius hastened to re-assure him. "He simply wants to enforce the rights which the will provides for him, the people and the soldiers. Of course, Octavian loved Caesar and wants to see his killers judged impartially by a court, not on the wave of emotion and events that followed the Ides of March, but he would never dream of exploiting his popularity to impose his will, nor of going beyond the prerogatives of the magistrates whose task is to apply the law and justice. He fervently hopes that you will believe in his good faith and the fact that, unlike Antony, he cares about the preservation of the Republic."

"Oh, how I wish I could," said the speaker, shaking his head. "I would so desperately like to. Young Octavian is the right person to save the state, I am convinced of it, as long as he does the right thing and follows the advice of those who have more experience. Which, so far, he does not appear to have done. You will admit that he has often behaved impulsively…"

"Octavian was thrown into a very competitive arena, and it is true that he has repeatedly acted impulsively," explained Pedius. "Only now has he realised that he needs someone to suggest the best course of action, and he is convinced that no one in the political landscape is wiser than you, Cicero. And who could blame him? You identified the threat represented by Antony before anyone else."

"Exactly. Precisely because Antony is such a threat, it makes little sense to neutralize the so-called 'liberators', don't you think? With them around, the rogue will not be able to establish the tyranny which he so evidently desires. Which is why I find that Octavian's haste for revenge misplaced at this time."

"This Octavian has understood," said Pedius solemnly. "He knows that Antony is now the real danger to the Republic, and he is willing to put aside his rightful anger over the murder of his father and place his now-considerable resources at the service of anyone who takes action to restore the normal course of the state. He is gathering many soldiers, all faithful to the name of Caesar and so also to his heir, with whom he can counterbalance the excessive power of Antony and march on Rome to convince the consul to take a different line."

"March on Rome? Like Silla? Never!" exclaimed a scandalized Cicero, looking almost as though he was about to rise from his chair. "I realize that, in his situation, he must necessarily create a private army – the precedents are so numerous that it would be tedious to list them and ridiculous to insist that he cease. But I think he should only threaten to mobilise them, and not actually go through with it. It is a practice which I abhor, but now, with Antony in possession of the Macedonian legions and the Gallic governorate, we need someone else in Italy who the consul fears, and I realize that Octavian is the only one with an influence equal to – if not greater than – that of Antony on the soldiers. But I would prefer that he did not act and that he came to Rome alone. Antony must be defeated legally, and I am preparing a series of speeches which, I assure you, will remove the ground from under his feet. After I have read them in the Senate, I doubt any of the patricians will still be willing to support him."

Pedius and Pinarius looked at one another and nodded, and the first spoke. "Octavian waits only for your advice. If this is what you propose, we can be sure that is the best for the Republic. We will immediately inform our cousin of your suggestions and, I am sure, he will act accordingly, so that you can return to the city in safety to work for the good of the state as you always have. Rome needs you, to curb the ambitions of Antony and prevent civil war from breaking out," he concluded, noting Cicero's smug expression.

Pinarius allowed himself a smile. Octavian was right: tickling the orator's vanity was the most direct route to obtaining his support.

*

Octavia watched Etain rock her daughter Marcella. The freedwoman's face still showed signs of the violence she had suffered, both in her features – still beautiful despite the swellings and bruises – and in her embittered, hardened expression. The gentleness that had previously inhabited her eyes and her movements had gone, and she wondered if this change had been brought about by the rape or was also due to the sentimental disappointment she had suffered at Agrippa's hands.

She would have liked to go to her and ask her how she felt, to try and explain to her that perhaps Agrippa had really loved her and had only behaved in that despicable way to serve the interests of the sect, but she was far from certain that the young man hadn't actually been enjoying himself with Fulvia, so she preferred to remain silent. She forced herself instead to eavesdrop on the talk of the other matrons who were bathing with her in the tepidarium of the baths. She had a job to do, and she intended to do it properly, in order to prove to her brother and the others that she was worthy of belonging to the cult of Mars Ultor. She was anxious to prove herself to those who were skeptical that a woman could be effective. Maecenas had voiced the proposal as a challenge, and she had agreed enthusiastically: she was to persuade the other women to plead Octavian's cause with their husbands, who for the most part were still wary of the young man, and to this end, she had invited the wives of some of the most eminent members of the equestrian class to the baths with her, renting the entire building exclusively for them, and had hired a bevy of masseurs, jugglers and cooks to ensure that they spent an especially pleasant time there.

Maecenas had explained to her that it was to the equestrian class rather than the senate that they must look to find support, converts and lenders. The senators were a gerontocracy, all hand in glove with one another and stubbornly hostile to newcomers and, in general, to anything new. They were conservative and narrow-minded, and Octavian would struggle to win them over before obtaining power. They were the type of people who could adulate one greater than them but never one who was lesser, however talented he might be. Conversely, the equestrian class was seeking authoritative representatives to safeguard their interests and elevate them to the same rank as the senators: many equestrians, including Maecenas himself, could now boast of assets and wealth equal – if not superior – to that of many senators, and wished to command the same influence as they did. Well, Octavian would be their champion, in the Etruscan's plan, and thanks to them and their money he would change Rome.

But first, Octavia had to convince them that her brother was the right person in whom to invest their money and their hopes of social and political ascendency.

And it was up to her to do it.

"You know, Cecilia, I'm very grateful to you for coming. I know that your husband was not fond of Caesar, and I was afraid you might be a bit wary of his family."

She was addressing the wife of Titus Pomponius Atticus, an important and wealthy member of the equestrian class and friend of Cicero, who Octavian felt it would be wise to bring over to his side. The woman, much older than she, was breast deep in the tub with her elbows on the ledge, enjoying the warmth of the water while a masseur worked on her neck and shoulders. A slave, meanwhile, had set in front of her a tray of fresh fruit, from which she took some grapes. Octavia looked around and saw that almost all the other matrons were equally at ease: as she had ordered, each was being attended by dedicated members of staff.

"Oh, my dear Octavia, Caesar never actually punished my husband for joining Pompey's party. Indeed, he was always very kind to him. He even pardoned two of his nephews who had fought at Pharsalus. So of course we hold no rancour towards you…"

"I'm so glad, my dear," said Octavia crouching beside her. "Because I would very much like us to be friends: my brother constantly seeks the consent and approval of Cicero, and everyone knows that the illustrious speaker is your husband's closest friend. Octavian has so many good intentions, but he needs wise friends and experts to implement them. And their support. My brother is convinced that the equestrians are the future of Rome: new men, open-minded, not conditioned by the antiquated ideas that keep the senators anchored in social and political stagnation which is detrimental to Rome and the Romans. If and when Octavian has some political weight in the city, it will be to the equestrians that he will entrust the economy and services, in his belief that they are the only ones with a real interest in the renewal and growth of common resources."

"In some ways you're right, my dear. My husband always complains that our class has little political representation. Something should be done – it cannot always be the aristocracy who command: they have nothing more than us, except their names. I live like the wife of a senator, if not better, and I concede myself even more luxuries."

"Well, talk with your husband, then. Octavian has clear ideas, and anyone willing to provide the means to assist him will see a thousand fold return on their investment in the future."

"I certainly will, my dear," replied the woman. "I've had quite enough of electing people who do not represent us!"

Octavia squeezed her shoulder in gratitude, then broke away from her and headed for another matron, ready to make the same speech to her. It would be a long day, much more demanding than the quiet, reserved ones she was used to, but she felt more and more alive, and had no intention of giving up her role. If only, at the end of the day, she was able to go and see little Marcus and sink into the arms of Gaius Chaerea then she would be truly happy…

*

Chaos reigned among the ranks of legionaries of the Martia. The news of the decimation had been completely unexpected, and the soldiers were too dazed and confused to react in any other way than with despair. Antony's bodyguards removed the soldiers chosen by the tribunes. Their closest comrades made some attempts to stop them, but they were shoved and forced back by the swords of the executioners. Meanwhile, the assistants had taken the first two soldiers onto the stage and made them kneel.

Agrippa had to get Gaius Chaerea, who he saw standing motionless at the head of his men, out of danger, but the urgency confused his ideas and prevented him from thinking clearly.

The *laticlavius* tribune called for the troop's attention. "This is what happens to those who undermine the authority of the magistrates of Rome and the efficiency of the most powerful army in the world." At his signal, the guards raised high their swords and then swung them down upon the necks of their victims. Two heads rolled onto the stage and down the stairs, leaving behind them vermilion trails.

"You still have time to denounce the seditionaries and troublemakers!" said the tribune. "Push them out of your ranks yourselves, and the decimation will stop immediately!"

No one seemed willing to do so, however. Agrippa was not surprised: the legion was united in its disapproval of Antony, and for this reason the consul was compelled to execute the soldiers chosen by auxiliaries without entrusting the executions to the troops themselves, as was the custom in those rare cases where the practice was applied. Usually, in fact, the convicted soldiers were forced to walk between two rows of their fellows, who clubbed them to death. But in this case, their comrades would not have lifted a finger against them.

Meanwhile, Antony's guards, along with the tribunes, were penetrating deeper into the lines and approaching the unit of Gaius Chaerea. Agrippa realised he had to act quickly if he wanted to avoid witnessing the execution of one of the followers of the sect.

Suddenly, he had an idea. Looking around him, he saw that the attention of the entire camp was focused on the decimation. He told his colleagues on the cart that he had smelled something that he did not like and moved cautiously toward the edge of the camp, reaching the storeroom and finding no sentries. The hay was still partly piled alongside the building: the event in front of the praetorium had brought even the storeroom workers to the parade ground. Near the warehouse, as in many other places in the camp, there was a brazier: it was late autumn and the soldiers and servants were accustomed to rekindling the fire to warm themselves during their evening and night shifts. He took some kindling and held it in the flames until it caught fire, then threw it onto the bundles of hay.

He watched for a moment as the fire took hold, and then, when he was satisfied with its intensity, ran back to the parade ground. When he reached it, he saw that Antony's guards had arrived in front of Chaerea's unit and had selected the first soldier: Gaius had a one in six chance of being chosen from among the centurions of his cohort.

Fortunately, he was standing outside the lines, and within earshot. Agrippa ran over feigning breathlessness. "Centurion! There's a fire by the storeroom! You have to put it out!"

Gaius looked disoriented. One of the auxiliaries pushed Agrippa away, saying, "Get lost, you!" and looked at Chaerea, undecided as to whether or not to choose him as his third victim.

"But the store of hay is on fire!" insisted Agrippa. "It could spread to the whole camp!"

This time it was the guard who looked confused, not knowing what to do, and in that moment the wind brought to them a whiff of smoke, which seemed to convince him. "All right, centurion, take ten men and go and put out the fire immediately!" he shouted.

Chaerea didn't need to be told twice: he called to him in quick succession ten of the closest soldiers and ran with them to the water tank, which was not far from the warehouse. Agrippa followed more slowly, calling to his fellows on the cart. When he reached the centurion, he and his men had formed a chain and were passing each other buckets of water with extraordinary precision.

Gaius noticed and approached him until he was close enough to whisper, "Thank you. Octavian will know what you did for me."

Agrippa looked at him for a moment.

"No. Not Octavian," he said flatly. "Tell Maecenas, if you

feel like it – he can pass it on, if he sees fit."

XIII

Octavia felt proud of her brother. As soon as she heard about his return to Rome, she rushed to meet him and give him the welcome befitting a relative who she had had no news of since his departure a few weeks earlier and who now appeared outside the walls with an army of ten thousand men like the great generals of the past. And he was only twenty years old. The real reason for her haste, however, was that she wanted to see him right away, so as not to be excluded from the meeting of the sect that Octavian, presumably, would be convening as soon as he entered the city. He and the others often did not consider it necessary for a woman to be present at the strategic meetings, and merely passed on to her decisions already taken.

But that was not what she had hoped for when she had decided to join the group. No, she had wanted to take part in the decision making – to have her say and influence events. She was certain she was more useful to the cause than either Lucius Pinarius or Quintus Pedius, both of whom she considered her inferiors. If only Octavian and Maecenas, the real brains of the group, had been given the opportunity—

Now, though, she had time only to greet her brother before he ascended the steps of the Temple of Castor at the edge of the Forum, and began to address the crowd. There had been negotiations before he came into town. Until Caesar, only Silla had dared enter the city's walls with armed soldiers, and the Romans feared that Octavian wanted to do the same. He did not intend to give the impression of violating the laws of the State, though: he needed to retain Cicero's trust and not completely lose the sympathies of the Senate, and so he therefore left the soldiers fifteen stadions from the walls, entering with only a hundred men, who now surrounded the temple area from whence he would speak to the people.

Veterans from Campania, whose only weapons seemed to be their grim faces, they had been lured by the clinking of gold to carry out the task of guarding their new commander. But in fact, as Pinarius had quickly told Octavia after a conversation with her brother, these men had daggers concealed under their tunics and were ready to face any eventuality. The mood of civil war was already in the air, and it was better to remain vigilant, he told his cousin.

Civil War... Octavia shuddered. They had created a cult to continue the work of Caesar in Rome and restore the peace that had enabled him, in times past, to build an empire, and now they were deliberately provoking a conflict. But she realised things needed making right – a conflict was already brewing between Mark Antony and Decimus Brutus in Gaul, and they were simply entering the battle. Without taking the side of one or the other, though.

She gave voice to her thoughts to Maecenas. She still couldn't understand why Octavian had made such a risky move.

"My dear Octavia, we do not want civil war," explained the Etruscan with the patronising tone of someone giving a lesson to a child. "Or at least, we do not want one with Mark Antony. We hope, rather, that he will realise he cannot fight on two fronts and so join with us against the murderers of Caesar, starting with Decimus Brutus. We need the consul, and if good manners will not convince him to join us, we will have to do it the hard way. We have an army now, so he must come to some agreement with your brother in order that revenge may finally be had. The more we scare Mark Antony, the more likely we are to be able to convince him to go along with our plans."

As though in confirmation of Maecenas's words, Octavian's voice increased in volume. "What would you do in my place, Romans?" he cried rhetorically to the crowd that had gathered at his feet. "Would you watch your father's killers running around the province, undisturbed by those who should punish them, chasing their own dreams of glory and doing nothing for the good of the state? Would you not do everything possible to obtain justice, and would you not try to force those who should take responsibility to fulfil their duties? Mark Antony is not only the chief magistrate of the Republic, he is also a relative of mine and of my father's, and was Caesar's most important lieutenant. Yet he has done nothing so far to punish those who so vilely assassinated the dictator. What is this? Cowardice or indifference? Because it must be one or the other! I can think of nothing else that might cause him to neglect a task that should have been his principal priority! If he now goes to Gaul to face Decimus Brutus, it is not out of a sense of justice, but for personal glory! He wants to hold all Rome in a vice, because for him, being a consul or proconsul of a province as important as Macedonia is not enough. No – he wants it all! He wants to be the ruler of Rome, and her tyrant, and he wants to frighten you into giving him what he craves. I am warning you, he has many legions and he will certainly not leave them outside the city, as I did, when his march brings him here. He will come with armed men, as did Sulla! No one should feel safe!"

Octavia looked at Maecenas. She was shocked by Octavian's vehemence, and wondered if perhaps her brother was going too far. It was true that they were learning how in politics you could speak evil of someone one day and then walk hand in hand with them the next, but in this way he risked an irreparable fracture. The Etruscan noticed her worried expression and smiled. "Don't worry," he said. "We have to make Mark Antony look like the aggressor in order to isolate him further – soon it will be even worse, I can assure you, and he will have no choice but to seek our support."

"What do you mean?" replied Octavia, annoyed at not having been informed of their plans.

"Wait and see," was Maecenas's cryptic reply, as he turned back to watch Octavian's speech.

The matron grimaced, deciding she needed to speak to her brother as soon as possible. She found it intolerable that she was considered of a lower rank simply because she was a woman. It was true that she had not done as much as Maecenas for the sect, but did not see, for example, why Salvidienus Rufus should know more than her. She had more influence in Roman high society than the tribune and was able to provide more valuable assistance to the sect than he was.

Soon she would show them, one way or another.

Etain only half followed Octavian's speech. Her mind was filled with a kaleidoscope of images that she had trouble holding back, although she wished with all her soul that she could remove them once and for all. She was assaulted by memories of the violence, the pain inflicted in that dark storeroom, the fetid breath of her attackers and their feral expressions, and felt again the disgust whenever their bodies came into connect with hers and the humiliation suffered at being an object in their hands. A waking nightmare that continued to haunt her – and her fear was that it would always remain with her. There had been no rest from that fateful day. In between one flashback and another, the memory of Agrippa crept into her mind, but not of their tender and intense meetings, which were all but lost in the fog of memory, but the spectre of his intimacy with Fulvia. She punished herself with imaginary frescoes of sexual relations between a man who told her he loved her deeply and Mark Antony's wife, and her stomach clenched in despair and disgust. She had begun her relationship with Agrippa with few illusions, as he was destined for greatness and soon would turn his attention to another – one who would be of more use to him and more suited to his social rank. But then she had been overwhelmed by his passion and persuaded by his words, and begun to believe that the relationship between them could last. The fact that they both belonged to the sect too had helped convince her that their relationship would be further strengthened over time, and that they would become something much more than lovers.

By the gods, she had felt like his woman then, and he had seemed to treat her as though she was! But instead, Agrippa continued to have his way with others. Who knew how many he had enjoyed while whispering words of love and pretending to be lost in her eyes... Or maybe he had lost his head over Fulvia, who was quite capable of getting anyone she wanted. And with Fulvia, thought Etain, she could not compete at all. Mark Antony's wife was not only one of the most beautiful and desired women of Rome, but belonged to a class to which Agrippa undoubtedly aspired. Etain felt that she could almost have understood him, if she hadn't been so angry about the betrayal and the lies that he had served up. She was glad that Octavian had expelled him from the sect, and didn't care that the reason was probably the revenge that Agrippa had taken upon her assailants. Though the idea of never seeing him again was genuinely painful, she was sure that with time she would learn to control her torment over her lost love as well as her feelings. Never again would she fall for a man's sweet words. Indeed, perhaps she would never let herself be touched again. The idea of a man's hand – any man's hand – caressing her made her feel sick.

"I heard what happened to you, and I am immensely sorry. Is there anything I can do for you?" A whisper tore her away from her thoughts. She turned and met the eyes of Salvidienus Rufus.

Another one who just wanted to have some fun with her, no doubt.

"I am trying to forget about it. Thank you for your interest, Rufus," she replied coldly.

He was not to be put off, however. "You didn't answer my question. Is there anything I can do for you?"

"You might leave me in peace," thought Etain, and was on the verge of opening her mouth and telling him so. But she restrained herself – after all, Rufus had done her no wrong. "For the moment I just want peace and tranquillity," she said candidly, hoping that he would take the hint to leave her alone.

But Rufus did not. "That is not really the aim of we of the sect of Mars Ultor – especially now," he said with a slight smile. "We might be on the brink of a civil war."

"What I want is inner peace. I know that what lies ahead is something else. We vowed to fight to the bitter end, until justice and peace have been brought to Rome," she replied flatly, emphasising the primary goals of the sect.

"Not necessarily," said Rufus. "If things go as we hope they will, we might limit the damage and prevent events from degenerating."

"Why? How should things go? Mark Antony seems determined to take everything for himself, and I see no other way of stopping the war."

"One way or another, you'll see that Mark Antony will calm down and you will find the peace of mind you deserve, and I hope I can help with one and the other," he said, with a smile full of tenderness.

"Doubtless a lie," thought Etain. Just like Agrippa's untruths.

In any case, it was clear that Rufus would not tell her what the leaders of the sect had in mind, and it made sense: she was a former slave, and furthermore a woman. Just manpower and nothing more, like those Germans Octavian had decided to engage.

"In all sincerity, I don't see how you could help me, Rufus," she replied.

"For example, I could keep you company once in a while, if you would allow me."

"I... I don't feel like being with anyone now."

"I understand that," he insisted, trying to sound reassuring. "After what you have been through I cannot blame you, and I suppose you're hurt at finding out about the relationship between Agrippa and Fulvia, too. But don't be afraid, I just want to talk to you. You are good company, and it would do me good to spend some time with you. The sound of your voice is so melodious, I feel soothed when you speak."

Etain felt touched by his words, but then remembered that she must not be seduced by the talk of a man. No doubt it was one of Rufus's tricks to get her into bed sooner or later, and she had absolutely no intention of allowing that to happen. However, if Agrippa were to learn that she was seeing his friend and rival, he might feel, if not regret, at least *annoyance*. It would give her a small shred of satisfaction, and would prove that she was not just a naïve little girl who hung on his every word.

"I'd like that," she said eventually, and the words came out so easily.

Rufus smiled and they both returned their attention to Octavian, who was sitting just above their heads, on the steps of the Temple of Castor and Pollux. But Etain saw that the atmosphere had changed. The young man was no longer speaking, and Maecenas was beside him. The two chatted animatedly. The soldiers Octavian had brought with him seemed agitated and someone had pulled out a dagger. Below, the crowd was becoming restless. Rufus left her and went up the steps to the podium of the temple.

She turned to the crowd to hear what they were shouting.

"We don't want war! Not on the streets of the city!" shouted a woman with a baby in her arms.

"I lived through the battles between Silla's army and Marius's supporters!" said an old man, "and I've no intention of seeing that kind of sacrilege in the city again."

"Antony has many legions! He could massacre anyone who dared to resist him! Just as Marius did when *he* returned to power."

"Mark Antony is a great general and he is also a consul! We

shouldn't have resisted! We should have sought reconciliation, not fought him." Etain noticed that these words were shouted by one of the veterans that Octavian had brought to the city as a bodyguard and now his own soldiers were shouting out their approval.

"I thought we were here to make peace, not to fight him. I will not fight against my old commander!" another soldier shouted.

Etain saw Octavia climb the stairs and talk to her brother then come back down soon afterwards and walk towards her as the crowd began to disperse, those who remained invoking peace.

The matron grabbed her arm and pulled her towards the litter that awaited them a short walk away, past the temple area. "We must leave," Octavia told her, as they walked briskly, "Mark Antony is coming with his troops. There is a risk of war in the city."

"What will we do?" She asked, getting up on the litter.

"We will do nothing. We will stay at home, just as Octavian orders. He will take shelter in Arezzo in the properties of Maecenas. Him and that Etruscan don't seem to be too worried. They are so reckless. Mark Antony now has immense power and could make them pay for opposing him. No one will be able to stop him, whatever laws he chooses to break! I knew it, we have bitten off more than we can chew… And if Mark Antony is heading to Gaul, there's no point in Octavian fleeing northwards. The consul will catch up with him…"

"Not to mention that it would look as though he was trying to escape. That would not make a good impression on the people," said Etain, as the bearers made their way through the stream of people returning to their homes.

"As far as I can gather from Maecenas, they hope, instead, that Octavian will be seen as a peacemaker and Mark Antony as a warmonger. The people are on our side, and especially now we need the support of the Senate. And we can get it only by showing we are the only real obstacle to the ambitions of the consul. In short, it's a risk we have to take."

Etain did not answer. She watched the frightened people running this way and that, troubled expressions on their faces. Some looked desperate and she wondered what good the support of the people and the Senate would be against a seasoned warrior with many legions at his command. Not even Pompey the Great himself had any luck against Caesar… and Pompey was a skilled commander. Octavian was little more than a boy, and a sickly one at that, and the only real military talent the sect once had was no longer with them…

*

"What are you doing?"

The optio waved his long stick under Agrippa's nose. He had just delivered new notes sent by Maecenas to the storekeepers, along with bundles of hay for the cavalry of the Martia legion. The young man looked guilty and frightened, and tried to climb up onto the wagon, but the sergeant ordered the storekeepers to stop him, and the two men grabbed him by the arms, pulling him down before he could reach the box.

"Let's see… what does it say here?" muttered the optio scrutinizing the small piece of papyrus. "Listen to this… 'Soldiers! Mark Antony is a leader unworthy of a Roman legionary. He will inflict decimation on you, he will neglect you, he will give you little more than symbolic rewards and he will make you fight against your fellow citizens. Do not make yourselves accomplices to his crimes. A criminal who, moreover, with every act he carries out insults the memory of your beloved leader Julius Caesar by refusing to avenge him'."

The optio contemptuously threw down the paper, walked over towards Agrippa and hit him with his stick. The metal ball on the end hit him in the stomach, winding him and knocking him off-balance. He doubled over and only managed to stay upright because the two storekeepers held him up.

"So it's you spreading sedition, eh?" The officer grabbed his hair and pulled his head back. "Who's paying you, little man? It's that boy Octavian, isn't it?"

Agrippa looked up, and opened his mouth only to spit on him. He received another blow from the stick, this time to the sternum.

"I asked you a question," insisted the optio, wiping the saliva from his face. "Who's paying you?"

He glared at Agrippa, banging the top of his stick into his palm as he did so.

"I... I do it on my own account..." murmured Agrippa. "I don't like Mark Antony."

The optio hit him again in the same place as before, which was still aching from the previous blow. Agrippa had never experienced anything like this in his life.

"Well, let's assume that your paymaster is Octavian," said the optio. "I want to know who your cronies are. You've been passing around plenty of these notes these last few weeks, first in Brindisi and then along the Via Appia. Apparently, we should have been looking among the grooms. This hay is poisoned," he quipped.

He waited, rolling the fearsome ball across Agrippa's face, from forehead to chin. But the young man knew that no one would touch his face – an optio was not allowed to mark the face of a Roman citizen, nor even to torture him. He was striking blows to his body so as not leave any visible signs, hoping to milk some information from him in order to make himself look good in front of his superiors.

His silence was answered with another blow, further down, this time, on his thigh. Agrippa took another two blows to the stomach before the optio decided that he was too tough to give in. "Well," said his captor disappointedly, "the tribune will decide to punish you as you deserve to be punished," he concluded, taking hold of him.

Agrippa could barely stand, and the two storekeepers had to help the optio support him as they led him out of the building. Once over the threshold, the optio called for two soldiers to come and help, and Agrippa was dragged in front of the praetorium, where the most senior officer of the legion lived. Along with the Martia, they had set up temporary camp near Ortona, in Sannio, having left the other three legions in Brindisi. The consul had sent them to Rimini while he had headed for Rome along the Via Appia, and the young man had never once stopped distributing the notes criticising Mark Antony to the troops. But now that he had reached the city, he had to do much more, and was trying his hardest to do so.

The optio sent for the tribune, who a few moments later came out of the building. He was one of those who had taken the place of the officers who had tolerated the sedition in Brindisi, and Agrippa had no doubt he was on the side of the consul. The tribune confabulated with the optio, then eyed the prisoner. "He has no intention of talking?" he asked his subordinate.

"I would say not. Even though I asked him so politely" said the optio.

"He is of no use to us, then. The consul ordered the death of anyone caught spreading sedition. See that he is executed immediately. You do it, optio. At my signal."

Agrippa felt the blood freeze in his veins. Everything was happening too quickly. In confirmation, the sergeant ordered the two soldiers holding the prisoner to make him kneel, then he laid the stick down and took out his sword. Meanwhile, the tribune climbed the steps of the praetorium, called the *cornicen* and ordered him to sound his horn. Agrippa was forced to wait on his knees, his head bowed. Around him, he felt the dust lifted by the steps of tens, then hundreds and finally thousands of studded boots.

"Soldiers!" cried the tribune. "We have discovered one of the grooms in *flagrante delicto* distributing propaganda leaflets against our commander in chief, and as the consul has ordered, he will now be executed so that each one of you can see how discipline is kept."

The tribune was silent. So were the troops. Agrippa shivered. No voice was raised in protest, no breath issued forth in his favour, and at any moment the optio's sword would fall on his neck.

"Gaius Chaerea, what are you waiting for?" Agrippa asked himself.

*

"He has come!" Quintus Pedius ran into the triclinium of Claudius Marcellus and Octavia's house with such enthusiasm that he overtook the caretaker who was coming to announce his visit. "Mark Antony is here, and he has come with an entire cohort in arms."

Octavia was playing with her daughter, who was sitting astride a wooden horse. Her husband, attracted from the *tablinum* by the commotion, also appeared in the doorway of the room. Octavia made a gesture of annoyance – with Marcello there, she couldn't speak freely to her cousin of what

Mark Antony's arrival meant for the sect, of whose existence her husband was unaware.

"Finally, someone who can sort out this mess!" said Marcello immediately, confirming once again that she had done well not to involve him.

"Do you not understand that if Mark Antony is in town with his soldiers," she said, "it is not to bring order but to frighten the people and the Senate?"

"It doesn't matter," shrugged Marcello. "If everyone is afraid, things will be calmer and everyone will do what he was elected or paid to do."

Quintus Pedius sat on a triclinium, even though no one had invited him to do so. Octavia immediately indicated to Etain to bring fruit from the kitchen for the guest. "In reality," said her cousin, speaking directly to the lady of the house, "it is not only one cohort – the consul has made camp a few miles from the city on the Appian Way, leaving there a cavalry garrison and the other nine cohorts of the Legion that he has brought with him. Meanwhile, the other Macedonian legions are moving up the Adriatic coast, theoretically heading for Rimini, to be used against Decimus Brutus."

"So if necessary, they could be diverted to the west and find themselves on the outskirts of Rome…"

"Why theoretically?" asked Octavia.

"Because this way they are on hand, and if necessary might detour westwards and, quite by chance, find themselves near Rome"

"So it's not certain that Mark Antony's first objective is Gaul," said Octavia.

"No, not certain at all," explained Pedius. "Although Mark Antony did approve a law at the time prohibiting the establishment of a dictator, he could now repeal it by force and decide he was no longer content being consul and proconsul of Gaul."

Octavia was sure that this would be the rumour spread by the sect. If what Maecenas had hinted at was true, the goal of Octavian, before leaving for Arezzo, was precisely that of painting Mark Antony as a potential tyrant, and indeed the consul himself seemed to be doing everything in his power to encourage the idea. It would not be difficult to make the people and the Senate believe it. But in the meantime, without enough troops to oppose him, the opinion of the people mattered little in the face of his military force.

Marcellus was unimpressed: "The more soldiers Mark Antony has, the more chance he has of averting a coup by one of the many hotheads running around the city. It seems to me that everyone here feels as though he is a Caesar." Octavia sighed: Marcello's comments always seemed to her to be insufferably dull.

Quintus Pedius bridled. "But he came into the city as if in triumph!" he said. "He came through the Appian Gate in a chariot drawn by four white horses wearing a robe covered with gold stars and a laurel wreath. Only the wagon with the booty was missing, because it was obvious that he intends to get his booty in Rome. Just think, he is heading now to the Gardens of Pompey where he lives, and he has the place surrounded by soldiers, who give passwords as though they were defending a camp – and since it is clear that he is on no campaign, it is obvious that he is celebrating his triumph over we Romans! The insolence of the man!"

"He is probably already taking his victory over Decimus Brutus in Gaul for granted," suggested Octavia.

"Or he will show that Octavian fled before confronting him and will celebrate a kind of victory over him," said Pedius. "I know that the Senate has convened for tomorrow, and is it said that they want to denounce your brother. I am seriously concerned. With all those soldiers putting pressure on the senators, they'll be able to get whatever they want from them…"

"Even getting Octavian declared a public enemy", thought the matron, feeling a shiver run down her spine.

*

"He who speaks the truth shouldn't be executed!"

The shout came from the crowd of soldiers deployed around the praetorium. Agrippa waited a few moments before breathing a sigh of relief. But much still needed to happen in order for their plan to work and above all, for him to survive.

But with the optio's sword hanging just above his head, it was more likely that the blade would hit his neck before the plan took shape.

"No more killing! That's not how a commander wins the esteem of his soldiers." Another isolated voice of protest. Too isolated. It must be one of those in the pay of Gaius Chaerea. Agrippa realised he had broken out in a cold sweat.

"Free him! He has only spoken the truth!"

"Mark Antony only thinks of himself!"

"He does not think of his soldiers!"

"Who will avenge Caesar, instead of thinking always of power?"

"Who will really pay the soldiers, instead of giving them alms?"

"Octavian is someone who pays – and his priority is avenging Caesar, not scheming for his own ends!"

"Yes, Octavian is better! He is Caesar's heir! He is his son, and the only one who cares about the welfare of the soldiers!"

Agrippa relaxed for a moment, as much as one who was expecting his head to be struck off at any moment could relax. This time, he thought, there were many different voices, not just the soldiers paid to incite sedition. He dared to raise his head and saw the officer above looking around himself in bewilderment. Then he moved his eyes to the soldiers. Most were looking menacingly at the optio and the tribune who, for his part, had taken a few steps backwards onto the steps of the praetorium, ready to cross the threshold and take refuge inside the building.

Good, the commander was no hero.

Agrippa saw unrest in the crowd. The crest of a centurion stirred between two soldiers and his vine staff hovered in the air. "Silence!" cried the officer as he bludgeoned the two legionaries. "Here we do what the commander tells us to do! This is a Roman legion, not some barbarian horde."

At the sight of the scene, the tribune became more courageous: "What are you waiting for? Execute the sentence!" he shouted to the optio, whose sword still hung in mid-air. The officer hesitated, as more soldiers took up the cries of praise for Octavian and insults against Mark Antony. Some advanced, and the optio moved away from Agrippa. He looked at the advancing legionaries, then the tribune, and remained immobile. Agrippa hoped that he was afraid of being lynched if he obeyed the commander.

But a few centurions emerged from the ranks and began

facing down the advancing soldiers. They began swinging their sticks through the air and forcing them back. There were insults and cries of 'lackeys!', but overall they seemed to be restoring a semblance of order.

Things looked bad again, thought Agrippa, especially now as the tribune, backed by the other officers, walked down the stairs. Annoyed at the optio's indecision, the commander snatched his sword from him.

"You're a coward, optio! I will take this matter further, be sure of that!" he shouted hysterically. "Mark Antony has no use for officers who are unable to maintain order in the legion."

Agrippa knew that he was lost. Above him he heard the tribune panting in agitation – the officer was not as confident as he was attempting to appear, and, like his subordinate, he feared the reaction of the troops. But he had to go through with it – if he pulled back now, he would lose all authority.

The soldiers continued to shout, and the centurions to inflict beatings. Agrippa waited for the blow that never came. He lifted his head and saw a single figure grab a vine staff from a centurion and snatch it out of his hand. The officer froze and had no time to avoid the blow to his helmet, which made him stagger and fall to the ground. Another centurion rushed towards the rebel with his sword unsheathed and pointed it at his throat, forcing him to drop the stick.

But in the meantime some space had opened up and other soldiers advanced, seizing stones and threatening to hurl them at the tribune.

The commander stepped back, distancing himself from Agrippa. "Now," the young man said to himself. "It's now or never." If the officers stayed together they could still recover the situation.

"Soldiers! Optiones! Centurions! We no longer have to obey Mark Antony! We have been and always will be soldiers of Caesar, and we cannot serve under the command of a man who does not take revenge!"

A centurion was climbing the steps of the praetorium.

Gaius Chaerea – finally!

Shouts of approval greeted his words, as well as voices of dissent and calls to order from his colleagues.

"He wants to take you to fight against Decimus Brutus in Gaul – not to avenge his former commander but to satisfy his own lust for personal power! We'll be sent to the slaughter, all of us. He would happily sacrifice us for his own ends! He attacks Decimus Brutus but he has not declared the murderers of your oldest and most glorious commander public enemies. The commander who made you proud to be soldiers of Rome, just as Mark Antony now makes you feel ashamed of it."

Some centurions raised their fists in approval, and immediately several optiones followed suit. Others accused them of treason and unsheathed their swords, but thought twice about using them – they had the soldiers, who were rallying against Mark Antony in growing numbers, to deal with.

Chaerea continued, and, though the tribune was still nearby, it was music to Agrippa's ears. "Octavian will pay anyone who intends to follow Caesar and put himself at the orders of his successor well. He will allow us to fight in campaigns that make us proud of our role as Roman soldiers, in battles for the glory of Rome, and not simply for somebody's personal advantage. Just as Caesar would have done! Caesar, who conquered for us the greatest empire on Earth, that of the Parti, following in the footsteps of Alexander the Great! Octavian does not want to lead us into civil war, but wants to make us participants, building an empire with clear, secure boundaries. What would you like to tell your children one day? That you killed a friend or even a relative in a fratricidal war, or that you went to the four corners of the earth, braving courageous and powerful enemies, to bring them the civilization of Rome?"

A chorus of cheers followed his words. Many were shouting the praises of Octavian, and no longer only the ones who had been paid to do so. Some of the more stubborn centurions had been disarmed and rendered harmless. The officer was shouting in an attempt to quell the insurrection, but when the first stone hit his breastplate he retreated back to the doorway.

"I say we imprison Mark Antony's toadies and send them back to him with our greetings," continued Chaerea. "I propose that from this moment on, the Martia should once again become the legion of Caesar. Let us give ourselves to his son and then march to Arezzo where Octavian will be waiting for us with cold, hard cash and sufficient reasons to recover our honour as soldiers."

Shouts of jubilation sanctioned the definitive shift in allegiance of the camp, and dissenting voices were silenced.

Agrippa finally let out a sigh of relief and, as neither the optio, nor the tribune were any longer near him, got to his feet.

He found himself standing beside Gaius Chaerea, who was looking at him with a mocking expression. He stared back disdainfully. "You took your time," he hissed.

The centurion smiled. "The situation was under control. I didn't take my eyes off the optio's blade for a moment. If I had intervened sooner, the other centurions would have stopped me. We had to stir up more discontent – wasn't that what we'd decided?" he replied, looking immediately over his shoulder and moving off towards the entrance of the praetorium to stop the tribune.

Agrippa wondered if, now that he was out of the sect, he were expendable. Who knew what Maecenas's real orders were? Maybe they had actually planned his sacrifice…

*

Lucius Pinarius saw Quintus Pedius among the crowd of senators hovering around the entrance to the Curia. He kept his colleagues at a distance, ignoring some and greeting others cordially, but he saw on most faces the same preoccupation which was probably etched upon his own – the convocation of the Senate that Mark Antony had requested immediately upon entering the city was not a good sign. Just as the presence of armed soldiers around the Forum was not a good sign. It seemed that Mark Antony wanted to wave martial law in the faces of the senators.

His law.

Pinarius heard the words of the other senators as he passed between them, trying not to engage with those who sought to catch his eye. They were all afraid that Mark Antony would impose a dictatorship and entrust all the key roles of the institutions to his own men. On the other hand, his brothers already had sufficient power at hand to determine the course of Roman politics. There were some who still remembered that when Mark Antony had attempted to put the royal crown on Caesar's head at the Lupercalia, the dictator had refused, with possibly false disdain. Well, it now seemed that the same crown was the goal of the consul.

"Do you hear them?" he said to his cousin when he managed to reach him. "They all have the names of the assassins on their lips…"

"Yes," agreed Pinarius. "They are all convinced that Brutus and Cassius and the rest are the only ones opposing Mark Antony. Nobody even considers Octavian."

"That's all we need. Now they will do anything that Mark Antony orders for as long as the consul is present, and then once he is in Gaul fighting Decimus Brutus – because Decimus Brutus will resist, there is no doubt of that – they will gang up against him in support of the deposed governor and his cronies in the East and in Africa. We are on the brink of a civil war of immense proportions, and we have not yet found our role in the conflict which looms," said Pedius, summing up the situation lucidly.

"Your cousin has certainly chosen a bad time to enter the world of politics," said another senator. "Between Mark Antony and the 'liberators' I see little room for anyone else."

Pinarius felt compelled to reply. "As Caesar's son, Octavian has a bevy of legions loyal to him. I'd say he has plenty of bargaining power."

"I don't know," insisted the other. "He might well have some nostalgic veterans willing to give him the benefit of the doubt, but he is too young and lacking in vigour to exercise any authority over the soldiery, and he cannot continue to buy them forever with the coin of Caesar's will. Sooner or later his resources will run out, if they haven't already…"

There was nothing to be done, thought Pinarius. No one was willing to consider his cousin a credible alternative to Mark Antony, Lepidus or the so-called 'liberators'. "I hope you're wrong. Octavian could prove to be of great use to the state," he said simply. But even he was not really convinced that there was any chance of this happening.

"Bah! I believe that the only ones of use to the state are the liberators. They are the only ones who can oppose Mark Antony and it is they we senators must support if we do not want to be crushed. For this reason, the others and I have decided to support the election of Servilius Casca as tribune of the plebeians. In that position he will be able to put a halt to many laws that Mark Antony will attempt to institute for his personal benefit."

Pinarius was appalled. Servilius Casca was one of Octavian's principal targets, the one who had struck the first blow at Caesar – and now they were making him tribune of the plebeians! The Senate intended to give him the role it had refused to give to Octavian, thus making him an inviolable person! His cousin would not take this well…

"He is coming! Mark Antony is coming!" he heard.

Pinarius and Pedius turned towards the space behind the Curia and saw the consul walking briskly in the midst of his lictors and with a retinue of soldiers behind him.

The phantoms that the senators feared most were materialising. On a wave of fear they would grant the consul whatever he asked, and everything would become more difficult for the sect of Mars Ultor.

Pinarius scrutinised the expression of Mark Antony, who now stood close to the stairway of the building's entrance. There was a wry smile on his face. Clearly, he was very sure of himself. In the meantime, his soldiers, in full military regalia, fanned out and began to arrange themselves around the Curia. No, there was no question about what the consul was after. Among the worried senators a deathly silence had fallen and many began to swarm into the building.

Pinarius and Pedius were about to enter when they saw a legionary run breathlessly up to Mark Antony and stop him on the top step of the staircase. They spoke animatedly, and the consul made a dramatic gesture of annoyance. He stood immobile for a moment staring into space before turning to his sergeants and ordering them to turn back. Soon after, the soldiers who had positioned themselves near the Curia fell in behind them. Before long, the small army had become only indistinct dots among the buildings that marked out the Forum.

The senators who were still outside the building were dumbfounded, and those who had entered re-emerged. A few citizens climbed the steps to speak to them, but for all Pinarius strained his ears he could hear only indistinct voices. He approached the senator with whom he had spoken a few minutes earlier and asked him what had happened.

"Mark Antony received unexpected news," he replied excitedly, "The Martia legion has mutinied and has taken up with your cousin Octavian – and immediately afterwards, the

IVth legion did the same!"

Pinarius looked at Pedius with a satisfied expression. Apparently Maecenas's plan had taken effect.

Now, the senators would have to take Octavian into account after all.

XIV

Ortwin peered at the horizon, where the line of the Asian coast had begun to take shape. His gaze seemed to wander along it, almost skipping past the coast and flying inland, where his memories dwelled. Veleda, who stood beside him at the bow of the ship carrying them towards their mission, would have liked to be able to see the images he was seeing in his mind's eye to understand a part of his life of which she knew nothing. With the only hand she had, the woman held his arm to show him that she understood his mood.

"You have many memories of this land, do you not?" she asked.

"Not so many, actually," he answered after a moment's hesitation. He looked at her with his one eye and smiled. "But the few I have are glorious. I came to these parts with Caesar and within a few days we had defeated Pharnaces, King of Pontus. We celebrated a grand triumph for that brilliant victory, and the commander coined a saying: 'I came, I saw, I conquered.' And he did just that. I remember the king's scythed chariots, with their rotating blades – they were enough to put the fear of the gods into you! And yet we wiped them out in an instant. And to think that Pompey the Great and the Roman leaders before him had worn themselves down fighting Mithridates, Pharnaces' father…"

Veleda knew Ortwin's admiration for the man he had served for many years. He could never mourn Caesar enough, while she had no reason to feel sorry about the man's death. It was he who had robbed her of her kingdom and caused the ruin of her father, Ariovistus. And it had been the dictator who had ordered Ortwin to cut off her hand when she had been captured among the die-hard defenders of a Gallic village. But she would never forgive herself for dragging Ortwin away from the work he loved into her own hopeless undertakings, and she regretted even more the eye he had lost after Munda, when he had torn her from the clutches of her abductor. "You have so much nostalgia for those days, don't you?" she asked. But it was a rhetorical question.

"Especially if I compare them to what we do now," he said with a grimace. "Then, we marched with an entire army to avenge the massacre of a legion and we conquered a kingdom, with the full approval of the institutions of the City. Now, we are just a handful of killers acting in the shadows, in a battle between Romans where we do not even know if we have chosen the right side. And one which, at the moment it seems we have not even the slightest chance of winning."

"We had no choice."

"No, we did not, not after Mark Antony rejected us. And in any event, if he has no intention of avenging Caesar, I will not serve him. The problem is that I do not know if Octavian will actually be able to carry it off, though he certainly seems to desire it with all his might. I will at least admit, however, that he is the only one of the people of rank who does not think only of his own political survival. Take Lepidus, for example – by now he will be in his province of Narbonne in Gaul and seeking agreements with everyone from Sextus Pompey to Decimus Brutus and Mark Antony. Did he lift a finger against the murderers of Caesar? No, he waited quietly for his consulate. Yet, when he was Caesar's attendant in Gaul, you couldn't speak to the commander without going through him first. And all the others as well, no one has said a word against the killers. They're all waiting to see who looks like he's going to win so they can lick his arse and remind him that they had never stood in his way."

"And you think that Octavian is different?"

"Octavian is different. Caesar would not have chosen him otherwise. He too thirsts for power, he too wants to survive politically and dominate others. But he has a long-term vision – a strategy. And he fights for Rome, not simply for himself. He really cared for Caesar, and he intends to avenge him. And moreover, it is for that reason that the two of us are here. Indeed, it is the only reason he hired us."

"He needed somebody to do his dirty work for him," replied Veleda. "He didn't want to bloody his own hands."

"He can't do everything. He's only twenty years old, and he has huge obstacles before him. He had the courage to take on the responsibility that Caesar had left him. A courage that many others would not have had. I'd like to see what those other supporters of Caesar would have done if they had been designated his heir! They would have enjoyed their inheritance and nothing else, I can tell you that! Or they would have used it to crush the others! Mark Antony first of all. He was convinced that he would be Caesar's heir, yet he never thought to avenge him, and now he thinks of nothing but tyranny."

"Even Octavian aspires to tyranny. Just as Caesar did, it is true." Veleda would rather not have said this, but throughout her life she had never been able to keep her thoughts to herself and she had never made it a secret that she considered Caesar a tyrant.

"I always felt that he was much more democratic than your father or any Germanic leader. He cared about others. Just as Octavian has the Republic at heart. He simply wants it to function as it should. Since I first began working for the Romans, I've never once seen the institutions working in harmony – there is too much bickering, too much animosity, too much ambition, corruption and immorality. The system is paralysed by too many leaders, too many setting vetoes and deriving personal gain from the situation. Nobody who matters is actually interested in changing things. Caesar tried to, and in Octavian I see at least a glimmer of the same aspirations. Yes, he is too young, inexperienced and sickly to succeed. He is no Caesar, and never will be. But if I look at the alternatives, that is already enough for me."

Veleda thought that Ortwin was mainly trying to convince and motivate himself – trying to ennoble the remaining solution after all their failures. But this time she did not say anything, because Dolabella, the consul, was approaching. Ortwin was right about one thing though. Dolabella, now proconsul of Syria, the province allocated by the Senate, had accepted their presence in his entourage solely because it suited him and allowed him to reap the benefits of the death of one of Caesar's murderers and acquire the province of Asia without too much risk and without getting his hands dirty. Ortwin hated him because he had been told that, shortly after the Ides of March, Dolabella was credited with being one of the killers.

"We will disembark at Pergamum. The latest news is that Gaius Trebonius is there. Then it's up to you barbarians to find ways to do what you have to do," began Dolabella in his usual vague way. "But you mustn't involve me, mind," he declared, reminding them in no uncertain terms what the deal was, and at the same time what he thought of them.

Veleda struggled to hold back her anger. For a moment, she hoped that Ortwin would grab him by the neck and fling him into the sea but he was, as ever, cooler and more meditative than her, and said calmly, "Fear not, consul. We know what we have to do, we 'barbarians'. All you have to do is point us towards our target." Well, if nothing else he had at least revealed some of his irritation.

Dolabella did not seem offended by the fact, though. For him they were just scum, and he completely ignored what they said. "Be careful, though," continued the consul. "Trebonius is working hard for Marcus Brutus and for Cassius, gathering troops and fortifying the border towns between the provinces, and I know that the go-between – Quintus Labienus, the son of that traitor Tito Labienus – is a very dangerous individual. If he is with Trebonius, you will find it extremely difficult to succeed in your task."

Veleda went cold. She looked at Ortwin and saw upon his face an expression which revealed all his anguish.

Quintus Labienus. The last man in the world he wanted to meet again.

*

"Why have the legions gone over to Octavian and not to the Senate?"

"Exactly! What is Octavian but a common citizen? By what right does he take legions that should belong to the people and the Senate of Rome? Who authorized this?"

Two senators had risen from the stands and dared to interrupt the speaker in the Temple of Jupiter while he held the chair of the illustrious assembly. All this was quite unusual – especially as, in this particular case, the speaker was none other than Marcus Tullius Cicero.

"This is looking bad," whispered Lucius Pinarius to Quintus Pedius, while their colleagues murmured to each other their assent to the shouts of protest. "I wouldn't bet on

Cicero the way things are going – and if *he* can't convince them to support Octavian, nobody else in here will."

Quintus Pedius nodded. "I am optimistic, however. Mark Antony still has four legions, auxiliary militias, the bodyguards and the recruits that he is gathering at the edge of Gaul. It seems that Lepidus is willing to make his four legions available. Decimus Brutus has only three plus his gladiators, and if he is surrounded in Modena, he will not survive one of Mark Antony's long sieges, especially if they are reinforced by Lepidus's troops. Now that Hirtius and Pansa have become consuls, what will they attack Mark Antony with? They need as many legions as possible, and there aren't many around which are still free. You'll see that they will make a pact to get their hands on those of Octavian – the Martia and the IVth in particular, are veteran units, and they are worth their weight in gold."

"Friends! Friends!" cried Cicero, waving his arms at his colleagues in order to speak. "There is a man abroad we should declare a public enemy and you are afraid of a young man who claims he wishes to make himself available to the Republic? A man willing to use the affection of the troops to serve his country and prevent a civil war? You know very well that, if we let him do so, Mark Antony will take Modena, kill Decimus Brutus, join Lepidus and perhaps march on Rome, one day."

"But we cannot today condemn yesterday's consul! We would be contradicting ourselves! You yourself praised him not so long ago, Cicero!" cried another senator.

"Friends, colleagues," said Cicero, while the Princeps Senatus demanded silence by banging the end of his staff on the podium. "Immediately after the death of Caesar, Mark Antony seemed to all of us to take his role as consul seriously, preventing riots and pardoning the liberators who, it seems, had intended to kill him too. He acted as peacemaker and showed no feelings of revenge, and for that we were grateful. But then we discovered that it was only part of a plan to consolidate his own power. He stole money from us, improperly managing Caesar's patrimony, which in part should have been returned to the state. He blackmailed the proconsul of Macedonia only to help himself to the troops which were destined for there, and then demanded Gaul Cisalpina, taking it from its legitimate governor. He also decimated the soldiers for their shortcomings

– and not for the sole and legitimate reason for rushing into such an extreme punishment – but for a word, or a laugh, or on the basis of random choice, without even subjecting them to judgement. And remember, he tried to march on Rome with his army, and might have actually entered the city in arms had Octavian not prevented him from doing so with another army. He now wants Gaul, no doubt as a base from which to move against us, just as Caesar did in his time, and you tell me that I should not be afraid? Now that this individual has shown his true colours? I warned you against Caesar before he showed his autocratic tendencies, now I am warning you about Mark Antony, and I say that our main instrument in opposing him is precisely the one Caesar chose as a son."

"How can you be sure that Octavian is not like his adopted father?" cried a senator.

"That's right! It is unwise to adopt a solution that might be even worse than the problem!" cried another.

"You do not know Octavian as I do!" said Cicero. "He is a young man of noble soul, who is learning to control his impulsiveness and his natural instinct for revenge. He is maturing quickly, and he realises now that some impulses have no place in politics. He sincerely has the salvation of the Republic at heart, and is willing to put aside his rancour towards those whom he believes to be the murderers in order to promote peace and the proper functioning of the state. I personally guarantee this, and you know, my friends, how much I abhor *any* meddling with the institutions. But in this case, we need him, and, in a moment as chaotic as this, we must give him something! Let us provide him with the opportunity to assist the institutions and let him take part! His age would not normally allow it, of course, but his birth, his passion, and the influence he has acquired upon the soldiers and the people now make him worthy of holding the most important positions."

Pedius looked at Pinarius. "You see? The old man is working hard for us. With these passionate pleas of his, he seems almost to be on our side. He actually believes that Octavian will allow himself to be manoeuvred by him and do his bidding."

"It means that we have done our job well," said his cousin, smugly.

*

Rufus hesitated before knocking on the door of Octavia's domus. According to his calculations, at that moment Octavian's sister should be with her husband visiting her mother Atia and stepfather Marcius Philippus in Velletri, and Etain would be alone. If he found the masters at home, he would nevertheless have the excuse of wanting to wait with them for Pedius and Pinarius' news from the seemingly endless sitting of the Senate at the Temple of Jupiter Capitoline. After all, it was in this meeting that civil war could be declared and the fate of Octavian would be decided, and he had stayed in Rome to inform the head of the sect, who was camped with his men in Etruria waiting for the outcome of the events, in particular the eventual news of his being given an institutional position.

Under normal circumstances he would have preferred not to stay in the city. Rufus was a soldier, a military man, and as far as he was concerned, mingling with civilians was not exactly the most pleasant way to pass the time. And anyway, now that Agrippa was no longer part of the sect, he felt like the group's military expert, and would have liked to live in camp. Above all now, as civil war was on the verge of breaking out.

But this time, when Octavian had asked him to remain in the City in order to liaise, he had welcomed the request. His thoughts had gone immediately to Etain, whom he could continue to see for a while before the war parted them for who knew how long.

He had taken advantage of this. The Senate did not want to do anything decisive until the two new consuls – in reality his armed wing – came into office, so he had had over a month to woo the girl and show her enough care, compassion, patience and gentleness to earn her trust. Now that Etain had overcome her initial reluctance, she spoke willingly to him, and the last time, when they had found themselves alone for a few moments, she had also let him touch her lips with his and caress her face without flinching in the way she had the two previous times.

Rufus knocked, and when the caretaker came to open the door, he asked politely if the owners were at home. The man shook his head, and so he asked for Etain. While the *ostiarius* was answering, she materialised behind him.

"Come in, Salvidienus Rufus. The masters will probably return soon and if you have the patience to wait you will be able to speak to them," she said with a sweet smile.

This was indeed a good sign.

"I will gladly wait, if you'll join me, Etain," said Rufus, returning her smile and entering. He almost pushed the disoriented doorkeeper, who moved aside, out of the way, and she led him into the triclinium, where she gestured for him to sit on a bench and ordered a slave to bring fruit.

She sat down next to him. "This gets better and better," thought Rufus.

"News from the Senate?" asked the girl after a basket of fresh fruit had been placed on the table in the triclinium.

"No, unfortunately. The session has been in progress since yesterday morning and none of the senators has yet come out. But I can't not say I'm sorry" he said, allusively.

"Why not?"

"Because when they do come out I'll have to leave to report whatever they have decided to Octavian, unfortunately, and afterwards won't have the chance to see you for a long time."

"I would be sorry. If you are to be absent for a long time, it means that civil war actually is going to break out and we of the sect will be involved, in one way or another – you, as an officer, above all."

"Would that be the *only* reason you would be sorry? Because there might be a war?" he inquired, looking into her eyes with all the intensity he could muster.

Etain held his gaze for just a moment, then she stared at the fruit on the table. "You're a man of experience, Rufus. You know only too well that it is not the only reason..." she murmured, her voice quavering.

"A man of experience? You mean I'm too old for you? Yes... I *am* slightly older than Agrippa..."

He saw her flinch at the mention of her former lover. He wondered whether it was contempt or because she still felt something for him, but didn't really care.

"That's not what I meant..." she replied with a smile, but her gaze was elsewhere.

She was ready, Rufus thought. Etain really seemed to have

decided to be his that day, without too much beating about the bush. Whether she was doing it to get back at Agrippa, to try to overcome the trauma of the rape, or simply because she liked him was irrelevant. He cupped her chin in his fingers, lifting her face up to his and pulled her towards him.

"So since you cannot explain it to me, I take it that you meant…" he murmured, a moment before placing his lips on hers to kiss her. Etain did not pull back immediately this time, nor did she limit herself to merely pressing her lips to his, but she opened her mouth and slid her tongue inside his. Rufus heard her breaths become spasmodic, and felt something that was not saliva drip onto his upper lip. He broke away for a moment – it tasted salty. Looking up, he saw tears trickling down Etain's beautiful face. He began to feel impatient, but forced himself not to show it.

"Do you not desire it?" he asked in the gentlest tone he could, softly caressing her at the same time.

Etain sobbed. "I… I desire it… but I cannot help but think of what I have suffered. I know you did not do me harm, Rufus, but I fear that, at any moment, you could turn into one of them…" she explained, while squeezing his arm.

All was not lost, thought Rufus. "That's understandable," he answered. And then an idea struck him. "You decide. You can do whatever you want," he added, smiling, and he dropped his arms to his sides and sat there passively. He hoped that she would feel encouraged. If she had decided to give herself to him, maybe in this way she would manage to overcome her fears.

Etain smiled back, embarrassed. She looked away but then sought him out again and reached out and stroked his face. Her soft fingers went down his neck as she gently pulled him towards her. This time there was a real kiss. Rufus was happy – he had chosen the right tactic. Etain had decided to overcome her fears, but she needed help, and he had given it to her. Now it would be easy.

As though in confirmation of his thoughts, she took his hand, pulled him to his feet and took him to her room. It was Etain who shut the door behind them, and it was she who approached the bed and unfastened her tunic and then took it off before removing her thong and allowing herself be admired, completely naked. Rufus longed for that white, velvety skin, marked only by the odd bruise and scratch from the violence she had suffered recently. She had the body of a young girl with long legs and breasts just beginning to develop. He decided that it was better if he stayed where he was, however. He had to show that not all men would jump on her. She waited a moment, then moved towards him, walking slowly, stealthily, as if she were trying not to wake someone.

When Rufus found her standing in front of him he restrained his urge to jump on her, throw her against the wall, turn her around and take her, but he knew that he would achieve nothing if he did. He let her lead, and once again he was not disappointed. Etain loosened his robe and threw it to the ground, then undid his tunic and pulled it off. The man waited to see what the girl would do with his loincloth. Etain had noticed his excitement, and the expression on the girl's face alternated between pleasure and fright. It was obvious that she was experiencing an inner conflict between what she wanted and what she feared.

Rufus decided that respecting her too much would not do her any favours, and perhaps would even create more inhibitions. He gently took her hand and brought it towards the loincloth. For an instant she stiffened and kept her hand on his erect penis as though it were red hot. She tried to remove it but he held it there, and after a while the girl began to caress it. Then she unexpectedly took off his loincloth and began caressing his buttocks, then surprised him even more by suddenly kneeling down and kissing the whole area, focussing her attentions on the place where he desired it the most.

It was time. After letting her work for a while, he could stand it no more, and hoped she felt the same. He lifted her delicately, picked her up and carried her to the bed, where she closed her legs and folded her arms as soon as she lay down. Rufus was not discouraged. He had expected this. His instinct was to lie down on top of her and force open her legs in order to penetrate her immediately, but he made himself once again be patient, though his groin was throbbing with desire.

He knelt beside the bed and ran his lips along the girl's legs, then between her thighs, kissing the soft hair there. He felt her relax slowly, and gently slipped his fingers between her legs. At first he found opposition in her tense thighs but gradually she relaxed and allowed him to spread them apart, and as soon as he had the chance, Rufus ran his fingers up and pushed them

231

gently inside her.

She moaned with pleasure, and this encouraged him to continue, pushing deeper and finding her ready. There was no need for him to open her legs now, it was she who opened them slowly while he stood up and gazed at her for a few moments, before laying down upon her as gently as he could. Etain made everything so easy for him. She welcomed him inside her, gently guiding him, echoing all his movements. A moment later Rufus felt overcome by that moist heat he had coveted and had been pursuing from the moment he had entered the house.

They reached the apex of pleasure at the same time, just before a commotion inside the domus forced them to hurriedly dress and rush out of the room. Pedius and Pinarius had arrived with news from the Senate.

*

Maecenas was struggling. He was aware he lacked the charisma and appearance needed to address even a normal crowd from a podium, never mind soldiers, who were far more demanding than civilians and used to dealing with decisive, stalwart, or at least sharp looking commanders. That was why, despite being aware of his dialectical and intellectual talents, he had always preferred to work from behind the scenes. He worked well with Octavian, and despite the fact that their collaboration had only begun a few months earlier, the partnership they had built up, with him providing the words and his friend their interpretation, was proving very fruitful.

But now Octavian was sick, and they needed someone to cool the spirits of the three legions who followed him. The soldiers had had enough, in fact, of doing nothing, knowing as they did that Mark Antony was laying siege to Decimus Brutus in Modena and that the Senate had not yet made a move. They had expected to march on Rome to demand the appointment of their young commander and be paid for fighting the consul, whose term had just expired in favour of his successors, Hirtius and Pansa.

"Legionaries," ventured Maecenas, realizing suddenly that his shrill voice was not suited to public speaking. "I know that you are eager to prove your worth and to avenge Caesar, but we must wait until the time is right. Octavian too thinks of nothing but avenging his father, but he is also concerned with winning the support of the Senate, so as not to have to face multiple enemies simultaneously. He must set himself one goal at a time, because if he tries to do everything at once he will be doomed to fail, and you with him. If it is necessary, and without a doubt will be necessary again in the future, for our young but influential commander to make the best of a bad lot and agree to temporarily put aside some of his primary goals – even that of avenging Caesar – if it serves to consolidate his position. Remember soldiers, you cannot avenge when you are weak. We must be strong and have many allies."

He was deeply convinced of this and for weeks had been trying to curb Octavian's craving for revenge, trying to convince him to put aside for the moment his hatred of his father's killers. He had managed to do it successfully with Cicero, who was now becoming useful – if only he could do the same with the others, beginning with Decimus Brutus. Now, in order for him to win the support of the Senate and be given a position, Mark Antony – and not Caesar's killers – had to appear as his principal enemy.

The soldiers continued to protest, despite his words. He was sure that if it had been Octavian speaking they would have quietened down, but as it was an awkward and chubby tribune hectoring them in a voice devoid of any authority, they wouldn't listen.

He was resigned to waiting until Octavian finished his latest fit of coughing, when he saw someone arriving in grand style – a horseman whom he immediately recognized as Rufus. Finally! No man had ever been awaited with such anxiety. His presence there meant that the Senate had decided.

Rufus had noticed that the soldiers had gathered on the exercise field located near the camp and had declined to cross the palisade. Seeing Maecenas on the podium, he headed towards him with a surprised, even amused, expression on his face. But the Etruscan did not intend to receive the news in front of everyone. Whatever it was, it would not be easy to manage in front of the soldiers. He alighted from the podium and went to meet Rufus.

"Come with me. We will go to Octavian. Do not dare say a word now!" he ordered, climbing onto another horse and moving closer to him.

Rufus smiled. "What's going on? The sight of you on the podium was enough to understand why you prefer to keep a low profile, despite your way with words. If nothing else, you have a sense of decency"

"Shut up, you idiot. Octavian is having one of his attacks and I hope you will be able to cheer him up a little with the news you bring," replied Maecenas, without rising to the bait.

'Well, if what I have to say doesn't cheer him up, I don't know what will…" said Rufus, and the Etruscan relaxed slightly.

They dismounted in front of Octavian's pavilion and the sentries announced them. Maecenas went in first, finding his friend lying on the bed with his personal physician, Glyco, sitting next to him. The young man must have been the only leader in the history of Rome to have a personal physician in tow during a military campaign. Fortunately, Glyco was an old, discreet and taciturn Greek who knew his place and felt at home among the attendants and slaves. It would not have made a good impression on the soldiery if his presence had been made known to all.

The Etruscan noticed that the sheets were stained with blood and that his tunic was covered with vomit and drool. Octavian lay there with a dazed expression on his face, and at first – probably because the room was in semi-darkness – did not give the impression of having recognised him.

"Octavian, Rufus has arrived. Let's hear the news from Rome."

"Rufus… I'm glad to see you…" murmured the sick man. "Do not… do not be alarmed by my condition. These attacks… they come and go. I live with them… I always have," Octavian felt compelled to explain at the sight of his friend's worried expression.

"So, Rufus, you have our ears," said Maecenas impatiently, as he sat down in a chair next to Octavian's bed.

Rufus cleared his throat and paused a moment longer. The Etruscan imagined that he was shocked by what he was seeing. As a soldier, it was probably disconcerting to see one's commander in such a precarious state of health, and no doubt he was asking himself some hard questions. This was precisely why Maecenas had not wanted Octavian to see anyone from the camp during the most acute phase of his illness. The morale of the soldiers would have suffered.

"Well, thanks to the support and eloquence of Cicero, the Senate has been generous with its rewards for you, Octavian," Rufus said, finally. "You are a *propraetor*, now, and can apply to the consulate – ten years ahead of the usual legal deadline. You can attend the Senate with the right to speak to the consuls. And a golden statue of you will be erected, just imagine…"

"What do I care about a golden statue!? What about the war and the army? That is what matters…" spat Octavian, who seemed to have suddenly regained his usual lucidity.

"The situation is complex. You have been partnered with Hirtius and Pansa, the chiefs of the army, but you will have to give them the two legions that mutinied against Mark Antony. In return, the state will pay the bonuses that you promised the legionaries in the case of victory against Mark Antony."

"So Mark Antony has finally been declared public enemy?"

"Erm… not really. They speak about it as though it were already so, but they still want to leave themselves a way out, in part because of the pressure of his supporters, and you will see that they will make you wait before heading north. Which is a good thing, because it gives you time to get better. They want to accept Macedonia in exchange for the Cisalpine, and meanwhile have praised Decimus Brutus because he didn't give up the province, justifying their trust once again."

There was silence in the tent for a while. Both Octavian and Maecenas were absorbed in their thoughts. After a while Rufus felt compelled to say something. "It's good news, though, right? *Propraetor* and senator at twenty years old…"

"Good news? What are you talking about? It's just form, with no substance!" shouted Octavian, banging his fist on the bed. His outburst was immediately followed by another coughing fit.

Rufus did not understand, so, to save his friend from the trouble of expressing the feelings he was sure they both shared, Maecenas began to explain. "You see, Rufus, it's obvious that a *propraetor* counts for nothing if he must act together with two consuls. The title is merely symbolic. What matters is that we had five legions, while now they have removed two, and the best two at that. They think it will keep us quiet, but in reality they are robbing us."

"And that's not all," said Octavian, after clearing his throat. "They are still being meek with Mark Antony and are going to leave him a way out. Moreover, they have reconfirmed their confidence in that murderous traitor Decimus Brutus, whom they clearly have no intention of getting rid of… Things could hardly have got any worse than this."

Rufus assumed a contrite expression "So what shall we do? March on Rome, like all the soldiers have been asking me?" he ventured.

Octavian did not answer, and began to reflect. Maecenas decided to speak up. "I would strongly recommend that you do not. We can be sure that Mark Antony will not give up Gaul to please the Senate. For him that would be humiliating, after all he has done to get it. Decimus Brutus will not grant it to him, above all now that we have had confirmation of the Senate's support. He will go to war, and in war many things can happen… but now, with the prospect of being rewarded, the soldiers will be satisfied and therefore more manageable."

Octavian suddenly rose from his couch with a vigour that surprised Maecenas. He called the slave and ordered him to remove his tunic, wash it and dress him properly, then quietened the protests of Maecenas and Rufus, who wanted him to stay in bed, saying, "Maecenas is right. We have to make the soldiers believe that we got what we wanted. I will make the ritual sacrifice for the investment ceremony of my new position and speak immediately to the legionaries. I will thank them for the command that has been assigned to me and will tell them that the Senate has confirmed what they had already told me. So when we are at war, they will listen to me, especially if they know they can expect further bonuses in addition to what they will be paid by the state. This way they will have double pay – that way, why should they follow the consuls? And then we'll see who the Senate listens to once the war is over."

"Yes. But let us remember that we have to win the war first," said Maecenas, trying to think of a way to involve Agrippa in it. They needed him more than ever, now.

XV

"Why are they are sending out ambassadors to meet us?" asked Dolabella. "They usually just let us enter without ceremony, don't they?" Veleda looked at the three men who had just come through the gates of the city of Smyrna and at the soldiers in the battlements. Some had arrows nocked, others swords drawn warily.

Dolabella was right – this was not the way one received a magistrate of the Republic of Rome.

The three men came before Dolabella, who was waiting impatiently a few steps from the walls. Dolabella, who had become proconsul of Syria, although all his subordinates continued to attribute to him the position he had held since Caesar died, was ringed by bodyguards which included Ortwin and his Germans. Even Veleda was now considered a warrior in every respect by the Romans. The magistrate had been confidently heading towards the entrance of the city when he saw the gate literally shut in his face, which had done little to calm his impulsive nature.

"Would you mind telling me what the hell is going on?" he asked the three legates before they could even open their mouths to greet him. "My men are tired and hungry."

"Consul Dolabella, the proconsul of Asia, Trebonius sends you his greetings and welcomes you to his province," said one of the three ambassadors. "He hopes that your trip from Italy went well and announces that the three days of supplies you and your army require are being prepared for you."

"Look, we are wasting time," snapped Dolabella. "Let me inside now and I will tell the proconsul personally what I need for myself and for my men. I need a nice hot bath and accommodation for a couple of days. The trip to Syria is long."

The man let out a sigh of embarrassment. "As I said, the proconsul is making the necessary preparations. If you would not mind being patient and waiting here..."

"I will not wait here! I am a magistrate of Rome, and have the right to enter into a provincial town as and when I please!" shouted Dolabella.

"The proconsul thought it unwise to let you in," explained the legate. "In this period of tension, two magistrates in the same city might cause problems. He cannot come out himself either. He apologizes for not being able to greet you but at the moment he is very busy and…"

"Of course! Busy working for his friends Marcus Brutus and Cassius! Do you think I don't know that Cassius went to Syria, my province?"

"I don't follow you, consul. I…"

Dolabella stepped forward and grabbed the man by his toga. "Listen to me, you piece of shit, you're going to throw open these blasted gates and let me in with as many men as I see fit, do you understand?"

"Forgive me, consul, I am only carrying out my orders… By tonight you will have received the victuals. You can make camp here in front of…" mumbled the legate, stepping back as soon as Dolabella released him. Then he took another step back, nodded a farewell, bowed his head, as did the other two, then turned around and retraced his steps. The heavy doors of the gate opened as soon as he approached the walls.

Dolabella, instinctively ready to take advantage of the moment to force his way in, moved forward and waved his guards to follow him. "That'd be a bit risky, consul, don't you think?" commented Ortwin, pointing to the men lined up along the battlements.

Dolabella stopped. He looked up, shook his head and said, "The bastard!"

The men around him, realising they were being watched, became agitated. Veleda looked at Ortwin, who gave her a reassuring look. He hoped that the consul would not do anything foolish, despite giving the impression of being the kind of man who would let his impulses get the better of him and do something stupid. Like trying to get through the gates as they closed.

But Dolabella did not move, and in the meantime the gates closed, swallowing up the three legates. The consul waited a few moments, perhaps in the secret hope of seeing Trebonius appear on the battlements. But the proconsul did not show himself. He had decided to stand his ground, it seemed.

This greatly complicated the task that she and Ortwin were to perform on behalf of Octavian and the sect, thought Veleda.

They had to get near Trebonius to perform the task, but it now appeared that things would be more difficult than expected. They had planned to act at night like assassins and make their escape immediately afterwards with Dolabella, like that time in Syria but, apparently, even the governor of Asia was aware of the opportunism of the former consul, and did not trust him.

"We will besiege them. We cannot allow them to treat a Roman magistrate in such a way!" exclaimed Dolabella. He turned to one of his legates. "Take the scorpios off the ships, and get to work on building a tower and a self-propelled ram. That will be sufficient to frighten them. We'll see if they won't open the gates then!" And he gave instructions to set up camp for his small army.

"Do you think building a few siege engines will be enough to induce Trebonius to open the gates?" Veleda asked Ortwin.

"Of course not," the man admitted. "Trebonius knows he is stronger, there are too few of us to expect to take a city with walls as strong as those of Smyrna. We will just look like fools."

Veleda had already realised for herself that they had no chance of getting inside. There was no need for Ortwin's confirmation – she saw other soldiers shaking their heads skeptically at the consul's decision. "How will we get to Trebonius, if he keeps Dolabella at arm's length?" she asked him.

"Bah! Maybe we could pretend to be deserters..." said Ortwin.

"And if Quintus Labienus is with him? He would recognise us... in any case, it would create problems."

Ortwin nodded, the gaze of his single eye lost in the void. The name evoked dark memories for him too. For years, Veleda had been a matter of dispute between them, and for a long time she had been the woman of Quintus Labienus, the son of Caesar's closest collaborator and then his most bitter enemy. He had raped her, and loved her in a perverse, obsessive way. Considered her his property, kept her prisoner and made her his slave. He had fought for her, risked his life for her even fighting against the eldest son of Pompey the Great, the late Pompey the

Younger, over her. Once his friend and fellow soldier, Ortwin had faced him on numerous occasions, from Italy to Greece to Africa, during the years of the triumphs of Caesar. They shared contrasting political views – one a supporter of the dictator, the other his archenemy – and their love for her, in a never-ending duel destined to finish only in Munda.

Or at least, Veleda had thought it had finished in Munda. After the battle, Ortwin had found her and Labienus and had the chance to kill his rival, but she had interceded for her lover and tormentor, and Ortwin, after defeating him in a duel, had let him go, despite promising to finish him off.

He had done it for her, for love, just as he had indulged her in her mad plan to recover her kingdom, despite not agreeing with it. The return to Germany had been a mistake, and now that Quintus Labienus was once again between them and their proposed goal, it looked as though allowing him to live had been a mistake too.

"If Quintus Labienus is here?" Ortwin finally said after reflecting for a while. "I will kill him this time. Octavian is not the only one who has a list…"

*

Octavian saw an arrow shoot by overhead. Instinctively, he ducked behind the top of the fence, but then his curiosity prevailed and he raised his head just enough to follow the confrontation taking place little more than a hundred paces from the rampart of his camp.

"Damn you, Galba, if you are not able to control your men, what are you doing here with us?" The consul Aulus Hirtius, standing next to Octavian, turned impatiently to the legate to whom he had entrusted the Martia, the legion that had rebelled against Mark Antony in order to turn itself over to Octavian, who in turn, had to return it to the Senate. The senators then assigned it to Hirtius who, in turn, had given the command to Servius Sulpicius Galba.

One of Caesar's assassins.

"Consul, sometimes it is impossible to calm the spirits of the soldiers. Caesar himself said this at Pharsalus, did he not? My cavalry saw soldiers assaulted by Mark Antony's cavalry and there was no way to stop them – they went out and they started to fight alongside them."

"'My cavalry'", thought Octavian with a wave of revulsion. "He called them 'my cavalry'!"

"Caesar knew when it was necessary to risk all, idiot!" cried Hirtius, soothing Octavian's anger a little. "But he would have kept them in line, if they even dared to step out of it! What did I say this morning? We must not accept provocation! We knew Mark Antony would try to flush us out and make us fight before the arrival of Pansa so as not to find himself with our armies in front and Decimus Brutus in Modena behind him. We knew that very well! We have no interest in fighting now."

"But even if there were a clash, Decimus Brutus might take advantage and attack Mark Antony from behind. We do not need Pansa. And moreover, his legions are made up of raw recruits and would only be a hindrance," said Galba's second in command, Quintus Pontius Aquila.

Another of Caesar's murderers.

"Oh really?" Hirtius's tone of voice was typically acrimonious. The dictator had considered him one of his closest aides, as much for his faithfulness and his ability as a writer than for any military or political competence. He had employed him to write up the last book of his Commentaries on the Gallic Wars but – knowing his limits – had never assigned him operational duties in war. Only now, after his death, had Hirtius assumed command of the Roman troops, and he was eager to show he deserved it. However, he was always argumentative and fixated on his goals, which made him rather obnoxious. For Octavian, however, he was less obnoxious than the assassins with whom he was obliged to co-operate. Especially when he was forced to take them back into the fold, like now.

"Oh really?" repeated the consul. "By the sound of it, I would say that you too lack experience. Pansa is coming and it makes no sense now to show ourselves. Decimus Brutus is on his last legs, his legions are starving and we cannot count upon their efficiency. Mark Antony is an experienced commander. If he has crossed the river Panaro and comes upon us, you can be sure that a part of his troops will still be outside the walls of Modena, commanded by his brother Lucius. Even if he wanted to, Decimus Brutus can do nothing."

The battle cries and the clashing of weapons rang out louder still, and all the general staff turned to look outward. Other squadrons of cavalry forded the river and, with an outflanking manoeuvre, swooped down on the flank of their troops, crushing them in a pincer movement. Galba's cavalry were now outnumbered, and it seemed as though they were certain to lose. Runaway horses fell heavily to the ground, splashing in the mud, their riders barely managing to get to their feet before having to dodge spears stabbing at them. Those who could were forced to fight on foot in the midst of a forest of enemies who were still mounted, until they disappeared inside a swirl of horses.

"We cannot just let them die thus! We must go out and help them!" exclaimed Aquila again.

"And give Mark Antony the battle he wants? No – they would slaughter us all," said the consul.

Octavian could take no more. Muttering a few barely intelligible words of apology, he broke away from the fence, went down the stairs that led to the bottom of the wall and vomited up a copious stream of bile just below the battlements. He felt a fit of violent trembling seize his body, and stood for a moment with his eyes closed trying to tame or at least manage it. He had to wait a long time before his nerves were once again under his control.

He was experiencing his first battle. Until then, the most direct contact he had with fighting soldiers had been his training in Apollonia, in the few months that preceded Caesar's death. But the noise, the clang of blades striking one another, the piercing screams of pain from the wounded, the vastness of a pitched battle where the men were being sought out to die, this was a new experience for him. He found himself wanting to share it with Agrippa, who was certainly more cut out for this sort of thing and had been waiting so long for an opportunity to not simply watch, but to actually participate in, a battle. He dismissed the thought immediately – there was no room for sentiment in the huge task ahead.

In any case, he was sure that it was not the upset or the fear that had made him queasy.

No. It was something else that was causing him this intolerable disgust. He wiped his mouth with the back of his hand, took a deep breath, puffed out his chest and climbed back up the steps, returning to his position. He immediately noticed that there seemed to be more fighters now, and realised that the number of Mark Antony's men had increased, causing Galba's troops to retreat. The riders were closer to the fort. Dangerously close to the fort. However their shapes had become more indistinct – they were not fighting along the bank of the river any more, and their movements did not raise mud but clouds of dust that enveloped them in a mist like gladiators in the arena.

"Hopefully they will not attack us! Young Octavian feels sick at just the sight of them, let alone having to fight them…" shouted Pontius Aquila, even finding time for a smile. Galba grimaced, making it clear to everybody there his sense of superiority, while Hirtius was too busy watching the developments of the battle to notice the verbal sparring.

Octavian bit his lip. He should have told him that he had vomited in disgust at having to collaborate with his father's murderers, but he knew he could not, so he said only, "If they get to the fort, we will see which of the two of us will face them with greater dignity, Pontius Aquila…"

In the end they arrived. Galba and Aquila had managed to convince Hirtius to lead out some of the troops, but the consul had not gone to help the scouts, so as to prevent the fighting from extending to the whole army. Rather, he had chosen to take five cohorts in an outflanking movement which threatened the enemy camp that Mark Antony had erected on their side of the banks of the river Panaro. In doing so, he hoped to force the enemy to give up its attempts at breaking through and force it to defend its own camp.

Gaius Chaerea approved of the commander's moves. It made good tactical sense and he had a good chance of succeeding: or would have done, had Mark Antony, whose troops were fighting under the walls, got close enough to attempt an assault on the camp.

The enemy had scattered almost all the cavalry sent against them and threw themselves against the protective barrier of the fort. It was the moment when Octavian had to take his first serious decision as commander.

Gaius Chaerea stared at him, while he gave the soldiers more orders. He seemed to have made a complete recovery. Hirtius had left him the responsibility of guarding the camp whilst he marched towards the enemy. They had opened the gates to let the fugitives in but immediately behind them came Antony's men, so they had been forced to close them again to prevent the enemy from entering. Octavian, who was on the battlements right by the gates, could not bring himself to give the order – there were still too many of his own horsemen close to the ramparts, and clearly the young man did not have the courage to condemn them to certain death.

But it was inevitable, and Chaerea approached him, urging him to act. Octavian continued to stare at the riders, many of whom were now on foot and being killed by enemy spears in their backs, in silence. He began to shake uncontrollably, his eyes full of dismay, but did not speak. He was paralysed by the responsibility, too much for a young man who had suddenly been catapulted to the front line, and one who was in poor health and unused to managing the lives of others to boot.

Chaerea felt compelled to intervene, and snapped him out of his daze by yelling in his ear, amid the cries and clamour of combat, to give the damn order. Octavian looked at him for a moment in disgust, and remained silent.

"Do you want to be defeated in your first battle? Do you want everyone to say that you were unable to defend the camp? How can you avenge Caesar, afterwards? Who will follow you then?" he had cried, throwing caution to the wind, and aware that he risked Octavian's hatred.

But it had worked. Octavian had come to, put aside his scruples and shouted for the gates to be closed. And then, instead of just standing to watch those he had left outside die, he called to the battlements the few auxiliary archers and spearmen available and ordered them to aim their projectiles at the enemy near the moat, and had them throw ropes down the walls and the embankment so the fugitives who managed to cross could hoist themselves up. But many were drowned, and others, though managing to reach the base of the embankment, were killed by enemy spears as they attempted to climb the fence. Few were actually saved in the end but, nevertheless, his enterprising spirit had earned Octavian the esteem of the men in the battlements.

Now the legionaries who remained in the fort could face the assault with the determination of those who had the utmost faith in their commander.

Suddenly, in fact, behind the riders, numerous cohorts of infantry had appeared. Approaching with determination, they fanned out, enclosing the fort on three sides. Many legionaries were advancing with material gathered from nearby to cross the dyke, and others followed them with makeshift ladders. Octavian gave the order to operate the scorpios, and their hissing darts began to mow down the enemy lines, albeit not quickly enough to slow their momentum.

"There's nothing we can do," said Chaerea after seeing how feeble the effect of the shooting and the few archers' arrows was upon the enemy's advance. "We'll have to wait and see if they try to cross the moat so that they're near enough for us to use spears, javelins and pilums on them."

Octavian thought for a moment and then nodded. "Centurion," he cried to the nearest officer, "spread the word among the other centurions to gather in the battlements with all the throwing weapons we still have and place them in regular piles for each of the units! Now!" As soon as all had heard the order, there was a burst of activity between the top of the fence and the inside of the camp which went on until they had rounded up every last available weapon. Meanwhile, Antony's men had begun to fill the moat with twigs and stones, piling them up to form small ramps. The camp had only been erected a few days before and the water had only filled the ditch up halfway, consequently not presenting much of an obstacle to the soldiers who ended up inside. It was rather the characteristic V-shape of the ditch that made it so difficult to get out of once you were in it, especially if there were attackers above you, as Octavian had ordered.

At his signal, in fact, from one part of the battlements after another the attackers were assailed with spears and weapons of every type, nearly all of them hitting their targets. The enemy legionaries, huddled around their makeshift ramps, were too busy watching where they put their feet to worry about keeping the shields up to protect themselves from the spears coming from above and, struck or knocked down, they collapsed to the ground or into the moat, often blocking the way so that the other soldiers were forced to scramble over their bodies in order to get past them, wasting even more time and exposing themselves to enemy attacks.

But there were so many more of them than there were of the

defenders that some of them did manage to reach the base of the embankment. A few, overcome by fervour, tried to go it alone, while others waited for their fellow soldiers to join them in order to form a kind of 'tortoise' by joining their shields together, but in the wait they were exposed to the attacks from the battlements and the narrow embankment was dotted with bodies that slid slowly down to the bottom of the ditch.

Every so often, however, one of the attackers would manage to hit their target – this was the price they paid for letting them get too close. Chaerea noticed that in the area to his left there were several dead and wounded men in the battlements and the few remaining defenders were no longer able to fire quickly enough. He saw a 'tortoise' of at least thirty shields forming on the embankment, and other soldiers from the ramp behind began to climb on top of it in order to jump over the fence.

Instinctively, he grabbed two soldiers and started to run. Octavian did not stop him, but raced after him and overtook him, reaching the threatened area first. A scorpio had been abandoned nearby, with no soldiers left to use it. "Come on, come here!" cried the young man to the other. He reached down and grabbed the pedestal of the machine. "Help me lift it!" he shouted to those following him. Together, they hoisted the machine up to the same level as the top of the fence. Chaerea looked down and saw that a soldier had jumped onto the platform of the shields and was running at them, brandishing his sword. He had almost reached the top of the fence, and was looking right at them with a wild sneer. In that moment, Octavian ordered them to throw down the scorpio.

The weapon flew over the top of the fence, knocking down the soldier, who had nearly reached them. He disappeared beneath the scorpio, which went crashing down upon the roof of shields with a sound of smashing wood, dented helmets, broken bones and inhuman screams. Chaerea gripped the edge of the fence and leaned over, to see their assailants rolling down the slope of the embankment and into the ditch, some unconscious or dead, and others simply knocked off balance as they were hit by their comrades or by pieces of broken weaponry.

Octavian gave a completely uncharacteristic cry of triumph and Chaerea looked at him doubly surprised: the boy had demonstrated remarkable sangfroid, putting his considerable intelligence at the service of military necessity and command. Behind that emaciated body and elegant figure hid an iron will and an uncommon determination.

The defenders of the nearest sectors had seen what had happened and began enthusiastically chanting his name. Below, the other attackers were hesitating, turning many of them into easy targets for archers on the battlements, as more gaps appeared in their ranks. It took only a moment more for the determination of Antony's men to collapse, irreparably. Some of them began backing off to get out of the range of the weapons, while those who had dared remained under the tortoise, realising they were becoming more and more isolated, eventually lost their nerve and, despite the shouts of their centurions, also began to pull back, until at last the order to retreat came from the rear. The forms of the besiegers grew smaller and smaller until they eventually disappeared round the curve of the river.

Only then did Octavian let out a deep sigh and let himself surrender to fatigue, walking over to the steps and descending them with his head bowed. For him, thought Chaerea , it must have taken enormous effort, and for a moment he feared that the young man might be seized by one of his coughing fits. Concerned that he might pass out at any moment, he ran to him, instinctively grabbing him by the arm to give him support, but Octavian pushed him away and started walking towards the centre of the fort, doing his best to puff out his chest and hold his head high.

"*Imperator!*" went up a cry from the battlements.

"*Imperator!* Octavian, son of Caesar, *Imperator!*"

"The new Julius Caesar *Imperator!*" By now the whole camp was acclaiming him as the victor.

The soldiers had found a new leader.

*

Maecenas began to regret having wanted to be part of the praetorian cohort sent by Octavian to escort Pansa's army. The places that his unit, led by the legate Decimus Carfulenus, had been forced to pass through that night were such hard going, so wet and gloomy, that he wished he hadn't come at all.

Fortunately, it was likely that they would not have to fight. It had been rumoured that Mark Antony had garrisoned troops at the entrances to Modena, but his scouts reported that they had encountered no enemy outposts.

On the other hand, the Etruscan thought, trying once again to scratch himself under his uncomfortable tribune's armour, no commander would place more than a few sentinels in a plain as unhealthy as this, where the ground oozed water at every step. Around there, in that very rainy spring, the Via Aemilia was narrow and impractical, and the landscape around them was made up entirely of pools, marshes, swamps and dense woods. In order not to be caught by surprise with his forces in disarray, Carfulenus had decided to widen the line, and so the less fortunate – those located at the wings – were forced to march knee deep in water.

The Etruscan looked towards the front of the unit, seeking Rufus. Octavian had appointed him second in command to Carfulenus, despite his young age. But Rufus was a soldier and not, like him, a civilian who was trying to prove to himself that he had enough courage to march with the troops. What he still did not know was whether he also had the guts to fight.

His awareness of the Etruscan's fragility had led Octavian to try and prevent him from taking part in any operation that might involve fighting, and when Maecenas had dug in his heels and insisted, he had told him to stay near Rufus if things started to go awry – and he had ordered Rufus to keep an eye on him. Beyond the friendship that had formed between them, Caesar's heir deemed the political acumen of the Etruscan too precious to risk losing it. For this reason, he wished him good luck, but sadly, as though he feared he would never see him again.

But what was there to worry about? Along with his praetorian cohort there was the Martia, and soon they would join up with the four legions that Pansa was leading towards Modena. Mark Antony, forced to leave most of his men guarding the besieged city and Hirtius and Octavian's camp, would not be foolish enough to attack such a large army with the few soldiers that he could spare. The enemy commander perhaps intended to surprise Pansa's recently formed units, which were all made up of recruits, but as soon as he noticed the presence of the veterans sent as re-inforcements, he would surely hesitate. At most, Rufus had reassured him a little while back, he might see the odd skirmish.

However, marching in such wild and inhospitable places, initially in the dark and then through the thick fog of dawn, made the Etruscan somewhat jumpy. The early spring dampness crept into his bones, causing him to sneeze occasionally, which – to judge by their eloquent expressions – the soldiers marching beside him judged a sign of weakness. Maecenas ignored their scorn, knowing that, at the end of the day, it had been his decision to mobilise them, and it was his money which motivated them. If they only knew that he was no humble tribune… But it pleased him to pass for an unimportant subaltern: he had never cared much for showing off. Only for influence.

The fog was still thick, and had it not been for Rufus's reassurances he would have been terrified of seeing the enemy suddenly appear in front of him. Not that he felt particularly at ease in that hushed atmosphere where the only sound was a disturbing mix of the rhythmic splashing of the soldiers' feet in the puddles, the birdsong and the chirping of crickets. He hoped that they were nearly at their rendezvous, and tried to calculate how long it would be. The night before, Pansa's army had been a few miles from Forum Gallorum, twelve miles from Modena, and now, after marching most of the night, the town had to be nearby. Comforted, he forced himself to march at a military pace, copying the legionaries beside him.

He saw a scout on horseback advancing towards the head of the praetorian cohort and whisper for a moment to Carfulenus and Rufus, before turning around and galloping over to the column of Martia, headed by the assassin Galba. Intrigued, Maecenas increased his pace and caught Rufus up. "Any news?" he asked.

"We are nearly there," was the answer. "Pansa is less than half a mile from here. We will stop and wait for him," he added, as Carfulenus gave the order to halt.

Maecenas breathed a sigh of relief. Fortunately, everything had gone well. His first act of war had been nothing worse than a nasty, cold, wet march through the night.

XVI

He was no longer consul, no longer proconsul, no longer even the conqueror of Smyrna. Dolabella was no longer anything, and it was plain to see. Ortwin sadly contemplated the man upon whom Octavian had relied to initiate his revenge upon Caesar's murderers. The German doubted that he had any further use at all. If he and Veleda wanted to bring some concrete results back to their real leader, he would have to take the situation in hand.

"How is it possible? How dare they take my Syria from me and give it to Cassius? They had given him Cyrene... what happened?" the commander of the ill-fated expedition whimpered, his head in his hands, venting his anguish upon one of his tribunes and ignoring the German guards who surrounded him in his tent.

"Cons... err... General," the embarrassed officer began, "at the moment the Senate is a weathervane. When Mark Antony was in its good books, it attempted to please him, and therefore you, who had been a consul together with him. But now that Mark Antony has become a sort of public enemy..."

Dolabella banged his fist on the arm of his chair, interrupting him. "Now that Mark Antony has become a public enemy and the Senate and the new consuls are at war, everything serves to strengthen the opposing party. Caesar's murderers have gone back to being heroes, just like in the hours immediately after the Ides of March. The senators see Decimus Brutus as the bulwark against Mark Antony's conquest of Gaul and will do anything to please him. They send him both consuls and the young Octavian as re-inforcements and give the major provinces to their friends and associates. And now what am I to do?" he concluded, querulously.

The officer held out his arms questioningly. "You could try to reach Syria before Cassius. He, too, is having troubles along the way, as you know..."

Dolabella looked at him with eyes red raw from crying. "Yes, that's what I will do. Let's get going as soon as possible and beat him to it. The Syrian legions will be mine, and I want to see how they will take them from me then."

Ortwin felt his stomach clench. The idiot was going to stop him from carrying out his primary mission, after spending three days camped pointlessly outside the walls of Smyrna. Bravely, he tried to intervene. "Forgive me, Consul," he ventured, using the title that he knew would most please his commander, "but would you grant me permission to bring up something important?"

Only at that moment did Dolabella seem to notice him. He looked over at him in annoyance, obviously surprised that a barbarian was able 'bring up' anything at all. By now, most of the Roman generals respected and valued the Celtic and German auxiliaries – but not Dolabella. But the commander, too disheartened to treat him with the contempt he felt, remained silent, and Ortwin took this as assent.

"If we leave after a failed siege here, it will not make a good impression, especially on the legions of Syria whose command you intend to assume," he said in a firm voice. After having spoken many times face to face with Caesar, he was certainly not about to be intimidated by a man like Dolabella, who was not a patch on the former dictator and had not one ounce of his charisma. "Moreover, even if you did reach Syria before Cassius you would have everyone here in the East – Marcus Brutus, Tillius Cimber in Bithynia and Trebonius in Asia – against you. In my humble opinion, you would do well to get rid of at least Trebonius, seeing as we are here."

"You make it sound so easy, barbarian!" Dolabella shook his head and stood up. He walked back and forth inside the tent. "Can you tell me how we can get into Smyrna? The few siege machines that we cobbled together didn't cause any damage to the walls or the gates, while their scorpios up on the battlements killed several men and beasts of burden."

He was right, of course. Thanks to the general's obvious military inexperience, the siege had begun in the worst possible way. All attempts to dig tunnels, approach the walls with ladders or place a ram in front of the gates had ended badly, halted by the attackers with ridiculous ease and with heavy losses to Dolabella's already meagre forces. In reality it was unthinkable to even try to conquer a city with such mighty fortifications as Smyrna without powerful machines and an adequate number of soldiers. Caesar himself would probably not have managed it, let alone a half-man like this mediocre subaltern, Ortwin thought to himself.

But right from the beginning of the siege, which his rich experience had immediately told him was an impossible undertaking, the German had devoted himself to finding a solution, and he decided now was the time to tell the commander. "General, we are not able to take the city. There are too few of us and we are too poorly equipped. Furthermore, if we stay here, we risk finding ourselves with Tillius Cimber on our backs. What we need is a rapid offensive."

"A rapid offensive? What does that mean?"

"You pack up and go. Or at least, make it look like you are giving up the siege," he said. "We 'barbarians' will do the rest."

Dolabella stared at him, then turned his head away, deep in thought. He could see that he desperately wanted to trust him. He was sunk so low, without position, province or army, that he was willing to believe anyone who would offer him a chance, but at the same time, it repelled him to have to depend upon a barbarian. Ortwin could only hope that the blunderer was so desperate he would ignore his own prejudices. He waited in silence for the general's decision, looking first at his men, then at Dolabella. The Roman took his time to decide. Finally he spoke.

"And if things go wrong?"

"If things goes wrong, my men and I will die. So it will no longer be your problem. Do you have anyone else willing to sacrifice himself, by chance?"

Dolabella gave up. The deed was done.

Now all he had to do now was take the city using eight men. And without that useless idiot, they might just have a chance.

*

Agrippa had rejoiced in wearing the legionary's breastplate again. Thanks to the good offices of Maecenas, he had enlisted among the latest recruits in Pansa's new legions, and had gone to the North to help the one who had thrown him out. The young man was looking for a cause to fight for, and could see none more worthy than the cult of Mars Ultor. And Octavian, who he had forgiven for his actions. Haunted by guilt for ruining his friend's plans and endangering the objectives of the sect, he had resigned himself to the idea of supporting the brotherhood from the outside without its leader knowing. What with all the creditors and politicians linked to Maecenas and Octavian, there were many working for the sect, but they were completely unaware of the fact that they were doing it for a group which was aiming to take control of Rome. Maybe they thought it was they who were using Octavian as their tool, or that they were building a faction around him in opposition to the other factions, or perhaps simply helping him to honour the memory of Caesar. He was fully aware, however, of the grand idea that his friend had in mind, and there was nothing he wanted more than to join him. For now, it was enough to know that Maecenas was following his movements.

"There! There's something moving in the bushes!" shouted a soldier who was Markhing in the same line of the column. Agrippa shook his head. He was surrounded by untrained recruits. Fortunately, that morning, thanks to the re-inforcements sent by Hirtius and Octavian, there was no risk of fighting, because these greenhorns would have had trouble putting up a decent front, but sooner or later they would have to take on Mark Antony's seasoned troops, and then they would see that in war the number of men mattered little. The majority of his companions were more or less the same age as him, but he had been fighting for over a year, and it was obvious.

"I can see something moving too!" croaked another frightened voice. "Maybe it's animals!"

"Yes, some sheep that have got away from their shepherd..."

"Or some peasant who is watching us, intrigued but scared..."

Agrippa realised immediately. Octavian's re-inforcements had not yet arrived and that group of so-called soldiers, hastily trained by the consul in Rome, wouldn't even have known how to deal with a gang of screaming barbarians, let alone veteran legionaries. It was better to make sure that there were no enemies in the area: even one cohort of Antony's men could sow panic among the ranks of the recruits.

He called the nearest officer. "Optio! I think we'd better

send someone to see what's behind those bushes and get into *agmen quadratum* formation!" he shouted.

"Don't talk rubbish! Hirtius's re-inforcements are apparently just ahead – no one would attack so many of us! It's just some animals!" said the officer, piqued that a foot soldier had dared to tell him what to do.

Agrippa was about to open his mouth again and answer, but the *optio* walked past him. With an angry gesture he left the formation and set off to see for himself.

"What are you doing? If he sees you, you'll feel his stick on your back…" whispered the even younger soldier next to him, grabbing him by the arm.

"Better to be beaten with sticks than have a pilum stuck in your chest," said Agrippa, continuing to walk away, until his feet were on the marshy ground. He drew his sword and headed for the bushes that bordered a wooded spot just off the Via Aemilia, towards which the men were heading. His feet splashed through the mud and felt heavier with each step. He began to push aside the bushes with his shield.

"What are you doing, soldier? I told you to ignore it! I'll show you, you idiot…" The *optio* had seen him, and was coming towards him, brandishing his long stick with a brass ball at the end. He looked intent on making him regret his actions.

Agrippa had to hurry. With extreme care, he moved more shrubs aside. Nothing. But it was a gloomy, foggy morning, with no hope of the pale sun filtering through the mantle of mist covering the plain. The looming trees prevented him from seeing anything. He took another two steps forward, whilst the squelching of the officer's boots and his laboured breathing grew louder and louder.

"Didn't you hear me, you idiot? If you don't need your ears, I'll remove them for you!" the *optio* shouted. He was getting closer. Agrippa, however, kept his eyes straight ahead. He knew that he was right when he saw a shadow emerge from behind the trees. It moved towards him, suddenly preceded by the glint of a blade. At that moment the *optio* appeared at his side, annoyed by his apparent indifference and prepared to strike him with his stick. Agrippa saw a legionary materialise in front of him and dodged to the side.

The legionary plunged his sword into the *optio's* ribs. He

remained immobile, his stick raised in the air, sporting an incredulous expression under his plumed and crested helmet, and Agrippa leapt forward to attack before the enemy could extract his blade from the officer's dying body. With a powerful jab, his sword opened up his opponent's side, ripping through the chain mail and thrusting into the man's flesh.

An instant later, more of Antony's men jumped out from the bushes in silence, all with their swords in their hands.

Agrippa drew his blade from the soldier's body, stepped back a few feet then turned round to make for his rank, shouting, "Alarm! Alarm! Ambush! Form up!" But his cries were lost amidst the terror of his inexperienced comrades, who had noticed what was happening. And he knew that his words were lost on the wind.

*

There was no army of friendly legions awaiting them, but a battle. Rufus cursed their inattention. There were many of Antony's men, he said to himself: too many to hope to scare them off without a fight, especially because Pansa's recruits were not up to the job – a fact none of the leaders had taken seriously enough.

The vanguard reported retreats that sounded more like routs among the consul's inexperienced men, and immediately Carfulenus and Galba had hastened to communicate to Pansa to leave to them the job of halting the attack with the few experienced men at their disposal and to wait for their arrival and keep the recruits out of danger as much as possible. But when Rufus arrived at the site of the battle, he realised that it was easier said than done. Mark Antony's soldiers were pouring out of the foliage and attacking from both sides of the Via Aemilia, and the recruits had no way of escaping, apart from meeting the oncoming Martia or returning to Forum Gallorum, where they would probably be picked up by the enemy, so they had ended up massing around the veterans, seeking their protection without being useful in any way and hindering their movements.

Exactly what Maecenas was doing to him, by Jupiter! The idiot had insisted on participating in the night march, and

Octavian had demanded that he kept an eye on him, without realising that in battle you need eyes in the back of your head just to cover your own arse, and now he would have to protect that Etruscan, who in the eyes of the chief was surely more important to the sect than he, and put himself at even more risk! Why hadn't Maecenas stayed quietly at the camp to give his good advice there, instead of trying to do the work of real men?

To protect him, moreover, he would have to reach Octavian's praetorian cohort, in which Maecenas was pretending to be a tribune. By the Gods – his first major battle and he was going to have to spend it playing bodyguard to that runt instead of proving his skill as a soldier! He was glad that Agrippa wasn't there – at least Rufus no longer had to prove himself better than him.

He noticed that Carfulenus had led the praetorian cohort to the left side of the road and his men, whose silhouettes were already blurred in the thick blanket of fog, disappeared into the dense vegetation. Next he saw Galba emerge above the helmets of his men and indicate to the centurions to move the cohorts to the right side of the road, where it seemed the enemy were present in larger numbers. Separating the forces seemed foolish to him, especially since none of them knew how many there were on that side.

Now, everything started to become more difficult. Rufus advanced through the marshes with a feeling of impending disaster, and the further he advanced the more he realised that they would have to fight on their own, despite there being five legions nearby. Where had Maecenas ended up? Had he already been done for? He was almost hoping so when an unmistakable clumsy figure appeared from between the trees in the swamp. The Etruscan was standing behind three soldiers who were defending themselves against at least five – he couldn't make out the exact number – enemy legionaries.

He rushed towards them, taking a diagonal trajectory that allowed him to spring up behind the attackers. He immediately stabbed one in the back and used his shield to knock over another, who ended up on the tip of one of Maecenas's comrades' swords. The three remaining attackers seemed disconcerted by his arrival, and in an instant none of them were left standing.

"Galba has delivered us to death!" wailed the Etruscan hysterically – his lucid intelligence had identified another reason why the commander of the Martia had wanted to separate the two units. Rufus realized that he was probably right – Caesar's murderers would certainly not want Octavian to become too powerful. "We of the praetorian cohort are too few to fight alone."

"So let's make sure we stay alive! Otherwise Octavian is capable of cursing my grave for having failed to protect his precious counsellor," said Rufus drily, grabbing him by the arm and dragging him along. "Let's try and join the others," he said to the other three soldiers. "Carfulenus has gone in too deep and he's broken up the unit – the only chance we've got of limiting the damage is by staying close together."

The others nodded, and together they began to advance parallel with the road in order to round up as many of their comrades as possible along the way. But instead they ran into a group of enemy soldiers.

"Stay behind me!" cried Rufus to Maecenas, as he and the other three prepared for the attack. The clanging of blades rang out through the trees, sending startled birds flapping away. There were none of the shouts of encouragement or insults which usually punctuate a battle – the soldiers fought in silence, as though enchanted by the hushed atmosphere, almost in deferential respect to the natural world which hosted their struggle.

From the corner of his eye, Rufus could see that Maecenas had advanced on their side, keeping up his shield to defend himself from the blows of one of the soldiers, but holding his right arm – the one which held his sword – limp and unprotected. He was completely useless, but at least he was keeping one of the attackers busy! Rufus, however, could not afford to let him be injured. He gave him a shove and pushed him back, but the Etruscan immediately returned to his chosen place. With a sigh, Rufus jumped between him and his adversary, hitting him with his shield. There was nothing worse, he thought, than defending a man who did not want to be defended and at the same time trying to save your own skin.

One of the attacker's lunges smashed his shield and Rufus felt the wood crack along his arm, which only served to make his attack all the fiercer. He reacted by swinging his sword horizontally and the blade cut clean through the enemy's neck, leaving his head dangling behind him. He heard a gurgling from Maecenas, and when he looked over at him saw that he was bent double, vomiting. What a soldier! But then another attacker – the one he had abandoned in order to defend the Etruscan – was upon him. He stumbled backwards and fell over Maecenas, exposing himself to the enemy blade and realising that he was done for.

Head down, the Etruscan threw himself at Antony's man, ramming his helmet into the man's thigh and knocking him to the ground. And suddenly there were two blades stabbing at him – that of Rufus and that of Maecenas, who plunged his sword in with both arms, pinning the soldier to the waterlogged ground. He tried to pull the blade out and remained motionless, exposing his back to the blows of an oncoming attacker, who Rufus just had time to block by retrieving his own sword and tackling him, then managed to catch him off guard and plunge the sword into his ribs.

"Look what I have to do for you…" he hissed at Maecenas, but not as acrimoniously as before. He had to admit that the Etruscan was doing his best, even though it was clear he was not cut out for it.

In any case, the enemy had had enough. The two survivors had chosen to make a run for it, and only then did Rufus realise that he had lost one of his own men, who was lying at his feet. There were four of them now, but then he noticed another group of fellow soldiers in front of them.

Among them was Carfulenus, standing over the carcass of his horse and struggling hard not to be overcome by the enemy.

And they were surrounded.

*

"Get back! Get back! Stand back, you over there! If you don't know how to fight just stay out of the way!"

Agrippa tried to advance, but the flood of new recruits retreating on the orders of their own commander dragged him back with them. Some centurions were attempting to keep order and direct the flow of Pansa's legions into a tight group at the rear to avoid obstructing the soldiers of the Martia. The veterans who had come to their rescue had hardly been able to swing their swords because of the disorderly press of frightened recruits.

No formation, no *agmen quadratum*, no centurion visible among the chaotic mass. The recruits clung to one another, huddling together on the road so as to avoid the woods and the possibility of being surprised from all sides. They had been ordered by their commanders to make room for Galba's legionaries, and Agrippa saw that they didn't seem to mind much about not fighting. But then, they were men who had only just finished their initial three months of training, and would never have imagined being catapulted into a real battle before getting to the battlefield proper.

But he *wanted* to fight. He was not a recruit, even though he was passing himself off as one. He would not regain Octavian's esteem by standing watching the men of the Martia being massacred. Even if one of their commanding officers *was* one of Caesar's assassins.

He began pushing against the tide and elbowed his way through, to surprised looks from the other soldiers who moved out of his way, until he reached to the front row, where he studied the situation. In almost total silence, the expert legionaries were fighting along one side of the road, from the verge to the woods, and staggering through the marshes. The only cries Agrippa heard came from the recruits who surrounded him. Suddenly he realized that this was not a battle, but a challenge. Mark Antony's men wanted revenge upon the legionaries of the Martia, who had abandoned their commander, and those of the Martia intended to avenge the inaction of their opponents at the decimation wrought by Mark Antony in Brindisi.

It was private business, and that was why they had sent the recruits away. The excuse of needing space to be able to fight properly was just a pretext.

He shared the feelings of the Martia, though, so he could not simply stand by and watch.

Suddenly, he shot forward. A centurion shouted for him to stop, but Agrippa ignored him. He rushed over the edge of the Via Aemilia and started making his way through the marshes beyond it. At each step, his legs became heavier and heavier and his breath shorter, and the increasingly dense bushes scratched at his calves. He passed the first bodies, which, hacked up and mutilated, lay half-buried in the mud, their bones broken, their faces twisted with agony and their innards scattered all around. He began to feel nauseous at the sight of what the sword in his hand could do to a man in a real battle.

Someone moaned, and he saw a man with terrible wounds dragging himself along. He had lost an arm and, holding it in his mouth by its fingers, was dragging himself along on his remaining one. Another, with a deep slash across his face and no nose, wandered on his knees, his arms outstretched. Yet another, a sword sticking out from just above his armpit, was staggering about and calling loudly for a doctor.

Agrippa felt as though he were living out his worst nightmare. He had always wanted to fight and excel in war: to show his courage and defeat an enemy as part of the admirable war machine that was the Roman army. But the reality was different from his dreams, and the road to victory and celebrity first had to pass through these horrors. Nothing in his training could have prepared him for what he was witnessing.

But courage presupposed also the ability to overcome the shock of those images. He decided he would not allow it to disconcert him, and set off again at a brisk pace, as fast as the muddy terrain would let him until he finally found himself in the middle of the battle. Only then did he feel the excitement of the challenge, which would allow him to prove himself among the veterans, mounting within him.

The legionaries, all older than him, fought with an expertise that he had never had the opportunity to see on the battlefield but only in training. They used their swords and shields with skill, making use of both of them in defence and in attack, changing places with one another without the need for communication, and fighting energetically both as individuals and as a unit even after a prolonged battle.

He had much to learn from such brave soldiers. Yes, it was there, among these men, that he felt he should be. And so he plunged into the fray.

*

Maecenas was almost happy that Carfulenus was in danger –

his duty to save the legate might finally force Rufus to slacken his guard over him, thought the Etruscan. So far he hadn't let up for a moment, as though he were looking after a child, and this was certainly not why Maecenas had wanted to go into battle. Of course, he was afraid of dying – terrified, in fact – but he was not willing to tolerate survival at the price of such humiliation.

Carfulenus was defending himself, together with a handful of men, from a group of enemy soldiers which surrounded him on all sides. Their attackers were few, but if they managed to pin him down there was the risk that re-inforcements would turn up. "You, with me!" the Etruscan ordered one of the soldiers who was with them. Then he turned to Rufus, "You take the other legionaries and attack this lot opposite while we spread out a bit and attack them from the other flank. Let's just hope they think there are plenty of us."

"No!" shouted Rufus, "We mustn't split up!" But it was too late. Maecenas had already left, and was making his way through the vegetation, feeling the damp of that insalubrious place, whose stagnant waters gave off a nauseating reek, penetrate his bones. He had to remind himself that it was he who had chosen to come here, and quickened his step until he found himself behind Carfulenus's group. A quick count of the fighters showed that the legate was left with four soldiers, while at least nine were attacking him on either side. The survivors of the cohort had made a barricade out of the bodies of their fallen comrades, piling them up between two trees so as to form a kind of wall. The fighting there must have been brutal, as it was heaped with dead bodies, and almost all the shields that had been abandoned on the ground bore the insignia of the praetorian cohort.

Then he saw Rufus and the soldier he had left with him attack three enemy soldiers who were too busy with the men of the cohort to notice their assault. He plucked up his courage and stepped forward with his own subordinate, his sword pointed straight ahead of him and his shield covering as much of his own body as possible. He spotted a soldier and headed straight for his back, deciding to strike him and at the same time try to knock off balance the soldier to his left with a thrust of his shield. He motioned to his companion to do the same to another soldier.

When he was close to his target, he took a deep breath and

leapt forward, lunging with all the strength he possessed. He cried out loud to give himself the courage to push his blade in deeper and deeper, for fear of not being able to penetrate the rings of chain mail that covered the attacker's torso, and was almost surprised when he felt the sword slide between the metal and the flesh, breaking bones, ripping apart organs and guts and even emerging on the other side of the attacker's body. He would never have imagined that he held such a potent weapon in his hand or that he had such a strong arm.

Even his shield had done its duty. When he had struck the soldier beside him in his back, the man had fallen over and ended up landing on the tip of one of the defenders' swords. But now the legionaries were aware of the attack from the rear, and at least two of them had turned their attention to Maecenas. He tried to regain his balance and recover his *gladio*, but his victim had taken his weapon with him when he fell to the ground and it was out of the Etruscan's reach.

He was disarmed. Fortunately for him, the soldier who was with him had not made the same mistake. He had hit his target with a blow to the neck, taking him out without losing his grip on his weapon. His speed made the two enemy soldiers turn their attention to him, giving Maecenas time to take the sword of the man he had killed, which was easier than retrieving than his own. He also wanted to keep an eye on Rufus, who had managed to penetrate the row of assailants and was duelling with a legionary who was positioned between him and the legate.

Suddenly, Maecenas realised he could no longer count on surprise in attacking the enemy: he was forced to fight on equal terms with experienced soldiers, now. The idea threw him into a panic – he must immediately put his superior brains to work, he thought, if he wanted to get away without losing his skin or being thought of as a coward. An idea came to him: while all the other soldiers were busy fighting, he backed off a few steps until he came upon a pile of corpses. With a quick slash he cut off the arm of one of the dead soldiers, then the other, and finally his leg. He picked up the three limbs and, struggling to control his disgust, held them between his torso and his left arm, which was protected by a shield.

Just in time. The soldier he had brought along had gone down after dragging an opponent to Hades with him, and the free legionary was now making for him. Maecenas did not run for it but stood his ground, the bloody arms hidden behind his shield. He let the leg slip to the ground in front of his feet and when his antagonist was in front of him – praying that he wasn't too seasoned a fighter for his trick to be effective – Maecenas kicked the severed limb, which was half hidden in the water and the vegetation, at him. It flew against the soldier, who saw it suddenly appear from out of the ground as though it were some demon of the underworld attempting to emerge from the bowels of the Earth.

The terrified legionary almost fell over in shock and, seeing his guard lowered, Maecenas threw one of the arms at his face. The soldier closed his eyes, giving him the chance to get close enough to strike a blow. By now he had learned that at that distance, he couldn't fail. The soldier collapsed to his knees, putting his hands to his face, as blood ran in rivulets between his fingers and down his arms, then fell back into the swamp, at Maecenas's feet.

"I can't wait to tell Octavian this," he said. Then he looked around. Now they had superior numbers. Rufus had freed himself of at least two enemy soldiers, without doubt fighting in the most orthodox way, he thought wryly, but he also saw Carfulenus on his knees, his hands grasping his stomach. He went to him, while the three surviving enemy soldiers retreated, chased away by Rufus and his men.

Maecenas focused his attention on the legate's wound, and what he saw shocked him into despair. Carfulenus was holding in his own intestines, which were protruding from a large gash just above his cingulum. He was doomed. The legate noticed his tribune uniform and whispered, "Take the survivors back to the camp... but hurry...", before collapsing on his side, his eyes wide open and glassy.

"By the gods, if you had listened to me maybe we would have saved him..." hissed Rufus, now free from any threat. "But at least you managed to save yourself, for now. Octavian cares more about you than about him, after all."

Maecenas did not know what to say without appearing unpleasant. And he did not like appearing unpleasant, so he changed the subject. "He said to rally the survivors and return to camp." He turned to one of the legate's soldiers and said, "You who were with him, do you have any idea how the battle went?"

The man held out his hands resignedly. "I only know that we of the cohort had to fight against at least two of Mark Antony's praetorian cohorts and his cavalry. It was a massacre, I doubt we'll find many alive. I have no idea what the Martia and Pansa's legions did, nor exactly where they fought. Maybe on the other side of the Via Aemilia."

Maecenas suddenly realised how difficult it was even for a commander to have a clear idea of the progress of a battle. The courage of a leader was inversely proportional to his ability to read the different stages of a conflict, and the more likely he was to plunge into the heart of the fighting to prove that he wanted to share the same dangers as the troops and lead by example the less chance he had of understanding what to do and what to avoid in order to achieve his objectives. The battles between massive armies took place on a chessboard which was so huge that only the use of couriers could allow commanders or individual officers to know what was happening even half a mile away on the opposite flank: but how could a courier reach a commander who was in the middle of the fray? And how could he do it in time to implement his orders and communicate them to the sector from whence he came?

That battle had made all these problems more evident. The road, the woods, the marshes, the swamps and the various units arriving from all points of the map had split the clash up into a series of isolated skirmishes, in which each fighter or official was ignorant of the fate of his comrades.

Fighting like this was totally pointless. Such battles could only be open-ended, however much carnage they caused. He made a mental note to reflect upon it further and to talk to Octavian about it. If they were going to show they were superior to all the other antagonists in this power struggle, they would need to adopt new military strategies.

He was about to tell Rufus to begin marching, but stopped himself: he had a natural understanding of people's souls, and knew that the young man was motivated, above all, by vanity. He needed to flatter him if he wanted to keep him firmly bound to the cause. It would be a bad idea to show himself his superior in military affairs.

"What shall we do, Rufus?" deferring to his decision.

"Do you even need to ask?" answered the tribune. "We

return to camp just as the legate told us to, of course – and at full tilt, too."

XVII

"Here they come," whispered Veleda, reaching Ortwin and the other Germans who were in the bushes where they were stationed. "You were right, they were following us."

"I was certain that Trebonius would send someone to check if Dolabella's army had really gone. How many?" asked Ortwin.

"Six," said Veleda, crouching down with them among the branches. "It'll be child's play," she added, running the fingers of her one hand along the sword which rested on her stump. It had been a long time since she had fought and she felt a great desire to do so in order to vent her frustrations and exorcise her failures.

Ortwin wasted no time. "You," he said, pointing to two of his men, "go immediately to Dolabella and tell him that we are ready – he can come back and start Markhing on the city right away."

The men stood up and walked towards the horses, who had been left in a nearby clearing. Veleda admired her man's assertiveness – he was a born leader, one who knew how to make his soldiers love him. One day he would command again, if things went as they hoped.

In the distance, they heard the clattering hooves of the horses that Veleda had seen previously. Ortwin motioned for everyone to be silent, gesturing for them to keep their swords at the ready. "Be careful," whispered the chief. "On my signal come out from the bushes and surround them immediately. If even one of them manages to escape all this will have been a total waste of time and energy. And remember – we need to take at least one of them alive."

The men nodded, and then they all waited for the knights of the garrison of Smyrna to come into sight. Veleda heard them approach, and gave a grateful look up at the sky: the cold, starless night and those dark clouds, heavy with rain, would help them with the ambush. The riders would see them emerge out of the darkness only at the last minute. She stood quietly, awaiting their arrival, looking first at the road, then at Ortwin, with whom she exchanged a look of understanding, certain that he felt the same excitement at going back into action as she did. The half-hearted siege conducted by Dolabella had done nothing but exacerbate the feelings of impotence and worthlessness which had never abandoned her since they had left Germany defeated.

The silhouettes of the riders appeared on the road – tiny shapes floating in the darkness which gradually became solid figures advancing in no particular order, occupying the entire width of the road. When they reached the Germans' position, Ortwin raised his arm and leapt out from the bushes, and the others followed suit, making no sound except that of snapping branches. The barbarians positioned four of their soldiers in front of the enemy line and four behind, while Veleda remained by the road and Ortwin ran along the other side. Before they had even noticed the presence of the enemy, the horsemen found themselves surrounded. The horses whinnied as Ortwin and the others grabbed them by their bridles and began to thrust their swords into the animals' legs. Some collapsed immediately, sending their riders crashing to the ground to end up at the mercy of their attackers.

The German's swords struck repeatedly, soon turning red with blood, but in two cases the horses reared up, giving their riders time to react. Veleda was unable to strike the animal near her, and her attacker managed to draw his sword from its sheath and began swinging it from left to right. Fortunately, his horse was moving too much to allow him any accuracy, and the woman was able to evade his counterattacks. She felt one of her men appear at her side and move into a position which forced her attacker to fight on both sides. The horseman looked around him and, seeing that all his comrades had been killed, gave up trying to hit them with his sword, turned the animal around and headed at full speed towards Smyrna.

No, this can't be happening, thought Veleda desperately. She couldn't be responsible for this undertaking failing too. She gathered all her strength, threw her sword to the ground and with her one hand grabbed the tail of the animal in front of her, before it could abandon the battlefield, grasping it tightly and trying to keep her feet. She moved her legs with the greatest possible speed, but could not prevent herself from being dragged along, ending up with her face between the animal's hindquarters, tossed forward in mid-air. She bounced once, twice, three times along the ground, but continued to hold on tight. A sharp pain shot across the palm of her hand but she continued to hold on with all the strength in her fingers, saying to herself, "If I can just slow him down... just slow him down..."

She couldn't have said how long she held on, nor how many times she banged her feet, knees and arms during her attempt to stop herself from being simply dragged along the road, and when she eventually let go, falling forwards onto her face in the dust, the feeling of defeat was even more painful than the bruises and cuts which covered her body. But immediately, she heard the horse neighing, its hooves clattering a few steps away from her, the unmistakable sound of swords and then a thud beside her. She opened her eyes and saw before her the glazed expression of a lifeless face, a torrent of blood pouring from its mouth.

"What got into you?" It was Ortwin's voice. He delicately turned her over onto her back and gazed at her, stroking her bloodied, tearstained face as he did.

"I... I didn't want to make you suffer another failure..."

The man smiled. "You've never made me do anything," he said. "I decided for myself to do what we did together."

"Did... Did any of them survive?" she asked faintly.

Ortwin did not answer. He turned to his men and gestured for them to come closer. They brought with them a frightened and bewildered soldier whose arm was wounded.

"Give us the password and you will die immediately. Otherwise, it might take a long time," said the German coldly.

The soldier looked at the grim faces of the warriors and tried to beg for mercy, but none of them said a word or moved a muscle. Ortwin motioned to one of his men, and the barbarian grabbed one of the prisoner's arms and then his hand, while another pulled out a knife from his belt and grabbed the Roman's index finger.

"The Ides of March! The Ides of March!" shouted the terrified prisoner.

"How imaginative..." muttered Ortwin, then nodded to his subordinate, who placed his sword on the soldiers's neck and slew him instantly.

*

All Agrippa had done had been to take the place of a fallen legionary, and now he found himself like a cog in a wonderfully efficient machine where everyone worked together with everybody else. He had not managed to get to the front line yet but – the *mutatio ordinis* meant that those at the front were constantly being replaced with fresh men – and it would eventually be his turn. All of them fought in a concentrated, ruthlessly efficient way and the centurions had almost no need to shout out their orders, because every soldier knew what to do and when to do it. They were professionals, aware of being among other veterans of war. And Agrippa loved it all, so when finally it was his turn to tackle the enemy face to face, it was with awe but also with the excitement of one eager to prove he was up to the job that he went.

In front of him was a legionary who, though elderly, was by no means slow or out of shape. He moved his torso little but his arms were always where they were supposed to be, his left constantly covered by his shield to ward off Agrippa's blows, the right always ready to attack and launch dangerous thrusts. Being the experienced soldier that he was, the man managed to conserve his energy by moving the bare minimum in order to injure others and to protect himself, and as they duelled, Agrippa tried to learn his method. He copied his moves and with each blow given or received, gave him admiring glances which the legionary would certainly struggle to understand.

It was hard for him not to complement the man, because more than once he found himself in difficulty, wishing that his opponent were not such a good soldier. At the same time, though, he wanted to use the opportunity to improve as a soldier and he hesitated to give his all, staying on the defensive. However, it occurred to him that sooner or later he would be replaced by his comrades to the rear, so he tried to hurry things up. Obviously, he found a serious obstacle in his attacker, who had no intention of letting himself be beaten – he was as steadfast and compact as granite, seeming never to tire nor make a wrong move.

Agrippa began to worry. He couldn't manage to strike his enemy, and at the same time realised that he was getting closer and closer. He managed to touch him a few times with the tip of his blade, but only ever hitting his breastplate. Gradually, his enthusiasm gave way to despondency at his own impotence. The young man lost his cool and began swinging his right arm almost blindly, deluding himself that he could penetrate the other's guard. But it was useless. The veteran, with his icy stare and tightly closed mouth, kept him at bay with his efficient moves.

Then, however, the soldier standing next to his opponent was run through by the legionary at Agrippa's flank, and fell sideways, right on top of the veteran, who was thrown off balance for a moment. The young man saw his chance, and immediately plunged his sword in horizontally. It took him an instant to realise that he had stuck his sword into the man's right armpit, and the man blinked as though he did not believe it either, then staggered and fell backwards.

Agrippa waited a second then let out a cry of triumph, which went unheard in that surreal situation where the only sounds to be heard were the breathing of the soldiers and the clanging of weapons. He prepared to face another attacker, feeling able now to take on anyone, but around him he saw that his line was moving back. The centurion ordered them to retreat. His men were losing ground, suffering under the pressure of the enemy and the high number of losses. His small victory meant nothing to them – it was important only to him.

He was forced to fight on the defensive, trying to keep off the attackers who were pressing his cohort while giving way to those behind him in order for them to retreat in good order, without ending up on top of them and breaking up ranks. But it was clear that they were losing – it was only a matter of time.

"The consul! The consul is coming!"

The cry ran through the ranks of the Martia legion, and immediately afterwards Pansa galloped up at the head of several squadrons of cavalry. The consul threw himself bravely into the front line, cutting through it in order to create a barrier between the Martia and the enemy, thus giving his unit the chance to regroup and launch a counter attack. While Pansa and his men kept Mark Antony's front line busy, Agrippa was sent back to the second row by a centurion. He was annoyed: he wanted to be up there at the front, ready for the battle, but resigned himself, knowing that it would soon be his turn again. And he was eager to put into practice what he believed he had learned from fighting with the veteran.

So he remained there, like the others, and watched the consul's men in action. Pansa rode back and forth along the front line, urging his men on and occasionally exchanging a few thrusts of his sword with the infantry. Agrippa couldn't help but notice that he was leading his troops and that Mark Antony was not. And just as he did, he saw the consul collapse over his horse, the shaft of a javelin sticking from his ribs.

He heard the men nearby cry out in dismay, and those near Pansa formed a circle with their shields to protect him. One of them led his horse by the reins and, slowly, they moved along the front in order to leave the battlefield. Pansa was still in the saddle, but sat immobile on the horse's back, presumably unconscious. Everyone wondered if he was alive or dead, while his men retreated with him, leaving the field between the Martia and the enemy line open once more.

Before even hearing the men cry out, Agrippa knew what the centurions' orders would be.

"Retreat! Retreat!"

His first important battle was a defeat.

*

Maecenas had freed himself from his breastplate and shield in order to be able to run faster and for longer. He enviously watched Rufus, who for miles and miles continued to alternate marching and running, whilst carrying all his equipment, without even getting out of breath. The Etruscan had tried to carry the same weapons as his companions, but unlike them he could barely hobble along under their weight, and in the end Rufus had told him to dump anything superfluous.

"Anyway," he said, "if they did catch up with us, you'd be no use anyway. And I've no intention of getting caught just because we had to wait for you." He seemed to have already forgotten that Maecenas had managed without his help during the fighting in the woods.

It was also true that luck did not strike twice in the same

place. Maecenas had killed an enemy soldier, of course, but if forced to bet on the next round, he would not have put his money on himself.

And from what they could see, more enemy soldiers would soon be upon them. They had reached the area near the Martia's camp, where the legion had just retreated. They were hiding at the edge of a forest, studying the situation and how to reach the walls of the fort, where many of the surviving legionaries were now lined up. Only the wounded had entered, carried inside by their comrades, along with those who had been disarmed. Others had decided to wait at the ditch for Mark Antony's soldiers, who had stopped a few hundred feet from them, to attack.

"Damn it, why aren't they going inside?" said Maecenas to Rufus, certain that he was asking the question that was on the lips of the other soldiers who were with them. Fifty survivors of the praetorian cohort, of the nearly five hundred that Octavian had sent to Forum Gallorum.

"This time, I can teach you something, Etruscan," said Rufus, almost amused. "You might be astute but you know very little about military manoeuvres. The legionaries of Martia lost the battle, but they are not willing to admit it, so instead of holing up behind the ramparts, which would force them to admit defeat, they want to show that they are still ready to fight and have only implemented a tactical withdrawal. This is a battle between veterans, my friend. Veterans who all want to put on a better show than their opponents. Nobody is willing to lose."

"And perhaps in this way they hope to dissuade Antony's men from attacking them, hoping that they are now tired from the battle and the chase," remarked Maecenas, after reflecting on what, at first, had seemed like an insane tactic.

Rufus looked at him with respect. "You always manage to surprise me, Etruscan. Yes – if they were fighting enemies who were fresh to the battle, they would be mad to wait for them with the moat and embankment behind them. There would be no chance of halting their advance and the moat would leave them nowhere to escape to. But in this way... if Antony's men do actually launch an attack, it'll be a feeble one, giving our men time to fall back into the fort and shut the gates behind them.

The problem is that the enemy has only a slight numerical

advantage now, so they cannot take too many risks. But in a little while, the other soldiers who beat us will be here and might succeed, notwithstanding their fatigue. Remember that our men are tired too…" he observed, staring at the soldiers of Martia who were trying to look impressive, standing erect along the moat and holding out their swords defiantly. But if he squinted at them he could see that their faces were sweaty and covered with dirt and scratches, their shields covered in dents and their armour thick with mud. They were in too battered a state to convince their enemy that they were an insurmountable obstacle.

"This means that we have to rejoin them before Mark Antony arrives with re-inforcements," said Rufus, bringing them all back to reality. They were not simply spectators at that moment – they had to reunite with the Martia if they were to have any hope of surviving.

The no man's land between the two armies was occupied by only a few isolated soldiers advancing on both sides, challenging each other to attack and shouting insults and accusations. But while the Martia were alert and well-deployed, Mark Antony's men, all from the XXXV legion, seemed to have lowered their guard – their lines were disorganized and many soldiers were sitting on the ground while others were scattered about in search of supplies.

"Logical," thought Maecenas, "they are not under threat of an attack." It was inconceivable that the soldiers of the Martia could do anything except defend their camp, after the drubbing they had suffered at Forum Gallorum. Nevertheless, Antony's forward scouts couldn't help but see Rufus, himself and the other survivors if they tried to get out of the woods and make for the fort. And for Mark Antony's cavalry it would be child's play to reach them.

"How can we do it? They'll be on us as soon as we step out of the trees," objected the Etruscan.

"We have to try," said Rufus. "They're searching the woods for of supplies and firewood, and they'll soon find us in any event. At a guess, it's a third of a mile from here to the nearest corner of the camp as the crow flies. If we head for that, maybe they'll only notice us when we are closer to our lines, and if they come after us the Martia will come to our aid"

"Good plan, excellent, well done!" said Maecenas,

ironically. "Thank the gods you're here to teach us about tactics! I'll tell you what we do. We wait for it to get dark and we don't move until then. It should be less than two hours, more or less."

"No way," replied Rufus. "In two hours they'll have come this way countless times and we'll be done for."

"I doubt it. They might pass by once, but there's no certainty of that. What *is* certain, though, is that they will see us and get to us if we try to cross the plain." That was the problem with soldiers, thought Maecenas – they always want to act. Waiting just wasn't in their vocabulary.

"I order you to move now, tribune. You are at my command," insisted Rufus.

"I don't think so. We are of equal rank."

The astonished soldiers watched this argument between the two officers until Rufus said, "At my signal, move out. I don't want to waste any more time." Ignoring Maecenas, he turned round, evidently convinced that they would follow him. But the Etruscan had no intention of moving and when Rufus headed out, only about thirty men went with him and not all at the same time. An irregular column formed, which made them even more visible. The remaining twenty legionaries who seemed to prefer Maecenas's strategy stayed where they were.

After a few dozen steps, Rufus turned for a moment to check the situation and saw that his friend had not followed him. He slowed down and stopped, then made a gesture of irritation and forced himself to lead his confused men back. He had been bluffing, and his bluff had been called.

But Maecenas saw that they had been noticed, and several riders were already heading in their direction. It proved that they would never have made it, but being proved right was little consolation now.

Suddenly, they heard trumpets in the distance, behind the lines of the XXXV legion, and the cavalrymen who were approaching Rufus and his men slowed to a stop and looked back. Suddenly, a commotion broke out in the ranks of Antony's men. All the soldiers who had been sprawled on the ground got up rapidly and stood to attention, while others hastily returned from patrols.

Another army was arriving. It could only be that of Mark Antony in person for the final attack.

They were done for, whoever it was.

*

At first, Gaius Chaerea had bridled at Octavian's decision to keep him at his side. Granted, he was part of his general staff and was obliged to stay at his side, but he was also part of the Martia legion and his unit had gone to meet the troops of Pansa coming from Bologna. The irritation had then turned into anger when there were reports of a direct clash with Mark Antony's legions. There was a battle going on and he was not with his men. The soldiers he had commanded over the recent months, the same men whose steadfastness in the face of decimation he had admired, and the same men he had convinced to abandon Mark Antony.

Now, however… now he felt immense satisfaction, even joy: a joy he would never have felt if he had marched with his unit before dawn. Yes, because instead of a defeat, he was participating in a victory and above all, because he was turning Mark Antony's success into a failure.

As soon as they had heard about the ambush lain for Pansa and Carfulenus by Mark Antony, the generals had assembled and resolved to send re-inforcements to the IVth Legion, another of those which had rebelled against the consul. As commander in chief, it was Hirtius who took the lead of the relief column, but Octavian had insisted that he be accompanied by his most trusted men, including Chaerea. He had marched in the front lines and so had been able to enjoy the show without paying the price. The surprise and terror of Antony's men who, a moment before Hirtius's appearance had lain sprawled on the ground, content and sated with blood, intent on enjoying the victory, their ranks scattered, simply awaiting their supreme leader with his praetorian cohorts to deliver the final blow to the Martia.

It had all been too easy, he told himself. Octavian had ordered him to act only as an observer, but he was a soldier, by the gods, and where there was a fight, there he went. Although, to tell the truth, the enemy had put up little resistance. Octavian couldn't have criticised him for leaping into the fray for the simple fact that there was no fray, nor risk. Antony's men had simply turned their backs and taken to their heels, without even taking along their shields. The only thing that they had put to test was his breath – they had eluded all his lunges and so, for a short way at least, Chaerea had actually tried to chase them.

He saw that some were gathering their comrades and trying to set up a line of defence in order to favour an orderly withdrawal. Their cavalry were trying to act as a barrier, or circled their pursuers to delay their advance. They were veterans who had already fought for most of the day and knew that they were too tired to fight fresh troops. They had given their best, fighting for hours on equal terms the expert legionaries of the Martia, and they had even beaten them: they felt they'd done enough for one day.

Theirs was not cowardice, he told himself, but a simple strategic retreat in order for them recover their strength. And it made no difference if it resembled a rout. On the other hand, he had no intention of there being a massacre and, if he could, he would not have killed anyone. These were men that he might one day command, given the switching of allegiance that characterised civil war. Hirtius himself had ordered them to be taken prisoner, if possible: considering the fact that if it was possible to persuade them to change sides it was a very good way of gleaning troops from Mark Antony and adding to theirs. But as long as the men continued to run away like that it was impossible either to kill them or take them prisoner…

Chaerea wondered, as indeed had Octavian when he had learned of the attack, what had become of Maecenas and Rufus. It was rumoured that the praetorian cohort was the unit that had suffered most losses, and the leader of the sect, afraid of losing his most valuable friend and ally, was desperate to know what had happened to them. Chaerea had the impression that it had already cost Octavian much to expel Agrippa from the sect, and perhaps he even regretted having done so. In all likelihood, he couldn't face the loss of his other old friend, especially to whom he seemed to have assigned pre-eminence over the others. With all due respect to Salvidienus Rufus, who didn't like coming second to anyone.

Finally someone stopped to fight him. Chaerea saw before him a feathery crest like his own – it was a centurion, one he actually knew by sight, and who blocked his sword while calling loudly to his men to form a line. Chaerea tried to press him, simply attempting to demonstrate his superiority in order to impress the man's subordinates and encourage them to surrender.

But the other man fought back fiercely, striking to kill, and had Chaerea not taken action, he would probably have been successful. Chaerea parried a lunge, then a direct blow and a backhand, this last striking his shield and making his arm vibrate. His rival was strong but slow, he thought, perhaps because he was tired, or more likely because of his massive size. He, though, was fresh, and intended to take advantage of the fact. He feigned to the left, then instead swerved to the right, leapt up, stretched out his arm and lunged with his sword from above, with a backhand into the shoulder of his attacker. The tip of the blade severed the wire mesh and reinforced shoulder straps and penetrated the flesh.

It was not much, but it was enough to put the centurion out of action. Chaerea turned his attention to the soldiers who had been watching the duel as they tried to get into a formation.

And he realized he was alone.

If they decided to attack him, he wouldn't stand a chance. For an instant, he looked each of them in the eyes and they looked at him, some with their swords pointing directly ahead and others squatting behind their shields. A shiver ran down his spine. He realised he was afraid. To cover up his fear he decided to take a risk. He walked slowly towards them, his sword outstretched before him. He felt beads of sweat trickling down from under his helmet and beneath his protective leather tunic, and the echo of his laboured breathing pounded in his ears.

Some of his attackers withdrew as many steps as he advanced. The others soon emulated them, with varying degrees of conviction. Just then, a group of their riders passed by at a gallop, and one of them shouted something to the group – something that Chaerea could not hear because of the noise produced by the horses' hooves. After a moment's hesitation, two legionaries threw down their shields, rushed over to the horse and grabbed its tail. The rider dug in his spurs, the animal set off at gallop and the two soldiers were dragged along behind, away from there.

The other riders gestured to the legionaries to do the same – and almost none of them thought twice. Within moments, the soldiers were already far away, running with the loping gait of those being pulled along by something much faster.

Chaerea now stood on the open plains and he could see the outline of the fort that he had come to save. The Legionaries of the Martia, reassured by Hirtius's intervention, had also got involved, and they were not as soft as their enemies, the consul's men. The clearing was full of small skirmishes that looked more like summary executions, above all when one of Antony's men found the road blocked by a group of enemy attackers. The only ones who escaped were those who had surrendered, the legionaries who had tried to form a defence barrier, allowing the others behind them to escape. However, now Antony's men had no way of escaping the vice that trapped them on both sides.

It was over for the day. The first battle of yet another civil war. Octavian maintained that he wanted to put an end to the infighting which had been continuous in Rome for almost half a century where whoever won now, lost later. It had always been thus. Marius and Sulla had beaten one another, and even Caesar had beaten everyone only to then be killed, and now Mark Antony had both won and lost on the same day. When Roman's fought amongst themselves, things always ended up back at the starting point. Today's winner was tomorrow's loser, and even a successful morning could have turned bad by evening.

The men who provoked these reversals of fortunes were so blinded by their ambition that they did not see that they were running round in circles, and making Rome run round in circles with them. But people like Chaerea, who must only obey, could see, all right. Civil wars could cripple Rome more than any external attack. Certainly, Gaius did not know what could be done – he was not a statesman, nor a leader. He hoped, however, that one of those ambitious men who had disputed power was more far-seeing than the others, and that, together with his personal goals, he also intended to pursue the goals of Rome.

He hoped with all his heart that it was the man he had chosen to serve.

Octavian.

XVIII

"Password?"

"The Ides of March."

The massive wooden gates, dotted with iron studs, of Smyrna began to creak open. The sound drowned out for a moment even the noise of the fierce rain that lashed down onto the six mounted Germans waiting just outside the city walls. Ortwin lifted his face and let the rain pour down onto it, feeling his tension subside and at the same time savouring the unexpected help that Wotan had sent him. That horrible weather had made the sentry guarding the door from the guard tower uninterested in checking their identity and uninterested in them, covered in mud as they were and even more unrecognisable in the clothing they had seized from the slain knights.

The gate opened just enough to let them pass. Ortwin hoped that the guards were not the same ones who had been on duty when the cavalry whose place they had taken had left the city. Their shifts were not normally longer than half a day, so nobody, even had they looked them in the face, should recognise them. And in any case, the terrible weather made them want to hurry everything up.

Just as he had thought – no one approached them once they had entered the city. The guards remained on the battlements out of the rain, deeming it sufficient to note that six riders had left and six had returned.

"Have they gone?" was the only question that one who must have been the chief guard asked.

"With winged feet, like Mercury," said Ortwin, trying to sound nonchalant.

The man told a subordinate who immediately spread the word along the battlements, and there were cries of joy and triumph, accompanied by howls of laughter at the pathetic impression Dolabella had made.

"Go immediately to the governor to make your report. He told me to wake him as soon as you returned, whatever the time," added the commander, before turning to join in the celebrations and forgetting all about Ortwin.

The German let out a sigh of relief. But the hardest part was still to come. He looked around him, trying to work out where to go without giving the impression that he was unfamiliar with the layout of the governor's palace. Before leaving the area around Smyrna, he had interrogated several villagers, getting them to explain the layout of the town and where to find Trebonius's residence, and now he tried to orient himself, but the dark and the heavy rain complicated the task and for a moment he was afraid his hesitation would betray him. He was almost glad Veleda had been wounded in the scuffle with the enemy knights – it had given him an excuse to exclude her from the group of six that had crept into the city, because she would certainly have expected to be a part of it, had she been fit enough.

He imagined her dressed as one of the men they had killed, maybe in the clothes of the rider she had helped capture with her sacrifice, with that mad scramble behind the horse which had perhaps cost her a few cuts, bruises and broken bones. He even managed to smile at the thought of how awkward that bulky costume would have been on her small but toned, muscular body, and, as always, he felt proud of her.

His principal concern was getting out of there. He knew he had to take the main street that branched off from the gate, which he heard closing behind him. They could no longer turn back – it was Trebonius or them now. He hoped at least that Dolabella was outside the walls with the vanguard: they needed to take advantage of that moment of euphoria in the battlements, the darkness and the rain to surprise them while their defences were down. It would be dawn in about three hours.

Three decisive hours for his future and for that of Veleda. There were no people around, of course – even though Smyrna was a big city, it was not under the order Caesar had imposed in Rome which allowed the entry of goods vehicles only at night, and the rain deterred even those who might have wished to venture out into the street from doing so. He tried to navigate his way through what was almost total darkness, save the few torches burning in the stands and those located under the archways and parapets that the rain had not put out. He turned right where, according to the instructions given him by his involuntary informants, he thought he needed to, but at the end of the street he found himself in a dead end. Irritated at looking stupid in front of his men, he retraced his steps and carried on along the main street until he came to another crossroads which seemed more like the one on the mental map he had prepared for himself before entering the city.

He began to feel anxious. Time was running out, and if he failed again, the chances of his plan succeeding would be reduced to a practically nothing. He could already hear his men muttering. Trebonius had to be removed before Dolabella tried to climb over the wall if he wanted to be certain that the assault would overcome the attackers. The sight of a building in the distance, lit by many lanterns, comforted him – it must be an important one, perhaps the most important of all. But it might also be the Curia of the city senate. He headed for it with renewed hope, comforted by the presence of the watchmen he could see: it must be Trebonius's residence – no one would guard an empty building.

He hoped the watchmen did not personally know the scouts that the governor had sent out after Dolabella and that there was no confidant of Trebonius amongst the dead soldiers.

He arrived before the guards, who were standing to attention under the arch which gave onto the courtyard and, without dismounting, said, "We are the scouts who were sent to follow Dolabella's army. We are to report to the proconsul."

The guard looked at him with curiosity. "German auxiliaries, eh? I'd have sent real Romans, myself... You can pass."

It was fortunate that Trebonius had Germanic knights in his troops. The legionary guard must be a veteran and his trained eye had immediately recognised them, without seeing anything unusual in their being there. Ortwin spurred on his horse and passed through the arched entrance, entering the courtyard and making sure his men were behind him. When he arrived at the entrance to the building, he dismounted, fastened his reins to one of the rings on the facade and presented himself to another guard, who in turn handed them over to a slave who walked them through the vestibule and towards a room, outside which he made them wait while he went in to wake the governor. After a moment, the man re-appeared and beckoned to Ortwin to enter.

Only Ortwin.

The German looked at his men for a moment. He had expected this, and they knew they could do nothing about it. He entered Trebonius's bedroom while the slave was leaving, and immediately saw the governor sitting on the bed, barely illuminated by a lamp on the bedside table. The assassin of Caesar wore a tunic untied at the waist, and peered at him in the dark. His hair was thick and matted, and he struggled to recognise him. He had aged since the last time they had met whilst following Caesar. For a moment, Ortwin remembered the praises that his commander had sung of Trebonius after the attack on Marseille at the beginning of the civil war against Pompey. Trebonius had forced Domitius Ahenobarbus to flee and gained control of that vital port city for Caesar's cause, earning the undying gratitude of the dictator, who rewarded him by promoting him to the highest offices. Gratitude which had not been reciprocated, and the German could hardly wait to make Trebonius pay for it. If Octavian had not been given him the job of avenging his adoptive father, Ortwin would have willingly taken on the task of his own accord. It was difficult for Veleda to understand, and he never talked to her about it, but for him, washing away the shame of the death of one of the most worthy commanders he had ever served under was one of the main goals left to him in life.

"So? What did Dolabella do?" Trebonius asked brusquely.

Ortwin was almost tempted to set upon him and kill him immediately, but he wanted to be recognised first, so that Trebonius would know that it was not one of Dolabella's men who had killed him but an avenger of Caesar.

*

Never was a council of war more tempestuous. Aulus Hirtius, supreme commander of the Republican faction, slammed his fist on the table and the sound echoed around the hall serving as *praetorium* where the other subordinate commanders and their lieutenants were gathered.

"Damn it!" exclaimed the consul. "It's been five days since the double battle of Forum Gallorum, and there's still no way to flush out Mark Antony! He's grown cautious since his defeat, the bastard!"

"If we don't hurry up and get him out of his camp, Decimus Brutus will give in and hand Modena over to him on a silver platter. His men are starving and I doubt they'll last more than a few days…" Galba shook his head in discouragement.

Hirtius, as touchy as ever, took this statement as an indirect criticism of his leadership. It was always important for him to prove he was worthy of the esteem in which Caesar had held him. "Oh yes? And do you perhaps know some magic formula to lure Mark Antony into battle when it is more convenient for him to wait? Especially now that Lepidus seems willing to send troops?" he said testily.

"Yes, Mark Antony is clever. The most able commander that Caesar had…" said Pontius Aquila, with the clear intention of provoking the commander in chief. Nothing, in fact, could make Hirtius angrier than a comparison with their enemy, who had certainly enjoyed greater consideration than he while Caesar had been alive.

Powerless to intervene, Maecenas watched the council of war. Octavian had told him to remain silent, whatever happened, so as not to further antagonise Hirtius. The Etruscan saw the consul trembling with indignation, and for a moment feared that he might set upon Caesar's murderer. He was certain that, in his heart, Octavian had hoped that Hirtius, Galba and Aquila would slaughter one another and that Caesar's two assassins would get the worst of it. This, however, would not have helped the republican cause, which at that time the sect needed to serve if it wished to maintain its objectives. Mark Antony had to be rendered impotent to be then used against the 'liberators'. This was what the members of the cult, and Octavian in particular, must always bear in mind until the last of Caesar's assassins was dead. Put aside the thirst for revenge, then, and concentrate exclusively on one objective: Mark Antony must be defeated and brought under control – by flattery, if necessary, but not annihilated. As Aquila had so rightly pointed out, he was the only really capable general around. At least until the members of the sect had gained sufficient experience…

Hirtius pulled himself together, breathed out heavily and said, "Mark Antony may be skilled, but he is nowhere near as skilled as Caesar was, and, all things considered, he is caught in the middle. We must take advantage of this. Communicating with Decimus Brutus is difficult, but not impossible. We need to plan a co-ordinated attack with him and catch Mark Antony in the middle," he suggested.

Maecenas had an idea. He whispered to Octavian, who nodded and intervened. "We should take Modena before it falls into Mark Antony's hands. It seems to me the only solution. If he saw us making a serious attempt he would do everything possible to prevent it, even if it meant risking the battle that so far he has sought to avoid."

All those present looked thoughtful. The proposal, Maecenas thought proudly, was at least worthy of consideration, and, for a civilian surrounded by all these military experts, that was a profound satisfaction.

Aquila was the first to speak. He shook his head, saying, "His cavalry is patrolling the perimeter of the besieged city, trying its best to open up a way in for the infantry. I don't see how we can break through. And we do not have enough riders to take on his cavalry – that is the only advantage they have over us…"

Octavian spoke again. "My Celt auxiliaries, who have had frequent skirmishes with Mark Antony's men, tell me that they have never managed to reach the far side of the city, and neither have the enemy cavalry. It is a hard place to access, almost impassable because of the marshes and swamps – it is a no man's land where, almost as though by unspoken agreement, no soldiers venture. What if we were to send one or two legions there while we kept Mark Antony's cavalry busy elsewhere?"

Hirtius's eyes lit up – he clearly liked the idea. Aquila, however, hastened to intervene, "If no one has ventured there hitherto, it means that the going is hard, and tactics should never be based on such problematic terrain – we are venturing into the unknown, meaning that failure is more than likely."

"It seems that the unknowns are multiplying with the passage of the days. Do we want to let Mark Antony continue to have the upper hand? The climate here is unhealthy, and will soon do for Brutus, as well as our recruits," said Octavian, and as he spoke the tension between the two came to a head – it was quite clear that, had they been alone, they would have challenged one another to a fight to the death. And Aquila, being much stronger and skilled in the use of weapons than Octavian, would probably have won.

"Of course, the unhealthy climate. It's not for you, young man," said Aquila. "A delicate type like you should go home to his mother and leave the war to men. Real ones."

Octavian glared at him, his eyes burning. Maecenas admired his composure: he didn't move a muscle, and his lips remained firmly closed. But his expression... the look was so piercing and full of contempt that even Aquila turned his gaze away, unable to bear it, and perhaps even awed by the force of will it demonstrated.

It was Galba who spoke up in defence of Aquila. The two assassins were prejudiced against the opinions of Caesar's heir, just as Octavian, for his part, was prejudiced against theirs. "We're not playing games here, boy, and we cannot afford to make mistakes," he said with obvious reference to the haste with which Hirtius and Octavian had sent the Martia and the Praetorian cohort to Forum Gallorum. "We need to think carefully about how we move. Sending two legions out into difficult terrain means exposing them to enemy attacks and, if we lose another battle, it's all over for Decimus Brutus. And for the Republican cause. Mark Antony would take Modena and he would join forces with Lepidus in Spain and become the new Caesar. Then we would have to kill him too, although he would probably be mindful enough of the fate of his mentor to take precautions."

Maecenas gripped Octavian's wrist, fearing that this time he would explode. What with all these constant references to his inexperience, his young age and to his adoptive father, they were giving him a real going over. The young man's disgust at having to work with Caesar's assassins must be immense. He whispered in Octavian's ear, "Let it be. You will see that Hirtius will welcome your proposal – he is too anxious to prove himself worthy of Caesar's esteem to remain inactive. He was waiting for a suggestion like ours. Now he has an excuse to act."

After a moment's reflection, Octavian spoke: "You are right, you who are experienced soldiers and politicians, to point out my inexperience, gentlemen. In fact, I am only here to learn, and you must forgive me if I sometimes express my ideas. You are certainly not bound to follow them and you do well to remind me that I am not the right person to dispense advice. But sometimes an outsider may have the intuition of the neophyte – good luck, let's say, nothing more. I ask you not to reject on principle what comes out of my mouth simply because I am so young."

"That's it, be humble, well done," thought Maecenas. In his heart he once again congratulated his friend. You had to cajole your enemy, first of all, if you wanted to get anywhere. It was the first lesson he had tried to teach him.

Predictably, Hirtius cut in, saying, "Time is working against us, so we have no choice but to act. Tomorrow, after carrying out surveillance, we will launch a series of cavalry assaults along the city walls, concentrating a column of two legions on the field chosen for the breakthrough. We'll see if Mark Antony stands and watches while we enter Modena without using his infantry to stop us."

*

After the war council had ended, Octavian asked Maecenas to convene a meeting with Rufus and Gaius Chaerea and to meet him in his tent. The Etruscan obeyed, but he took his time. There was another person he had to meet first. He left the camp and went into the one nearby which housed the recruits of Pansa who had fallen under the command of Hirtius after their commander, now bedridden and suspended between life and death in Bologna, had been injured.

There he found Agrippa intent on polishing his weapons, while the companions of his *contubernium* were losing their pay in a game of dice. The young man had a bottle of wine to hand, though, and from his reddened, staring eyes it was clear that he had already drunk plenty. He was a good lad, generous and brave, Maecenas thought, and it was inexcusable that he was no longer part of the sect simply because he had made a mistake in a moment of despair. He didn't trust Rufus completely, but he did trust Agrippa. Octavian needed his loyalty, which was almost blind devotion, and his skills. It was impossible to find others like him in Rome. But if his plan succeeded... He was sure that Octavian already regretted his decision and was simply too proud to admit it and change his mind. All that was needed was a pretext, and he was working on one.

"Tomorrow there will be a new battle, if all goes as predicted," began the Etruscan, getting straight to the point.

"And will I participate?" asked Agrippa, the undiluted wine he had drunk audible in his voice.

Maecenas felt tenderness towards the boy. Agrippa was desperately seeking motivation: scorned by his closest friend, abandoned by his woman, who had been raped and psychologically devastated, he had tried to forget his sorrows by keeping himself busy – throwing himself into the war to use his vast reserves of energy. He was no longer interested in strategies and tactics, he just wanted to fight and take out all his frustration on the enemy, and learning that there was a battle imminent could only please him.

"Two legions will be involved, at least initially and I will make sure that your unit is one of them. I am sure that Octavian will want to participate too – at the moment he is healthy and doesn't want the soldiers to think that he lacks the makings of a leader. Now I'm going to speak to your centurion. A nice little cash bonus should convince him to turn a blind eye tomorrow and leave you free to undertake diversions. Stay close by, ready to take over at my command, and if we are lucky, you'll soon be part of the sect again. Because that is what you want, isn't it?" he asked.

"Of course it is. I have nothing else now," said Agrippa, grabbing the wineskin and taking another mouthful before going back to polishing his shield.

Maecenas hoped that all would go well. If the plan he had devised failed he would be powerless to stop the boy's downfall and they would lose him forever.

*

He's taken the bait, Rufus told himself when he saw Antony's legionaries arriving. Now they had to keep them there, to induce the enemy commander to send for other re-inforcements and thus transform the clash into a real battle between the two virtually full armies. The enemy unit prepared to charge, advancing with their *pila* grasped tightly in their hands. Hirtius commanded the legion to switch from marching to battle order, and the legionaries turned forty-five degrees without breaking formation. Having foreseen the attack, the formation the consul had adopted was almost inevitable, with the three companies in which a legion was usually disposed already prepared for battle.

Meanwhile, the legionaries' enemies had increased their pace and were approaching. Rufus nodded to Gaius Chaerea, and the centurion gave the order to close ranks. The other centurions did the same and in a few moments, all along the line, each legionary positioned himself at the right-hand side of the legionary in front of him. Immediately, a wall of shields was formed, while the soldiers kept a tight grip on their swords, still sheathed on their right hips.

Rufus moved to the side of the cohort under his command. For the occasion, Octavian had wanted him to be part of the Martia. Hirtius had decided to add to the unit of Pansa's veterans another made up of recruits, to use as bait and tempt Mark Antony to attack and massacre them. The consul's plan was that the unit of veterans would avert a rout while the recruits would entice the enemy to continue the battle, attracting other legions to them.

And no one was to throw their javelins. They did not want to risk making Antony's soldiers flee immediately, so it would be necessary to face their thrown *pila*. And throw they did. Hundreds of javelins arched across the sky between the two armies, but Hirtius's men, who had not broken ranks in order to throw themselves, limited the damage. The rain of projectiles fell upon their shields with almost a single thud, but nearly all the soldiers came through unscathed. Some fell to the ground, injured by a javelin, while many others found themselves unable to remove the spears stuck in their shields, leaving the shaft dragging along the ground, hindering the soldier's movements, forcing many to discard their only source of protection.

Gaius Chaerea immediately ordered the soldiers without shields to move to the rear, and their place was occupied by fully equipped soldiers, who drew their swords, forming a front line where each shield corresponded to the jutting tip of a blade.

And then, the impact.

A deafening sound of shields clattering against each other, of men screaming battle cries to exorcise their fear and of the clanging of swords – all at the same time, as deafening as a sudden explosion, resonating for miles around.

Rufus was on the flank. There was no one to the side of his shield and he could move at will along the outside line, just like all the high-ranking officers. A few steps away was the flank of Pansa's legion, commanded by Hirtius, and he could almost choose whether to fight against the enemy soldiers of the Martia or those of the other units. Octavian had told them not to take risks, but he was sure that even the leader of the sect would take some that day – he had much to prove to the soldiers, and could not allow himself to appear inferior to Hirtius and Pansa. But Rufus too had something to prove: he knew that he would have to confront the ghost of Agrippa, and even though the young man had never fought in a real battle, Octavian seemed convinced that he would fight like a lion in any situation. Well, Rufus was determined not to make him regret losing his old friend and to show him that he had lost nothing by sending him away, because he was there now, and able to do even better.

He threw himself against the nearest legionary, knocking him off balance with his shield and going at him vehemently until the man dropped to the ground. Rufus kicked him, knocking off his helmet, and plunged his sword into the soldier's mouth, seeing the tip of his sword protrude from the back of his neck. He pulled out the blade, dripping with the man's blood, and instinctively slashed sideways, keeping the next man away. He was about to attack him when he saw him fall to the ground, stabbed in the side by one of the legionaries from his unit. And then he noticed Gaius Chaerea who was a few steps away within the formation. He was egging on his men and constantly lashing out, severing limbs and ripping open faces. Rufus gestured for his attention and once he had it, pointed in front of him making a circular motion with his arm. Chaerea nodded, calling three men to follow him and they began to push the attackers with their shields, forcing them to retreat several steps.

Rufus advanced using a circular motion in order to keep at a safe distance and then, suddenly, swerved to the side of the line and sank his sword into the back of one of the soldiers Chaerea was holding back. After removing his blade, he did the same with the next fighter, while the third, having now noticed him, moved to defend himself from an attack from behind and was skewered by Chaerea.

Rufus and the centurion exchanged a quick smile of satisfaction, and then Chaerea began lashing out again. The tribune caught his breath and looked around him, taking the opportunity to see how the recruits were doing. Predictably, they were moving back under the pressure of Mark Antony's men, who were much more experienced and determined, even though there were only a few cohorts of them against the entire legion that Hirtius was commanding. No one fled or broke the lines – they simply yielded ground gradually, until Rufus was now no longer by the front line of the recruits but of the attackers.

Some groups of soldiers were still holding out, though, and the front line was uneven. In some places it was further back, while in others wedges had taken shape among the enemy soldiers. If their opponents continued to give ground, they were threatened with being cut off from their fellow soldiers and would be surrounded and isolated. But they were not dissuaded, and perhaps hoped that their example would encourage their comrades to stop moving backwards and instead try to reach them.

One group of Hirtius's legionaries in particular was grouped in defence of the far wing and had enemy soldiers on three sides. He was tempted to go over and give them a hand, but could not leave his own unit – the soldiers were awaiting his orders. But he was fascinated by the determination with which the soldier who had gone further than anyone else fought. He didn't fight like a recruit – he was a fury, with full control of his movements and seemingly equipped with eyes in the back of his head, to judge from the way he moved quickly, dodging just in time whenever an enemy soldier threatened him from behind. The man's moves seemed familiar to Rufus, who watched him carefully, trying to identify the face beneath the helmet. He knew many legionaries and perhaps had already had dealings with him.

When he finally recognised him, he could scarcely believe his eyes.

At that moment, he heard a muffled scream behind him, and realised that he had turned his back on the battle of which, until then, he had been a part. He turned and saw a soldier collapsing to his knees in front of him, eyes staring blankly, a sword sticking from his back.

The gladio of Gaius Chaerea.

"What are you doing, admiring the view?" asked the centurion who had just saved his life.

Rufus did not speak. He turned and, with an outstretched arm, pointed to what he had been watching. But now there were only Antony's men.

"What?"

"A moment ago… Agrippa was there…" said a disoriented Rufus.

*

Agrippa parried yet another lunge from his opponent and, as always, returned the blow. He hit home, as he frequently did, opening a deep gash in the arm of his attacker. The soldier stood there incredulous, the wounded limb hanging by his side and looking as though it might fall off at any moment, then fell to his knees with a cry of horror, and Agrippa finished him off, running him through at the base of his neck.

The next legionary hesitated before attempting to tackle him – the sight of his mangled comrade was far from encouraging. Agrippa took advantage of his disorientation and leapt forward, jumping over the body of his first victim and rushing against the shield of the second. One, two, three strikes and the wood cracked, breaking on the fourth – it must have already been damaged in the previous battle. The soldier threw away his shield, trying in vain to strike Agrippa. He took his dagger from his belt, holding it as a reserve weapon, and faced his attacker with two blades, one in each hand. But without a shield to protect him, he refrained from attacking.

Agrippa had no time to lose and lunged at him. The soldier instinctively brought his left arm up to protect himself, his dagger sticking into the young man's shield. Agrippa jerked his left arm about, unbalancing the soldier who was still holding his *pugio* and flinging him on his side and then onto the ground. Agrippa put his boot on his stomach and plunged his sword into the soldier's chest.

He pulled his weapon out from the still twitching body and looked around him. He was in the heart of the battle, and he was doing all he could to prevent the rout of the recruits alongside whom he was fighting. Hirtius, who was commanding the legion for the occasion, couldn't help them: his men were retreating. But as long as there were those like him holding out and keeping pockets of resistance going, one could always hope that Octavian would arrive, bringing extra manpower to attack the enemy from behind.

At least, that was what Maecenas had hoped the night before.

Hirtius had been too optimistic in hoping that his units could represent an anvil against which Mark Antony's men would be beaten by the hammer of Octavian's re-inforcements, which would attack them from behind. In theory, it was a good plan, but probably only the Martia would hold out, and the collapse of the legion by his side would compromise their tactic.

What Hirtius and Octavian did not know was that among their recruits, there was one who was special – one who moved and fought like a veteran and one who would not back down when faced with the superiority of Mark Antony's men. Agrippa almost laughed. Octavian was about to perform a pincer movement without knowing it, or even knowing that they were working together! Maecenas certainly seemed to find the idea ironic and he himself would have thought so too, had he not been too busy trying to save his skin. Hirtius's formation had, in fact, been bypassed, and there was a tight, chaotic scrum. No soldier could ever know if the fellow at his side was a friend or a foe, and the swings that landed did not necessarily land upon the enemy. Legionaries who fell to the floor were completely covered in mud when they climbed to their feet, and clumps of wet earth flew everywhere. It was almost impossible, now, to distinguish the symbols on the shields and recognise a comrade or an enemy soldier. They all resembled clay giants – members of one single army of shadows.

But they resisted, and that was what mattered.

And he was still alive. And only if he survived could he hope to support Maecenas's plan and perhaps obtain the only thing that interested him now: Octavian's forgiveness.

And the forgiveness of Etain, of course. But that was another story, to which he would turn his thoughts at a later time. If he survived.

He continued to sink his sword into human forms which

were increasingly indefinite – impossible to say whether because of the mud which covered them, the fog of fatigue clouding his exhausted eyes or the difficulty of breathing in those terribly cramped spaces, crushed by the bodies of the living and the dead, who sometimes had no room even to fall to the ground. Often it was simply a matter of pressure: those who prevailed exercised greater thrust, finally unbalancing their opponent, pushing him against the man behind him and impaling him when he was no longer able to move. Agrippa, with his muscular physique, always won out – it would have taken a colossus to knock him off balance, and he hadn't met one yet.

Suddenly he was elbowed in the face, and his helmet did little to protect him. It had probably been one of his comrades trying to ward off the blows of an attacker. The helmets of legionaries were not equipped with a nose guard, and the blow hit him between his upper lip and nose, causing blood to spray all over his face and intense pain between his eyes. Everything went red and the figures around him became even more blurred. He wiped his face but it didn't help much. He noticed a silhouette coming towards him and he thought he saw the glint of a knife pointed at his waist. Instinctively, instead of using his shield, he leaned with his right arm and crossed swords with his attacker. The sound of the impact, metal on metal, rang in the cacophony of dissonant sounds. But he had been too late in his attack, the force of the impact with his enemy caused him to lose his grip on his weapon, and the sword fell from his hand.

He was done for: no more pincer movement with Octavian, no reconciliation with his best friend, no rise to power, no part in the salvation of Rome, no second chance with Etain… The attacker, whose muddy face was split by a cruel grin which revealed his white teeth, stepped forward to finish him off, raising his sword ready to strike the deadly blow.

But no blow was struck, and the one who fell was his attacker: someone had pushed him from behind, he had lost his balance and stumbled over him. The legionary ended up on his face, and the young man was able to turn and plant an elbow in his back, preventing him from moving. But he could not finish him off because he felt other boots trampling him. Mark Antony's soldiers were passing almost above them, pushing forward. Voices were raised among the cries of encouragement and of death that he had been hearing for a long time now.

"There's another enemy legion coming!"

"There are many of them! Maybe two legions!"

"They're surprising us from behind! Turn around and fight, don't run away."

The hammer had arrived and he could still serve as an anvil. The pincer movement had done its job.

*

So Agrippa was still with them, and still on the battlefield, and still alive, too, thought Gaius Chaerea, while enjoying the spectacle of the Martia's enemies being forced to hurriedly move out of the way in order to avoid being caught in the pincer.

It must have been Maecenas' work, just like in Brindisi – who knew what that Etruscan had in mind, this time! Surely something to convince Octavian of the necessity to reconcile with his old friend. Unlike Rufus, who had always seemed jealous of Agrippa and perhaps glad that Octavian had quarrelled with him, Maecenas was doing everything possible to bring the two old friends back together, without worrying that Agrippa's return might affect his own importance.

He heard Hirtius order his soldiers to counterattack, but now Mark Antony's legions were trying to avoid combat and were attempting to move backwards before Octavian's men swooped down upon them, forcing them against the Martia. Rufus shouted to march forward but Gaius Chaerea soon realized that they would have to run if they did not want to lose contact with the enemy in retreat. The principal concern was to conquer Mark Antony's camp – any other outcome would mean the day was undecided, despite the heavy losses the enemy had suffered. Modena could fall at any moment, and if the ex-consul took possession of it he would be able to turn around any eventual defeat on the battlefield.

The centurion urged his men to follow him, and together they moved behind Antony's soldiers, who were trying to maintain a compact formation as they retreated. He waited until he had at least fifty men with him and then launched himself against a unit that was retreating more slowly than the others. He attempted close combat, but it wasn't easy – the enemy was voluntarily giving up ground and they were merely defending themselves, and the attackers' blows hit their shields most of the time. Gaius Chaerea continued to flail unnecessarily and urge on his men, but the results he obtained – an occasional victim in the enemy ranks – did not justify the outlay of effort. In part because the others were not offering him much support – both sides seemed to be fighting quite half-heartedly, now.

This was clearly a moment of transition and of patience: Hirtius, seeing that Antony's men were now determined to fall back to their camp, was content to stalk them without wasting his soldier's energy on interim skirmishes, awaiting the decisive battles near the enemy's fortifications. Mark Antony, on the other hand, was counting on his soldiers to make every effort below the fortifications, where they would have the support of the troops that had remained inside and of his artillery.

Both parties, therefore, were preparing for the decisive phase of the battle.

Gaius Chaerea allowed himself to relax for a moment, and his thoughts returned to his home. To his son and his wife, whom he had left hurriedly without saying goodbye to them in the way he would have liked – by making passionate love to her, as he always did before leaving for a campaign, and by playing with his son, Marcus. Against his will, the image of Octavia superimposed itself over that of his family, disorienting him. Something had happened since they had begun seeing each other again – she was no longer the fragile little girl, enchanted by his strength. Now she was an important woman, with a prestigious husband, a daughter, and a brother whose cause she had joined, and yet... and yet she still seemed to be attracted to him. Despite what he had done. And he was still attracted to her. More than before, when she had been so fresh, innocent and pure and he had not managed to ignore his base impulses. But now there was Fabia. The woman he had been close to these last few years, who asked only for his love. The woman who had taken care of bringing up Marcus, even though he was not her son, and who had done it with such dedication that the child never doubted that she was his real mother. As far as he could remember, the most serene moments of his life in recent years had all been spent with her, and there was nothing, absolutely nothing, that could justify a relationship, or even just a fling, with another woman.

Octavia would never really be his but Fabia already was, and there was nothing that made him think that it would not be forever.

Did he love her? Yes, he loved her. Did he also love Octavia? It was hard to say, but if it was so, at least part of that would have been an illusion. This time he would dominate his impulses, and not simply because Octavian would never forgive him if he found out. Simply put, he was happy with what he had and no changes in his love life would make him happier, whatever they might be.

At that moment, events brought him back to the present and to the awareness that all these reflections on life would be completely pointless if he died. And what he saw made him expect the worst. He was in view of the enemy's camp, now, and an unbroken line of armed soldiers were deployed in front of the ramparts, while another, almost equally unbroken, was visible above the battlements. They would have been an insurmountable barrier were it not for Antony's retreating men who, because of the pressure of the republicans pursuing them, arrived at the camp in complete disarray, ending up practically on top of their fellow soldiers and breaking up their ranks.

Mark Antony had miscalculated, Chaerea thought with a grimace of satisfaction. He had aimed to move the fight to favourable ground where his back was covered, but now he found himself with an army that was unable to get into formation. He could not even avoid fighting or open the gates to let his men in to entrench themselves behind the walls, as he knew that if his own soldiers entered so would the enemy.

Gaius Chaerea hoped that Hirtius would give the order to attack immediately – they needed to take advantage of the confusion that reigned among the enemy ranks. He didn't have long to wait: the trumpets sounded and the legionaries prepared themselves to attack the soldiers thronging the ramparts. They set off in unison, one continuous line of *centuria* and maniples that advanced with a converging manoeuvre on three sides of the camp, like the giant claw of an eagle ready to seize its prey.

There were no more javelins thrown – they had all been used in the previous skirmish. Only swords now, and with his sword held tightly in his fist, Chaerea urged his men to move faster and threw himself against the enemy legionaries, quickly covering the distance that separated him from them and falling upon their confused lines at the same time as thousands of his fellow soldiers.

He had recovered his strength during the previous lull in fighting, and began slicing his way through the mass. The enemy soldiers were so tightly packed between the ramparts and Octavian's men that they were in each other's way, and could barely move their swords or shields. It was like attacking immobile targets – training dummies who could do nothing else but suffer their blows. Stabbed, sliced, mutilated and ripped open, they fell one after another under his sword, and once on the ground were trampled by the feet of their fellow soldiers.

Chaerea was overcome by a kind of megalomania. Faced with this tide of powerless soldiers he felt invincible, and he was sure that his comrades felt the same way. His strength seemed tenfold, and he launched blow after blow relentlessly, alternating downward blows with lunges like a man possessed, without ever feeling any hint of fatigue. Only gradually did he began to realise that his blows were mostly landing in empty space. He tried to regain some sense of reality. Squinting, his eyes covered with beads of sweat, he saw that the enemy soldiers were fleeing.

That could mean only one thing.

Mark Antony had opened the gates.

XIX

"It would seem that consul Dolabella has departed, governor." Ortwin answered Trebonius's question with the same abruptness with which it had been asked.

Trebonius's astonishment at the German's tone showed in his face, and he scrutinised him more closely. "It would *seem*? What do you mean? Why do you think I sent you after him? Didn't you follow him? Who chose my officers?"

Ortwin continued to toy with him. They had met on several occasions, a long time ago, and Trebonius should have remembered a man who had never been just another auxiliary but the commander of Caesar's bodyguards, even though now he only had one eye. But he preferred to wait before letting himself be recognised – before carrying out the act that would be both his duty and pleasure. So despite the shortness of time, he left him hanging a moment longer, in the meantime beginning to move imperceptibly closer to him so as to have him as near to his knife as possible when he reacted. "I didn't need to follow him to Syria to realise he was gone, Sir. I imagined that you would be in a hurry to know whether or not to worry about his presence," he replied, with a vaguely mocking tone.

"Listen to this idiot... I'll have you whipped for your insolence and for your obvious ineptitude, and... Wait a minute. I know you. You're..."

He didn't have time to finish his sentence. With feline dexterity, Ortwin pulled the dagger from his belt and pounced on him, squeezing his neck with his strong arm and covering his mouth with his hand.

"Yes, it is I, Ortwin, former commander of the Germanic auxiliaries, the man you betrayed. Octavian sends you his greetings," he whispered in his ear, before exchanging his arm for the blade and drawing it cleanly in one fluid movement across Trebonius's throat. A stream of blood poured onto the bed without touching the German, while Trebonius floundered, choking, seeking something to hold onto – something that he would never find – and vainly trying to call for help. Only a few inarticulate sounds emerged from his mouth, though, and his lifeless body fell to the floor, splashing the elegant marble with red.

Ortwin looked at him contemptuously for a moment. They had been told that Trebonius had not been among those who had stabbed Caesar. It seemed that he had been keeping Mark Antony busy outside the Theatre of Pompey, chatting away amiably with him while the others did their dirty work. But in any case he deserved to die that way. Of all the assassins, apart from Decimus Brutus and Marcus Brutus, he was perhaps the one the dictator had rewarded most. He was the first of his commander's assassins to die and Ortwin felt proud to have been the one to do it.

Now an unpleasant task awaited him. Or rather, it would have been unpleasant to treat anybody else in that way, but in Trebonius's case there was no need to be fussy, he told himself. He looked around and, seeing the murderer's toga on the back of a chair, wrapped it around himself to avoid being spattered with blood, then knelt down and began patiently to sever the corpse's head, digging at the gash he had made at the time of the killing, pressing down with the tip to break the bones. When he was done, he lifted it by its hair, took off the blood-soaked toga and wrapped the head up inside it, then pulled a bag from his belt and put the trophy inside and briskly left the room. In the antechamber, he met the gaze of his men, with whom he exchanged a nod to confirm his success.

"The proconsul has gone back to sleep and does not wish to be disturbed," he said to the slave who had escorted him into Trebonius's cubicle, then walked towards the door, followed by his men.

But it was not over. Now came the third part of the plan which, unfortunately, needed the participation of that idiot Dolabella. Which meant that it was the most dangerous part of all.

Ortwin walked through the halls of the building as though nothing had happened.

He descended the stairs and reached the hall, ignoring the few staff and guards he happened to meet. Fortunately, the grim faces of his men dissuaded anyone from approaching them, and he soon found himself at the entrance to the courtyard, where he met the guard with whom he had exchanged a few words when they had arrived. Dawn was breaking. Dolabella should be ready.

"So? Was it worth waking the proconsul?" asked the legionary.

Ortwin just gave him a fleeting nod, hoping the other wouldn't recognise him. He had to answer, but only did so as he mounted his horse at the same time as his men. "I would say so. I brought reassuring news, so now he can finally sleep peacefully," he said.

The veteran moved closer, standing in front of the muzzle of his horse. He eyed him quizzically and suspiciously. "We don't need to suffer the siege any more, then?" he asked, more to prevent him from leaving than out of any for real interest, it seemed to Ortwin.

"Just so. The usurper has vanished." He was about to turn his horse around and spur him to leave but the guard grabbed the reins.

"Your bag. It's dripping. You didn't have it with you when you arrived. Did the consul give you a bonus?"

"My pay."

But the man continued to hold the reins.

"It's dripping, I said."

"Is it? I hadn't noticed," the legionary extended a finger and with his fingertip collected a drop that was oozing from the leather bag, put it in his mouth and, with surprise, said, "But... it's blood."

"By Wotan! I must have cut myself somewhere while I was scouting" said Ortwin, pretending to look at his chest and legs, knowing that the man wouldn't believe him. But he had to buy some time. His men were lined up all around him, ready to set off on their mounts.

"Let me see inside the bag, you one-eyed barbarian," the guard ordered as he moved towards him, pulling out his sword and pointing it at him.

He could beat about the bush no longer – in no time at all they would have the entire garrison of Smyrna to deal with, unless Dolabella attacked, and they had not managed to complete their part of the plan. Seized with sudden inspiration, he took the bag and threw it towards the German farthest from the sentry, shouting, "You and two others, go to the gate – do what we agreed to do and show it to the soldiers."

Immediately, the band of barbarians split into two. Three of them set off towards the walls while Ortwin and the others drew their swords and pounced on the two sentries. The legionary was ahead of him and swung the first blow, but Ortwin spurred his horse and the blade, which was aiming for his thigh, ended up in his saddle. Meanwhile, his men simultaneously stabbed the other guard in the shoulder. At this point Ortwin, freed of the sentries, would have left too, but the brief commotion had attracted the attention of other guards from inside. Four of them came into the courtyard, swords in hand, moving faster as soon as they realised what had happened. Now with the first faint glow of dawn it was possible to make out more than just simple silhouettes.

Ortwin was annoyed. He could no longer leave. They would raise the alarm and the defenders in the battlements would be on the alert, preventing his three companions from opening the gates. Followed by his men, he rode towards the enemy, but there were now six legionaries and he found himself surrounded. With attacks coming from both sides, he lashed out at a soldier, but felt a stinging sensation in his leg. At that moment, he heard a loud scream at his side. He did not have time to turn round but he realized that one of his soldiers had fallen. He managed to hit another attacker, who fell to the ground but then someone went for his horse, which in turn collapsed to the ground, throwing him from the saddle and trapping one of his legs beneath it. At that point, an authoritative voice ordered the soldiers to stop fighting. Ortwin saw that there were at least four of them just inches from his face.

"I have sent someone into the private apartment of the proconsul, barbarian. If anything has happened to him, I wouldn't bet a sestertius on your life." Ortwin lifted his head and saw that the speaker was a centurion, who was evidently in charge of guarding the governor's palace.

The German looked around for his two companions. He saw both of them lying in the dust, immobile. His already meagre band of followers had been reduced yet further, and perhaps a third would soon join them at Wotan's side. Or maybe all six, if Dolabella did not arrive in time…

A visibly upset slave came to announce that they had found the headless corpse of Trebonius, and a murmur of surprise ran through the ranks of the men in the court. Meanwhile, from the palace they could hear cries of despair.

"I get the feeling you're done for, friend. But first you must tell me for whom you did it," said the centurion, kneeling down next to him.

"For Dolabella, of course," replied Ortwin unflinchingly. "And Dolabella is outside, ready to enter. Because you can be sure that as soon as the men in the stands see Trebonius's head, they will surrender without resistance and open the gates. And so will you… what sense is there in fighting for someone who no longer exists and who you barely knew? Give up, and you will not be harmed. The proconsul needs good people to assert his right to Syria."

The centurion laughed. A sign, if nothing else, that he was certainly not grieving the death of Trebonius and that he would be bought with ease. It was always a question of price. "It seems to me that the Senate has declared Dolabella a usurper and a public enemy, in truth."

"Be careful, centurion," warned Ortwin. "In these days, things change quickly in Rome. Yesterday Dolabella was official proconsul of Syria – today he is not, perhaps, but tomorrow, especially if he prevails here, he may be again. Do you know that there is civil war on the border with Gaul? Whoever wins will impose his own will on the Senate. He will reward those who have fought at his side…"

The centurion seemed struck by his words, but remained unconvinced. "I don't hear any armies entering the city," he said, pointing his sword at his neck. "I think you might just be telling me a lot of nonsense."

Curse Dolabella! Where was his signal? Without that, his three men could not act. "Wait and see, then." He did not know what else to say.

"I don't have a lot of patience, barbarian, and I don't trust you. You've stopped a good source of income for us: Trebonius was generous, through his friends Brutus and Cassius. I ought to kill you just for that…"

"And Dolabella will be even more so. He has even more important friends behind him, such as the son of Caesar."

"That sickly boy? Pah! Trebonius spoke ill of him, and I don't see how he can defeat his opponents. Right, that's enough – time to die, you bastard."

The only thing Ortwin could think about was that he would never see Veleda again. He lifted his head and stared at the officer who was preparing to kill him.

Suddenly, one of the soldiers let out a cry of surprise. "A fiery dart in the sky! We are under attack!"

Dolabella had arrived at last.

*

Maecenas grabbed Octavian's arm, preventing him from throwing himself into the press of the two armies in Mark Antony's camp. The gates were unmanned, the soldiers in the battlements were under attack from the front and from behind and the battle had now moved inside the walls.

"I have been thinking," he said. "Don't go in until the situation is more under control. It is never wise for a commander to throw himself into the fray."

"What? Not wise for a commander to guide his soldiers?" exclaimed his outraged friend. "What do you imagine the legionaries would think of a leader who was fearful?" He spurred his horse again, but this time his friend grabbed the reins.

"Not fearful – intelligent," Maecenas pointed out. "And some battles which are almost won can be lost if a commander falls. His death may dishearten the soldiers – without a guide, they do not know what to do. They no longer see why they should die. And if you're in the middle of it all, you cannot make decisions – you cannot monitor the progress of the battle and take countermeasures. You might be defeated simply because, despite only needing to move some troops to a threatened area, you hadn't had the chance to realise what was going on. No, a true commander should observe combat from a privileged position."

"But Alexander the Great…"

"Alexander the Great died at thirty-three. Do you want to end up the same way? Don't you have a few things to do before you die?"

Octavian was silent. He looked at the walls which were under attack and the flood of fighters who were pouring inside.

"Hirtius was one of the first to go in…"

"Hirtius has never been a good commander. Not surprisingly, Caesar never gave him front line military positions. He is still the same, even now. He knows he is not really considered much of a general and he desperately wants to prove to everybody what he is worth. He couldn't wait to fight and he thinks that showing a little courage by throwing himself headlong into battle makes him look like a great leader. He will just get himself killed. Maybe that's what he wants, who knows? But look at the others – Galbus, Aquila… they look after their own skins and follow the soldiers, instead of leading them."

Octavian did not speak. He looked over at the panorama of screams, blood and flashing blades that was unfolding before his eyes. Maecenas knew that he was weighing up his words, and trying to convince himself that they were right. He didn't like fighting, and his body would not allow him to for long, nor effectively. The only reason he wanted to fight at all was to maintain the esteem and affection that his soldiers had bestowed on him since he had first appeared on the political scene – and the soldiers, more than any other part of society, were the key to ascending the heights of the state.

"People will say that I waited too long before throwing myself into combat. Mark Antony would love it, and the last thing I want is to give him another excuse…"

The objection was a good one, but Maecenas had already considered this aspect of the matter. "We will make sure that he knows you were admirable in battle. Don't worry – you should have learned by now that people, and soldiers in particular, are willing to do anything for a bit of money. And what the enemy says doesn't count. The enemy is the enemy and has every reason to disparage you. In any case, if Mark Antony loses, he will have to come to terms, sooner or later, and would derive no benefit from speaking ill of you."

Octavian seemed convinced. He began to watch follow the battle in silence, surrounded by some of the men of his praetorian cohort. Maecenas tried not to let his concern show. There was another reason why he had persuaded his friend to delay entering the fray. In the chaos of that moment, it would have been impossible to carry out his own plan.

With his desire to prove himself a more worthy leader than his reputation allowed, in fact, Aulus Hirtius had begun attacking madly, risking his own life and defeat in a battle that had almost been won. If the consul had not thrown himself into the fray, the two armies would have faced each other with greater order, and he, Maecenas, would have been able to locate all the unknowing protagonists of his scheme. Now, instead, everything was more unpredictable.

"They're taking over the camp. I cannot wait!" hissed Octavian suddenly. "Men, with me!" he shouted, urging the others to follow him with a wave of his arm and spurring his horse on. Maecenas could hardly blame him – by now the fighting had moved to Mark Antony's side and although he feared that they would find indescribable confusion there, he indulged his friend and promptly set off after him.

When they entered the Praetoria gate, the sight that met their eyes was completely different from what they had expected. They had imagined that they would find Antony's men almost overpowered, but instead they were still fighting on equal terms, and in fact, the republicans were pulling back, and some were even trying to escape from the camp.

"Propraetor! Propraetor!" It was Gaius Chaerea, coming to meet them. He was out of breath and there was a small wound on his arm. "The consul has fallen, just when he was about to storm Mark Antony's praetorian tent! The men disbanded soon after. The body is still there and we cannot approach it."

Maecenas shook his head, then looked round at Octavian, who gave him a look of gratitude and respect. It was proof of his foresight. What came next was so obvious that the Etruscan did not dare suggest it to his friend, for fear of offending his intelligence. Fate and the stupidity of one consul had just offered him a golden opportunity. He discovered right away that there was no need to advise him further.

"Gaius! Gather the soldiers and tell them that Caesar's son will lead them to recover the body of Hirtius and complete the conquest of the praetorium! Run!" cried Octavian without hesitation, then he raised his sword, calmed his horse, which had risen up on its hind legs, and cried out for the attention of the soldiers around him.

"Legionaries of the Martia!" he shouted. "You who have forsaken Mark Antony for me, for the son of Caesar, to honour the memory of my father! You who have had the courage to oppose the abuses of Antony's men! You veterans of so many battles! Follow me to avenge the consul Aulus Hirtius and wash away the shame of how Antony's supporters have treated you! I will lead you to vengeance and to victory!" The soldiers who had heard shouted their approval and gathered around him, while others who had been about to leave the camp came back to put themselves at his disposal. Octavian turned his horse to gaze upon them all with his fiery eyes and remind them that he was a worthy son of Caesar. In that moment, thought Maecenas, he really did seem like Alexander the Great: beautiful and regal, charismatic and almost divine, willing to do anything to conquer the whole world.

The legionaries, who shouted the praises of the son of Caesar and were actually impatient to counterattack, seemed to think so too. Octavian did not make them wait long. With a new cry of encouragement, he began to gallop along the Praetorian Way without even looking back. Maecenas followed for a while, looking around him in the dim evening light at the fighting amongst the tents. But many soldiers, on seeing Octavian pass, joined those following him, until a small army had gathered near the centre of the camp, surrounding the square between the circumferential praetorium and the principia.

Mark Antony was not there, but many of his soldiers were. He had probably left them there to cover his retreat. Maecenas scanned the faces of their opponents. Those who had not fled or been killed had barricaded themselves into that relatively small space. But they were afraid, now. Octavian had managed to instil new confidence in an army which had felt defeated as soon as it had lost its commander. The young man did not hesitate and immediately urged his men to attack. Wisely, he did not lunge forward with them, but allowed them to pass before dismounting from his horse and walking towards the tent brandishing his sword.

Maecenas did not follow. He had other things to do now. His plan was beginning. He looked around. He was near Mark Antony's tent now, where the battle had been focused, and he had no doubt that the actors in his little play were all there – always assuming that they were still alive. He had no need to go looking for one of them – Agrippa appeared of his own accord. He was covered in blood, but he moved with such agility that

Maecenas had no doubt that it was him. What a tremendous fighter! They nodded at each other, and the Etruscan asked, "Where is Pontius Aquila?"

"Probably with his chief, Galba. They were fighting along the Via Principalis," said Agrippa.

"Let's go. But follow me at a distance," Maecenas ordered him, abandoning his horse and Markhing in the direction indicated by his friend. There were clashes behind the tents, and groups of soldiers slaughtering isolated legionaries, foot soldiers facing one another in single combat, larger groups looting or burning or fighting with other groups of equal size, while others fled and others still stopped to catch their breath. He saw Galba with his staff, and immediately afterwards spotted Pontius Aquila. He was duelling with a centurion and was getting the worst of it. No one could help him because all of his comrades were engaged in other, isolated battles – between the tents it was almost impossible to adopt compact formations.

He had an idea. He pointed Agrippa to the murderer of Caesar, and the young man knew what he had to do. They both approached Aquila and, swords in hand, surrounded his adversary. He reacted with shock at the sight of new enemy soldiers appearing, and the fear remained etched on his face when Agrippa plunged his blade into his side, almost to the hilt. When he pulled it out it dragged with it tissues and organs, which fell at Aquila's feet. Aquila, a burly man almost as big as Agrippa though more flabby, wore a scowl on his face, and it remained there even now that he was out of danger.

"I would have managed by myself…" he whispered.

"Thank you for allowing me to feel useful, then, tribune," answered Agrippa, sarcastically.

Their exchange offered Maecenas the opportunity he had been waiting for. He liked to gather information on the character of his enemies, and knew that Aquila was particularly thin skinned and irritable. "That is not how it appeared, Pontius Aquila," he said sweetly, "and while you are apparently unable to overcome a single enemy soldier, Octavian is busy taking Mark Antony's tent. I doubt you will dare give him any more lessons in the next war councils."

Aquila looked at him disgustedly. "Ah! It's you, his effeminate minion! Well I will give him a lesson even now!" he cried. "I've never seen him at the front line during battle, and now he wants to take the credit for the conquest of the praetorium? He can forget it – I will always be at least one step ahead of that little boy!" he roared, and set off immediately towards the centre of the camp.

Maecenas looked knowingly at Agrippa. Too easy, he said to himself – by knowing and exploiting a man's weaknesses, you can make him do anything. They both followed at a safe distance.

The first part of his plan had been a success. But now came the hard part.

*

The wave of legionaries that swept through the area around Mark Antony's *praetorium* were fierce, and Octavian felt proud that it was he who had brought this about. He had inherited some of Caesar's charisma after all, even though he would never have his spirit, courage, determination, endurance and strength in battle. The qualities that had commanded total commitment from his soldiers. But maybe one day, men would be willing to die for him too. At the moment, they were doing it for the republican cause, or to take revenge on Mark Antony for his decimation, but in the future they would do it to implement the Rome that he had in mind. The Rome which was head of an immense empire where everyone had enough to eat, where soldiers received regular pay, where there were no institutional conflicts and where a traveller could move from one place to another, by land or sea, without danger.

And perhaps he would even be a great leader, if he could follow Maecenas's suggestions, putting the overall vision of the battlefield at the service of his remarkable intelligence – not a leader like Alexander the Great, but a co-ordinator. A new type of commander in chief: a more modern one, one who would transfer to the battlefield the same global vision that he had of Rome.

He joined the legionaries, who were gaining ground at every step. Although the soldiers tried to make room for him, the crush was oppressive and the inevitable jostling and elbowing soon had him feeling short of breath. His temples throbbed, his vision became blurry and his breathing laboured, and he began to fear that the effort was too much for him – that his body would abandon him just at that moment, exposing him as a weakling in front of his soldiers. A leader who fell to the ground right after his first battle would be a laughing stock. He was afraid his mother had been right. She had always warned him not to do anything too physical and, more so, not to risk attempting to take up Caesar's legacy. The exaltation of a few moments ago gave way to despair – was it all an illusion? Were his perhaps the pathetic dreams of a crippled boy, for whom even a sitting in the Senate would represent an impossible effort?

The prospect of failing so miserably and of exposing himself to public ridicule terrified him more than death itself. He imagined the jokes that Mark Antony, though defeated, would make, the mockery of the soldiers who had welcomed him with such trust, and the disappointment of the small group of friends who were devoted to his cause, and decided that he would kill himself if his knees even once touched the ground because of his frailty. He let out a cry of encouragement – this time to encourage himself – and leapt forwards against the weakness that pressed more heavily upon him than even the enemy. The others did not know that he was fighting two battles, one against himself and one against Antony's men. Everything was so much harder for him!

He continued his advance, but at every step his legs grew heavier, and the soldiers seemed to be swirling around as though mocking him, but he was still conscious enough to understand that it was his head which was spinning and depriving him of all points of reference. He began to cough, and after taking a few steps he became aware of the bitter taste in his mouth – the taste that he knew so well. A trickle of blood mixed with saliva ran down his lips, his chin and down onto his neck, but he forced himself to ignore the messages that his body was sending him. He kept walking, trying to focus on the shapes before him and to distinguish, at least, if they were friends or foe.

"General! Are you ill?" asked a soldier, grabbing him by the arm and staring at him.

No, not this, he said to himself. He shook off the man's grip violently. "I'm fine! *Fine!*" he answered almost hysterically. Then he raised his arm and his sword and lunged forward, head down, pushing even his comrades in front of him out of the way. At the sight of him racing forwards, his men imagined he wanted to lead them and made room for him, and he felt the air circulating around him once more. Suddenly, his lungs began to function as they should, his vision cleared and his head stopped throbbing. He was still struggling, but was no longer afraid of collapsing and could at least clearly distinguish everything around him. A fire next to the praetorium had begun licking at Mark Antony's tent, where a squad of Martia legionaries was fiercely defending Hirtius's corpse. A group of Antony's legionaries was running towards the decumana gate, another group had barricaded itself between the quaestorium and the pavilions of the tribunes and was attempting to resist the assault. Scattered soldiers entered the tents of the tribunes from the Forum and looted them. He had two clear objectives. He moved towards Hirtius's body, urging on his men. "Hold them back, legionaries," he shouted. "Let us defend a hero of the Republic, a loyal follower of Caesar!" And he positioned himself at the far end of the line that they had formed, warding off blows at the same time. The enemy soldiers recognised him and tried to converge upon him, but his legionaries reacted promptly and the fighting moved to the flank. Octavian himself managed to exchange a few sword thrusts, attacking the enemy soldiers, and when he saw that the shields of the soldiers at his side protected him, he began putting more energy into his swings and became more enterprising. When he managed to hit the arm of one attacker and make him drop his sword, allowing a legionary to finish him off, there were loud cheers for his first, albeit indirect, victim. He plucked up courage, ordered two soldiers who were not as busy, to remove the body of Hirtius and continued fighting, feeling strength coursing through his body and an excitement he had never experienced before.

He closed his eyes and struck out relentlessly, until he realized that he had slashed open an enemy soldier's neck. And suddenly, Mark Antony's legionaries, who an instant before had been standing in front of him, vanished. He saw only their backs and heard a shout of triumph from his subordinates for his victory. It could be said, without fear of contradiction, that it was he who had retrieved Hirtius's body. Excellent! Now he headed for his second objective: Mark Antony's tent. He marched towards the pavilion, inviting his soldiers to follow him. A thin line of legionaries defended it. This time, still feeling exalted from the battle, he made no plan and simply threw himself against them without waiting for the shields to protect him.

The enemy soldiers stared at him almost in awe and, seemingly intimidated by his enthusiasm, didn't even fight back as much as he had expected. He struck out and warded off blows without effort or opposition. It seemed that they were afraid to hurt him. He saw another of his opponents fall, but could not say where his hail of blows had struck him. Other republicans arrived, breaking through the enemy line and the battle broke up into a series of smaller skirmishes around the tent. Another torch next to the pavilion toppled, and a flap of leather caught fire. He had to hurry to get inside. He picked up a shield from the ground and used it to push aside the two enemy soldiers who obstructed his way, then made for the entrance, but when he crossed the threshold he bumped into someone with the same idea.

He looked at the man and was about to order him to make way for Caesar's son, but then, in the light of the flickering flames, he realised who he was.

Pontius Aquila, one of Caesar's assassins, was looking at him with a gleam of defiance in his eyes. Sharing that moment of triumph with the man seemed the cruellest joke that the gods could play on him. He wished only for his death, and when he saw that there were two soldiers armed to the teeth inside the tent busily throwing Mark Antony's abandoned documents into the flames, he realized that Aquila's death was highly probable.

As was his own.

*

Things were going as Maecenas had planned, thought Agrippa as he watched Octavian and Aquila enter the pavilion of Mark Antony at the same time. But what not even the brilliant little Etruscan could have predicted was what they would find in the tent and how things would go afterwards. The fire had spread to one side of the pavilion which would soon become a death trap for anyone who remained inside. Agrippa threw away his shield and made his way hurriedly through the throng, pushing both friends and enemies out of his way, his eyes fixed on the flap of leather that had closed behind the two men.

He jumped at it and charged recklessly in, but what he saw in the darkness illuminated by the flickering of the flames gave him a moment's pause. Two enemy soldiers were threatening Octavian and Aquila with their swords, and it looked as though the two men weren't sure whether to attack their enemies or one another, while at the same time the fire was spreading through the tent at great speed.

All the protagonists of this incredible drama stood there for a moment, immobile. Agrippa noticed Octavian's shocked expression at his appearance, and then threw himself between him and Aquila and pounced on the two enemy soldiers. He grabbed the table that separated him from them and pushed it towards them, knocking them off balance and sending them flying against the back of the pavilion. He made for one of them immediately, cutting his throat with one stroke, then turned to the other, who had recovered his balance and was awaiting his assault with both his blades ready.

Agrippa heard the clang of metal behind him. Again Maecenas had been right – once again, Octavian and the murderer of Caesar could not help but challenge one another to death. He wanted to turn around to see how Octavian was doing, but it was unthinkable to turn his back on the enemy soldier even for an instant. He had to have faith in his friend and hope that he would manage to hold Aquila off. He tried to force his own opponent into a corner, but, with a sudden move, the man slipped away. Agrippa turned to follow him, ending up with his back to the fire. He felt its heat reaching out for him, burning his skin, and instinctively leaned forward. Which was just what his attacker, who stood ready for him, his two blades in hand, had been waiting for. The young man just managed to avoid his opponent's first lunge with the dagger, whose blade was only long enough to scratch his arm. But now his attacker was trying to squeeze him into a corner, to push him into the flames. Agrippa tried to throw himself to the side, but was surrounded by blades threatening him on both sides and was trapped in a confined space. Meanwhile, the sound of the crackling fire was growing louder, as was the clanging of blades and the heavy breathing of the other two fighters…

He threw caution to the wind and slashed at one of the soldier's forearms, exposing his body to the other's sword. As he had expected, the other dodged his attack and was forced to fight back. He saw the blade of the sword coming towards him and swiftly moved to the side, but the tip just had time to catch his side, breaking through the rings of chain mail and reaching his skin, cutting and tearing his flesh before catching in the back of his armour.

"Just a scratch. It's just a scratch," Agrippa said to himself as he gathered his strength and unleashed the only swing he had the opportunity for. His sword ended up in his attacker's cheek, ripping the bone out of his face and causing an explosion of blood that went everywhere.

He didn't even watch him fall. He pulled out his knife and, hardly able to breathe, turned to face the other two men in the tent. A few feet away from him, Octavian was lying unarmed on the ground, his right arm covered in blood, and Aquila, with one foot on his chest, was preparing to deliver the final blow. Agrippa saw that the murderer had his back to the fire. His sword held forwards, he threw himself at him, parrying the blow which was intended for Octavian and, with his body, throwing Aquila backwards.

Into the flames...

Agrippa heard him scream and rolled on top of his friend, then turned his gaze towards the man he had sentenced to burn alive. Aquila had ended up falling back onto the burning flaps of the tent, and being enveloped by the flames. His body had become a blazing brand.

Only then did the young man roll over, freeing Octavian from his weight and slumping onto the leather floor. He heard the trampling of feet ringing in his ears, felt himself lifted up and he thought he heard the voice of his friend giving orders. A hand gripped his wrist. He tried to focus on who it belonged to, and saw Octavian's face.

But he could not read his friend's expression. He had never been able to – not even in the past, for that matter.

He couldn't think any more. Fatigue overcame him, followed by darkness.

XX

Veleda attempted to rise from the stretcher as soon as she saw Ortwin making his way through the crowd of soldiers to reach her in the Forum of Smyrna, but the grazes on her elbows were burning too much so she let herself fall back just before her man embraced her.

"They… they told me that you hadn't made it. I was afraid you were dead," she said between sobs and gasps, her stretcher shaking from the accidental jolts of Dolabella's soldiers, running in and out of the gate of Smyrna, celebrating and fraternizing with the defenders.

"For a moment I feared it myself, to tell you the truth," said Ortwin holding her tightly but taking care not to press her wounds. "That idiot Dolabella made us wait, damn him, and we all risked death."

"You managed to open the gates, though… He didn't have to fight…"

"Not me. I had a centurion's sword at my neck when the signal appeared in the sky. Then the three of our men who had managed to escape took advantage of the guards' distraction to open the gate, and calmed the reaction of the defenders by showing them Trebonius's head. At that point, none of the garrison had the will to fight any more and they let Dolabella's men inside."

Veleda squeezed his wrist and looked at him tenderly. On impulse she wanted to tell him that she would not have known what to do if he had been killed, but as always, regal pride prevented her from freely expressing her emotions. She hated herself for not being able to, but could do nothing about it – it made her a worse person, she knew, but as long as Ortwin continued to love her and tolerate her, she had no need to change.

She looked up and watched the legionaries celebrating. Dawn was breaking and a hint of sunlight brightened the sky which in recent days had been full of clouds. Soldiers were shouting the praises of Dolabella the conqueror, offensively ignoring the role they had played in the fall of the city – particularly because, in fact, the only two victims were Germans. As she gazed around her, her eye fell upon a curule seat placed upon a grandstand at the centre of the Forum. She squinted and made out upon it a head. She pointed it out to Ortwin, asking, "Is that it?"

Her man looked at it. "Yes, that's Trebonius. Dolabella wanted it to be placed on the chair where justice is administered. And to think that only a few months ago our commander boasted of having collaborated with him in the murder of Caesar…"

"You're the one who admires the Romans, not me…" She could never help her caustic remarks, but she knew that Ortwin didn't mind. Or at least not too much. He did not answer, though.

At that moment a chorus of laughter attracted their attention: some legionaries were dragging a naked corpse by the arms. But then Veleda noticed that they weren't pulling it by the arms but with their swords, which they had stuck into its hands. One soldier stumbled backwards when his blade came free, splitting the corpse's hand in two. The others laughed even louder, and when the man returned to the body, he hurled insults at it and spat upon it. Only then did Veleda realise that its head was missing. She looked at Ortwin, who nodded. It was what was left of Trebonius.

Someone else plunged his sword between its legs, then pulled out some bloody pulp with his hand and hurled it at one of his companions, braying with laughter as he did. His friend pretended to lose his temper and set about hacking off the proconsul's foot, before picking it up and throwing it at the others.

"This is what happens to traitors." Dolabella had emerged from the crowd and materialised next to them. "The legionaries simply could not tolerate the man who had killed their commander, even though he was one of his lieutenants."

Veleda was glad that it was Ortwin who had to answer. If it had been up to her, she would not have been able to hold back from saying that *he* had pretended to have killed Caesar, the man who had appointed him consul, and now he had had the man whose comrade and ally he had not long ago professed to be, killed. *Twice a traitor*, then. Worse than Trebonius.

"Yes, he was a traitor and I'm glad I killed him," said Ortwin, limiting himself to underlining – or so it seemed to Veleda – his not insignificant role in events.

"Your plan worked, Ortwin," conceded the general. "Even though it was too risky to really be considered a decent one. Fortunately, I arrived in time. But we might have to do something like that in Syria, if Cassius gets there before us. Work on it for next time," concluded the proconsul, or whatever he now was, giving Ortwin a pat on the back before walking off towards the platform.

Veleda looked at her man, who stared back at her, his eyes full of self-pity. Sometimes, he made her angry with his calm, condescending way... Without even complimenting him, that hideous individual had practically said that the Germans were nothing more than expendable soldiers who could be sacrificed to conquer a city without him needing to do anything. And if they didn't manage, well, never mind – in the end it had cost him nothing.

"Was he there?" she asked Ortwin, not needing to specify his name.

He understood immediately that she was referring to Quintus Labienus. "I didn't see him. Anyway, I was not aware that he was even in the city. Do you care so much about seeing him again?" There was a hint of jealousy in his voice.

Veleda was pleased. Every so often he did betray some emotion, after all. "Of course not! I only feared that he might endanger your life," she replied – and then asked herself if that was the real reason for her interest.

She hesitated a moment too long before answering herself that it was, but then she was distracted by the sight of Dolabella climbing up onto the grandstand to the undeserved cheers of the soldiers, taking Trebonius's head and hurling it into the crowd. Soon after, some of the legionaries picked it up and began to throw it about as though it were a ball.

She looked at Ortwin again, her mystified eyes asking him why he admired the Romans so much.

*

Octavian felt Maecenas's gaze upon him. He moved away from the flap of the tent where he had been secretly observing the hospitalised Agrippa, and saw the Etruscan gesture with his head for him to go inside. He quickly looked away – he didn't need to be told what to do, damn it! He knew that himself. He just… had to find the right words first. It was not easy to admit you had made a mistake, or at least, that you had gone too far. Yes, *gone too far* – that was a good way of putting it. He would follow that line of thinking. Agrippa was the best person he had ever known, there was no doubt about it, and his closest friend to boot, but the choices they had made in their lives meant that he was also his subordinate – or at least he would be once more now that he had saved his skin – and a leader could not lavish too many apologies on someone who was under his command.

He was tempted for a moment to ask Maecenas to accompany him inside, but then realised it would be a sign of cowardice. The night before, at the end of the battle, he had a good excuse for not going to see Agrippa – he had immediately sent Glycon to take care of him, and the doctor had told him that the patient was unconscious and needed rest, so he had used that pretext to spend the night deciding on the right words to say to readmit Agrippa to the sect and make him understand that his affection for him had never waned. But now… Now he could put it off no longer. By the gods, of all the things that he had to think about after being seen as the winner of the battle, this was the most difficult. Immediately after the fighting, the only thing that had occupied his mind was how Agrippa had happened to be there, covering his back.

He had realised straightaway that Maecenas must have had a hand in it, and had gone straight to the Etruscan to ask for an explanation, ignoring the many requests of the officers about the recovery of the dead and the care of the injured, as well as the guarding of Mark Antony's camp. His friend had told him only that he had done it to ensure that Agrippa never really left the sect. "Unyielding with enemies, forgiving with friends," he had added by way of suggestion.

"Damn!" he said, as he finally made up his mind to cross the threshold. He saw that Agrippa was awake and conscious, lying on the bed, poorly illuminated by a lamp, while Glycon was replacing the bandage that covered the young man's entire torso, for he had received serious burns to his back and been stabbed in the side.

In order to save his life.

"How is he?" he asked the doctor right away, avoiding Agrippa's eyes and standing next to the bed.

"Our friend is as strong as an ox," said Glycon cheerfully. "I'd say that he will pull through. The burns on his back are mild, and I have stitched up the wound. He'll be stronger than before."

"Excellent. We need him," he said, in order to introduce the theme of which he felt obliged to speak.

The doctor sensed that it was time for him to be off. He hurriedly finished his work then stood up and wished them farewell, while the two young men remained silently staring at each other. Octavian saw how full of expectation Agrippa looked, and felt a surge of affection for him that he wished he could manifest. He wanted to embrace him, but he stayed where he was, even after Glycon had left.

He sat in the doctor's place and limited himself to grabbing hold of Agrippa's wrist. Agrippa was silent. For a moment, Octavian thought that his friend was about to start trying to explain himself – after all, he had forbidden him to show his face and had instead had found him where he had least expected him and when he needed him most, like some kind of guardian deity. "Unyielding with enemies, but forgiving with friends," he reminded himself. It was time to speak. He sighed deeply and said, "You saved my life."

Agrippa's eyes filled up. Whether from the pain or from emotion, he could not say. "You would have done the same for me. I'm sure," he said. Octavian was glad to hear his voice again.

"And you also killed Aquila, one who was on the list. The first we have taken revenge on, to my knowledge."

"Your objective has always been mine, Octavian. I too loved Caesar."

Silence again. Then he said, "I should be angry with Maecenas for having schemed behind my back, but I cannot bring myself to… I'm glad to have you with us again."

"And I'm glad that you've forgiven me. If he has allowed me to earn your forgiveness, then I too must thank Maecenas."

"Who knows, perhaps you needn't have gone to such lengths. In my heart, I knew that it was my pride which was guiding me, nothing else." As soon as the words left his mouth he almost regretted saying them – it seemed almost as though he was prostrating himself.

Agrippa grabbed his wrist with both hands to show that he knew what it cost him to speak thus, and that he appreciated his friend's candour. They looked at each other in silence and Octavian felt comforted. He wondered how he could have been so foolish as to renounce this invaluable friendship at such a delicate time in his life. Now, more than ever, their relationship was the most noble element of that series of challenges which would certainly bring out the worst aspects of his character: the only ones that would allow him to survive in that perverse situation in which he had chosen to play a role.

"So how are you going to take advantage of the victory? By the look of things, you're the one deciding the strategy now," Agrippa said finally.

"Yes. Good question," nodded Octavian. "I never expected to find myself in this situation, but I'm determined to exploit it in the best way possible. Hirtius is dead, Pansa is in a bad way. In the absence of the consuls, a propraetor assumes command, but I still need to talk to Pansa in Bologna. It would irk the Senate were I to take over – they are just waiting for me to take a false step and give them a pretext for getting rid of me. As far as they are concerned, I'm nothing more than a means to an end. And the feeling is mutual…"

"It all depends on what Mark Antony plans on doing, I suppose," agreed Agrippa.

"Exactly. I have to play a double game. At the moment, now that Decimus Brutus is on his last legs, I am the only resource that the Senate has in the field, but Mark Antony is the only one I can really use to gain credibility and importance in the eyes of the senators and curb the power of my father's murderers. In essence, I need him, and I have given orders not to put too much pressure on his camp. As long as he is considered a threat, the Senate will be forced to rely on me."

"You're playing with fire. Mark Antony is a dangerous character, and things could easily get out of hand. What do you hope to achieve?"

At that moment, the curtain was pulled aside, letting in a ray of dazzling light. It took Octavian a moment before he was able to make out the form of Rufus. He saw that his gaze had fallen upon his hands, which were still holding Agrippa's, and seemed to sense irritation on his face. Rufus did not greet Agrippa, but he shifted his eyes to Octavian and announced in an unusually neutral voice, "Greetings, Agrippa. Glad to see you alive. Mark Antony has dismantled the camp and is leaving, and Decimus Brutus sent a messenger to request a meeting with you, Octavian. What shall we do, deploy the army to stop Mark Antony in the meanwhile?"

"No. Tell the officers that the men are still tired from the fighting and we would risk a defeat. Let it be. I'm on my way now. Assemble the other members," said Octavian, then turned to Agrippa. "What do I hope to achieve? Precisely this: let Mark Antony still be a threat... Or at least give that impression," he concluded, getting to his feet and walking towards the exit.

*

Rufus felt confused. Ever since they had told him that, yes, it had actually been Agrippa on the battlefield and that he had saved Octavian's life, he had been torn between a desire to be sincere with him and the annoyance of finding him in his way once again, coming between him and Octavian. And maybe even between himself and Etain. When he realised that the two friends had reconciled, he felt a surge of annoyance that he could not control. He wanted to set aside that unpleasant feeling, and also to congratulate him on making up with his friend, as Maecenas and Gaius Chaerea had already done, but something held him back from doing so. He had been barely able to speak to him when he had entered his tent.

Now, Octavian would consider Agrippa his principal military aide and his greatest friend, and in the chief's eyes, Rufus would always be in second place in the sect. Or maybe even third, considering the now inescapable presence of Maecenas.

No, he was not happy about the re-appearance of Agrippa, he admitted to himself as went to meet Octavian by the river, where Gaius Chaerea and Maecenas were already waiting. But he was aware that it was only envy, and promised himself he would try to beat it. And to beat Agrippa too, by proving that he was better than him. One day he would force Octavian to admit that it was he who gave something of importance to the sect, and not this overvalued lad.

"You see, Rufus?" Octavian welcomed him when he reached the river bank. His friend waved Decimus Brutus's message under his nose. "That murderer has the good manners to admit that I helped free him from the siege, and asks for a meeting with him to agree on a joint strategy to continue our fight against Mark Antony. He also wants to explain himself, he says. He even claims that it was a demon which convinced him to kill my father and that he feels sorry for what he did..."

"But in the meantime, as soon as he saw Mark Antony breaking up camp, he destroyed all the bridges as though *we* were the attackers," added Chaerea, indicating the nearest one, which Brutus's engineers had reduced to a pile of rubble. "The 'liberator' must be quaking in his boots – without Mark Antony between him and us and with his strength reduced to the limit he is already in our power and he knows it."

"Decimus Brutus is awaiting Octavian there," said Maecenas indicating an island in the river, so close that an arrow could reach it. "It could be a trap, of course. But it may be that he is now willing to do anything to save his skin and is actually contemplating the idea of an alliance."

"But I do *not* contemplate it!" exploded Octavian, making the messenger who was waiting for a response shake. "Tell your superior that I did not come to save him, but to fight Mark Antony!" he shouted. "Perhaps I will be able to reconcile with Mark Antony sooner or later, but my character does not allow me even to *speak* to Decimus Brutus, nor yet look him in the face, the traitor!"

Maecenas squeezed Octavian's arm, inviting him to control himself. It was not part of the strategy of the sect to manifest their intentions so openly. He pulled his young friend towards him and said softly, though loudly enough for Rufus to hear, "Calm down, my friend. Don't you want the Senate to reward you with the consulate in place of Hirtius? Persuade, if you want to be persuaded. You won't get any rewards by insulting Decimus Brutus, who is the darling of those old windbags."

Octavian nodded, and pulled himself together. He let out a long sigh and said, "You are right, of course. But I have no wish to seem willing to give up on my principles altogether either. Remember that if I have earned the respect and support of the army, it is certainly not because of my military prowess but rather because I set out to avenge Caesar. Many legions abandoned Mark Antony because he was willing to make agreements with my father's murderers. If I do the same, what impression will it give? The soldiers are my only support for the moment, and probably the only tool that will allow me to force those damn senators to give me a few concessions."

Maecenas opened his arms and spread his hands. Both arguments – that of his friend and his own – were irrefutable, thought Rufus, glad that it was not up to him to make decisions regarding the high politics of the sect.

Octavian walked over again to Decimus Brutus's messenger. "Excuse my intemperance to the proconsul," he said, "and re-assure your master – the Senate wishes to save him, so he has nothing to fear from me as long as those in Rome are happy." A good compromise, Rufus said to himself – and he hadn't even had to lie.

The frightened messenger nodded and hurried back to the boat in which he had arrived. He soon reached the small strip of land in the middle of the water, where they saw him conversing with Brutus. Octavian turned round, ostentatiously turning his back on them. "Let's go. That abject being deserves no attention. I am only interested in speaking to Pansa before he leaves us."

"And a recommendation from him to assign the consulate would be decisive," Maecenas said.

"Not to mention the celebration of a triumph or at least an ovation. After all, it is you who has won this war," said Rufus, who could already see himself parading through the streets of Rome behind the chariot of the victor.

"And let's not forget the rewards promised to the soldiers," said Chaerea. "The state took upon itself to pay them what you had promised them, and now they must pay through you. It must be quite clear to the troops that it was you who procured that money for them."

Suddenly, they heard Octavian's name on the wind. They all turned in unison and saw that the proconsul was trying to attract their attention: the shouts were coming from him. Decimus Brutus waved the document in which the Senate had given notice of his appointment as proconsul. He approached the edge of the island, descending into the water up to his waist, in order to make himself heard better and continued to shout. Now they could hear him clearly.

"'The Senate of Rome, with the favour of the immortal gods'," read the magistrate from the papyrus in his hand, "'nominates Decimus Junius Brutus Albinus proconsul of Gaul Cisalpina, with the right to dispose of the legions stationed there for the good of the Republic, and grants him judiciary powers and the associated duties of tax collection.' The conscript fathers wrote this for me. I am here because of the senate and the people of Rome! You cannot do anything to me, you boy! Do not dare to cross the river – without consuls, you're nothing! You cannot even enter a province if the magistrate who governs it does not allow you to! Not even to chase Mark Antony! You have no official position, and I, in the absence of the consuls, am responsible for waging war against him: it will be me who follows him."

"Unfortunately, he's right, the bastard," said Maecenas. "He feels that his back is covered by the Senate."

"But his legions are falling apart," protested Rufus, "and furthermore they are all recruits and gladiators! We have more soldiers, and they are in excellent condition. It makes no sense for him to continue the war."

Octavian did not respond to the shouts of the proconsul. Ignoring him, he turned away and strode off towards the camp, a frown on his face. The others followed. Only Rufus had the courage to ask him a question. "Why don't we attack? As things stand we could do it in one go... Even the soldiers would be happy to take the head of that traitor," he suggested.

"I would like to. I would like to more than anything else, Rufus. But it is a luxury we cannot afford at the moment," replied Octavian, continuing to look straight ahead.

*

Pansa's face had grown even more ashen since the last time Octavian had visited him, but the young man forced himself not to be influenced by the desperate condition of the consul, who at their last meeting had used his suffering as an excuse for being evasive in the face of his incessant demands. This time, he would get his support, even if it killed Pansa in the process.

Octavian saluted and sat down beside the deathbed of the consul, who looked at him with glassy eyes, barely moving his lips to greet him. He waited for Pansa to dismiss his Secretary and the slave who were in the room with him, then forced himself to ask the customary questions about his health.

"I think you can see for yourself, how I am, propraetor," mumbled the consul. "I'm dying. The doctors were unable to stop the infection, and the evil demon is consuming me from the inside. Not even your Glycon – who, by the way, I thank you for having sent me – could do anything but look to the gods. A blessing for you, Octavian – with both consuls out of the game, you'll have more chance of indulging your wildest ambitions... Until they elect new ones, you have the army that defeated Mark Antony in your hands..."

"Are you mocking me, consul?" said Octavian, testily. "Have you not heard? The Senate has already put a stop to my alleged ambitions. Your friends the senators have not even mentioned me in their decrees, despite having established some fifty days of celebrations for the victory over Mark Antony, fifty! More than for any other war! My report on the battle was not even read to the people, while yours was, and all they have done has been to glorify Decimus Brutus, as though he were the consuls' only ally. They have decreed the triumph for him. They have assigned to him the legions that had passed to me from Mark Antony and that they had then given to you. They have also set up a commission to award gratuities to the soldiers, and – would you believe it? – they have not mentioned me there either! This is a provocation... No – an insult."

"Yes, my dear friend, I know and I am sorry," answered Pansa, although Octavian was certain that he was not sorry at all. The man was merely an expression of the Senate. "But it is clear that, since Mark Antony is on the run, they do not need you any more. You enjoy too much consensus among the troops, and for this reason the nobles fear you, because you are the heir of Caesar, for whose death the majority of senators rejoiced. They had hoped that you and Mark Antony would fight each other – you did, and you weakened him and allowed us to defeat him, and now you have outlived your usefulness."

Octavian shook his head then put it in his hands. "They wrote to Lepidus, to Plancus Munatius, to Asinius Pollio... To all the provincial governors who supported Caesar, urging them to attack Mark Antony – and not to me… Not even a letter."

"Come, what did you expect? With Caesar's death, the Senate saw an opportunity to take back the reins of the state, and it will continue to rely upon the dictator's murderers because they are the only ones upon whom they can really count to be left free to govern: Marcus Brutus, Cassius Longinus, Decimus Brutus, Trebonius… they are the Senate! And instead, Mark Antony, Caesar's Lieutenant, Lepidus, the *magister equitum* of Caesar, and you, Octavian, Caesar's adopted son… You are all potential dictators! They will use whatever weapons they have at their disposal to put you out of the game."

"Then you must help me, Pansa. If you really cared for Caesar, if you didn't betray him as all the others appear to have done, you must help me."

"And how? In my letter, I commended your ability on the battlefield and suggested to the conscript fathers to let you have my legions, but you have seen for yourself that it was pointless. All I can do now is give you some advice."

"That would be very welcome, Pansa."

"I've already given it to you, Octavian. You have the army in your hands, and no decree of the Senate would convince the soldiers who abandoned Mark Antony because he did not avenge Caesar to march under the banner of one of his killers. It is too ridiculous to even consider, and their decision shows their political myopia. Those legions will remain yours, one way or another, so use the fact to your advantage and keep the pressure on them. You must find a way to make them take you seriously… Caesar learned that, when they start raising their voices, all you need to do is raise yours even louder and they turn into sheep. And then…"

"And then?" Pansa's reflections were extremely interesting, Octavian said to himself.

"And then, as I told you… You, Mark Antony and Lepidus have a common interest in collaborating. The Senate has its champions in Caesar's murderers, and does not want you, nor will it ever. It has done everything to turn you against each other, because it knows that together, the three of you would easily impose your will. And you fell for it. Mark Antony because he is impetuous, you because you are still young and inexperienced and Lepidus because he is a lazy good for nothing. If you had made some kind of agreement right at the start, Caesar's killers would not have been able to consolidate their power in the eastern provinces. If only you had stopped fighting amongst yourselves, they would be too weak for you… But perhaps now the time is right. You have no choice, if you wish to survive politically – or simply survive. Whatever your brains neglected to make you do, your survival instinct will. How much do you want to bet that when Mark Antony crosses the Alps, Lepidus will not attack even if the Senate orders him to?"

Octavian reflected a moment. Pansa was wisely suggesting playing a double game. Let Mark Antony come back stronger than before in order to induce the Senate to reconsider Caesar's despised heir as his opponent, but at the same time seek an understanding with him, as indeed he had wanted to do from the start. He'd had the intelligence – it was Mark Antony who was too dull to understand, the fool! He, Octavian, was not the enemy at that moment, and he had to make Antony realise that once and for all. Pansa had just imparted a profound lesson in politics and he felt deeply grateful to him.

He looked at him with gratitude, but saw that the consul was at death's door. The effort of explaining had exhausted him and his breathing had become more laboured. His eyes were wide open with the effort of trying to breathe, his mouth twisted into a grimace. Octavian had really squeezed the last drops of energy out of him. But he had got what he wanted.

He stood up, satisfied, and said goodbye to him, squeezing his shoulder, affectionately. The magistrate nodded and closed his eyes, spent.

Pansa had helped him. Now he knew what he had to do.

XXI

Agrippa nodded to Gaius Chaerea, and the centurion passed him the wineskin. The young man reached over to take it, and the effort of doing so made the wound in his side throb. He tried not to let the pain show, but Chaerea noticed his face and moved closer to offer him support. Agrippa stopped him with a wave of his hand and took a step toward the coals which burned before him: Octavian had allowed him the honour of playing an active part in the funeral of the two consuls and he had no intention of letting his friend down.

He looked over at Octavian, who nodded, then made his way over to what was left of Hirtius and Pansa and began to pour the wine over the burning brands. Immediately Agrippa, Maecenas and Rufus did the same, and from the single pyre rose sparks and smoke which carried off into the surrounding air the delicious smell of the unguents scattered among the remains of the fallen leaders. The soldiers, arranged in two rows between which the bodies had been paraded, extended their right arms in the military salute.

The heat of the smoke sent tingles of pain down the spine of Agrippa, who was still suffering the after effects of the burns he had received in the battle with Aquila. He reached for more wine and repeated the ritual until the glowing embers were only dim flickers, and only then did Octavian step back, inviting his friends to do the same, and let the servants take over and pour milk over the bones the fire had not completely consumed. They then took two shrouds from one of the adjacent wagons and, using tongs and scoops, placed the bones and ashes upon them.

One after another, the legates, tribunes and centurions filed by to say a final farewell to the two consuls. Each stopped for a moment in front of the shrouds and murmured a few words before moving on to make way for the next. When it was the turn of Galba, the conspirator looked askance at Octavian and, after paying homage to the remains, approached him.

"I will never forgive you for not giving permission to celebrate the funeral of poor Pontius Aquila together with them," he whispered, loudly enough for Agrippa and his friends to hear.

"And I will never forgive you for killing my father. So we are even, murderer," hissed Octavian, casually holding his gaze.

Agrippa had to stop himself from smiling. Asking his friend to celebrate the funeral of one of the murderers of his father was a sign of Galba's infinite arrogance, and he was certain that he had done it to provoke him and make him lose his temper in front of the soldiers: the legate had sent him a request to that effect by letter, and Octavian's refusal had been categorical. There was no point in returning to the subject unless it was to pick a fight.

Galba did not answer. He turned his gaze once more upon the embers and walked on; who knows what would have happened, wondered Agrippa, if he had known that Aquila had not fallen after being killed by Antony's men when they took the field, but had died at his hands? He told himself that if he ever had a chance to take revenge upon the legate, he would tell him – before killing him.

When the ranks of the officers had finished, they rolled up the shrouds and placed them back upon the cart, which would soon leave for Rome, where Hirtius and Pansa would have civilian funerals organised by their relatives and the Senate. With a wave of his arm, Octavian declared an end to the funeral, and the soldiers cheered their gratitude at his having taken the trouble to celebrate the services of their commanders. Then the young commander walked to his headquarters, his aides behind him.

"Well, it is to be hoped that the Senate appreciates what you did for two of their most prominent leaders as much as the soldiers did, and begin to accord you due respect, Octavian," said Rufus, with whom Agrippa had not yet had a chance to speak since he had returned to being a full member of the sect.

"I doubt it. After all, Hirtius and Pansa were not just senators – they were also supporters of Caesar, and among the few who didn't actually betray your father," said Maecenas. "These days, anti-Caesareans are more in vogue than Caesarians…"

"I think that the senators will feel obliged to recognise my importance after they hear the latest news from Forum Iulii," said Octavian, a satisfied expression on his face.

"Why, what's happened?" asked Agrippa.

"That's right, you don't know – this morning you were resting, and as I knew that you would insist on putting yourself through the funeral, I left you in your tent," explained Octavian. "It seems that, instead of attacking him as the Senate had ordered, Lepidus welcomed Antony with open arms. Their soldiers have fraternised and now it is Antony who commands them all: his legions plus Lepidus's seven. If we add the three of Publius Ventidius, who had already joined him before he came to Spain, Antony is stronger than ever, and represents a serious threat."

"And Decimus Brutus, who was counting on capturing Antony in a pincer movement by attacking him from behind while Lepidus blocked his front, can do nothing. Especially since a pestilence has apparently broken out in his ranks," added Maecenas. "I have the impression that we will soon be receiving communications from the senators. In Rome they have no legions to defend them if Antony decides to march from Gaul and occupy the city, and Marcus Brutus and Cassius are too far away to help. They have no choice but to resort to our eight legions…"

"It was a blessing that the Martia and the IVth legions did not follow Decimus Brutus," said Octavian. "He is too weak to do it by himself, and it gives me a powerful advantage for my election as consul. In Rome, the chaos is such that elections for new consuls have been suspended, and I intend to take advantage of the fact. I wrote to Cicero to propose a joint consulate, with him as senior consul and I as junior, to tickle his vanity, expressly stating that I would leave all the decisions to him."

"Has he answered?"

"Ah! He would have been in favour, of course. But his proposal didn't pass. The senators are well aware of how sensitive that old windbag is to flattery, and though he fell for it, the others realised that I was manipulating him. He's no more use to us politically now. He no longer has the authority he used to, and is adrift on an ocean of his own self-importance. Pansa was right: our most valuable ally can only be Antony now. And after him, Lepidus."

"But Antony still bears you a grudge" said Rufus.

"We will make him understand that he has no reason to. At the moment, he should be more afraid of the Senate than of Octavian," said Maecenas. "Our army is now the needle of the balance between him, the senators and Caesar's murderers: four military and political powers which make the current situation more complicated than any other in the history of Rome. I have the impression that in this game you are playing not only for our destiny but for that of the Republic too. Whoever wins, the city will not be the same as it was before."

"We can reduce the four contenders in this match to two by creating coalitions," added Octavian. "Antony and I on the one hand, the Senate and the murderers on the other. I offered myself to the Senate, but those old fools prefer the killers: well, for all the ill Antony has done me, I find it less sickening to make an agreement with him than with anyone who was involved in my father's murder."

"And when you have too many options, the best strategy is to do nothing at all and wait for their number to shrink of its own accord," declared Maecenas solemnly. "Let's see what the Senate will do under the pressure of Antony's threat and then act accordingly. But one thing is certain – we will not do them the favour of provoking Antony…"

*

The tribune was standing to attention in the middle of the praetorium. Seated behind his desk, the end of his stylus pressed to his lips, Octavian watched him, tapping occasionally on the wax tablet Maecenas had just placed under the nose.

"It's the release order, *propraetor*" said the Etruscan, addressing him in a formal tone. "This man is called Decius and was serving in the Second Legion when he was taken prisoner near Modena."

Octavian decided to affix his signature to the document. "Well, Decius, you are free," he said, with a smile. "You can go back to your commander and give him my regards."

The officer seemed confused. He remained silent, looking around as though he feared he was the victim of a bad joke.

"What is it, tribune? You may speak, if you wish," urged Maecenas.

The man looked at Octavian, requesting confirmation. The commander nodded. "Erm…" he began, finally, "I wonder, if I might… What do you think of Mark Antony, sir?"

Octavian smiled mirthlessly. "I would say that I have already given clear proof of my feelings in that regard, for those capable of understanding… And for those who are not… well, a thousand words would not suffice. You may go, tribune."

The officer appeared no less confused than before. He hesitated, then bowed his head in a respectful farewell and left the tent.

"And that makes forty-seven prisoners released over the past ten days," said Maecenas. "In addition to the one hundred and two who left of their own free will when we announced that anyone who wanted to return to Antony could do so."

"He too must have heard that the Senate had decided to entrust me with conducting the war against Antony with Decimus Brutus, and will have seen that I have not moved from here. At this point, I think I have done enough to show him that I no longer consider him an enemy…" mused Octavian.

Outside they heard shouting, and soon after, Gaius Chaerea appeared in the doorway. "*Propraetor*, the *decemvirs* charged with establishing the bounty for the legionaries have arrived from Rome," he announced.

"Gods! How ridiculous that a committee of which I should have been part comes to *me* to ask my opinion!" replied Octavian impatiently. "Well, let them come."

"Erm… In truth they do not wish to speak to you, *propraetor*," muttered Chaerea.

Octavian jumped to his feet. "What do you mean they do not wish to speak to me?"

"They… They went straight to speak to the soldiers. Promising them half of the bounty now and the other half when the war ends, if they go over to Decimus Brutus. And there's more."

Octavian opened his arms and raised his eyes to the heavens.

"*More*? What more could there be than *that*, in the name of the gods?"

"Errr… They only made the offer to the Martia and the IVth: the legions which have abandoned Antony. They ignored the

331

others."

The young man looked over at Maecenas. "Of course – they want to foment rivalries and jealousies to set the soldiers against me and the legions against one another."

"I'm not surprised," admitted the Etruscan. "After all, they tried to soften you up by giving you a shared command with Decimus Brutus, and now that they've seen you're not doing anything about Antony, they're trying to steal the troops."

"What did they expect? To buy me off with a command post? I asked for the consulate and a triumph, and they give me a sweetener? Quintus Pedius wrote to me that when my name is mentioned in the Senate, the senators call me 'boy'. But I'll show them, the stupid bastards: I'm going to make a speech to the soldiers."

Maecenas held him by the arm. "Wait. It'll look as though you're begging – they'll think you've lost control and are desperate. Let me go first. We need to prepare them."

Octavian paused, reflecting on his friend's words. Then he nodded. "Very well. I'll give you an hour to work on them."

Maecenas put his arm around Gaius Chaerea's waist. "Gaius, accompany me to the field of camp of the Martia and the IVth. Let's see what we can do."

*

When they arrived, they saw that the word had spread and that, in addition to the delegations of the two legions, there were also delegations from the others who were camped in neighbouring forts. The officers and representatives of the soldiers were crowded around the podium of the exercise field, leaning against the rampart. On the platform, the ten envoys of the Senate chatted animatedly with those closest to them.

"Go among the crowd and tell the soldiers what I told you, and hurry up!" cried Maecenas to Chaerea. "I will do the same with the officers."

The Etruscan pushed his way through the crowd until he had reached the knot of people beneath the platform. He saw a tribune he knew, grabbed him by the shoulders and shouted in his face, "How dare you speak to this committee in place of your commander? Have you not seen how the Senate has made fools of you so far? How can you trust them?"

The officer looked embarrassed. "We're just curious, Maecenas... We just wanted to see what they were offering, that's all. I..."

"The Senate considered the bounty that Octavian promised you its responsibility, but you were never paid it. And now they are promising you *half*. What makes you think that they will give you the rest? At least Octavian has shown himself to be a man of his word by paying all that Caesar had decreed even at the cost of getting himself into debt."

Meanwhile one of the ten *decemvirs*, noticing the presence of one working against them, raised his voice and addressed the crowd.

"Soldiers! Do not pin your hopes on one man. Believe in the Senate, the only body whose power has no limits over time! The only one upon which you can truly rely."

But Maecenas did not give up. "Is this the price you ask, legionaries, to serve the murderer of your late beloved commander? Half of what Caesar's son has promised you?"

An increasing number of soldiers seemed to listening more closely to the words of Maecenas than those of the *decemvirs*. Even the men on the platform had stopped paying attention to the emissaries in order to listen to him.

The Etruscan summoned up all his courage and went on, hoping that Chaerea was doing the same.

"Was Octavian wrong, then, to consider you heroes, loyal and brave? Is your venality such that you will abandon the cause you once reputed so just that you allowed yourselves to be decimated by Antony simply because he did not pursue it? And do you wish to set your comrades, alongside whom you have fought, against you by accepting a payment that they will not have at all?"

More and more people thronged around him, and the soldiers relayed his words to those behind them and they to their fellows, until his message was spreading at incredible speed. He noticed that the soldiers of the other legions were paying close attention too, and had begun to shove those of the Martia and accuse them of being greedy and ungrateful.

He immediately seized the opportunity. "And you, you legions of soldiers unlucky enough not to have been offered anything by the Senate, how you can tolerate such a difference in treatment? Are you not outraged to know that the senators have decided to reward only a few legions, even though you have all shared the dangers and sacrifices in equal measure? Do you not understand that they want to set one against the other so that they can steal power and influence away from the son of Caesar? Do you not see that they are trying to make you argue and even fight amongst yourselves?"

"Curse the Senate!" came a cry.

"Octavian is our commander! Let him speak with these idiots!" shouted another, immediately followed by a chorus of assent.

"We should not deal with the messengers of the Senate without the son of Caesar! It is he who protects our interests!"

Soon the mass of soldiery began to flow away from the platform and Maecenas felt himself transported in the opposite direction to that of the fort, until the crowd suddenly stopped moving.

"There he is!" voices shouted. "He has come! Octavian is here! Praise be to Octavian, who has came to take care of us!"

The Etruscan peered about in search of his friend and only after some time did he manage to make him out in the crowd. The young man was making his way among the soldiers with a confident step, and the legionaries let him pass, backing out of his way and shouting words of praise and encouragement. Octavian reached the grandstand and climbed up without deigning to look at the representatives of the Senate, just as they had ignored him.

There was silence among the soldiers. All present hung on his words. Maecenas looked at the face of his friend, who before speaking levelled his blazing eyes upon each of the legionaries in the front rows, and knew that he knew.

"Soldiers! Until today, you and I have been united in believing that the memory of Caesar should be safeguarded and his honour vindicated," he said. "The Senate is dominated by the relatives of those who murdered him and who have always opposed justice being done. By going along with the Senate, and thus, indirectly, with the killers of your commander, you would kill Caesar a second time – and you would have no guarantee of receiving land or money, just as I would have no guarantee of my own survival. I speak not out of personal interest: you know that I am not ambitious and I act only out of a sense of gratitude and affection for my father. And I am willing to accept my fate and to make any sacrifice because I think it honourable, such is my desire to avenge him. But it is for you that I am afraid – you, who have shown yourselves to be so valiant, who have volunteered in such great numbers to obey my orders. Who will protect you, who will act in your best interests, if you allow me to face my enemies unarmed? At this point, I see only one way out for me and for you: that with your help I be elected consul. Only in this way will you receive everything my father promised you, and even more – that which *I* promise you: lands and colonies, and justice for the murder of your commander, before being freed of the obligation to fight more wars and enjoying a well-earned rest."

He stopped. And began to look at them, one by one, as they stood there in stunned silence.

"To Rome! To Rome!" a voice in the ranks cried out suddenly.

"Yes, all to Rome! Octavian for consul!" rang out the answering cry, which others soon began to pick up. Maecenas looked at him proudly. They had survived even that hurdle. And now it was time for the final challenge.

*

Gaius Chaerea felt a sense of awe rise up in him that he had not even felt the first time he had met Julius Caesar himself. He watched the plain mass of the Curia of Pompey loom majestically before him at the rear of the quadrangle surrounding part of the theatre built by the man who had been Caesar's greatest opponent.

He wondered if the source of his discomfort lay in having to enter the hall where the dictator had been killed or in the obligation of facing the entire Senate, right there, in the place where historic meetings which had decided the fate of the world had been held.

Now it was he who had to determine the fate of Rome, with an act of force which would probably go down in the history books.

He stopped at the entrance of the building, where the two confused sentries on guard seemed not know whether to bar his

335

path or run away screaming. He looked behind him, as though to ensure that the four hundred officers he had brought to Rome to support him in braving the infinite arrogance of the cream of the Roman aristocracy, were still there.

Yes, they were, ready to back him but each glad that it was he who would be speaking and not them: he was sure that none of them wished to speechify under the stern gazes of the senators on their benches.

To steel his nerve, he had told himself that Octavian must nurture great respect for him to have put him at the head of the delegation that was to force the issue in the Senate. It had also occurred to him, however, that perhaps it was actually because Agrippa was still sick and Maecenas and Rufus were too useful at the front: the war against Antony and Lepidus, now officially declared public enemies by the senators, languished somewhat. Indeed, contact between the leader of the sect and the two rebels had intensified and a sort of truce was now in place, but Octavian was playing a delicate and complex game, and the slightest thing would be enough to upset the balance.

"I am Gaius Chaerea, senior centurion of the Martia legion," he said finally to the guards, who were clearly awed by the sight of the four hundred soldiers now deployed along the façade of the building. "I come with my fellow soldiers in the name of Octavian, Caesar's son, to confer with the Senate."

"It… It isn't usual for armed soldiers to circulate in the city. Nor to enter the holy place where the Senate gathers. And as for conferring with the senators…" It had taken the guard all of his courage to answer this way, Gaius knew.

"This time, we will make an exception," he said resolutely. He knew he could go whenever he wanted. And so did the sentry.

"You cannot *all* go in though – there are too many of you…"

The objection was a reasonable one. He had never been in that now hateful hall. He knew it was huge, but four hundred soldiers would be truly excessive. He did want to strike fear into those old fools, though, and so he told the men he was leading, "A hundred of you, inside with me! The others form a cordon around the building!" Then he turned to his *optio* and ordered him to split the soldiers into two groups. When the selected number were ready to join him, he had the guards open the heavy doors.

The senators were waiting for him: he had made sure that his arrival was announced, requesting that the Senate find itself in session. Chaerea hoped a sufficient number of senators were present to make any decision he managed to extort from them official. And he hoped that they had taken his threat to go and collect them from their homes if they had failed to present themselves seriously.

Creaking loudly, the doors opened and before Gaius's eyes appeared an imposing backdrop which dwarfed all within it: the statues in the exedras, the windows high up in the walls, the podium at the far end, the benches of the senators, and the senators themselves, present in a number which he immediately found comforting. Instinctively, he looked around him for the infamous statue of Pompey beneath which Caesar had fallen under the blows of the conspirators' daggers, and when he saw what he assumed must be it on its podium, he felt his stomach tighten with emotion.

He turned his gaze to the senators, sitting to his left and right along the side walls, and the feeling was replaced by another type of emotion. He had to talk now, and people like Cicero would be listening, levelling at him all their contempt for what they no doubt saw as his violation of the sanctity of the place.

He walked the short distance to the foot of the podium. The platform was empty, as were the two high-backed chairs of the consuls – naturally, because both positions were vacant. For a moment he was tempted to stand between them, but he decided to climb only a few steps. The senators were observing him and the soldiers silently, without daring to say a word. Their hostility was increasingly tangible and it was not easy to speak, but he could not disappoint Octavian, and so he steeled his nerve.

"Distinguished Senators, I am Gaius Chaerea, a centurion of the Martia legion, and I requested a meeting with the Senate to present to you the claims of the soldiers, who consider themselves wronged by the Republic for which they have fought and endured many sacrifices."

His audience fell silent again as a subdued murmur rose among the other officials. He was surprised by the echo that his words produced but, since no one was interrupting him, he forced himself to continue.

337

"We have recently finished enduring the labours of a civil war, fighting against Antony's troops on the basis of promises made to us by our commander Octavian which were later taken up by the state. But so far nothing has been paid, and in fact we have recently learned that only half of what was promised will be paid, and then to only two legions out of eight. Well, we demand the agreed upon amount."

He paused. It was curious to see the reaction of his audience, and wait for an answer. It did not come immediately, but in the meantime several of his officers echoed his words, re-iterating his demand for money.

"But the war against Antony is not over… Why should we pay you now?" said a senator Chaerea didn't recognise.

The murmuring of the officers increased, and Chaerea had to raise his voice to be heard. "The compensation is due to us for that which we have already done, Senator. We have fought two battles and an entire campaign. Whatever happens now, there will be another battle. And the compensation promised us by Octavian, which you undertook to pay, was a form of engagement, and was to be paid in advance." He hoped he would continue to have effective responses – Octavian and Maecenas had trained him to perfection.

"But the Treasury is almost empty, centurion. Between Caesar and Antony, there is nothing left," said another senator whose face meant nothing to Chaerea.

"Allow me to doubt that, Senator. And in any case, you could pay us in land. It is our legal right!" Maecenas had told him to use an intimidating tone after the first few phrases, and Chaerea did not hesitate to do so. Behaving aggressively allowed him to hide his embarrassment and shyness.

"Even were we to give you the last of the state's resources, we would do so because you take orders from a proconsul, and not from the propraetor. Decimus Brutus is currently the most senior magistrate among those we trust, and it is for him that you should be fighting." Another senator, another load of shit. But Octavian had foreseen that they would try once again to antagonise the soldiers.

"There is, in fact, one irksome problem to solve first," pointed out Chaerea. "It was Octavian who won the battle. Decimus Brutus managed to hold out barricaded inside the city, and that only thanks to us. None more than Octavian deserves to lead the army – the eight legions that are placed under his command – and to do so as consul. And it is in your interest too: he would gain the prestige necessary to lead the troops into the taxing challenge of taking on Antony and Lepidus together." That Octavian and Antony had now in fact agreed to a truce was not something that the Senate needed to know: it was important to make them believe that the consulate position would convince Octavian to resume the war.

"But the son of Caesar received an order from us to resume fighting Antony, yet did nothing, and has not even joined Decimus Brutus," objected a senator.

"Because without high office he feels that his hands are tied…" replied Chaerea.

"He's too young to be a consul!" cried another of the senators indignantly.

An objection that Octavian had foreseen.

"Young? Was not perhaps Scipio Africanus young when he assumed his consulate? And what of Scipio, then? There is no lack of examples even in times closer to our own – what of Pompey the Great and Dolabella? And did you yourselves not authorise Octavian to apply for the position ten years before the usual legal term? Come, this is a ridiculous pretext: give him the consulate and we are all happy!" he ordered finally, following the script that Maecenas had taught him.

"But it is unheard of! This boy sends his soldiers to us and demands that we make him consul, otherwise the state will lose eight legions in its fight against the enemies of the public."

"This is blackmail."

The senators summoned up their courage and began to remonstrate with vivacity. Too much vivacity. Chaerea drew his sword and banged the blade on the bare marble several times. The other officers followed suit, and soon the ominous sound of a hundred swords echoed around the room, bouncing off the walls and deafening those present.

There was no need to call for their attention a second time. "I expect you vote right away: five thousand sestertii each for all the legions and the consulate for the son of Caesar." In accordance with his instructions, he was to make it appear that this was entirely an initiative of the soldiers, and that Octavian had simply accepted it.

"This is an outrage! We are facing a new Caesar!" came a cry from the farthest benches. But the rest of the senators fell silent. Chaerea held up his sword, as though wishing to display it to all, and said, "If you do not want to give the consulate to Octavian, then *this* will give it to him."

There followed a cheer from the other soldiers, and then silence. The senators had become even smaller than they appeared from the podium. Another of them stood up, and this time it was one that Chaerea recognised: Cicero. At last the old fool had woken up!

"If this is what you ask, soldiers, then we can do nothing but give it to him!" he said, before sitting down again.

Was that it? Chaerea was disappointed. But then, it was exactly what Octavian had predicted: at this point, Cicero was able only to expose himself to ridicule, and there was no point deluding themselves otherwise, he had said. Even if he had spoken in his favour, it would not be thanks to him that Chaerea would see his demands met.

The sword. The sword was the only resource that could move these people, the centurion said to himself.

*

The door shook under the excited blows of someone knocking urgently. Chaerea woke with a start, startling Fabia next to him and little Marcus, who had crawled between them during the night. The man sat on the bed for a moment, letting the swirl of thoughts with which he had fallen asleep settle inside his head. It had been a long time since he had felt so satisfied: after obtaining from the Senate everything he had requested, he had decided to spend a night with his family before returning to Octavian and escorting him to Rome with all honours to receive his consulate. And he had fallen asleep happy: civil war seemed averted, Octavian had achieved the most important of goals, he had carried out his task well, and finally, after months of war – both imminent and actually fought – he had also been able to enjoy domestic calm with the people who were dearest to him. Things could not have gone better.

"Were you expecting someone so early?" asked Fabia, who was also now awake.

"No – no I wasn't," he replied, perplexed, staring at the half-closed shutters of the window and noting that the light outside was still dim. He got up, gripped by a vague sense of unease, while outside the knocking increased in volume. Opening the door, he found himself facing a visibly agitated Lucius Pinarius, his toga wrinkled, unshaven and with the disheveled hair of a man who has spent a sleepless night or who has dressed in haste.

He went out through the door. He did not want his partner listening to the business of the sect.

"Gaius Chaerea, the Senate has changed its mind," said Pinarius quickly. "After the closing of the session yesterday afternoon, it was learned that the legion requested from Cornificius, the proconsul of Africa, has embarked and will soon be in Rome, and thus during the night the relatives of Caesar's assassins convinced the others to revoke the decree that gave you your money and Octavian the consulate."

"This is a fine mess," said Chaerea bitterly.

"And that's not all. They expect Octavian to react, and I learned from one of the senators of the opposing faction who is in our pay that they are planning to take his sister and her mother hostage. You must go to them immediately and escort them to safety."

Chaerea was appalled. "By the gods, we cannot risk a civil war with the Senate and the conspirators without having any idea of what Lepidus and Antony are going to do! We're between two fires, damn it!"

"What matters now is rescuing Octavia and Atia," urged Pinarius. "I've already spoken to the chief vestal: she will give them hospitality."

"Yes, of course… But I only have a few men available. I sent almost all the rest back to Octavian with the good news that we received yesterday."

"You'll have to manage with what you have. Pedius and I will come with you. I'll see you at Octavia's home in an hour. Gather as many men as you can," concluded the senator, climbing back into his litter before disappearing into the alleys of the Suburra.

Chaerea walked back into the house, rushing towards the chest where he kept his equipment. He washed his face in a basin and began to dress, throwing a last look at his son, who had fallen back to sleep in their bed. He wondered if he would see him again: the situation was degenerating, and Octavian's back was now against the wall. A new war was on its way, and it would be worse than the one that had just ended.

"You have to go to her, don't you?" asked Fabia.

"I have to take Octavian's family to safety, now," said Chaerea after a moment's hesitation. How did she know?

She sighed, but said nothing and helped him to dress in silence, handing him his breastplate and adjusting it so that it adhered to his statuesque chest without creating folds in his tunic. She handed him his helmet, and only then did he find the courage to look into her eyes. He saw there anxiety and sadness.

He gently took her shoulders. "Listen. You have nothing to fear: it is you that I love and you that I have chosen. Because it is you that can make me happy, not her." Then, without waiting for a reaction, he held her to him, took a last look at the little boy, and left, hoping that she had believed him.

And hoping that it was the truth.

He had too little time, and could only scrape together eight men from among the centurions and *optiones*. He took them with him to the Aventine as the sun, surfacing over the top of the Esquiline, the easternmost hill of Rome, was starting to become a more defined disc. The families of Marcius Phillipus and Claudius Marcellus lived next to one another in two separate but adjacent *domūs*, and when it came to splitting the soldiers into two groups to take one with him into one house and the other into the house next door, he hesitated: he wanted to take care of Octavia.

But he went to Atia.

*

Etain burst into Octavia's room with unusual animation. Octavian's sister was not in the habit of sleeping with her husband, and at first, half asleep, she thought it was Marcellus, come to claim his conjugal rights. When she realized that it was her maid, she relaxed. At least until she saw the girl's agitated expression.

"*Domina*, they are knocking at the door. It's soldiers, and the doorkeeper doesn't know whether to open up: it's still so early, your husband's people haven't even turned up yet..." said Etain, touching her belly: Octavia was still not accustomed to seeing her unfortunate assistant's slender figure with the bump of pregnancy.

"Soldiers? What does Marcellus say?" The matron could not help feeling disturbed in turn.

"Your husband did not come home last night. They came to call him from the Senate when you had just gone to sleep; apparently, there was another secret session after the meeting yesterday, right in the middle of the night."

Octavia could not help but wonder if there was a connection between her husband's absence and the presence of soldiers at the door. But she also knew that Gaius Chaerea was in the city, and she hoped that it was him. Perhaps he had come to inform her officially of what she already knew, namely that Octavian had finally been granted the consulate! Meanwhile, the banging had become so loud and insistent that she could hear it clearly from her room. She had no choice, she thought. She feared that they would knock the doors down, and ordered Etain to tell the doorkeeper to open up. Then she stood up, quickly pulled on a robe, and stood at the mirror attempting at least to make her hair acceptable. If it was Gaius, she did not want to appear before him looking as unkempt as his wife.

She had just started to insert some hairpins when the door of her room burst open again and one of the slaves presented a centurion she had never seen.

Octavia jumped up saying, "It is deplorable that the visitors do not await in the vestibule."

"He wouldn't wait, *Domina*..." explained the slave.

"My lady, I have orders to protect you, and I was told not to waste time," said the centurion sharply.

"And who might have given you that order, centurion?" said Octavia, standing up. She noticed immediately how much she had changed since the Ides of March last year when the soldiers had raided her house to take her into custody: she no longer trembled and was able to maintain her proud bearing in front of him.

"By order of the Senate, my lady," said the soldier. "There may soon be fighting, and the senators wish to make sure you are safe."

The faint hope that he had been sent by Gaius Chaerea died altogether. Octavia felt disheartened and looked about her for a chair to drop into. Perhaps she was not so very changed, after all. However, she forced herself to stay upright. "I am the sister of the consul elect. You should speak to him first, I think," she ventured.

"There is no consul elect, my lady. This morning the Senate will issue a new decree to overturn the one of yesterday."

Octavia swallowed. Now it was all clear. Almost.

"Did my husband approve the provision that affects me?" she asked, trying to keep her voice steady.

"Your husband proposed it, and it was approved immediately," was the centurion's curt reply.

That was the final blow. Downcast, Octavia slumped into her chair. She knew that Marcellus did not approve of her support for Octavian and he hoped her brother would fail, but she would never have imagined that he would use his own wife as a hostage against her brother.

"You'll have to carry me out," she found the courage to say, "because I am not going anywhere." She wanted to see if Marcello had also authorized the use of force. A year of grappling with politics had not been spent in vain: even she had gained a little steel.

The centurion looked confused. Octavia gave a fleeting smile. It was evident that Marcellus had not expected her to put up resistance. But she soon realised that the soldier was not willing to disobey an order from the Senate. He advanced toward her.

"Don't make me use force, my lady," he whispered with a grim look that made her tremble "I was given a command and I intend to obey it." But she forced herself to resist. At the very least, she would make her husband pay for what had happened.

"I am not moving from here."

The centurion shook his head, clenched his fists in anger and looked around him in search of inspiration. Then he noticed Etain, who had just entered the room. He walked over to her, grabbed her throat in his hand and pulled out his sword. "I'll start with her, my lady. You'll have no more slaves left unless you obey the order of your husband and the Senate."

Octavia faltered. She knew she could put up no more resistance, and yet felt a sense of frustration in knowing that she was a hindrance to Octavian, rather than a help. Etain was shaking, but said nothing, showing more courage than she. In her condition, with her pregnancy now visible, she must be terrified, and yet it was she who appeared to be keeping her nerve, perhaps sure that her mistress would not let anything happen to her.

Or perhaps simply because she was braver.

"Let her go. I will do as you are commanded, "said Octavia eventually, inevitably. She remained motionless in her chair, dejected for not having immediately thought of taking shelter from any changes of mind of the Senate instead of rejoicing stupidly for a decree of which she had no confirmation. Her brother would be disappointed by her behaviour.

The centurion kept his grip on Etain and shouted for his men, who were waiting in the vestibule. At that moment, she heard an answering shout, strangled and gasping, and soon after the clanging of weapons. Without letting go of the woman, the soldier moved to the door of the room, calling out again. But instead of one of his soldiers, Gaius Chaerea appeared. Again! Octavia felt as though she were reliving the events of a year earlier.

"Let go of that woman, centurion," Chaerea said, his sword levelled at his fellow soldier.

"I can still hear fighting," said the other. "It doesn't sound as though you've overwhelmed my men, so you're in no position to give me orders, centurion."

Chaerea hesitated a moment, then said, "We took them by surprise, it's only a matter of time. Let her go, I said."

"Let's wait and see what happens, then," the centurion challenged him.

There was a tense silence. Octavia looked around for something that would make her feel useful. She rose from her chair and pretended to walk nervously around it, but as she did walked over to her dressing table and, without taking her hand from her dress, grabbed a large hairpin. The centurion, seeing nothing worrying in her movements, returned his eyes to Gaius Chaerea, and paid her no more attention.

But Chaerea had noticed, and Octavia saw his bewildered, frightened expression: evidently, he did not want her running risks, and thought she was incapable of helping. She would show him that she was not just a burden for the sect, she decided. Or the little girl he had known so intimately.

She continued walking around her chair, but this time moving in a widening circle until she had reached the point where the centurion was standing with Etain. The deafening beating of her heart, the sounds of fighting coming from the vestibule, the eyes of Gaius which she felt upon herself even when she wasn't looking at him and the danger which Etain was in took her anxiety to levels she was not certain she could manage. She gathered up all her strength and, when she was certain she would be able to rapidly reach the centurion, she released her pent-up tension and threw herself at the man and her freedom, using her right arm to strike him a blow with the hairpin and her left to push away Etain.

An instant later, a violent hot spurt flooded her face, neck and arms. She realized that the soldier had dropped his sword and, with piercing screams, had clasped both hands to his eye, his fingers clutching her make-shift weapon. Etain was falling forward, and Chaerea shot forwards with his sword outstretched. The blade disappeared immediately into the neck of the wounded man, who collapsed on the floor, his screams fading into a gasp. Octavia ran over to Etain and helped her to her feet, making sure she was all right. The girl nodded, so she turned in the direction of Chaerea, feeling a powerful urge to run over and embrace him. But the centurion had vanished, no doubt to lend his support to his comrades who were still struggling in the vestibule.

She embraced Etain, whose liberation had released the tension which had built up inside her, making her burst into tears. Octavia caressed her face and made her sit down in the chair, and soon only muffled sobs accompanied her tears. They strained their ears to hear the sounds coming from the other parts of the building – the screams, the clanging of swords and the sounds of breaking furnishings that, for a time, seemed endless.

Then nothing. For a moment, silence hovered over the house, broken moments later by the sound of footsteps.

Studded shoes approached her room. Octavia clung to Etain, who in turn clung to her. A shadow appeared at the threshold, and it was only when it entered that they realised with immense relief that it was Chaerea. Behind him, three men appeared at his command, all covered in blood which was clearly not their own.

"Get your daughter and let's leave, my lady," ordered Chaerea. "Your cousins Pedius and Pinarius are with your mother, in the house next door. We will take you to the house of the Vestal Virgins, where none may touch you."

Octavia nodded to Etain, who nodded and went to get little Marcella. Once they were alone, the matron went over to the centurion. "This is the third time you have saved me in a year..."

He looked away, uncomfortable. "I was only just in time. I went to your mother's, but when my men saw that soldiers had already been sent to you by the Senate they called me and we burst into your home together."

She moved still closer to him. "I mean... you seem to know how to do it better than anyone else," she whispered, her mouth now only inches from his. She stared at him with all the intensity she could muster, waiting for him to react.

Chaerea looked back into her eyes with just as much intensity, raised his hand slightly and began moving it towards her cheek, then stopped.

"That's why I will continue to do so forever, whether the sect orders me to or not," he said, swallowing and closing his eyes for a moment. She took his hand and raised it to her face. She was about to move it lower, but he took a step backwards, putting more distance between them.

Octavia released his hand. "Why not?" she managed to say.

He hesitated. "Because I love my wife," he mumbled.

"Are you sure?"

He hesitated again. "Yes."

"Some men... many men... love their partners, but they have no trouble having... having *intimate relations* with others."

"Not me."

"Why?"

Chaerea did not answer. He turned and left the room with a deep sigh.

"Because with me, it would be much more than that," she answered her own question. She watched him leave. She was safe. Nevertheless, tears of sadness trickled down her cheeks.

XXII

Dolabella leant over the bow of the trireme and stared at the walls of Laodicea, whose silhouette towered along the Syrian coast. The sea breeze blew back his long hair and his cloak flapped behind him, giving him the appearance of a flesh and blood figurehead. He seemed so eager to land and take possession of that which, in spite of the circumstances, he considered his province, that Veleda almost expected him to jump into the water and swim to the shore.

"The elders of Laodicea await me, sirs. They have declared their support for me, and not for Cassius, and this is a sign that the gods love me," he said solemnly to the staff behind him, with whom he was forced to include Ortwin; and in turn, the German had demanded that Veleda be present too.

"Rumour has it that Cassius has put together eight legions now. And we only have two," Ortwin pointed out.

Dolabella did not turn round. He stared at the approaching profile of the walls and said, "You are forgetting the legions I requested from the queen of Egypt. I didn't tell you, barbarian, but Cleopatra responded just before we raised anchor in Cilicia: we will find here at Laodicea four of the ones remaining along the Nile after the defeat of Pompey the Great by Caesar. And with all the messengers that I sent to Lycia, Pamphylia and Cilicia itself, I count on receiving additional re-inforcements in the coming weeks. In this city, one can easily get hold of anything by sea – I chose it for that reason. Cassius might have reached Syria before me, but without Laodicea he has nothing."

Veleda imagined Ortwin's irritation at discovering such important information had been kept from him: that was not what the former consul had previously agreed to with Octavian.

"He can get re-inforcements too," said the German, attempting to maintain a neutral tone. "Don't forget that Marcus Brutus and Tillius Cimber are on hand for him. Or that he is highly respected by the Parthians, from whom he could

348

obtain assistance. But you… you cannot even expect relief from Rome until Octavian convinces the senators to revoke the decree against you."

"I've had enough of you, you cursed barbarian!" replied Dolabella testily, as he always did when Ortwin forced him to look closely at his plans.

And he was the only one to do so, his other lieutenants all being too busy trying to please him. "We will find plenty of reinforcements around here. They mourn Caesar, and will assist us against his killers," said one officer, provoking theatrical gestures of assent from the commander. But Veleda knew that, with the exception of Egypt, the East had always been the land of Pompey, and thus of Caesar's killers. She saw that Ortwin did not intend to continue the discussion, and followed suit: she had learned that it was pointless with that stubborn, prejudiced dullard Dolabella.

Their ship docked in the port shortly afterwards, and Ortwin was forced to admit that, for once, it seemed Dolabella was right: the notables greeted him with a show of great welcome. They learned that Caesar had gratified the city with the intention of using it as a base for the war against the Parthian kingdom, and it was for that reason that its representatives reserved a warm welcome for those who professed to be his followers.

When they had quartered behind the town, along the isthmus that connected it to the mainland, Veleda thought she would be able to relax, at least for a while. As soon as they were alone after dinner in the tent reserved for them, she moved over to Ortwin and helped him take off his breastplate, which the warrior habitually wore at all times, so as to maintain his martial bearing and demeanour in the face of the Romans, and then continued, removing the rest of his clothes as well. He stretched out on one of the blankets laid on the ground and she sat on top of him, guiding him to remove her tunic and feeling his rough, strong hands squeeze her breasts.

When Ortwin was fully erect he undid her loincloth and Veleda allowed him to make his way inside her, then began to move above him, while the man's hands ran up and down her sides, following her movements, and she continued to rise and fall until Ortwin, with a roar, climbed to his knees, grabbed her hips again, positioned her on all fours in front of him and took her again: this was his favourite position, the one that gave him the most pleasure, and she always let him do it, using her hand to help them climax at the same time. It worked this time too – they were in unison in everything now. They slumped on the blanket, face down on top of each other, and fell asleep in that position, without having to say a word. All Veleda needed was to be lulled by his breathing in her ears: it was the most contentment she had experienced in her whole life. One day or another, she would have to find the strength to tell him…

*

Screams all around them woke her with a start. It was dawn, and shadows darted about outside the tent. They dressed hastily and raced outside without Ortwin having putting on his breastplate but with sword in hand: the cries of their fellow soldiers camped nearby showed them which way to look.

Inland loomed an endless line of armed men, a short distance from the city and the coast.

Cassius had already arrived, and with a number of legions evidently greater than their informants had reported.

"Come on, hurry!" he shouted to Veleda, returning a moment later into the tent to seize the rest of his equipment. They hurried towards the main gate, which had been left open only to allow the soldiers camped outside to re-enter, and Ortwin immediately rushed off in search of Dolabella. He asked where he was and was directed along the fortifications. They reached the general, who as soon as he saw them waved a message under Ortwin's nose.

"By arrow, he sent it to me. By *arrow*. But I had him shot, that damn archer who dared almost hit me!" he said, before handing it over.

Ortwin read it, and let Veleda read it too:

> Greetings, braggart of victories which are not your own. I would inform you that you are occupying a territory which does not belong to you, and which the Senate has bestowed upon me. I know you have only two legions, and thus would suggest you do not even attempt to resist my twelve. Yes, because there are now twelve, dear Dolabella: unfortunately for you, those that Cleopatra sent you encountered my army on the way and, as their commander felt they had no chance against an army twice

Ortwin handed the note back to Dolabella. "What are you going to do? Give up?"

"Are you joking? He will kill me as soon as he gets his hands on me, never mind all this talk of trials!"

"Then we run. Let us take to the sea immediately," said the German.

"Perhaps. But to do so, we will have to fight."

Dolabella pointed behind him. Ortwin and Veleda turned, and saw the stretch of sea in front of the harbour teeming with ships.

Cassius had them surrounded.

*

"Caesar managed it with a single legion. Why should not I succeed with eight?" thought Octavian, staring at the waters of the Rubicon which flowed by calmly. The stream seemed prepared to allow the easy passage of his troops.

Then he turned and passed his eyes over his legions. The legions which had offered themselves to him when he had not yet even been an official in the Republic, and those formed of veterans who had returned to service especially to carry out his orders and avenge their old commander, Julius Caesar. He knew he could count on them, as his adoptive father had counted upon the Thirteenth legion and on all the others who had fought for him in Gaul. Of course, he must not appear weak, irresolute or militarily unskilled; but for that, he had Rufus and, above all, he once again had Agrippa, at whom he cast an affectionate glance.

He looked upon his closest associates who stood, all in religious silence, aware of the significance of the moment. Caesar's life had changed dramatically when he had crossed that negligible little stream, and no doubt his would now change just as radically. Agrippa, Rufus, Maecenas and Gaius Chaerea – who had just returned from Rome with the news that had forced him to follow in his adoptive father's footsteps – wanted

351

him to do it. They wanted it as much as he did.

An eerie silence hung all around them. Even the soldiers made no noise, aware as they were of being part of something which was destined to go down in history. The farmers of the surrounding countryside had vanished, knowing what the deployment of a battle ready army along the river which defined the border between Gaul and the sacred Italian land meant. A land which could not be trodden with arms drawn, except with the consent of the Senate.

An authorization which had been denied.

Silla had been the first to march on Rome. He had held absolute power until he had given it up of his own free will. Then Caesar had done the same, and he had achieved absolute power, until they had killed him. Now it was his turn.

He would demonstrate to the Senate that he was no boy, and Caesar's murderers could not hope to go unpunished. To Antony, that he would have him to deal with. To the soldiers, that he was worthy of the legacy of Caesar. To the members of the sect of Mars Ultor that he had dragged them into a just and triumphant cause. To his mother, that she had been wrong to suggest that he give up the inheritance. And to Caesar, that he was deserving of the decision the dictator had made to choose him. Crossing the river meant all of this, and the thought sent a shiver down his spine.

He was surprised that none of the fifty thousand men who followed him, neither the soldiers nor the officers, had anything to say when he informed the army that he wanted to cross the Rubicon. Either it had become the norm for anyone aspiring to power, or it seemed to them the only way to obtain the money and glory that the Senate seemed determined not to give them. Yet the dangers that weighed upon the company were even greater than those which had faced Sulla and Caesar. The first had only had to deal with Gaius Marius, the second with Pompey the Great: both had one enemy to face, who they would battle to assume control of the City.

But that day no one, from the tribunes down to the last sutler, was ignorant of the extraordinary number of threats which surrounded them on every side. To the south, they would meet the three legions that the Senate had ordered to Rome, and which would probably have defended it had Maecenas not been so adept at his tireless work of corruption. To the east, the conspirators were gathering legions in the provinces they had occupied, and might plunge into Italy at any moment. To the north, Decimus Brutus could attack them from behind, and to the west, Antony and Lepidus could break the tacit truce which had prevailed with Octavian for the last few weeks and attack him with their many legions.

Those two were the keys to the precarious equilibrium: the young man hoped to have softened up Antony's position, flattering him repeatedly and agreeing not to help Decimus Brutus and to obey the orders of the Senate; Caesar's former lieutenant must have understood by now that increasing the power of the dictator's heir, constituting as it did an obstacle to the Senate and to Caesar's murderers, would be of mutual benefit. However, Antony might also have thought that, once consul, Octavian would agree with the Senate to finally declare war upon him. After all, Octavian had already changed sides, making himself at first available to the Senate and the consuls against Antony, and now turning against the senators and offering him a tacit alliance. What was to stop Octavian from changing sides again?

Nothing. Because that was how things stood – if it was in his interest, he would do it and that was an end to it. And Antony knew that very well. But there had been one constant in his attitude: revulsion at the idea of collaborating with the murderers of Caesar and a desire to see justice done for their crime. Octavian hoped Antony understood him, and that he would always oppose those murderers, and this gave those who had eyes to see and a brain with which to think the opportunity to distinguish a pattern in his seemingly contradictory actions. He had even explained it to him in a letter a few days before, although he held no illusions that his words would win over the general. Only his common sense could persuade him of Octavian's good faith. No answer had arrived, but Octavian did not expect one: Antony wanted to stand by and watch, hoping that the 'boy' and the Senate came to blows, wearing each other out and thus leaving the field free to make an agreement with the winner, whoever that was. He was a necessary and indispensable ally, but just as treacherous and dangerous as any other.

Octavian looked up to the sky. The sun was losing the orange of dawn and its semicircular shape and becoming a disc of a bright yellow which bathed their imminent undertaking in gold. He sighed. Never as then had he needed the help of Mars Ultor, but also of Venus, his ancestor. He called upon both in his thoughts, re-iterating his promise of a temple to the first, and to the second to glorify her more than any other deity in the future.

"Are you ready?" asked Agrippa, riding at his side. "I'm ready," he replied without hesitation.

"Well, as Caesar said in similar circumstances… 'the die is cast'," said Maecenas.

"No. It was already thrown the moment I accepted his legacy," he answered, before adding, "And now, I must try to collect my winnings." Spurring on his horse, he raised his arm and entered the water.

*

"Let us give them the money! Let us give the money to all the legions! If we can turn the soldiers against him, he will no longer be a threat!" cried a senator, drowning out the ritual words of the *Princeps Senatus* which confirmed the start of the emergency session.

Another rose to his feet. "We could have given him the *triumph*, at least. It would have satisfied the boy's vanity and he would have behaved himself. But no, we made him and the soldiers dissatisfied, and now we have both of them to contend with."

"The truth is that we should not have gone looking for trouble while Brutus and Cassius were both far away in the East. Who will defend us?"

"Decimus Brutus will defend us! We must resist. We have three legions at our disposal. Octavian is advancing quickly with only four, and we also have the walls to defend us. By the time the rest of his army arrives, we will have received re-inforcements. I say we resist!"

"You can resist, if you like! I already have a boat docked at the Forum Boarium awaiting me, with all my belongings aboard, ready to set sail to Ostia."

"Why should we accept yet another tyranny? I prefer to defend myself to the death rather than live in slavery as I did with Caesar! Did we fight Antony to prevent him from seizing total power, just to then give in to this boy? Never!"

Lucius Pinarius and Quintus Pedius looked around them in bewilderment at the confusion that reigned in the hall. "There is no unity of purpose," said the first. "At the end of the day, that works in our favour."

"But they're still not terrified. They are ready to resist. If it had been Antony marching on Rome they would surrender immediately. Octavian is not frightening enough, unfortunately. They still consider him a relatively harmless boy," replied Pedius.

"Yes. At least until they find his legions deployed outside the walls."

Then, suddenly, the cries ceased. At the entrance of the hall had appeared the unmistakable figure of Cicero, and a sarcastic murmur immediately ran through the ranks of senators. It had been days since the great orator had shown his face, and many thought that he had gone to Arpino or Campania, as he usually did when events degenerated.

"And what do you think, Cicero?" said one senator. "As you have deigned to honour us with your presence, it would be interesting to know your opinion."

"I have heard what many of you think, distinguished colleagues," said the old consul after reaching the podium. "You fear endorsing a new tyranny. You know well that I, more roundly and before anybody else, have always denounced all forms of autocracy. I identified early Catiline's ambitions, and later those of Caesar, to which I never bent. I also made against Antony the most incisive speeches of my long career. Yet I will tell you right now, until our 'liberators' are once more back strong and ready, far better the supposed tyranny of an inexperienced young boy than that of a man as intemperate and unscrupulous as Antony. Him, we cannot control or guide, but Octavian we can! The boy is devoted to me and respects me, and I believe I can direct him to behave in ways which are not harmful to the Republic. So I suggest choosing the lesser evil."

The murmuring that had continued all through his speech exploded into a chaos of shouting.

"Don't be ridiculous, Cicero! You want to rule us through that boy."

"You're the same old coward! Or you've let yourself be bought off!"

"Go back to where you came from, we've no use for you here!"

"Let us get his soldiers off him, rather! Let us use our private reserves to deplete his troops."

"Yes, let's pay them. If we give them an advance, they'll abandon him."

"Yes, let's send the troops a shipment of gold immediately. You'll see how quickly they come over to our side. He no longer has a sestertius to his name!"

"Of course! His soldiers are dependent on his money and will obey him until it runs out. Our three legions, however, are the State, and obey the Republic, and hence we do not need to pay them."

"Yes, let us send the payment tonight!"

"Nothing doing," whispered Pedius in Pinarius' ear. "They're preparing to resist. We must act. But not in this session."

"I agree. Let's inform Octavian of the trick they're preparing for him."

*

It was nice to be back in action. Feeling alive. And above all, being part of something again. For the first time in a long time, Agrippa was happy: Octavian had given him the opportunity to test his convalescent physique, entrusting him with the command of the detachment in charge of ambushing the gold the Senate had destined for the legionaries. When at last the young man saw the little train of carts appear along the Via Flaminia, he was almost disappointed: at the head of the column were five horsemen, and there were the same number at the rear, while on each side of the vehicles, driven by civilians, marched a dozen legionaries.

When he had been given the task in the camp in Upper Etruria, he had hoped it would be more of a challenge. Octavian and Maecenas, acting on the information received from Pedius and Pinarius in Rome, had asked him to prevent the shipment of gold from reaching the legionaries: many of them might have settled for the handout from the Senate and pulled out. The soldiers needed to be motivated in order to get them to march against the city – nothing could drive them better than the desire for money and revenge, and Octavian had to look like the only one in the institutional framework who could provide them with both. For this reason, the squadron that Agrippa had brought with him – experienced Celt auxiliaries, veterans of Caesar's Gallic Wars – were sworn to secrecy about the mission: no one could trace with certainty the source of the plan to the dictator's heir, what with all the armies and commanders roaming around Italy and the neighbouring provinces.

Agrippa whispered to the *decurion* to await his signal to leave the woods in which they were stationed. And he reminded them not to kill: those same soldiers they were about to attack might quite soon come under Octavian's command. For the ambush he had chosen a gorge between the Tiber and a cliff, beyond which the Romans could fall back and defend themselves.

He drew his sword and immediately all the others followed suit. With his arm, he motioned to the *decurion* to take half the squadron towards the vanguard, stopping the convoy from travelling further, while he took the rest of the unit and headed for its flank. He wanted to leave the soldiers coming from Rome a way out, so they could immediately inform the Senate that the delivery had not been successful, thus inducing the senators to abandon all thoughts of resistance.

When the carts drew level with his hiding place, he sprang out of the bushes together with the Gauls. The walking escort drew their swords and took up defensive positions around the chariots while the horsemen dismounted and lined up next to them. Agrippa rushed at what seemed to him to be the highest-ranking member of the escort and launched a flurry of jabs – making sure none actually landed, even when his adversary let his guard down giving him the perfect opportunity to run him through.

As he fought, he shot occasional glances left and right to check on the progress of that surreal battle. One soldier had lost his sword and shield under attack by a Gaul, and had raised his hands in surrender: the Celt struck him a blow to the head with the boss of his shield and, despite his helmet, the Roman was knocked unconscious and collapsed by the wheels of the cart.

Agrippa continued to press the commander of the escort,

forcing him to move backwards and hoping to hear at any moment the word he was waiting for. But in the meantime, he saw, blood could not help flowing: to his side, a spear had hit a Gaul, thrown with such violence as to slice through the double layering of his breastplate and shoulderplates, and he had collapsed, dropping his weapons. Blood gushed from the wound, and the warrior, though still on his knees, was no longer moving. One of his comrades gave a wild scream and set recklessly about the aggressor, levelling blows against him until he managed to hit him in the thigh, cutting it deeply, then finishing him off with a blow to the neck when the unfortunate instinctively bent forward to steady his leg.

Blood gushed from the soldier's almost detached head, and, curiously, it was the sight of that which led Agrippa's adversary to shout the words he had been waiting for.

"Retreat! Towards the gully behind us, hurry up!" the officer shouted, releasing himself from the young man's attack. But the Gauls were too enraged by the death of their comrade to give him a chance. A second Roman fell, and then another went into the river, then a fourth collapsed to the ground, and the Gauls took out their rage on his body. If it went on like this, things were likely to get out of hand, Agrippa told himself, and rushed in front of a group of Celts, positioning himself between them and the three legionaries who they had cornered against a cart. He almost had to fend off more blows from his own men than from the Romans, and in at least two cases had to block thrusts with his shield before they realised who he was and regained control of their tempers.

At the same time, though, he neglected their opponents, as he realised when a sword struck his shoulder, but fortunately the blade slipped off without injuring him. He just had time to twist his upper body and strike a blow in return, which put his opponent on the defensive and gave him some breathing space. The Roman soldier gave up and backed off with his fellow soldiers while Agrippa stood unmoving, his statuesque figure blocking the Gauls' anger, before advancing again but attacking only feebly, dictating thus to his men the intensity of the fighting.

The carts, which the drivers had turned round, reached the gully with the legionaries by their wheels, and two of them were set crosswise so as to form a barricade and obstruct the passage.

Now there was no way to get round them, but neither could the Romans advance without having to fight their way through: it was the stalemate that Agrippa had hoped for. Meanwhile, the Gauls had started running individually or in small groups towards the blockade, provoking their opponents to a confrontation. One, screaming, attempted to climb the sides of the wagons, but was driven back by a crowd of legionaries leaning round the side of the vehicle.

Agrippa ordered his men to stop attacking and led his Gauls out of range of spears, then commanded them to rest and sent for the horses. Now it was just a question of waiting and making it clear to the Romans that they had no intention of leaving...

*

Maecenas looked at the long line of people who emerged from Ponte Sublicio and walked along the Via Aurelia with wagons of household goods in tow. He squinted, and it seemed to him that there were not only the poor but also aristocrats who had dressed modestly in an attempt to pass unnoticed; to a keen eye, though, they could not hide their haughty demeanour and well-looked after figures, wagons full of belongings and retinues of slaves even from this distance. Along the walls next to the Tiber, in the western part of the city, numerous guards manned the battlements and towers. The river itself was teeming with boats and the pier in front of the Tiber Island was crowded with people awaiting a boat for Ostia.

Apparently, he thought with satisfaction, the situation had got out of hand for the Senate, who had been able neither to re-assure the citizens nor to prepare them for the resistance to the bitter end they had pompously declared they would. So the people no longer saw Octavian as a boy who was more capricious than dangerous, as the Senate had always attempted to make him seem: he was as feared as was Caesar when, six years before, after having subjugated the whole of Gaul, he too had set about taking possession of Rome.

It was right that he should be feared, but they also had to avoid him being hated. And Maecenas was there for that reason, too. After Agrippa had prevented the money from the Senate reaching Octavian's legions, the senators had resolved to resist, but no one really wanted civil war to come to Rome, so it was necessary to show that Octavian, despite appearances, wanted it even less than anybody else. The people considered his claims justified and the wrongs he had suffered evident, but didn't have the strength or the means to support him. Now, it was time to convince those who *did* have the means to do so, so as to wear down the Senate's will once and for all.

"Decurion! Go into the city and re-assure the people, as you have been ordered," he said to the commander of the *turma* who accompanied him. "Leave me only two cavalrymen for my needs. I will see you at the Milvian Bridge in the early afternoon."

The squadron commander nodded solicitously and, together with almost the entire unit, galloped back down the slopes of the Janiculum Hill, which they had partially climbed to enjoy a wider view of the City. Maecenas, however, had a more specific task. He motioned to the men who had remained and, instead of going down, went up the slope to the advance garrison that the Senate had posted on top of the hill. He came in sight of hastily assembled fortifications with a ditch in front, and as he approached the guard ordered him to stop.

"I am the tribune Gaius Cilnius Maecenas, sent by Octavian. I wish to speak to the commander of the garrison," he said.

"The legate Gaius Cornutus cannot talk to a rebel unless expressly authorized by the Senate," answered the guard.

"Even if that might avoid a war?" asked Maecenas. "Do you really wish to take that responsibility, soldier?"

The other did not answer, but remained motionless for a moment before disappearing behind the rampart. He re-appeared with a superior officer, recognizable by his Attic helmet with high red crest and anatomical cuirass. "I am the representative of the Senate, Gaius Cornutus," he specified. "What do you want, tribune?"

"To parlay with you, if you will allow me to enter, legate."

"I am not authorised to do that. Say what you have to say, and then go."

"Do you think that's wise? I'd rather talk to you in private."

"I do not speak in private with the messenger of a public enemy. If you do not like it, you can leave."

Maecenas snorted. A stubborn man of integrity. Well, he

might as well turn his stubbornness against him.

"As you prefer. I just wanted to let you know that my commander Octavian has no intention of waging war on the city, the Senate or the Roman people. He has only come to accompany his soldiers, who demand payment of what was promised to them by the senators. It is they who took upon themselves a promise made by Octavian himself. And as he is in Rome, he also intends to candidate himself for the consular elections."

"Why are you telling me? Go to the Curia of Pompey and tell the Senate…"

"I am telling you because you are a soldier, Gaius Cornutus. And as such, Octavian believes that you and all your soldiers are also entitled to the promised bounty… And he would stand guarantor that you too would receive the agreed upon five thousand sestertii… as a reward for keeping the peace."

A murmur spread through the fortifications. Maecenas saw soldiers whispering among themselves and other silhouettes appeared over the top of the battlements, as though to verify that there really was someone there in the mood for giving out gifts.

"That is not what the Senate has established. Go back to your master, tribune," said Cornutus, without any inflection in his voice. He was stubborn alright.

But his soldiers were not, as the Etruscan had expected. He saw a centurion approach the legate and talk animatedly with him. Other soldiers gathered around him, and several clusters formed along the battlements, where lively discussions arose. Cornutus seemed to get quite angry with his subordinate, and another centurion approached the two and spoke with obvious anger.

Maecenas smiled. He was done there – the seed had been planted. Now it was time to pay a visit to the other garrison instituted by the Senate for the forward defence of the city: the one at the Milvian Bridge.

XXIII

"It's not Cassius any more, I tell you," said Dolabella from the battlements, watching the movements of the commander who had kept him besieged for two months in Laodicea. After two naval battles and numerous failed sorties, they were more stuck than ever inside the city: they had lost most of their ships, which had been sunk in the fighting, and along the isthmus Cassius had placed a barrier of rocks and material of every sort that he had raided from suburban villas and tombs to prevent them from setting off en masse for an attack.

They were not even receiving supplies, and would soon be starving.

Ortwin sighed as he climbed the stairs to the fortifications. He'd had enough of Dolabella and his impulsive decisions, which were leading them to rack and ruin. Now his defence was merely a pointless wait for re-inforcements, requested directly by sending a message to Octavian in Italy. "If you want your revenge," he had written, "have my position legalised in the Senate and send me some legions." But Dolabella was not and never would be able to ensure Octavian the revenge he had sought against his father's killers. Backing him would only mean wasting time: Octavian would not support that idiot any longer, nor would he send any legions which might well be appropriated by Cassius, depriving him of his showdown with the other murderers of Caesar. A showdown which would happen sooner or later, Ortwin told himself as, together with Veleda, he walked to his position on a tower from whence they could observe the entire besieging army, which had grown enormously over those two months.

"You mean Cassius has left someone else here to accept our surrender?" he asked Dolabella defiantly, when they reached him.

The proconsul looked at him with a dismissive smile. "One day I'll cut out your tongue, you insolent barbarian – when the legions I have requested from Octavian arrive, I will no longer need you and your miserable crew, and then you'll pay for your irritating air of superiority. Yes, it seems that Cassius believes we are done for and has left one of his lackeys to finish us off: it is irritating to know that when we fight back, that worm will not be there and I will have to chase him through the Orient to shove his arrogance down his throat…"

Ortwin gave Veleda a dismayed look. She too must have realised that Dolabella was now lost in a world of his own which had little to do with reality. He did not answer, and looked out over the city walls, in the direction in which the general's attention was concentrated. The scene, in fact, was monopolised by imposing ramps of earth that the attackers had built to allow their siege towers access to the walls. The sappers worked hard to pile up the soil and hold it in place with strips of wood: self-propelled siege towers and mobile bunkers covered with fire-resistant hides offered those engaged in the work protection from the projectiles hurled by the defenders, and the work proceeded with such speed as to cause concern that in a few days the embankment would reach the base of the walls. And at that point, nothing would prevent the attackers from gaining access to the battlements. It was hard to believe that Dolabella had not realised it.

The enemy commander, recognizable by the personal guard which accompanied him, and from the red cloak that wrapped around his anatomical cuirass and his crested Attic helmet, was up on an artificial hill built by the besiegers to the side of the leading edge of the ramp. He was just outside the range of the scorpios in the battlements, but his figure was clearly distinguishable.

He looks familiar, Ortwin said to himself.

He turned to Veleda, and realised that she was thinking the same thing. She knew that way of walking better even than he.

The two of them were likely to be wiped out at any moment, to be killed supporting a commander in whom they no longer had any faith at all, and who could no longer be of any use to the sect of Mars Ultor. In fact, at this point Dolabella had become an obstacle to the vendetta that Octavian intended to pursue, and had had his day. But that was not all: there was also a real danger that their conqueror would be the man who had had more effect upon their lives than any other after Julius

Caesar.

The man who had them at his mercy, and who they could have eliminated if only Veleda had allowed Ortwin to sink the sword blade he held pointed at the man in all the way.

The last man to whom Ortwin would ever have wanted to hand himself over to or would have wished to see smiling in triumph after having defeated him.

Quintus Labienus.

*

The massive doors of the Porta Collina were still motionless in the darkness. An unusual fact, since Caesar had determined that vehicles could only enter Rome and circulate at night, in order to limit the traffic during the day. Octavian looked at Agrippa and Rufus quizzically, wondering if he should advance further, with the risk of moving into range of any archers who might be in the battlements.

"Do not worry," Agrippa assured him. "If Maecenas wrote to us that tonight he would find a way to open the door, there is no reason to doubt his word: that wily Etruscan never misses a trick." Rufus, instead, did not speak. In Agrippa's presence, he hardly ever did.

"Maybe something's happened... Maybe he's been arrested, or worse..."

Octavian felt more shaken than he had since he had learned he was to be Caesar's heir. The presence of his legions camped a mile from the walls did not re-assure him. As he wanted to avoid the risks and uncertainties of a siege, he had to come to Rome alone, with only his praetorian cohort to exploit the ground that Maecenas had prepared for him; but once inside, there were still three legions which could quite easily overpower him, if the Senate had managed to recover control. After all, if the gate was closed it was because the senators still exercised authority in the city.

"Who, Maecenas? Even if he *had* been, he'd manage to convince his captors to release him – probably by showering them with gold. If I were you, I wouldn't worry," replied Agrippa.

Octavian continued to stare at the gates. He was anxious to

see them open, but at the same time was afraid: for all that Maecenas had re-assured him and all the confidence he had in that extraordinary Etruscan, he still had too many powerful enemies in Rome to feel completely at ease. He wondered if the risks he was taking sneaking into Rome were not after all greater than those of besieging it.

And at that moment, he thought he saw the doors move, and a crack of flickering light confirmed to him that they were in fact opening up. A dark shape came out and walked towards them.

"You must have a lot of confidence in me, Octavian, to be waiting so far from the walls." Maecenas's unmistakably theatrical voice allowed them to recognize the young Etruscan before they could make out his features.

"You never know," said Octavian, smiling broadly to release some of his pent-up tension. "There might always be someone who gets it into their head to do the murderers of Caesar and the senators a favour and come and kill me in the hope of a reward…"

"And no doubt there are those who would pay handsomely," said the Etruscan, embracing him. "But we will not give them the chance, because we can offer more. The treasury's money is on the Janiculum at the moment. Something tells me that tomorrow we will be able to take it for ourselves."

"Isn't there a legion defending it?" asked Rufus, finally breaking his silence.

"At the moment. But I do not see why soldiers should risk their lives defending something that is not theirs and which they themselves desire, if they can take it with no risk… Everyone knows that you are anxious to pay the legionaries and that, on the contrary, the Senate is somewhat tight-fisted."

"If you say so…" said Octavian, who found Maecenas' tranquility contagious. "Shall we go?"

They let half of the cohort go ahead, then set off themselves, crossing the threshold after some of the soldiers, followed by the others. Octavian looked up and saw that the watchmen on the towers to either side of the gateway were saluting him. Somewhat timidly, he returned their salute, then trotted on, leaving the city walls behind. Climbing the slopes of the Quirinal Hill, they passed the *campus sceleratus*, the piece of land where those condemned to death and vestal virgins who had betrayed their vow of chastity were buried, these last whilst still alive. A shiver ran through him at the thought of being buried alive by his own enemies, and once again he hoped that Maecenas had done his work well.

The Etruscan seemed almost to guess his thoughts. "We are expected on the top of the hill. And it is a meeting that should dispel any lingering doubts you might have," he said.

The cohort continued down the *Vicus longus,* forcing the wagons they encountered to move aside and make room. The drivers watched the passage of the soldiers with expressions of surprise mixed with fear, probably connecting the presence of Octavian's army outside the walls, of which all were now aware, with this nocturnal march. On occasion, the young man heard his name whispered, and at least once heard a cry of encouragement.

"See? Even the people are with you. The Senate cannot afford to confront you face to face, because they know that the people would oppose them," said Maecenas. To confirm his words, in some *insulae* along the street lights came on, people looked out their windows and, despite the presence of the soldiers with their hands on the pommels of their swords, there were even those who came out into the street and joined in the praise.

"It's about time someone helped those senators make their minds up!"

"That's the way, Octavian! You're a worthy son of Caesar!"

"Give them what for!"

"I'll vote for you at the consular elections, if they let you stand!"

"You showed Antony! Now it's Cicero and those other old halfwits turn!"

"You're smart, lad! Avenge your father!"

"Caesar was the greatest! It looks like he did well to choose you!"

Octavian thought that a commander parading on a chariot during a triumphal procession must feel the same thrilling sensation that he felt in that moment. He looked over at his close friends, and they all smiled back at him, understanding perfectly how he felt.

The people wanted *him*.

They reached the top of the hill, where Octavian was able to make out the dark outlines of the buildings of Rome. It was many months since he had been in the city, and he struggled to orient himself and make out its principal landmarks. Instinctively, he sought the Theatre of Pompey and the Curia of the same name, but he could only guess in which direction they might be. At the same time, a shudder went through him and he felt a strange thrill, seeing there at his feet the centre of power from which he had been kept away these last months – the place from whence everything which had guided his life since the Ides of March last year had begun, and towards which all were destined. His every thought had revolved around Rome, his every move came from Rome, every threat came from Rome, and his fate itself was linked to Rome, and now that he was finally there, breathing the fetid air, heavy with the stench of rubbish and excrement, he could sense the nocturnal chaos, but at the same time was awed by its majesty and uniqueness.

Maecenas took Octavian, Agrippa and Rufus to an elegant house, and led them through the vestibule and entrance hall and along a corridor, emerging into a small garden surrounded by walls covered with ivy. On a bench sat two men in praetexta togas, who rose smartly on their arrival. The August weather made the night air pleasant.

Maecenas made the introductions. "Octavian, this will be your base for the next few days. And these are your hosts: if you do not recognise them, know that they are the urban praetor Marcus Gallius and the peregrine praetor Gaius Crassus. The commanders of the garrison of Rome."

Octavian shook hands with them, without being able to resist giving his friend an admiring glance.

By the gods – he had actually managed it!

*

Octavia tried to look happy when her mother came to call her. Octavian had arrived with a retinue of clients and beggars, some even of rank, who crowded in front of the Temple of Vesta and the House of the Vestal Virgins, where the two women had taken refuge during the march of Octavian towards the heart of Rome. While Etain completed her make-up, passing kohl over her eyebrows and blue pigment around her eyes, she attempted to convince herself that she *must* be happy. Her brother seemed close to achieving the first important goal he had set himself, and she would soon be one of the most influential matrons of Rome. Octavian had also made it known that he had already forgiven Marcellus for having voted against his election as consul and intriguing against him. And her daughter Marcella was growing strong and healthy.

In short, everything seemed to be going well. So why did she feel sad?

There was no need to answer that question. She was fully aware that she could not be as happy as Gaius Chaerea's woman, who had the certainty of having her man with her. And that she was raising the son of the man she, Octavia, would have liked to be with.

"Will you hurry up, Etain?" insisted Atia impatiently. "It will already be hard enough to get a moment with Octavian, what with the crowd out there and the people coming to pay their respects, without us letting other people get there before us!"

Octavia stopped Etain's hand as she was about to draw a fake mole on her cheek, as she sometimes had the habit of doing on special occasions. She got up, hoping that she would not catch the eye of Gaius among her brother's bodyguards: she would struggle to stop her tears from ruining the make-up around her eyes.

She left the room the head vestal had given her and walked down the colonnaded corridor which led to the main entrance. When she reached it, she looked admiringly at the magnificent spectacle of a jubilant crowd chanting Octavian's name while a cordon of soldiers surrounded the podium of the temple her brother had climbed, letting the petitioners past one by one. And only those wearing praetexta togas.

Two legionaries came over to collect her and Atia and lead them across to the sacred building. Octavian had wanted their meeting after so many months to be public, to show the people that among the wrongs he had suffered there was also that of having to hide his family to avoid reprisals. Theatre – but Octavia had learned that theatre was the essence of politics.

As she approached the podium, she couldn't help looking around her in search of Gaius. She saw him among a group of soldiers surrounding a man whose arms were tied with a rope, and forced herself to look away immediately: she did not know how she would react, and in public she must maintain decorum. There would be time to cry once the celebrations were concluded. She smiled when she finally met the gaze of her brother, who, at the sight of her and his mother, spread wide his arms and softened the expression which was part of the role of ruler of the city: to all intents and purposes he looked like – and perhaps actually was – a conqueror who had stormed the city, despite having done it bloodlessly. And that made Octavia even more proud of him, and proud of having contributed, albeit in a small way, to his success.

Atia's joy was, however, irrepressible. She waved her arms at her son, extolled his qualities and talked incessantly, with little matronly decorum, considering her rank. Octavia had to put a hand on her arm and squeeze her wrist to call her back to greater dignity. The soldiers parted to let her pass, but just then came Gaius Chaerea with the prisoner. For a fleeting moment their eyes met, but just as quickly the two, as though by tacit agreement, turned away. The centurion said to the soldier who was escorting her, "Legionary, I need to speak to the general urgently. And you, ma'am," he added, turning to Atia out of respect for her age, "please forgive me if I pass in front of you, but it is an urgent matter which your son will wish to deal with as soon as possible."

The soldier obeyed, and Atia too had no choice but to comply. "We're only a few steps away from Octavian and yet we cannot embrace him!" was all she said, as she stood waiting with folded arms.

Chaerea climbed the few steps that separated him from the podium of the small circular temple, the smoke of the eternal fire of Rome rising through a hole in its conical roof, and brought the prisoner before Octavian. "General, you recognize the praetor Crassus. We caught him early this morning trying to sneak out of the city."

The heir of Caesar looked the magistrate without saying a word, and Crassus too remained silent, actually looking away when he felt those eyes focus on him like an unquenchable, burning flame. An expression of disappointment crossed the young man's handsome face. "Is this how you support me, Crassus? Your attitude disappoints me greatly," he said.

"I... I am sorry, Octavian," said the other. "It was rumoured that the Martia legion had rebelled. I learned that the Senate had convened an emergency meeting, and I was told to assemble an army to come to our aid in Picenum."

"It was I who started the rumour of the rebellion," said Octavian. "The city had handed itself over too easily, and I needed to see whom I could really trust. And so I see you still take orders from the Senate, even after our agreement..."

"The institutional situation is unclear, I don't know *who* to take orders from... You are not yet a consul, and the army has not had its money... Forgive me," said the magistrate.

"On that, I can only agree with you. The institutional situation is not yet clear. But we will ensure that it becomes so very soon," said Octavian drily. He turned to Chaerea. "This man is pardoned. He is not responsible for his actions. Send out soldiers and tribunes of the people so that the people may know that I use clemency towards those who have joined my cause only for opportunism or venality."

He did not stay to hear the profuse thanks of the incredulous Crassus, but descended a few steps and went to meet his mother and sister with open arms. The soldiers parted again to let Octavia and Atia pass, and finally there it was – the theatrical flourish which Octavian had so much wanted for the purposes of propaganda. Octavia could not help but wonder how happy her brother was to be embracing them both safe and sound, and how much for the cheers of the crowd, obviously gratified by this happy ending. It must have been the wily Maecenas who had thought up this little performance, she thought, feeling a little used.

"I thank Vesta and the people of Rome for having protected the people I love most in the world," said Octavian addressing the people before even talking to them, in confirmation of her suspicions. But then, finally, he turned to them and said, "You must excuse me, Mother, but tonight we will talk properly. At the moment, everything I do has a purpose, as you can well understand," he explained, and Octavia brightened. All she needed was to know that Octavian was aware of the lack of sensitivity he was showing towards them. Politics before everything else – and everything was politics.

"Do not apologize, my son," said Atia quickly. "You have proven you know what you are doing. Keep it up, and you will surpass your father... the adoptive one, I mean!" she added with a laugh. Since she had told him to give up his inheritance, her mother's position had changed – and changed a great deal, Octavia observed to herself.

She wanted to re-assure her brother, too, if he needed it. "Octavian, know that we are proud of you. And I…" She had to stop. Another centurion had appeared in front of him and was trying to get his attention. "Commander, Senator Cicero wants to pay you homage," he said as soon as Octavian turned his gaze to him. The young man suddenly seemed to forget the presence of the women and nodded, and the centurion sent over the famous orator.

Cicero too seemed to ignore them. "Dear, dear boy! I'm so glad to see you. I was so worried about you, and I'm sorry I was not ready to give you the advice for which, with great kindness, you had always asked me," he cried unctuously.

Octavian's mouth curved in a smile while his eyes remained dispassionate, and he grasped the hands the senator had stretched theatrically toward him. "You are a true friend, Cicero, the *last* of my friends to appear before me. I was just about to leave the *pomerium* and the city to await the results of the elections. Just as required by law for candidates to the consulate."

Octavia could barely suppress a smile. Her brother had become so powerful that he could afford to be sarcastic to the great Cicero…

*

Etain observed the cheering crowd that thronged around the Temple of Vesta, looking around for Rufus, but with the hope in her heart of seeing Agrippa too. She knew she shouldn't think about that: she was pregnant by Rufus, and had shown such contempt for Agrippa that she could not imagine he would even speak to her again; but she realised that, for as much as she might ever love Rufus, what she had felt for Agrippa was another thing entirely.

And perhaps he had even forgiven for what she had done.

But she could never have him back. And perhaps she didn't really want to. She was Rufus's woman now, and the life that was growing in her womb proved it. And anyway, Agrippa now would feel free to go back to that wicked, disturbing woman – that Fulvia who had made him and dozens of other men in Rome lose their heads. But who would never be entirely his. Surprisingly she found comfort and consolation in the cruelty of the thought.

She suddenly spotted them together, the only two men she had ever loved. They appeared at the side of Octavian, with Maecenas, Lucius Pinarius and Quintus Pedius: the General Staff of the sect of Mars Ultor, apart from those of lowly rank, such as her. She returned to the doorway of the house of the Vestals hoping that at least Rufus would notice her, but had to wait some time before Octavian's lieutenant became aware of her presence. The crowd was still growing, and the cheers now resounded around the entire Forum.

She thought that Agrippa looked in her direction, but then saw Rufus leave the podium of the building, push through the cordon of soldiers and make his way through the crowd to come to her. She put aside any thoughts of her former lover and tried to focus on the current one, who she welcomed with an embrace when she finally saw him appear through the crowd which filled the space in front of the home of the priestesses of Vesta.

"By the gods, how I've missed you!" exclaimed Rufus when he reached Etain through the crowd. "I've often thought of you in these months of war. And every time I did, I couldn't help but touch myself!" he added in a lower voice. That wasn't exactly what the girl wanted to hear, nor the kind of thing Agrippa would have said to her... But still, she was glad to hear that Rufus seemed to care about her.

"I've thought about you a lot too. And I had a special reason for doing so." She could hardly wait to tell him.

"I have a special reason too," said Rufus enthusiastically, kissing her hands repeatedly. "I realised that you are the woman I like making love with best. There hasn't been one I've enjoyed myself more with in the last few months."

Etain felt disappointed, but then could not have imagined that Rufus would be faithful. And on the other hand, Agrippa hadn't been either. They had made no promises to each other, and rightly he had considered himself free to indulge his impulses. If nothing else, she was glad that those fleeting encounters had convinced him she was his ideal companion.

And letting him know that he had made her a mother would doubtless encourage him to be even more responsible.

"I suppose I should be happy," she managed to reply, a lump in her throat.

"Of course you should! I couldn't wait to return to Rome to make love to you again. I think about you naked all the time – that innocent sensuality of yours drives me crazy. Can I see you tonight?" urged Rufus.

"Of… of course," answered the increasingly perplexed Etain. Each man had his own way of loving, clearly. "Only, as told you, I have some news to give you first."

"Of course. Tell me everything!"

"I… I'm pregnant," she said with a forced smile, lowering her hand to her already pronounced belly. For some reason, she had thought she would feel happy when she told him. Instead, she felt a bitter taste in her mouth as the words came out.

"Pregnant?" frowned Rufus, looking at her from head to toe, only then noticing her condition, which was now evident despite the stole that covered her. "Who by?"

"What do you mean, 'who by?' By you, of course."

"How do you know? Those two had been having their way with you at Antony's, only a few days before me…"

Etain felt dismayed. She didn't want to believe her ears. "What do you mean, a few days! It was weeks before. And anyway, a woman knows these things," she protested.

"But a man doesn't. And who knows how many others you've been having fun with while I've been away. A lusty woman like you can't live without sex…"

Etain felt herself trembling with indignation. She clenched her fists and repressed an urge to slap him, too enraged even to answer him.

"So now what do you want from me?" asked Rufus with a suspicious expression. Every trace of enthusiasm was gone from his face.

"I… I told you because I thought you would be happy to be the father…" she mumbled, in the hope, which even she could not help but consider absurd, that he would soften.

"I would never be father to a bastard. And frankly, the idea of making love to a pregnant woman makes me nauseous," Rufus concluded, turning and walking away with the same haste with which he had come over to her.

Etain felt hot tears stream down her face. She looked over in the direction of Agrippa, but her eyes fogged and she could see only indistinct shapes. She felt a powerful urge to run to her former lover, before concluding that men were all the same, and that he too would only treat her like a whore. And perhaps he had more reason to than Rufus...

*

Seeing Etain again had depressed him. As Octavian had ordered him to in front of the Temple of Vesta, Agrippa walked toward the Janiculum with a certain melancholy in his soul, in spite of his satisfaction at the apparent victory they had just achieved. He had tried to wipe away the memory of the only woman he had ever loved, but the sight of her had aroused in him a wave of images that he struggled to control. He wanted to run to her before carrying out the task assigned to him by his friend, and tell her that he still hoped for her forgiveness. But the reality was that it had been Rufus who had done that, and that she had received him with joy. Because she was his woman now. And he had heard Atia say that they had not brought her to the temple in the middle of the crowd with them because she was pregnant. By Rufus, no doubt.

Too much had happened in those months for him to even hope to get back together with her. It was a closed chapter, and he might as well resign himself to the fact and concentrate on how best to carry out the delicate task ahead.

He crossed the western part of the city on horseback, escorted by a *centuria* of the praetorian cohort, going out past the walls and the Tiber Island and climbing the slopes of the Janiculum. Once he had reached the garrison there, he told the sentries to announce him to Legate Cornutus, but saw that they seemed rather disoriented. He waited impatiently for them to open up, but it took much longer for the doors to begin to move than he had expected. It seemed strange, because the soldiers had been largely forewarned of what Octavian had intended to do. Out came a *primus pilus* centurion who walked towards him escorted by two legionaries.

"*Ave*, Agrippa. We have been awaiting for your arrival," the officer greeted him.

"*Ave*, Centurion. Where is the legate? Is there a problem?" he replied, without dismounting.

"Well... in theory, no," said the centurion, sounding embarrassed. "But you will not be able to see the legate. At least, not alive."

Agrippa stiffened. "What do you mean?"

"Let's just say... that he didn't agree with the men's feelings... and rather than give in, he decided to commit suicide. We found him a few hours ago with a *pugio* planted in his belly. In fact, we had placed him under arrest in his *praetorium*."

"I understand," nodded Agrippa. "Should I therefore infer that the only obstacle to the operation has been swept away and that I will not be hindered?"

"You shouldn't be, tribune – you shouldn't be."

"I shouldn't or I won't?" asked Agrippa, who needed to know how intimidating he should order his centurions to be.

'Well, some of the officers believe that... forgive me... That a theft is in progress... And that Octavian will not pay the soldiers with his own money, as he claims, but with that of the exchequer. But I doubt there will be anything worse than a bit of rowdiness: it's a minority."

"Good. Explain to them that much of the money of the exchequer comes from Caesar's bequest to the soldiers, and therefore, as Caesar's bequest is destined for Octavian so that he may distribute it *to* the soldiers, there will be no theft here, despite what you may have been led to believe by the Senate and the murderers of the dictator, who are the only real thieves at large around here."

The centurion nodded. "I agree. Come, tribune, I will lead the way," he said, finally inviting him in. Followed by his men, Agrippa rode his horse across the threshold and proceeded down the *Via Praetoria*, passing the tents on either side of the road from whence emerged legionaries eager to see the man who had come to pay them.

The expectant silence was broken by a shout. "Finally!"

Many others soon followed.

"It's about time!"

"May the gods protect Octavian, the only one who keeps his promises."

"What are you waiting for? Give it us right away."

"Yes, I want it right now! I've been waiting too long!"

"I've thrown ten years of my life into the civil wars. I'm not waiting another day!"

The shouts became more aggressive, and Agrippa began to anticipate trouble. When they arrived at the *principia*, the centurion let him in and took him to the *sacellum*, where they had stored the treasury's money, and when the young man entered the shrine of the legion, where the unit's banners were usually kept, he was taken aback by the number of chests full of money, gold and jewels for which, from that moment on, he would be responsible.

"Commandeer all the available wagons. I want them outside in half an hour," he ordered the centurion, who nodded and walked quickly from the room. After opening a few chests to check the contents and finding more wealth than he had ever seen before, Agrippa closed them again and left the room. Once outside he saw that the wagons had already arrived, but in the meantime a crowd of soldiers had gathered around the pavilion.

On their faces was a strange mixture of joy and anxiety. They looked like beggars who, instead of begging, were about to start making demands. Some of them had even lined up.

He turned to the centurion of his unit and ordered him to start loading the available wagons. The officer ordered half of the centuria to line up in a row and pass the chests out of the shrine, while the other half formed a semicircle in front of the pavilion to protect operations.

"So? What about the money?"

"Where are you taking it?"

"They said you were giving us the money."

Agrippa felt obliged to speak, even though he knew he was no good at making speeches. On the other hand, if he wanted to become a general, sooner or later he would have to learn how to address soldiers. He raised his arms aloft, waited for them to quieten down, and said, "Legionaries! No one said that would have your money right away! In the coming days you must present yourselves, unit by unit, at the place which will be designated in the Campus Martius, where General Octavian's army has now assembled, and each of you will receive what was promised. It is right that we start with the legions who have followed Octavian since the outset of the campaign, and who shared with him the sacrifices and sufferings in the war against

Antonius. But it will be your turn soon, don't worry – Octavian wants to put you under his orders when he is consul."

A dismal silence greeted his announcement. For a moment, the only sound was that of the heavy breathing of the soldiers engaged in passing one another the treasure and the thud of the coffers being loaded on wagons.

"It's a lie!" shouted someone at the back.

"Yeah, you're only going to give it to your men!"

"Then let's take it for ourselves, right now! Otherwise that'll be the last we see of it!"

Some began to advance. Luckily they were not armed. Agrippa called the *primus pilus* centurion he had spoken to earlier.

"I require you to enforce discipline, centurion," he hissed, and the other, after a moment's hesitation, went to talk to an *optio*, and the pair of them went over to the soldiers closest to the wagons. There was some jostling, and Agrippa also saw the spiked club come down on the back of more than one legionary.

Meanwhile, his centurion came to say that loading operations were finished. With growing tension, Agrippa ordered the driver to move off with the wagon train and ordered the convoy towards the main Praetorian gate, then remounted his horse and made his way back to the Principia, but this time there was no friendliness on the faces of the soldiers of the garrison, who were still crowding along the sides. They watched him and the centurion with overt hostility, and when he was halfway towards the gate, the young man noticed some legionaries with their swords in hand, and others going into their tents, only to re-emerge immediately, armed.

He saw a soldier grabbing a pilum, and watched him from the corner of his eye until he saw that he was about to pull back his arm to throw. As soon as he was close enough, he spurred on his horse, drew his sword and lunged, forcing the other men to leap out of his way in order to avoid being trampled. The soldier with the javelin looked shocked but attempted a throw anyway. The weapon left his hand just before Agrippa was upon him, and only missed its target by a hair, while the horseman, leaning out of the saddle, stretched and swung his blade through the air. A slash appeared across the neck of the soldier, who fell to his knees, swayed slightly and remained still, while his head slowly peeled from his body and fell to the ground in front of his body.

"This man will not have a sestertius. Would you rather end up the same way or get your money in a few days?" shouted Agrippa loudly, so as to be heard all the way along the street, which was now enveloped in a ghostly, amazed silence.

He received no answer, but the faces of the men were telling: this time it was a strange mixture of awe, fear and respect – or so, at least, he interpreted it thus.

With the feeling that they no longer needed to look around themselves, he returned to the head of the convoy.

He had convinced them.

Epilogue

"Gaius Julius Caesar Octavian."

"Gaius Julius Caesar Octavian."

"Gaius Julius Caesar Octavian."

Octavian savoured every syllable of the words the substitute Pontifex Maximus had just uttered, and which the people, gathered in *comitia*, repeated aloud. He closed his eyes and repeated them to himself several times, as though to convince himself that, finally, he really was the son of Caesar – by law now, and not simply by inheritance.

Immediately after his inevitable election to the consulate, in fact, he had demanded that the ceremony of the *lex curiata*, under which the adoption was no longer just a matter of possessions but became also legal, be carried out, and now for all intents and purposes he was the son of Julius Caesar, as though he had actually been begotten by him. Given that the only son of the dictator was in Egypt with his mother Cleopatra, and could certainly not represent an alternative, he could boast of a privilege unique in the Roman world: that of being the legitimate heir to the greatest man – together with Alexander the Great – who had ever lived.

He greeted the people who had gathered in the precincts of the curiate assembly in the Campus Martius, under the watchful eye of the army deployed in front of the camp set up just beyond the Tiber, to oversee the smooth running of the ceremony.

In the same way, his armies had supervised the voting for his election to the consulate, where only two candidates had presented themselves and both been inevitably elected. His occupation of Rome had allowed him to avoid haggling or compromise: he would not have to share power with some colleague who was a representative of the opposite party, as Caesar had to do with Bibulus during his first consulate. The conspirators had been manoeuvred completely out of the game.

He embraced the relatives and close friends who were there with him, and who had mostly helped him to achieve his three aims. He embraced his mother Atia and his stepfather Marcius Philippus, then he kissed his sister Octavia and shook hands with Claudius Marcellus, re-iterating once again his forgiveness. He exchanged a quick glance with Gaius Chaerea and embraced Lucius Pinarius, then seized Maecenas, Agrippa and Rufus and embraced them at length, drawing them into a huddle to show the strength of a friendship which he hoped would last forever.

Only Quintus Pedius, who had already begun to deal with the third goal that Octavian had set himself within the year, after the consulate and the confirmation of the adoption, was missing. He invited his relatives and friends to follow him to the Forum: they too must witness the culmination of that journey which he had painfully undertaken in the aftermath of the Ides of March of the previous year. It was the most important moment – the one most longed for by all those who had loved Caesar, and he wanted to share it with them.

He marched between the lictors due to his new position, anticipating the event that awaited him.

It had started with Pontius Aquila, who Agrippa had killed outside Modena. And just a few days before, news had arrived of the death of Gaius Trebonius, the infamous traitor: Ortwin had done his job well.

Two down.

Now it was up to others, perhaps with the help of Antony, whom he aimed to meet as soon as possible and with whom he intended to make an agreement, despite the Senate's hopes to set them against one another. But he wanted it to be a court that condemned Caesar's surviving murderers – he demanded that they be judged as criminals according to justice and prosecuted by the law. They must go down in history as criminals and murderers, and therefore he had to wipe away the reputation as 'liberators' that they had built up thanks to the backing they enjoyed in the Senate.

He reached the tribune of the Rostra, where he had ordered the summary trial for the murderers to be held, so that it would be as widely seen as possible. Quintus Pedius was seated on the podium in his curule seat as the president of the court, and was intent on listening to witnesses. In front of him, at the foot of the tribune, more chairs had been set up for the jury, made up almost entirely of senators. Further back was a throng of the public which had come from attending the committee for his adoption.

Octavian noted with satisfaction that the people were anxious to attend the trial, and the court was full of members of the public who flocked around the Rostra from every street.

"Hail, senior consul," he greeted his cousin. "How goes the hearing?"

With a gesture of his hand, Pedius stopped the witness who was speaking, rose from his chair and walked over to him, leaning upon the railing that overlooked the bronze rostrums.

"Hail, young consul," he replied with a smile, enjoying the sound of the title. "I'd say everything is going well. I have only one problem: there are many people denouncing not only the material murderers – who we know well and had already identified some time ago – but also other people who were complicit in one way or another. And frankly, in some cases they seem to me to be a bit of a stretch. At this rate, I'll have to draw up a list of the convicted that runs into hundreds of names... And just hearing them all will require several days."

"No," replied Octavian flatly. "The *Lex Pedia de interfectoribus Caesaris* you had approved by the Senate provides that the trial lasts one day only. It should focus exclusively on the material perpetrators. If the defendants fail to appear and the allegations are proven, you will proceed immediately to the confiscation of property and exile. The cult of Mars Ultor will do the rest."

"As it happens, none of them has turned up. Not even the tribune of the people, Cascus, who was in Rome until a few days ago."

"Very well. Then let us get it over with and issue the judgment."

Pedius nodded, returned to his seat and summoned the chairman of the jury, who, after speaking to him in a low voice, went back down into the forum and urged all the senator jurors to vote by a show of hands: those who found the defendants guilty should raise their arms. It seemed that all promptly raised them, but when the chairman asked if there were any who did not agree, one juror held up his hand.

"Who is that?" said Octavian to Pinarius.

"He's called Silicius Corona. He is a great friend of Marcus Brutus."

The president of the jury nodded toward Pedius, who rose to his feet again, approached the edge of the platform and said, "I hereby declare the trial established on the basis of *senatus consultum* which approved the *Lex Pedia de interfectoribus Caesaris* concluded. With the complaints collected, witnesses heard and votes of the jury received, and in view of the judgment of the majority, I hereby declare guilty of the murder of the dictator Julius Caesar – and condemn in absentia to the interdiction of fire and water – the following individuals; Gaius Cassius Longinus, Marcus Junius Brutus, Decimus Brutus Albinus, Gaius Servilius Casca Longus, Publius Servilius Casca Longus, Lucius Tullius Cimber, Publius Sextilius Nasone, Quintus Ligarius, Minucius Basilus, Rubrius Ruga, Marcus Spurious, Caecilius Bucolianus Major, Caecilius Bucolianus Minor, Quintus Antistius Labeo, Gaius Cassius Parmensis, Petronius, Publius Decimus Turullius and Servius Sulpicius Galba. Since Trebonius and Pontius Aquila are no longer alive, be it known that, being found guilty of the same crime, they are subject to a posthumous conviction."

Octavian applauded, and his relatives and friends immediately did the same. So did the members of the jury, while the crowd which had gathered gave cries of approval.

Justice was done, the young consul told himself. Now began the second phase of vengeance.

*

The two centurions appeared like flashes in the darkness, their armour gleaming with reflections of the lantern one of them was carrying to light the way. The other held the document Ortwin and Veleda were anxiously awaiting. He held it out to the woman, who immediately pulled it out of its case, held it up to the light and studied the text: after a moment she nodded to Ortwin. It was the safe conduct pass they had requested.

And, ironically, it was Quintus Labienus who had provided them with it. His signature, which Veleda had no difficulty recognising, stood prominently at the end of the text, which referred only to 'the bearers of this pass'.

"Did you explain that the ship which must be allowed passage to the open sea is the one with a figurehead in the shape of mermaid?"

"Of course," replied one of the two officers. "You should have seen him: he could hardly believe that he was being handed the city, the few soldiers still in it and Dolabella on a silver platter without needing even to scale the walls. On the other hand, he can boast to Cassius of having conquered Laodicea with no losses."

Veleda had no difficulty imagining Quintus Labienus as happy as a child at the prospect of being able to effortlessly succeed in an undertaking that had cost his commander so dearly for so long without results. Her former lover's unstable character meant that he became excited easily at success and just as easily depressed by failure. She was certain that he would have welcomed the opportunity without hesitation, and without wondering why and by whom it was being offered. And she was equally certain that he would not leave Dolabella alive for even a moment once he got his hands on him, so great was the satisfaction that taking the man's head to Cassius would give him.

It had not been easy to arrange everything in two days. The decisive attack was imminent, and their flight must take place as soon as possible. For this reason, Ortwin had contacted the centurions who were most unhappy with Dolabella and had convinced them – with the promise of rich rewards if they joined him and Octavian – to go to the enemy headquarters and propose the opening of the doors and the delivery of Dolabella in exchange for a pass to Europe. And of course, the Germans would not be involved: officially, it had been the initiative of the two officers, who had had enough of the proconsul's ineptitude. Ortwin and Veleda had then gone to the captain of the trireme, who had shown himself impervious to the commander's whims, and persuaded him that Octavian would be mightily pleased with him if he took them home and abandoned the incompetent Dolabella to his destiny.

And now everything was ready.

"When did you arrange to open the gates?" Ortwin asked the two Romans.

"In two hours. We have just enough time to go and leave them ajar, as agreed. A small group of attackers who will be waiting just outside in the dark over the ditch, will take care of guarding it until the main forces have advanced. In the meantime, we will have gone down to the harbour and will have already embarked."

"Good. I would say that we can go, then, before that idiot Dolabella wakes up and starts creating problems for us," said Ortwin, urging his few men to follow him. Then he turned to the two centurions.

"We will await you on the ship for a little less than two hours, then we will give the order to sail. So waste no time." He had no intention of risking a meeting with Quintus while he was in that position of weakness. Veleda could not blame him, even though something inside her made her want to look again into the eyes of the man who had made her suffer so much, but who had also loved her madly – unlike Ortwin, who for a long time had not had the courage to.

The German must have noticed the slight look of regret in her eyes, because without saying a word he seized her stump and dragged her off towards the harbour, as though wanting to emphasise that she was his. And although at any other time she would have considered it an affront to her royal dignity to be treated thus in front of the men, she let him, without resisting. In fact, she was glad. She needed him to demonstrate to her powerfully that it was he who had won her. It was a way of making her feel like a coveted and important prize, despite the failures of her life.

They reached the port through dark, smelly, narrow, winding streets and boarded the ship, where everything was ready for departure, the rowers already seated upon their benches and the captain ready to take advantage of the slight westward breeze. Veleda leant on the bulwark, staring at the city which Quintus would soon enter. When the two breathless centurions arrived just before dawn, the trierarch set sail and the ship pulled away from the jetty, sailing toward the harbour mouth and shortly afterwards passing the lighthouse and heading unimpeded out to the open sea.

Ortwin moved closer to her and put his arm around her waist. With his usual respect, and with the sensitivity that she had always recognised in him, he had known she wanted to be alone, and had granted her the time she needed.

"All in all, I think Octavian will be satisfied with our work," he said. "We've killed one of Caesar's murderers for him, just as he ordered, and we've condemned Dolabella to his doom."

"Perhaps he will not be so happy to have sacrificed an ally…" objected Veleda.

"Oh yes he will," smiled the German. "Before we left, he told me that when we no longer needed Dolabella I could make him pay for his boasting of having participated in Caesar's killing. In fact, he was on the list too…" he concluded, throwing a last look at the increasingly indistinct outline of the Asian shore.

We hope you enjoyed this book!

The next gripping book in the Rome's Invincibles series will be released in Winter 2016

Find out more
http://headofzeus.com/books/isbn/9781784978938

More addictive fiction from Aria:

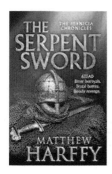  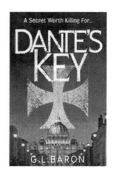

Find out more
http://headofzeus.com/books/isbn/97817849788221

Find out more
http://headofzeus.com/books/isbn/9781784977474

Find out more
http://headofzeus.com/books/isbn/9781784977511

About Andrew Frediani

ANDREW FREDIANI is an Italian author and academic. He has published several non-fiction books as well as historical novels including the *Invincible* series and the *Dictator* trilogy. His works have been translated into five languages.

Become an Aria Addict

Aria is the new digital-first fiction imprint from Head of Zeus.

It's Aria's ambition to discover and publish tomorrow's superstars, targeting fiction addicts and readers keen to discover new and exciting authors.

Aria will publish a variety of genres under the commercial fiction umbrella such as women's fiction, crime, thrillers, historical fiction, saga and erotica.

So, whether you're a budding writer looking for a publisher or an avid reader looking for something to escape with – Aria will have something for you.

Get in touch: aria@headofzeus.com

Become an Aria Addict
http://www.ariafiction.com

Find us on Twitter
https://twitter.com/Aria_Fiction

Find us on Facebook
http://www.facebook.com/ariafiction

Find us on BookGrail
http://www.bookgrail.com/store/aria/

Addictive Fiction

First published in Italy in 2015 by Newton Compton

First published in the UK in 2016 by Aria, an imprint of Head of Zeus Ltd

975312468

A CIP catalogue record for this book is available from the British Library.

ISBN (E) 9781784978884

Jacket Design © Head Design

Aria
Clerkenwell House
45-47 Clerkenwell Green
London EC1R 0HT

Printed in Germany
by Amazon Distribution
GmbH, Leipzig